GEEKOMANCY

MICHAEL R. UNDERWOOD

PRAISE FOR *GEEKOMANCY*

"*Geekomancy* is a glorious blender of genres, like a sweet candy shell filled with pop culture and high heroism. Absolutely stellar."

– Seanan McGuire, New York Times bestselling
author of *Discount Armageddon*

"Magic in geekery, mysticism in celebrities, the Ree Reyes series by Mike Underwood is a celebration of everything that makes being a geek cool. Can't wait to read what he has in store next."

–Stephen Blackmoore, author of *Dead Things*

"If Buffy hooked up with Doctor Who while on board the Serenity, this book would be their lovechild. In other words, *Geekomancy* is full of epic win."

– Marie Lu, author of the Legend trilogy

"If you took wish-fulfillment, ground it into a powder, and shot twice the recommended dosage into your eye socket, the result would look a lot like *Geekomancy*. I want to live in this world, where all the books and shows and movies and games I love are a source of power, not only in psychological terms, — which they already are — but practical, villain-pounding ones."

– Marie Brennan, award winning author
of *A Natural History of Dragons*

"Modern, sleek, and whip-smart, *Geekomancy* is a wonderful blend of geek and pop culture — you'll find yourself grinning knowingly at least every other page. And Ree is the perfect protagonist to navigate Geekomancy's world — geek enough to hold her own, yet human enough for me to be deeply invested in her struggles. I can't wait to read the next one!"

– Cassie Alexander, author of *Nightshifted*

"Underwood's Geek Fu is strong-and he's not afraid to use it. *Geekomancy* is fun, fresh and full of geek culture references that will have you LOLing to the very last page. This book is one hundred percent pure awesomesauce and totally FTW."

– Mari Mancusi, award winning author of
The Blood Coven Vampire series

2nd Edition
Copyright © 2012, 2022 by Michael R. Underwood
All rights reserved, including the right to reproduce this book or portions thereof in any form whatsoever.
For rights inquiries, contact info@morhaimliterary.com
ISBN: 9780998060637 (paperback)
        9780998060620 (ebook)

Cover by Deranged Doctor Design (derangeddoctordesign.com)
Also available in Audiobook from Audible Studios

First edition by Simon & Schuster Pocket Star Books July 2012
1st edition ISBN: 9781451698138

MORE BY MICHAEL R. UNDERWOOD

The Ree Reyes Geeky Urban Fantasy Series
Geekomancy
Celebromancy
Attack the Geek
Hexomancy

Genrenauts
#0 – *The Data Disruption*
#1 – *The Shootout Solution*
#2 – *The Absconded Ambassador*
#3 – *The Cupid Reconciliation*
#4 – *The Substitute Sleuth*
#5&6 – *The Failed Fellowship*
#7 – *The Wasteland War*

The Space Operas
Annihilation Aria

Other Books
Shield and Crocus

The Younger Gods

Born to the Blade
(with Malka Older, Cassandra Khaw, and Marie Brennan)

The first one goes to Mom and Dad, who always believed.

CONTENT NOTE

This novel contains violence and dramatized references to suicide. *Geekomancy* is written for an adult audience and would carry a PG-13 or R rating as a film.

Did You Say BOOM!?

Zombie Cafe was nestled gently (read: "squashed improbably") between a high-art gallery, which seemed to never have anyone in it but still managed to stay open, and the around-the-corner side of a bank.

The owner-manager, Bryan Blin (Strength 14, Dexterity 11, Stamina 15, Will 15, IQ 16, and Charisma 14—Geek 6 / Barista 3 / Dad 4 / Entrepreneur 3), paid a premium for the location, just a half-block up a side street from one of the main drags in Pearson's University District. Zombie Cafe was the city's premier coffee shop/comic store/gamer hangout, and in a geek town like Pearson, that actually meant something.

The formula was simple. The café served a normal assortment of coffee for the walk-ins as well as geek-themed coffee and treats to help it stand out. Additionally, its decor and staff fostered a social atmosphere to help convince customers to pick up that role-playing game book or graphic novel they'd been on the fence about buying for the last three weeks. It was a perfect geeky home-away-from-home.

Rhiannon Anna Maria Reyes, (Strength 10, Dexterity 14, Stamina 12, Will 17, IQ 16, and Charisma 15—Geek 7 /

Barista 3 / Screenwriter 2 / Gamer Girl 2) was Bryan's secret weapon. Rhiannon (known to practically everyone as "Ree") kept the café in fabulous baked goods, talked authoritatively about subjects from *Aliens* to *Zork,* and drew the attentions of countless lovelorn geeks.

She got hit on, sure, but the guys were easy to let down, and no one had made a scene about it in a while. They came in, saw her across the room like they had just walked into a meet-cute, and then proceeded to try to cast her as their own Manic Pixie Dream Girl.

Ree fit the bill—visually, at least. She wore thick glasses (which she needed to see more than six inches away from her face), had long black hair that she kept braided in a variety of styles (to keep it out of people's lattes), and had an "ethnically indeterminate" look that came from the mix of her Irish and Puerto Rican heritage. Ree's figure was more boyish than bombshell, though, despite her teenaged prayers to fill out a C-cup.

In truth, Ree wasn't anyone's dream. She was a near-broke frustrated screenwriter who would rather just talk with a guy for an hour about the ideological condemnation of super heroes evident in Alan Moore's comic work during the mid-to-late '80s—without them going straight to imagining her naked.

Zombie Cafe was a twenty-by-twenty front room, with a small prep and office area in the back and a basement accessible from the street. Nearly every inch of the front room not devoted to walking space was filled with something. The front half of the store was dominated by tightly-packed round tables and their corresponding chairs. A tall shelf of graphic novels lined one wall, matching shelves filled with RPG books and miniatures on the other side. A six-foot-tall shelf-on-wheels held the comics, currently pushed forward to allow Ree to move out into the seating area. Bryan had painted the walls with a mural, decked with planets, spaceships, super heroes, and java-bean alien monsters, to round out the look.

As of eleven in the morning on this particular blustery Thursday, there had already been the normal AM rush of young techies and professionals stopping in for their triple mocha lattes and chocolate espresso breakfast bars and then . . . nothing.

And for Ree, that nothing was scary.

Taking a lap around the Internet on her phone, she was eager for distraction. Nothing useful in email, but she had three voicemails, including one from her dad.

Not dealing with that now, she thought. She'd call him when she got home.

The other messages were from Priya and Anya. Ree didn't think she could handle the outpouring of support from her friends right now. She just had to lie low until her heart put itself back together. A burst of emotion bubbled up in her mind.

Fuck you, Jay. "We're not on the same path anymore," my ass.

Red crept into the corners of Ree's vision, and she flailed mentally, trying to find something to do, something to keep from losing her shaky equilibrium.

Ree looked over and saw Charlie, the other full-time cash-wrap monkey, straightening some comics and staring absently out the window. Ree squatted down and checked the food case, starting a mental list of what they'd need to bake to replenish the store.

As she was counting the Mario 1-UP cookies, a theremin-tune door chime rang, signaling another customer. Ree looked up to see a vaguely familiar young man in a polo shirt and khakis. He was on the skinny side, with medium-brown hair, a soft jaw, and the start of laugh lines. Ree was sure she'd seen him in the café before, but she didn't remember anything in particular about him other than that he was one of the shy ones.

"Hello," Ree said, but got no answer. The customer wove through the sea of tables silently and pulled an issue of *Action Comics* off the shelf, shifting his weight side-to-side as he read.

Ree turned to Charlie, who had come back to the counter. Charlie French (Strength 13, Dexterity 13, Stamina 15, Will 15, IQ 16, and Charisma 14—Geek 5 / Barista 2 / Social Media Ninja 4 / Trekker 2) was five-five, had sandy red-blond hair that was consistently a mess, and was in the top twenty for the "install a phone in my brain, please" wait-list.

Ree asked, "You want to start bake prep or should I?"

Charlie reached down to a coffee mug and drew out two d20s. Ree nodded and took one. Roll-offs solved nearly all trivial arguments at Zombie Cafe, per Bryan's lead. Ree cupped the die in both hands, blew on it, and shook, warming up its inherent magic. Charlie shook his d20 in one hand near his head, then threw. Ree rolled as well, and the dice kissed on the counter, Charlie's nearly rolling off the far side. His read 13. Ree's: 18.

Charlie sighed, then knelt to fiddle with the music station, an iPod permanently plugged in to their PA. Bryan was eight months into a XM discounted-rate trial, but Charlie only baked to Weird Al. He queued up *Running with Scissors* and set to work.

Ree slid around him and tried to get the customer's attention. "Looking for anything in particular today?"

The customer looked up briefly at Ree, opened his mouth as if to speak, then looked down again, his cheeks red.

Make that "one of the really shy ones."

Ree waited for a response. A beat passed, and she said, "Let us know if you have any questions."

She waited another moment for the customer. He was unresponsive, immersed in the comic.

Okay, whatever, she thought, nonplussed. Some folks just wanted to read in peace. The café wasn't a library, but if she took to banishing customers for loitering and reading comics, they'd run out of customers pretty damn fast.

Charlie made a sad-angry face at his phone as he picked up Ree's bake list.

Ree asked, "What's up?"

"Tweet linking to a news story. There's been another suicide in town."

"That's the second this month, isn't it?"

Charlie nodded. "I don't know if these things are happening more or if I'm just psyching myself out by reading all of the news all of the time."

Ree put a hand on Charlie's shoulder. "Maybe you don't need to follow every news outlet on the planet through Twitter."

"But . . ." Charlie said, then nodded. "Still a shame."

Ree nodded back at him, ducked down, and turned up the Weird Al a notch. "Maybe put down the phone for a while?"

Charlie laughed, disappearing into the back for the construction phase of the baking. Ree heard the sound of the fridge and freezer opening as Charlie gathered culinary forces to wage delicious war.

Ree killed time by cleaning the espresso machine and the counter, keeping an eye out for movement or indications of help-needing-ness from the silent reader. He eventually replaced the comic and left without a word.

×✕×⊛×✕×

Charlie clocked out at two, leaving Ree to woman the fort by herself.

The alarm for the peanut butter chocolate d6 cupcakes went off, and Ree spun in place from the register to grab the robot-claw hot mitten and shimmy through the narrow behind-the-counter walkway to the oven. The lack of customer traffic gave Ree the chance to slide off her wobbly plateau of emotional stability right back into her least favorite, yet most frequent, train of thought: Jay.

Jay. The man who had been, up until last Sunday, the love of her life, the guy she thought she might actually marry, against all odds. Instead, he announced that they'd "grown apart," that he didn't think they could make it better. And that there was this girl from work . . .

And so Ree had spent each of the last three nights drinking heavily and trying to keep everyone else out of the splash zone of her self-destruction. Last night she'd drunk mojitos until Anya and Priya carried her home so Sandra could stay with her in the bathroom and hold her hair. Ree was, in retrospect, not doing so great.

On top of that, yesterday she'd heard back from the friend of a friend in Pasadena who had pulled some strings and gotten her script, *Orion Overdrive,* in front of Damon Lindelof. No comments, no invitation to send more, just a "no thanks." She'd spent a year writing and rewriting the script, trying to make something fun, feminist, and optimistic, but so far it had gotten even fewer nibbles than her far-less-awesome but very hook-y SpaghettiWesternCthulhu mashup, *Shoggoth Showdown.*

Even with the one-two whammy of that rejection and Jay's bombshell, she couldn't miss work. So this morning, she had picked herself up off the floor, put on her big-girl pants, and dragged ass down to the café.

Ree sighed and checked her hair to make sure it hadn't spontaneously changed into an Emover.

She set the cupcakes on the cooling rack under the counter and checked on the coffee. It had been on for two hours but was still hot enough to serve. Back at Big Corporate Coffee Land, they'd had strict regulations about coffee rotation, but Bryan wasn't much of a stickler. They stuck close enough to health code regulations that the place had never gotten more than a warning.

She looked around the empty room and felt the shadow of Jay creeping back in.

This was going to take some intervention. If she was left by herself, alone with the cupcakes, the angst would run on repeat.

She checked her texts.

Sandra: I'll be home at 6:30. I can make dinner, or we can go out. I hope things are ok at work.

Priya: U ok? Sandra said you had a pretty bad night. Movies tonight?

Anya: Call me anytime. Have laptop, will travel.

Ree looked over her shoulder to check the cupcakes, then texted Anya: *Can you come to the cafe?*

Three minutes later, Anya: *What's up?*

Ree: Tide-y Bowl of Emo.

Anya: Got it. On my way.

Ree distracted herself with more baking, despite the fact that there were no customers. The food she made today would still be good for Friday, which should be busier. Since Zombie Cafe didn't believe in throwing out food if at all possible, anything left over after that would go home with the closer. Conveniently, Ree always made sure there were plenty of treats that she wouldn't mind eating all weekend if need be.

Hearing the theremin-tune motion detector, Ree looked up to see Anya Rostova (Strength 7, Dexterity 12, Stamina 15, Will 15, IQ 16, and Charisma 15—Musician 5 / Geek 2 / Scholar 3 / Opera Diva 2), wrapped in trendy jeans, a jacket, and one of the fabulous brocade scarves that Ree frequently plotted to steal from her but never quite managed to. Anya was Russian in the way that movies in the '80s said Russians always must be: thick black hair, sharp features, and an enviably curvy (if short at five-three) figure.

Ree coveted Anya's curves sometimes, having inherited a fairly sticklike figure from her mother's side of the family. Ree wore her hair long so she didn't get mistaken for a boy. It mostly worked. Mostly.

Anya, on the other hand, managed to look amazing every single time Ree saw her, which was impressive and somewhat frustrating, since as a doctoral student, she made even less than a comic shop lackey. But Anya was a diva-in-training, and fabulous was part of that job description.

Ree's own wardrobe consisted mostly of jeans, T-shirts, more jeans and T-shirts, a handful of skirts, her three "date outfits," and a smattering of business-wear for her occasional bank-breaking trips down to L.A. to pitch producers or attend conferences to woo agents.

"Step one: Can I get a chai?" Anya asked.

Ree nodded and grabbed a mug off the top of the espresso machine. "Done. Step two?"

"Step two happens when you're done here, but step one and a half can be where I tell you about how wild my show is."

Ree listened while on chai autopilot. Zombie Cafe used a chai concentrate, which made the drink comically easy to prepare. Since Anya had forsworn real dairy in her drinks, Ree started steaming some soy milk. Ree spoke up to be heard over the machine. "I do so love wallowing in the misfortune of others."

Anya cracked a smile. "It's one of your best qualities."

"True story. Now spill." Ree leaned over the counter, chin resting on one fist.

"So we're doing *Carmen,* right?"

Ree nodded. Since she'd met Anya, Ree's opera knowledge had gone from 0 to no more than +4, but even she knew *Carmen.*

"We're doing it Steampunk-style, so the toreador is fighting a steam-bull, right?"

Ree nodded. "Perfectly reasonable."

Anya continued. "And the director wants me to wear a corset so freaking tight, I can barely breathe. Then she yells at me when I can't hold the notes."

Ree raised an eyebrow. "Shouldn't she know that corsets do that? And that's it—a corset? Don't you at least get a clockwork arm or something?"

Anya chuckled. "I get a fan. As Madame Wesselmann reminded us, 'I performed the role of Papagena wearing a corset that brought my waist down to 18 inches—and we got rave reviews in Chicago.' So I get to 'suck it in.'"

Ree made a sour face while giving a thumbs-down, and Anya nodded.

"How was I supposed to know I should have been deforming my organs since I was twelve in order to properly function in my first operatic leading role?"

"That's really the kind of information they should put in your grad packet, at least, right?" Ree mimed a neutral voice-over tone: " 'As a part of the University of Pearson vocal performance program, here are some tips on how to best abuse your internal organs. Remember, organ failure is temporary, but glory is eternal!' "

Anya laughed.

At that particular moment, as Ree was happily settling into Listen-and-Support mode, a clear key-shift away from her post-breakup funk, the door burst open, hitting the near wall before the door chime could finish. Through the door lurched a scruffy man in a dirty black trench coat that Ree could have sworn was *smoking*. The man grabbed the door and slammed it behind him, muttering something under his breath. He was around six feet tall and looked somewhere between forty and fifty-five. He had a couple days' growth of beard and, oddly, several bruises on his face. The biggest bruise swelled one of his Capital-G-Green eyes nearly shut.

The man leaned back against the door to keep it barred. Then he looked to Ree and asked, breathless, "Do you have any Grant Morrison *Animal Man* trades?"

Ree had seen some rushed customers before, but this guy was asking about a comic book the way a Western hero who'd just walked ten miles through the blazing sun asked for water.

Ree casually scanned the wall for the section with Morrison's work and said, "Um . . .sure. I can get one for you, but they're on your left, between *Seven Soldiers of Victory* and *Batman & Robin*."

He turned to his left and pawed at the trades with gloved hands. His left glove was bloodied, several of its fingers torn and hanging off his hand.

"Is it less than twenty dollars?" he asked, fumbling with his wallet.

What the hell is up with this guy? Ree wondered. "19.95 . . ." she said.

The man pulled out a crumpled twenty and slapped it on the counter, leaving blood on the bill and the glass. "I don't need a bag, thank you."

He turned on his heel and pulled the door open, rushing out of the store while flipping through the book.

When the door was shut, Ree traded a *WTF?* look with Anya and said, "There's my weirdo for the day."

"You get one of those a *day?*" Anya asked.

Ree shrugged. "Most of the customers are nice, but there are some weirdos. He at least was in a hurry." *The real winners are the ones who corner me to talk about their RPG characters for hours, don't let me get a word in so as to actually participate in the conversation, and then leave without buying anything.*

A minute later, once Anya had resumed ranting about the wild antics of her director, Ree heard a *BOOM!* from outside. Ree guessed from the echo that it came from the alley by the gallery, but mostly, she focused on the fact that there was a *BOOM!* at all in a neighborhood/age where/when one should not hear a *BOOM!*, especially one that sounded more like a bomb than a backfiring engine.

"The *hell?*" Anya asked.

"Watch the store for a sec?" Ree said more than asked, grabbing the crowbar from under the counter. Said crowbar had +2 *N3wb Bane* engraved on the back, one of Bryan's many personal touches. She rolled back the comics shelf and strode out of the store, past the gallery, then into the alley, scanning the street as she went to look for people who looked capable of making a *BOOM!*

The usually boring alley was fifty feet deep, holding several Dumpsters and ending with a tall wooden fence that was the other side of a local church. There was no immediate evidence of a thing that would have gone *BOOM!*

Instead, Ree saw, halfway down the alley, a pile of colorful shredded paper that looked not quite like newspaper. She approached and looked over the pile and saw that it consisted of shredded snippets of a graphic novel. Several strips of comic page were plastered to the wall, with what looked like bloody prints on them. Ree walked over to the wall and saw from the slivers of art that they were pages from the book she'd just sold.

Ree tried to add up the situation and make it resemble sense in her mind: *So this guy comes in looking like he's a Backstreet Boy in '99 chased by crazed fans, buys a graphic novel in a crazed rush, and then runs out to shred the comic in an alley, does something to a wall, and somewhere in there, there's a BOOM!*

Ree shrugged. "Above my pay grade," she said to the alley, and then walked back into Zombie Cafe.

"I've got nothing," she said upon returning to her perch. She replaced the crowbar and leaned back against the rear counter. Anya raised an eyebrow, which Ree answered with a *what can you do?* shrug.

⨯✕⨯⬡⨯✕⨯

Anya stuck around for a couple of hours, long enough to help Ree settle back into a state of relative Zen. A few more customers came and went, mostly the awesome regulars who would buy drinks, stay to chat for a few minutes, then go on their way.

After they left, a couple of *Yu-Gi-Oh!*-loving teenage boys came in, bought one booster pack each, and then played several excited games, discussing school and the girls they had crushes on as if Ree couldn't hear them.

The people-watching and overheard conversations were one of the best perks of working retail or food service. *When you're out doing your own thing, it's easy to forget that the person in the uniform T-shirt or polo shirt is their own person.*

While the *Yu-Gi*-tots played, some students swung by for coffee, talking about classes and midterms as they waited for Ree to make their macchiatos.

Just after five, Jeff the Lawyer came in for his comics (*Batman*, *Astro City*, and *Morning Glories*) and a recap of the week's television (*Fringe, Community*, and *The Walking Dead*), but after the *Animal Man* guy, the day had reverted to normal.

Still, when business reached a lull, Ree occasionally replayed the *BOOM!* and the frantic customer's visit in her mind.

The sun started to set, orange lights pouring in from the west-facing windows, and Ree closed up the shop. She set the still-good-tomorrow pastries and baked delectables in the fridge and boxed up the ones that were no longer fit to sell. She traded pastries for bagels with the folks at Sue's Bagels, and cookies for veggies with Rachel at the co-op near her apartment.

Said apartment was affectionately known as "The Shithole" due to Ree's deep belief that the ancient idea of giving your kids crappy names to protect them from evil spirits and SIDS was applicable to apartments as well. The Shithole was actually quite nice for its price. But thanks to its thoroughly unappealing name, no random spiteful gods of housing would come around and rob her and Sandra of an apartment that was affordable, cute, and large enough to have friends in without A) being run by a slumlord or B) residing in the "Good Luck Not Getting Shot by Drug Dealers" part of town.

However, The Shithole was a fifth-floor walk-up, which had nearly killed Ree and the handful of friends who had helped when they moved in two years ago. Now that Ree and Sandra's stuff was safely ensconced on the fifth floor, Ree had no desire to move—ever, if possible—though she was willing to make a concession if Joseph Gordon-Levitt or Christina Hendricks asked her to run away with them.

Just inside the door was a pair of couches that formed the

TV nook, one of Ree's favorite spaces on Planet Earth. The nook's walls were lined with overburdened plywood bookshelves and a pair of hard drives that contained her preposterously large movie and TV collection. Across from the TV nook was the dining area, with two card tables shoved together and a collection of metal folding chairs, three folded down and another three leaned against the wall.

The kitchen was mostly Sandra's domain, since she'd spent a semester in culinary school before dropping out, just like she'd dropped out of nearly everything. Like Ree, Sandra was still on cruise control post-college (though in Sandra's case, it was post-college-the-third-time and post-AmeriCorps-which-she-didn't-even-finish-because-Thank-You-pneumonia). Currently, Sandra worked as a receptionist in a dental office and remained severely lacking in what Ree's dad would call "life direction." Ree had a life direction; it was just a seemingly impossible vector pointing to Hollywood.

Sandra wasn't home, but the kitchen still somehow smelled like fresh bread. Ree put on some water for tea and walked through the living room to her bedroom. She took one step toward her bed and lobbed her bag to bounce off of it into the corner. Her bed was a mattress and box spring stuffed against two walls, with burgundy sheets, a black duvet, and a pair of pillows. She'd used a bed frame for a while pre-Shithole, but the "feeling like a grown-up" bonus hadn't yet overtaken the "it's an extra thing to move" negative.

Ree changed into sweats and returned to the living room, settling in until Sandra got home from the crosstown commute and they could make dinner or go out. Sandra's boyfriend, Darren, would be by anytime, so Ree soaked up the solitude while it lasted. It was a different thing being home and alone instead of at work and alone. When she was at the café, there was always something theoretically to do; a customer could walk in any minute, and the coffee had to keep getting refreshed and the orders processed.

At home, she could just *be*. And so she was, splayed out on the couch with the TV on mostly for background noise. It was a Syfy original, and the horrible CGI monster looked like the redheaded stepchild of the baddies from *Ernest Scared Stupid*. She wrapped herself up in a blanket, and as she dozed off, her thoughts strayed to the weird customer and his desperate, inexplicable Morrison kick.

CHAPTER TWO

Tunnels and Trollops

A few minutes later, as she was nicely burrowed into her couch den, Ree's phone started playing her dad's ringtone ("Piano Man," his favorite). Ree extricated herself from the blankets and fetched her crooning device.

"Hi, Dad."

"Hey, love. How's the daily grind?" Ree could hear his self-satisfied smile through the phone—the one he used when he was patting himself on the back after a horrible pun. She couldn't help but grin.

"Rough only because it was smooth. Boring day, save for one weirdo. Anya swung by to chat for a while. What's the word from the world of hair?"

Ree's father was a hairdresser (for now) and had stuck with it longer than any of his previous careers. In the years after her mom left, Ree's dad usually worked long hours at multiple jobs to keep them afloat. Only recently had he been able to stay afloat without overtime.

"Fortunately, it's a growth industry. I had a few referrals this week, which helped. Any word on the writing?"

Ree's dad was her biggest (sometimes it felt like only) fan.

And he was thankfully taking her request from their last conversation to *not* talk about Jay. Any topic in the world was preferable to that jackass.

"Nothing since yesterday. I'm out of options with *Orion Overdrive*, unless one of the agents who never responded to submissions before actually writes back this time. I sent out another dozen submissions to agents last week, including the guy who said that he wanted to see something else from me when he rejected *Shoggoth Showdown*. But the Lindelof lead came back with nothing."

She could feel the smile in his breath. "Well, you're staying on it. What are you working on now?"

In truth, she hadn't written a word since the breakup, even when she opened a new document intending to free-write to get the anguish out of her brain. The words just didn't come. She had gone back and looked at *Orion Overdrive* after the last rejections, to try and see what didn't click, but her heart wasn't in it.

It wouldn't do any good to lie, so she said, "Yeah, about that. I've been in kind of a funk."

Her dad *hrrm*'ed in the phone. "Anything I can do?"

Ree shook her head by instinct, though of course her dad couldn't see it. "I'd rather not have you running from the law on an assault rap, so probably not."

"You know I'd do time for you, love."

"Of course, Dad. But you'd last about a millisecond in prison."

"What about all that Taekwondo you taught me? I've been practicing the roundhouse kick." Her father trying to do Taekwondo was hilarious, charming, and completely unintimidating.

"Take a knife-fighting class and then maybe we'll talk."

"We're talking right now."

Ree groaned. "This is me rolling my eyes."

"I'm not going to acknowledge that. How are the Rhyming Ladies?"

"They're fine. Pretty soon Priya will disappear down the hole of end-of-semester papers, and Sandra's been extra busy since one of the other receptionists is out sick."

A thought struck Ree. "Hey, any word back from banker lady?"

"Alas, no. I left a voicemail, but it's all echo chamber."

"Her loss," Ree said with a smile. Her dad was awesome, and he'd been single for way too long.

"I'm not exactly the world's most eligible bachelor, dear, your bias aside."

"Bias my ass, you're awesome and you deserve to be happy."

He chuckled. "Thanks."

The locks on the door opened one by one, and Ree looked over the couch to see her roommate walk in. Sandra gave her an only-the-wrist-moves wave.

Sandra Wilson (Strength 15, Dexterity 13, Stamina 13, IQ 17, Will 12, and Charisma 13—Geek 3 / Scholar 3 / Dancer 1 / Teacher 1 / Waitress 1 / Chef 1 / Professional 1) was just over six feet tall, had long curly black hair, a perfect olive complexion, and a build sufficiently Amazonian that Ree occasionally had to choke down a bout of homicidal jealousy.

Every group of friends had the hot girl, the funny girl, the smart girl, etc. The roles were usually visible only in contrast. Like in a sorority where all the girls are gorgeous, one is maybe a shade more camera-ready.

But Ree, she was the funny girl, the jester for her Rhyming Ladies, a crew who dated all the way back to college. Technically, the three women's names didn't all rhyme, it was just the name that had stuck. Ree had tried Ree and the Holograms, The Fabtastic Four, and The A-Team, but in the end, and prompted by her father's humor, they were the Rhyming Ladies.

Most of the time, when people scoped out her friends, they zoomed in on Sandra's statuesque figure, Anya's marvelous curves, or Priya's look-straight-through-you eyes.

Yes, the geekboys headed for Ree *if* a conversation ensued

that showed off her massive geek cred. But the rest of the time, well, she got to watch and make jokes.

Not helping, she scolded herself. Focus. Be positive.

Ree returned to her father. "That's Sandra. I should go, there needs to be dinner or I'm going to eat the couch."

"Take care, love," her father said.

"Love ya, Dad," she said, then hung up.

Sandra slung her purse on the coatrack and said, "We're going out tonight," as she turned toward her own room across from Ree's.

Ree called after her, getting off the couch. "Is something wrong?"

As Ree caught up to her, Sandra snorted in frustration. "Freakshows on parade today, so I need a drink. Plus, Darren's about to start his term papers, so he needs a drink. And I want to see him one more time before he's swallowed by term papers."

Darren was a graduate student in history at the University of Pearson, focusing on the gender politics of proxy wars conducted by the USA and the USSR. You'd think that would be interesting, but from what Darren said, it was mostly seeing how many times he could flatter his professor's research while quoting Foucault, Butler, and Hardt & Negri to prove his theory chops.

"Where are we going?" Ree asked as Sandra switched out of her business clothes into a skintight top and skirt that were less "dinner with grandma" and more "dessert with boytoy."

Sandra grinned. "Trollope's Trollops."

Trollope's Trollops was a college bar with more grad students than frat boys in the clientele, weekly burlesque shows, and open-mike debates. It was Darren's favorite, strangely more for the debates than the burlesque shows. At least until Sandra joined the burlesque troupe, at which point he declared it his boyfriendly obligation to attend every show. According to Darren, said duty was "truly torturous."

Ree clicked off the TV, silencing the comically gross trolls. As she walked into her room, she shouted, "Activate Bar Crawl outfit!"

Trollope's Trollops was fairly busy, since Thursday had been claimed by the drinking weekend years ago in Pearson. Darren was already there, splayed out in a corner booth to claim space. Darren Hudson (Strength 15, Dexterity 11, Stamina 14, IQ 18, Will 16, and Charisma 13—Scholar 7 / New England Heir 3 / Grad Student 3) was even taller than Sandra, with light brown skin and a bright smile. Darren stood to embrace Sandra with a deep kiss, then gave Ree a quick hug before the three of them took their seats.

Ree's heart rushed with vicarious excitement at her friends' kiss, then went *klunk* with a dull ache. She was in no condition to date, not for a while. If she did, it would be desperation and loneliness, not desire. And that way lay madness and more hurt feelings.

Plus, whom would she pick? She didn't have a shortage of suitors, but going home with one of the customers at Zombie Cafe would invariably be read as an invitation for all of the other regulars to ask her out, and then she'd have to kill them all, sleep with them all, or quit. Not a great set of options.

They ordered a pitcher of Urban Ale-ian, a local microbrew, which Darren paid for. Despite being a grad student— the larval form of the notoriously low-earning Professional Academic—Darren had money to throw around because of a gloriously bourgeois family background.

Oh, to have a wealthy family.

Ree had no such family fortune, so instead of a trust fund, she had student loans the size of Mount Rainier. If there was a continuum of financial savvy with Warren Buffett on one end, then Ree lived pretty close to the opposite extreme.

Most of the time, she blamed her continued brokenness on budgeting for the L.A. trips, but that was a convenient excuse. No one had come to break her kneecaps yet, so she took it as a win.

Ree sat back, letting Sandra and Darren chatter. She looked over the bar to take in the laid-back energy. She needed to recharge her social batteries, which had been flashing red most of the day, barring Anya's visit. Priya texted a few minutes into the pitcher, saying she was stuck at home with laundry.

Two beers later, Sandra asked Ree a question, but Ree hadn't been paying attention.

Ree shook her head. "Sorry, what? I zoned out."

"Do you want to go down to Turbo's for a slice?" Their pitcher was empty, and Turbo's was fantastic drinking/drunk food.

"Is the pope naked in the woods?" Ree said.

Darren raised an eyebrow, but Sandra laughed.

Ree and company donned their coats again and made their way through the bar. Ree licked her lips in anticipation of the pizza. *Why didn't I think of this earlier?*

The trio walked up the stairs to where the bar emptied out into an alley that was as likely to host a game of Hacky Sack as a homeless guy selling tube socks.

As she reached the door, Ree heard a shout.

"Gorram frakking piece of go-se!"

If Ree hadn't placed the voice by itself (which she did), the dense geek-speak cursing and the fact that there were more strange noises coming from an alleyway were enough to assure her that she was hearing the frantic customer from the afternoon.

Ree ducked around the corner and saw the man from earlier in the alley, holding a prop lightsaber and looking even worse for wear, if that were possible.

And then things got *really* weird.

Facing him was a twelve-foot-tall, green-gray-skinned beast with a bulbous nose and eyes so beady that they deserved their own craft fair. It was, for all Ree could tell, some kind of troll.

Except for the fact that trolls didn't exist and sure as hell didn't belong in the University District on a Thursday night when all she wanted to do was find someplace to drink in peace without running into one of her exes or any of the eccentric customers from her job.

> **break** *(n—Archaic English)—a thing that cannot be bought by one Rhiannon Anna Maria Reyes.*

Darren and Sandra both screamed when they saw the thing. The strange customer stepped forward, raising his lightsaber, which made the whirring hum of a high-end prop. Except that the glow was too good, too bright, for any of the sabers that Ree had ever seen. Ree kept a pretty close eye on the designs on the Web, to see if anything was cooler for practical use than her Force FX, but she hadn't found anything yet.

And the plastic or glass or whatever on this one was way too thin to be practical—she couldn't even see it through the glow.

And then the guy twitched forward with a quick kendo slice that cut off the troll's hand.

What.

The.

Eff.

The troll's bellow echoed through the alley, shaking dirt from the walls. The other side of the alley was a dead end into a building, so it wasn't not like she could escape, except back into the bar.

Sandra and Darren screamed from behind her; then Ree heard the door slam shut.

Well, crap.

The troll took a lumbering step toward Ree, and she found

her mind split in two. One part of her was so scared that she wanted to dig through the concrete to get away. But another part of her was strangely unimpressed, instead buzzing with excitement, saying, *The troll from that crap movie was better-looking than this thing.*

The logical part of her brain said to the suddenly fearless part, But, self, that thing was on TV, and this one wants to tear your liver out your nose. Run.

Before she could decide, the troll brought down its other massive hand toward her head.

Without thinking, Ree dove into a shoulder roll to the right of the beast's blow. She composed a letter in her mind as she rolled.

Dear Dad,
*   Thank you for enrolling me in Taekwondo when I was five and not letting me quit until I had my black belt.*
*   Love, your doting daughter*

P.S. Trolls are real. I know, right? Wild.

Ree rolled up to her feet, wondering how in the wild wild west she was going to joint-lock or jump-kick a twelve-foot-tall monster. Then the increasingly sane-seeming customer jumped forward and slashed again, his lightsaber cutting the troll's legs off at the knees. The beast howled in pain as it collapsed to the ground. Ree scrambled back and jumped clear of the falling troll's head, which crashed into the ground at her feet.

Over the troll's body, she saw the man standing in a perfect Force Unleashed stance. He watched the troll, standing ready. After a moment, he relaxed and touched a button on the lightsaber.

The too-realistic blade blinked out in a moment with the requisite sound. Deactivated, it looked like an expensive prop hilt.

"Are you all right?" he asked.

"The *hell?*" she answered, pointing at the maimed troll. It rolled over once, flailing for the man. *Aaah!* she thought, and shuffled away another couple of steps.

The bearded man jumped out of the beast's reach, unfazed. "Are you hurt?" he asked.

Ree dusted the street off her legs. A few scrapes, nothing bad. "No, but 'confused as hell' would apply."

"Understandable. You'll want to step back a bit more."

"Why?" she asked.

A second later, the dying troll popped like a burst balloon and gushed out into a puddle of viscous green-gray goop. Ree hopped back, but the wave of goop caught up to her, lapping over the sides of her boots.

She cursed absently, walking over to the man. "So who are you?"

"Call me Eastwood," the man said.

Ree put her hands on her hips, thoroughly past "unamused" and approaching "HULK SMASH."

"First name Clint?" she asked, one eyebrow raised.

"It's a nickname."

Taking another step toward Eastwood, Ree said, "I'd like to return to my earlier question: The hell?"

Eastwood gestured with his head to an open manhole in the street. "It was a troll, came out of the sewer."

Ree gave him a skeptical look. There was no way something that big could fit through a manhole. Not to mention that she still hadn't gotten a good explanation on the whole "trolls exist" fact.

Eastwood nodded. "You have questions, and I can provide answers. The fact that I've saved your life means you owe me the chance to explain, something I intend on doing." He took another look around the alley. "Looks clear. Come with me now before the Doubt settles in."

He pronounced *Doubt* with a capital letter, much the same way that her dad could say "Rhiannon Anna Maria

Reyes, come here Now" when she was in trouble. Which happened a lot, between her childhood science experiments, Nerf war escalation, and the avant-garde haircuts she gave their golden retriever, Booster.

She said, "My friends are back there, so I'm not leaving. You can explain right here or I can call the cops."

Eastwood harrumphed. "In less than five minutes, they won't remember this happened at all. That's what the Doubt does. But it won't affect you. I can explain why I came into your store and why the troll was here, but we need to get out of this alley before something worse arrives." He looked over his shoulder again, scanning the street.

Ree snorted. "Are you some kind of back-alley Kenobi? Come to teach me the ways of the Force so I can become a Jedi like my father?"

Eastwood flashed her a surprised look, then shook it off and pulled the lightsaber prop from his coat. "It's what I had on hand."

"Either you're drunk or I am. Wait here," she said, not waiting for him to respond. *But only one of us just came out of a bar, Ree,* she told herself. *Bah.*

Ree turned and opened the door again. Sandra and Darren weren't in the stairwell, so she walked down the stairs to see them looking around the entranceway of the bar. Sandra looked up and said, "Oh! I thought you were still in the bathroom. Ready for pizza?"

Not to sound like a broken record, but the hell?

"What are you talking about? We were just outside, it was kind of memorable?"

Darren gave a wordless humph of bemusement. "That joke wasn't that good, Ree. Firefly doesn't have to make sense to be fun."

You've got to be kidding me, she thought. "The troll, remember?"

Two blank faces looked back up at her. They didn't remember. Which meant Eastwood was not totally full of it. One way or another, it looked like the rabbit hole was inevitable. That or a padded room. Not a terribly appealing choice, really.

"Sure thing." Ree scaled the stairs two at a time and returned to the alley to see Eastwood using a cartoon mop to soak up the troll goop.

Huh, she thought, her mind the model of erudition.

"So?" he asked.

"Not now. Gimme your cell number," Ree said.

He laughed. "Just meet me outside Zombie Cafe at midnight, and we'll go from there."

"I have to work tomorrow. Gimme your cell and I'll call. My life isn't so crappy that I'm going to fall over myself asking for the blue pill, okay?"

Eastwood smiled and produced a smartphone. He pressed one button, and a second later, her phone started ringing.

Ree looked down, and the phone showed [Blocked]. She held it up to check with Eastwood that it was, in fact, him calling, but he'd pulled a Batman, vanished without a trace.

Ree turned to the door of the bar but jumped back as it opened quickly, revealing Darren and Sandra with confused looks on their faces.

And Fanboy somehow has my cell phone number. Great.

Stalker has the lead over Kenobi, 4–1, but the pool is still open.

CHAPTER THREE

As You Know, Bob

Shaking off the experience in the alley, Ree accompanied Sandra and Darren to Turbo's so they could all enjoy a glorious communion with the gods of pizza as incarnated in the basil pesto, tomato, Italian sausage, mozzarella, and feta pie. When they were done, Ree kissed Sandra goodbye and wandered down the street. Ever since the time Ree had gotten frustrated and shouted the couple's scores through the bedroom wall in a Russian accent, Ree had taken to lagging behind and giving the two some privacy. And this time, it was a convenient excuse.

When they were gone, she called Eastwood. The phone rang three times.

"Here's what you do," he said.

Ree recoiled from the phone. "Hello to you, too."

"Go south on Wilco ten blocks from Main, then turn left three times and knock on the first door on the right."

"Give me an address. I'll Google it."

He scoffed. "No go, girlie. That'd do you less good than telling it to give you a walking route from Hokkaido to Beijing."

Sighing, Ree said, "Whatever. Text me the directions."

"If you really want the scoop, Ms. Digital Native, you'll remember the *frelling* directions."

"Are you always this much of an ass?" Ree asked.

"This is my nice side, *mei–mei*."

"I'm not your sister."

"Just follow the directions."

And then he hung up. Ree stared at her phone, wrinkled her face in annoyance, and started walking.

She pulled her collar up as she crossed the street. If she were smart, she'd just go to a café and have some tea, then head home and pretend that the whole bullshit episode hadn't happened. Sandra and Darren had apparently r out the sight of the troll, but Ree couldn't help but see the damned thing every time she closed her eyes. She could still hear the pitch-perfect hum of the lightsaber as it cut through the monster's knees, so she continued following the directions Captain Analog had spouted. There was something seriously screwed up in Pearson, and investigating it was way better than going home and wallowing in misery, though possibly just as bad for her mental well-being.

And that's when she lost it, Doctor, Ree imagined Sandra saying as she looked down at a future Ree, locked in a padded room.

Wilco was mostly empty at 10 PM on a Thursday night. There were students here and there, a few homeless people, and the random unplaceable folks in clusters of ones and twos.

Making her way through the sporadic crowds, Ree reached Auburn, which was ten blocks south of Main. She'd left the U-District and entered a boring neighborhood filled with offices and apartments where rich kids from Cali and New England lived. This allowed them to attend U of P without ever having to deal with the inconvenience of seeing any parts of Pearson besides their classrooms and bars.

Ree walked a block, then turned left again, walked one more block, and turned left a third time. Why Eastwood couldn't have just said "Go south nine blocks and then go in the first door on the right" was hard to say, but maybe he had a yen for folklore. Or was a jackass with a yen for folklore.

Remembering the rampant awesomeness of the lightsaber, she knocked on the door, hoping to get answers. She waited a few seconds, and then the door swung open with a reassuringly archetypal creak. The genre-loving part of her brain chuckled in approval as she stepped inside to see a stairwell going down.

Ree pressed the Record button on her voice memo app and started down the stairs. If nothing else, she'd be able to turn this into some kind of one-act.

"Eastwood of Eden"? No. "East by Eastwood"? Nah. "Ghosts and Grognards?" Yes. That'd do.

There was another door open at the bottom of the stairs, lit by one naked bulb flickering consistently enough that she wondered if it was Morse code.

The room beyond looked like a cross between the Science Fiction Museum and the dealer's hall at Origins. Stacks climbed to the ceiling, forming narrow, dimly lit rows across the room. At the far side of the room, Eastwood stood in front of a desk piled high with books, yellowed paper, and a leaning tower of laptops. The far wall was covered by flat-panel TV screens.

Eastwood threw open his hands and said, "Welcome to the desert of the real." His voice carried easily through the long room, the air still.

She snerked. "Morpheus, eh? Your coat needs to be bigger, and you need that awesome gap between your teeth."

"Whatever. Just come in and close the door. We don't want to be interrupted, and you may have been followed."

"What, by fratboys?"

"If only," Eastwood said. "I can deal with the Bromance crowd."

Eastwood said the phrase with surprising seriousness. *Curiouser and curiouser.*

Ree made her way across the room, sneaking a look at the boxes and artifacts on the shelves. There were a lot of bound manuscripts, some old Betamax videos, DVDs, long-boxes of comics, and costume pieces from TV shows and movies across the 20th century, among others. She stopped and looked at a piece that looked like Gort's head from *The Day the Earth Stood Still*.

"Okay, I'm here. Lay some exposition on me, donor figure."

"That's Folklorist talk. Did you go to Berkeley?" Eastwood asked.

"Didn't. Dated someone who did." Ah, Berkeley, home of the best Folklore program south of the Mason-Dixon Line. Now, *that* had been a wild six weeks. Ree's romantic history had several advantages, namely all the strange nonweapon proficiencies she'd picked up over the years from her partners. Do it right and you can get a general studies degree from dating widely, or an honorary doctorate if you stick with one person long enough. Ree hadn't made it past the B.A. stage, though she'd learned more than a few handyman tricks from Jay.

Her stomach dropped at the thought of Jay, and she took a deep breath with her eyes closed, trying to push the feeling away.

When she opened her eyes, she looked up to Eastwood, who was waiting. He rolled a chair out in front of her. "Have a seat, this might take a while."

"You have any popcorn?"

"That's some impressive Snark Armor you have. I'd say +3 at least. Urban Outfitters?"

"ThinkGeek." Ree considered and raised her hands. "Sorry. I'm here to listen, so talk."

Eastwood picked up a mug from his desk, took a long sip, and started. "You're a geek."

"Yes . . ."

"You grew up watching sci-fi movies, reading fantasy novels, hiding under the covers after watching *Alien*. You probably played with lightsabers, maybe you had your cowboys fighting Picard and the spandex crew on the holodeck."

"Close enough. But what does that have to do with the big pile of ugly back at Trollope's?"

Eastwood waved to his stacks. "We tell these stories for a reason. They let us simultaneously remind ourselves of what's out there while reassuring us that they're not real. Humanity can't quite manage to stop telling the tales of the monsters and beasts, gadgets and robots. We keep the warnings alive, even in ridiculous contexts: monsters that eat co-eds and aliens that kidnap nubile maidens to Mars."

Ree sat forward. "Wait, are you saying these things are real because of the stories or despite them?"

"Good question," Eastwood said.

"You don't know?"

Eastwood started to pace back and forth, talking with his hands but never making eye contact with Ree. "There are a range of opinions, most of them crappy and none conclusive. Some say we told stories to explain the shadows at the edge of the cave, and in the telling, they became real. Some say that the shadows at the edge of the cave were already alive and our stories made them whole, bound them to individual forms that could be known, and when they were known, they could be killed."

"And what about this Doubt thing? Sandra and Darren don't even remember stepping out into the alley."

"The doing of some jackass a while back, during a massive throwdown in Europe during the Enlightenment. It was a virulent meme, spreading with humanism and rationality and all that rhetoric. The Technomancers wanted to be the alpha and omega of magic, so they tried a massive retcon, wanted to write the creatures out of existence."

Eastwood swiped one hand through the air. "Sadly, like any good meme gone viral, it took on a life of its own. Instead of eliminating the beasts entirely, the Doubt just settled into our minds and let us *MIB* ourselves out of believing such things exist when we do run into them. When they realized what had gone wrong, the Technomancers got into the secret-police gig. As they spread around the world with the various empires, the Doubt went with them. It's not fully settled in everywhere, and some people are immune, like with chickenpox or common sense."

Ree took another deep breath, processing the backstory while delaying judgment on whether she believed it. "So maybe you're telling the truth. Maybe you're some whacko predator with a damn fine hologram generator. And maybe you had someone slip something in our beer. How do I know you're for real?"

Eastwood nodded, walking around the corner into one of the stacks. Ree heard the sound of rummaging, and a minute later, he returned with a gray-white sphere. It looked for all the world like the training remote from *A New Hope*. Eastwood pushed a few buttons on the sphere, raised it to head level, and let go. The remote stayed in place, hovering and spinning slightly. Then Eastwood pulled the lightsaber prop out of his coat and handed it to Ree.

"You know what to do—elegant weapon, civilized age, all that good stuff."

Ree smiled. "Can you put on some John Williams?"

Eastwood smiled and pressed a button on a remote she had never noticed him pick up. Luke's theme started playing on the massive sound system, and a chill washed over Ree.

Okay, this is pretty cool. She had to admit, the prop was damned pretty. The metal was cool to the touch, and its rubber grip was sturdy but flexible in her hands. She found what should be the activation switch, then struck a stance she remembered from *The Force Unleashed* and flipped the switch. The saber jumped to life with the appropriate sound, but the blade didn't feel any heavier.

Ree smiled from ear to ear. "Wow."

Eastwood grinned. "Right?"

"So if I can't use the Force, how am I supposed to keep from chopping my own hand off?"

"I've tweaked it so that it won't cut through matter, but it will absorb the blasts. Speaking of which." The drone spun and floated to the left, shooting out a white bolt of energy. Ree tried to bring the blade across her body to parry, but missed. The bolt hit her in the left shoulder, hurting like a bee sting. She let go of the lightsaber with her left hand and curled the arm up in pain.

"Sonofa . . . But this is all stuff you can do with a good animatronics department and a roofie," she said, not sure she believed herself. Or what to believe at all.

The drone spun and moved to one side, then fired another bolt.

Ree continued trying to block the zaps while Eastwood talked. "Really? Or are you just trying to keep from freaking out? You accepted the troll's existence when it was about to crush you into smithereens, but now that you're only getting stunned, you feel like you can play Doubting Thomas."

Damnit. He was right. There were too many weird-ass things to be able to brush them all off with roofies or David Blaine sneakiness. Eastwood might be a stalker, but he was giving her more answers than she'd had before, and the weird had stacked up way past the level of prank. Was her lingering skepticism good old human logic, or was it all the Doubt?

Ree walked up toward the drone and grabbed it, looking for the off switch. "Okay, that's enough drilling for now. Keep spilling your guts about these Technomancers, but first go to the part that tells me why you came into the store and why there was a troll in the alley but I've never seen anything weird before today."

"It could be that you've never run afoul of any creatures or magicians before today, or maybe someone's been protecting you, or maybe you've had encounters before but this time the

Doubt didn't cover it up . . . What do you think?"

"Is this some kind of test?"

Eastwood shrugged. "I actually don't know, but I'd like to hear your opinion. In case you didn't notice, I'm no Dumbledore, and I have better things to do than spend all day educating nascent Geekomancers—but you do intrigue me enough to figure out why you fell through the cracks."

Ree walked back to the chair, sitting and feeling it roll toward the stacks. She reached out and stopped herself before she hit anything. "Well, for one, I wouldn't know if someone's been protecting me, since, to my knowledge, this is the first time I've seen something that would make normal people run screaming for Prozac or the psych ward. And what the hell kind of title is 'Geekomancer'?"

Eastwood shrugged. "The name stuck. It's no less ridiculous than Bromancer, Plutomancer, Celebromancer, or any of the other schools of magic."

"How many schools are there?"

"Seems like it changes every day. Blame postmodernity, it's an easy scapegoat."

"Really? I'd expect it to be dodgy, full of unstable referents and all."

Eastwood cracked a smile. "Touché."

"So what was up with the Grant Morrison trade?"

"I was tracking an *oni,* and I needed a power boost to follow it up the walls and over the rooftops."

Ree cocked her head to one side. "So the comic let you climb walls?"

Eastwood nodded. "That's my thing. I take artifacts and use their power. In a pinch, I can take a manuscript or DVD or tape and break it to take on something from the story. Animal Man trade paperback plus my portable shredder equals instant animal empathy for one hour."

"Let me parse that for a second. One: *Oni* are real, like big-gnarly-teeth Japanese-demon *oni.*"

"Yes."

"And two: All of the comics in my store might as well be single-serving superpowers as far as you're concerned."

Ree looked over to one of the stacks and saw a dusty pile of individual comics issues, including three beat-up copies of *Marvelman*. Ree restrained the urge to swipe one and stow it in her coat. She'd never read it in paper, only scans.

"Not just that," Eastwood said. "They can be used in rituals, too. It's slower, but you get more bang for your book."

Ree took a breath and voiced a question. "So why don't you just carry copies of *Superman* around and channel Kryptonian badassery all the time?"

Eastwood nodded, thoughtful. "You can do that, but even with the artifacts, you're still channeling power. An average collector-level issue is good for at best one post-Crisis Kryptonian punch. To get any kind of sustained power, you need ridiculously important artifacts. I saw someone rip up an *Action Comics #15* for power once." A doofy grin passed over his face. "It was astonishing."

Ree opened her eyes wide as her mind contemplated the possibilities. *This is either the coolest or the craziest thing that's ever happened to me. Probably both.*

"So the bigger-league the power you want to channel, the less uses you get? Like magic item charges or a mana pool?"

Eastwood nodded. "Exactly. If you have a larger supply, you can learn to squeeze more out of an artifact over time. I don't want to think about the number of Star Wars special-edition DVDs I've melted in my crucible."

Ree laughed. "Well, in that case you're doing the world a great service."

"Not a fan of the fiddling?"

Eyebrow raised, Ree asked, "Have you met anyone who is?"

Eastwood shrugged. "Lots, actually. Mostly Cinemancers—they'll tweak movies to get different effects out of them."

"So what's the difference between you and a Cinemancer,

then?" Ree felt a headache coming on from all the weirdness. It was worse than watching a David Lynch film. *Maybe I should be taking notes.*

Then she remembered that she *was* and pulled her phone out of her pocket, seeing the clock run on the recording. She stopped it and started a new one; it'd be easier to load them back onto her laptop that way.

Eastwood said, "They're more specialized, I'm more a generalist. And I focus more on artifacts and memorabilia; they play more in celluloid and iMovie."

"And you called me a Geekomancer, too. What makes you think I can do any of this?"

"How many trolls have you fought before?"

"None, but I do have a black belt in Taekwondo and Hapkido."

He nodded, processing. "And what was the last movie you watched?"

Some zombie flick from last night, before the drinking. No, it had been that Syfy troll movie, playing in the background while she waited for Sandra.

"Why does that matter?"

"It's rare, but one of the strongest effects of Geekomancy can be genre emulation—watch a movie and you can replicate the powers or skills of a character. If you'd watched *Star Wars* before coming here, you could have blocked every one of that drone's bolts with a little bit of the right focus."

"Why haven't I been doing it before?" Ree asked.

"Probably the same reason you've never seen a troll before. When people affected by the Doubt do magic, they never remember it. Anyone passionate about something can be a magician, focus their emotional energy into impossible effects. They might never remember it, write it off as luck, or rewrite their memory so that it doesn't break their brain."

Eastwood paced over to the edge of his desk, then turned around and continued back, talking to the air more than to her. "Some types of magic are harder than others. Genre emulation is rare, from what I've seen. Like some of the more powerful talents, it seems to run in bloodlines, sometimes lying dormant for several generations. There's more magic in the world than you'd think, which is actually really cool." Eastwood turned the corner and walked down an aisle, still talking. "If people knew the effect they were having on the world, it'd be pretty amazing—then again, magic isn't all sparkles and rainbows up your *pi gu,* so maybe it's not so bad."

He emerged from the aisle holding a comb-clip-bound manuscript, paging through it while humming a song that Ree half-remembered from her youth—'80s TV show, maybe?

"What now?" Ree asked.

"Good question. I don't take apprentices, as a general rule, but I do need help with something, so I'm willing to make a trade. I show you the ropes, you help me with this case."

"The *oni?*"

Eastwood shook his head and grabbed a newspaper off his desk. He handed it to Ree and said, "That was a one-off. This is my real problem."

A short article below the fold on the cover was circled.

Recent String of Teen Suicides—Parents Panicked

Ree scanned the article. Three teenagers in Pearson had committed suicide within the last month. To the parents' knowledge, none of them had been bullied.

Ree handed the paper back to Eastwood. "Okay, so this is horrible, but what does it have to do with your mountain of memorabilia?" She gestured to the stacks behind her.

"I've psychic-papered my way onto the crime scenes, and there's been a stink of magic at each site. And I've dug up another link between the kids—they all had breakups within a week of their suicide."

"Who would benefit from making people kill themselves? Some demon worshipper?"

A shadow passed over Eastwood's face. "There are . . . a lot of people who might take an interest in this—which is why I could use some help. I think someone's following me, but they might not be able to follow you at the same time. I want you to go to the family of the third suicide. Angela Moorely, 4710 Washington. See what you can find out about her, especially the details of her breakup. I can't help but feel that there are some other connections between the kids that I haven't cracked yet."

Ree stood up and gave Eastwood the *quoi?* eyebrow. "And how I am supposed to get them to talk to me?"

Eastwood pulled a leather-bound wallet from his coat, then opened it toward Ree. At first it was blank. Ree blinked and saw lettering fade in as a gold badge appeared on the other side, identifying Anthony Eastwood as a detective lieutenant with the Pearson PD.

"Psychic paper."

Eastwood nodded. "It'll work for you, too. When you show it to someone, just focus on making them believe that you belong."

"These aren't the droids you're looking for," Ree said.

"Except this time, you *are* the droid they're looking for."

"I have to pose as an android detective? Will the ID say Deckard?"

"Are you capable of ever not being snarky?" Eastwood asked.

"Only if I try really hard. Plus, this situation is so preposterous, this is the only way I can keep from freaking out."

"Call me when you've had the chance to talk to the Moorelys, and we'll go from there. In the meantime, watch an action movie where the main character never gets hurt, or maybe a Looney Tunes. Something to make you tough—until we can do more training."

Ree checked her watch and did the mental math of how much sleep she'd be able to get before rising from the dead in the morning to open Zombie Cafe. Less than six hours. Not great. But weren't all the best detectives insomniacs, anyway? Maybe it would help.

She slipped the papers into her coat and left the basement lair. Outside, the chill winds of autumn had picked up. They sliced at her face and legs on the way home as she pondered.

So, am I actually going to do this? Question the families of suicides, tag along with an eccentric magician?

That can be Future Ree's problem. Right now, bed.

By the time she reached The Shithole, she was rubbing her face to get the feeling back in her nose. It wasn't supposed to get this cold in the Northwest, not unless you were way inland. *Portent or random vagary of weather?* Ree harrumphed at the fact that such questions were now a valid part of her life. There were no lights on in the apartment, except a crack of white at the bottom of Sandra's door. Ree poured a glass of water and took it to bed, placing bets with herself on what wild-ass dreams she'd have from the day's events.

CHAPTER FOUR

A Study in Sherlock

When the air-raid-siren alarm on her phone went off in the morning, the first thing Ree did was grab the phone to paw at the snooze button.

The second thing she did was groan in dissatisfaction at having to be up at an hour that was beyond monstrous, beyond unearthly: It was Shift-X painful. During college, Ree had been the No Classes Before 10 AM sort, finding that her natural hours for sleep were 2–9 AM. After that, the barista schedule tried both body and soul.

The third thing she did was stare at the leather fold-over that contained the slip of seemingly psychic paper.

Which meant the whole thing was in fact not a dream, and that she had for realz fallen through the cracks in the world and discovered that magic works and trolls lurk in alleys.

Clearly, the only thing to do was take a shower.

As the paper was still there when she was done with her shower, she accepted unreality and dressed for work. She slipped on a pair of work jeans and a black cami, then a Superman Kingdom Come T-shirt, and a hoodie over that. *Layers, kid, layers.* That was one of the first lessons she'd learned when she moved to the Northwest with her dad, after he'd moved them around from job to job and place to place before landing in his current cosmetics cooperative. She topped off her outfit with a Wonder Woman beret to hold back her hair.

Properly equipped for the day, Ree grabbed the wallet off her dresser and stuffed it into a pocket to keep it safe. And maybe a little to let her prove she wasn't hallucinating.

There wasn't any use in having breakfast at home, since there would be pastries to eat at work. But in deference to "healthiness," she poured herself a bowl of cereal and wolfed it down to the dulcet dorkiness of the last night's *Daily Show* on her laptop while catching up on email.

While Ree was eating, Sandra emerged from her turn in the shower, and they talked for a few minutes in that glorious sliver of time while the world was waking up, before the day started in earnest and the weights of life came dropping down like globs of snow falling off trees during a thaw.

×✗×⬡×✗×

Bryan was already at the café when Ree arrived, oven wafting the comforting smells of sugary carbs throughout the room. Xombi's owner and manager was a fairly typical geeky guy of fortyish, with bushy brown hair, a full beard, and a bit of a paunch that had expanded in the last few years alongside his family's expansion from one child to three with the arrival of the twins. His wife, Amy, worked for a restaurant goods wholesaler, currently selling from home so she could stay with little Luke and Leia full-time.

As Ree walked through the door, keys jingling, Bryan greeted her. His warm voice was always reassuring. "Good morning. Looks like it was a slow day yesterday?"

Ree nodded. "Steady morning, then practically nothing in the afternoon."

Except the guy who came in for a graphic novel and sent my life spiraling into bizarroville.

But Bryan didn't need to hear about that. Who *did* need to hear about it? Was she going to tell anyone about this? Would anyone believe her? She didn't know how much of anything worked on the Flip Side.

They Might Be Giants played on the stereo, the two Johns serenading her with scientific singsong about the sun. Ree settled into the café's routine, baking and brewing and then serving and squeezing through the tiny service area as she and Bryan dodged each other to accommodate the Friday-morning rush. The chatter about comics and movies and the latest political dustup helped Ree find her feet again, get grounded in the rhythm of the real world.

At 3 PM, Bryan's eldest walked in, dumped his backpack on an empty table, and stepped up to the counter for a drink.

"Hola," Ree said.

Aidan Blin (Strength 12, Dexterity 11, Stamina 11, IQ 16, Will 14, and Charisma 15—Geek 3 / Prodigy 1) took after his dad, standing just on the tall side of average, neither skinny nor thick, with a mop of unruly oak-brown hair and an easy smile. He also kicked academic ass and took names, having become a high school senior at the ripe age of sixteen.

Aidan gave her the half-smile (also inherited from his father), then asked, "Can I get a vanilla Italian soda with one shot of strawberry?"

Ree nodded, spinning in place to make the drink. She talked over her shoulder as she worked, hands remembering where everything was and leaving her brain free to chat. "Any word from Stanford?"

Aidan and his girlfriend had both applied to Stanford for early decision. The responses were due by the end of the month, and over the last week Aidan had turned into a coiled bundle of nerves.

Aidan responded as he returned to his table. "Nothing.

I can barely pay attention in class, and I got my phone confiscated during math for checking email."

"You're not supposed to be using your smartphone during classes anyway," Bryan said.

Aidan rolled his eyes. "You didn't have the temptation of instant gratification when you were in high school, Dad."

"Thank the goddess I didn't. I'd have been a nervous wreck!" Bryan said, laughing. Aidan huffed.

That's what you get when you have a trickster for a dad, Ree thought, suppressing a laugh.

Aidan looked down to his laptop screen, clicked at something, then sighed again.

Oh, the Joy of the Endless Refresh, Ree thought. Aidan had a high standard to live up to. He'd been in Gifted & Talented programs his whole life, had skipped 8th grade, and was intending to declare pre-law. Ree had never had a plan like that—"become a famous screenwriter" was both more nebulous and more unrealistic, though she could pursue it on her own time frame.

Aidan took off his headphones and rubbed his temples, looking tense even here, among family and friends, goofing off.

Not a good sign, Ree thought. Time for a Spanglishvention.

"Hang in there, kid," she said in Spanish. Not her normal "I grew up speaking this with my dad" Puerto Rican Spanish, but "horribly pronounced if grammatically correct" Spanish, with an accent that sounded like it came from a Valley kid drunk on cheap tequila.

Aidan perked up and responded in equally bad Spanish, "I am not Hang in There Kitty."

Ree cracked a smile, which Aidan matched. She ruffled his hair, and he brushed her hand off, scrunching up his face in mock annoyance.

"Whichever way the universe goes, you're going to do great," Bryan said from behind the counter.

Aidan nodded at his dad and went back to his laptop.

At 3:30 PM, Ree finished up her shift, hugged Aidan on her way out, and headed home.

If I'm going to try this and something explodes, it should be my something, not Bryan's, Ree thought. There was also the whole magic-in-public thing.

Ree returned to The Shithole, made sure Sandra hadn't randomly come home for an unknown reason, then set to work.

She had done as much research on the local suicides as she could during downtime at work, reading the news articles and chasing some of the chatter across social media sites from impromptu digital memorials that the girls' friends had put up and set to public. It was an intriguing puzzle, with seemingly no connection between the victims other than their romantic circumstances. That'd be one hell of a specific serial killer, assuming there was malicious intent. Ree had no idea what magic could or couldn't do to people's minds. It was disturbing, the same kind of disturbing that led Ree to stay up too late at night watching horror movies.

Setting her mind to the task, she changed into one of her "I am serious screenwriter" outfits. This one was a charcoal pantsuit with two buttons, a hint of extended shoulder, and an orange silk blouse. With that, she should be able to pass for a young and casual Someone Important.

Next she pulled the first series DVDs for the BBC *Sherlock* down from its shelf and popped it in.

All right, so I need to focus, internalize the awesome. But is it about the character or the show? The writing or the feeling?

Probably the feeling, she decided, hoping she wasn't about to explode thousands of dollars of tech.

Ree smirked internally at how wild it all was. But as much as it was wild, it was also exciting. *Magic. Real magic. And monsters and superpowers.* She shook out the nervousness and queued up the first episode, "A Study in Pink."

As she watched, Ree dialed in to Benedict Cumberbatch's Sherlock Holmes, his mannerisms and speech; as she did so, she couldn't help but smile again at the great shot composition and use of the soundtrack.

She'd just finished the scene where Sherlock uses his deduction-fu on the woman with the pink coat when the doorbell rang.

Damnit, don't lose focus. If she had to start over, she'd lose time, maybe miss something.

Ree went to the door, still watching the show out of the corner of her eye, with the intention of brushing the visitor off. She peeped through the eyehole and saw the building's superintendent. She opened the door a quarter of the way, leaning against the wall.

As her eyes scanned the super up and down, her mind went into overdrive, a buzzing in her mind driving her thoughts.

She looked down, and superimposed text popped in over his feet, the same font as in *Sherlock*.

It read: Left leg .5 inches shorter than right.

Her eyes scanned up the man's leg to a patch of exposed skin where his stained shirt failed to cover his side.

A line of text popped up over his waist: *Surgical scar above the left hip.*

She noticed a metallic flash from a coin on a chain tied to his belt. *24th Infantry Division Challenge Coin.*

Holy crap, it's working! Ree thought as her mind raced.

She looked up to the man's shoulders, then saw more text: *Right shoulder displaced. Improperly healed.*

Then she looked him in the face. Sun damage. Crow's-feet. Wrinkles.

As the super opened his mouth to speak, Ree jumped the gun, saluting her super. "You never told me you had a Bronze Star, Sergeant."

The superintendent took a step back, crossed his arms. "Excuse me?"

Ree continued without thinking, agape at what she was doing, her mind on Sherlock overdrive, jumping from fact to inference faster than she could keep track.

"Your left leg is half an inch shorter than your right. There's a surgical scar on your hip, suggesting extensive reconstructive surgery. You never wear shorts, even during the hottest parts of the year, because you're self-conscious about your prosthetic leg. The displaced shoulder indicates that you pushed a squadmate out of the way of something, I'm assuming a vehicle. Maybe during military action. More likely during an accident. You took the brunt of the damage along your left leg, hence the prosthetic. But you also displaced your shoulder when you landed, thrown by the vehicle. The sun damage on your face but not your waist suggests you were exposed to extensive UV radiation that, combined with the age suggested by your crow's-feet and facial wrinkling, indicates that you could have received the injury only in Desert Storm. Casualties were rare in that action, but accidents can happen anytime."

The superintendent rocked back on his heels, his eyes wide. Ree wanted to stop, but the words kept flowing. "And any soldier who saves one of their squadmates would receive not only the Purple Heart but a Bronze Star, likely with a Valor Device. That heroic act and the two tours it would take to have sun damage that extensive indicates you would have left the service as at least a sergeant. Had you achieved higher rank, it's unlikely that you would become only a superintendent, though that could be due to the injuries. I've heard there have been great advances in artificial legs since then, but I imagine you'd have them by now. Troubles with the VA, perhaps? A shame."

Both thrilled and somewhat shocked at the frankness of how she was addressing the man, who could have her evicted from their beloved Shithole for any one of the many, many regrettable things she and Sandra had done over the years,

Ree continued, "Regardless. Your service and your sacrifice make you a war hero. So I thank you, sir."

Ree extended her hand to shake without thinking about it.

Her super stood speechless. He did not meet her hand, instead wiping his on his pants leg.

Ree marveled at the twisty road of deduction she'd sprinted along. But in showing off that skill, she'd embarrassed the super and created a big bucket of awkward.

The show still ran, off to her right, as she regarded the clearly uncomfortable super. "What can I do for you?" she asked, conscious of each word to make sure she said what she wanted, not what the Sherlock magic would have her say.

The superintendent took a second, then said, "I just wanted to tell you that we'll have to shut off the water in a half hour so we can fix the water main."

Ree nodded, and the super, whose name she couldn't remember for all the Geekomancy in the world, took a step back and walked down the hall.

Another set of Sherlock text popped up as he walked.

Right leg stride length 22"

Left leg stride length 20.5"

Wow, Ree thought. It really works. I wonder what else I can do.

Thinking back, she realized the little details had been there all along—the coin, the stride—but she'd never considered them much, and she'd never known how to identify challenge coins by sight.

Ree closed the door and turned back to the television. Her vision focused on the DVD wall, and as she read titles on the boxes, the possibilities popped up in her vision, the text layering like a typewriter wound back to write and rewrite over the same page hundreds of times.

Superstrength. Wire-fu. Romantic serendipity. Cartoon invulnerability. Organic web-shooters. Superskill Intersect. Eidetic memory.

Ree closed her eyes and shut out the text before it

overwhelmed her.

I really hope this gets easier, she thought as her mind continued to race.

She took in another breath, trying to hold back whatever part of her that was the rampaging intellect on a Sherlock binge.

Right. Time to go play girl detective before I lose this. And try not to freak out everyone I come across between now and then.

The winds were gentle, so Ree decided to walk the couple of miles to the Moorelys' house. Listening to Massive Attack on the way, she tried not to look too long at any one person so as to avoid the creepily accurate Sherlock-read until she needed it.

A half hour later, she reached the 4700 block of Washington and saw the squad car parked outside.

Bloody hell, there's already someone here.

The psychic paper should get her in, but would it convince a detective or patrolman not to ask her questions she couldn't answer? Ree had taken only a couple of criminal justice classes, more to help with her writing than for real use. She could wait until the car left, but how long would that be?

Almost certainly longer than she could hold Sherlock in her head without getting an aneurysm.

Affecting her best official-person look, she walked up the steps to the front door. She knocked three times, holding the psychic paper in her hands and repeating in her head, *I belong here. I belong here. I belong here.*

A middle-aged man with salt-and-pepper hair answered the door. He had bags beneath his eyes larger than what you'd expect to see in a Long Island housewife's arms the Saturday before Christmas.

"Hello?" he asked.

Ree held up the paper and said, "Agent Reyes, FBI. Are you Victor Moorely?"

"Yes. May I help you?"

"I'm here to ask some questions for our profile on your daughter, Mr. Moorely."

"Why is the FBI involved?"

And now the B.S. skills. Here goes nothing.

"The FBI is taking a direct interest in the national teen suicide rate, and we have task forces established across the country. May I come in?"

It sounded better than she'd expected.

"Please." He stepped back and opened the door, ushering her inside.

The interior of the house was pleasantly decorated, but there was a pall of sadness and neglect. Moorely pulled out a chair for her from their dining table, and they both took a seat.

"First, I'm very sorry for your loss," she said.

Moorely nodded, clearly trying to find a small smile to utter his thanks.

"Do you mind if I ask a few questions?"

He nodded again, though a twinge of pain hit his face as he realized what was coming. How many times had he already answered A Few Questions? Had the media been here? How many outlets? His story would be rehearsed by now, for better or worse—in *Lie to Me*, Timothy Roth had told her that rehearsing a story made it more rote, but there would still be indications of deceit, if she could pick them out. Maybe she should have watched *Lie to Me* to prepare instead of *Sherlock*.

"Mr. Moorely, how long had your daughter been seeing William Smith?"

"They had been going out for about four months—they met through a local stage company."

"Angela was a singer, yes?"

Moorely smiled, then half-choked, half-sobbed. He took a breath and said, "Since before she could walk."

"Can you tell me what you think happened last night?" Ree had to fight the urge to step back and watch herself in the role. It was an ridiculous cocktail: empathy for the Moorelys, curiosity, fear, and the strange detachedness of the Sherlock Brain—not to mention the niggling claws of her own relationship anxieties trying to personalize everything.

"William came over at seven, and we had dinner—Angela, William, my wife, Alexandra, and I. At about eight, they went upstairs to talk. William left at nine, and at nine-fifteen, we heard sobbing from upstairs, so Alex went up to check on Angela."

"Is your wife home now?" Ree asked.

He shook his head. "She's in the middle of a case and couldn't get any of the junior counsel to take over. She should be back by six."

There went the afternoon. "If you don't mind, I think I'll wait to speak with her as well. Sorry to have interrupted. What can you tell me about William?"

Victor Moorely sat back in the chair, a mix of anger and friendliness passing over his face. "He's a good kid—he gets good grades, he's funny. I was excited for Angela, thought maybe she'd been one of the lucky ones to meet a good guy so early. My wife and I didn't meet until we were in our late twenties."

Ree nodded. She'd need to talk to William as well. *Sigh.* This was going to become a full-time job, and all for what? The chance to LARP her favorite TV shows?

"Have you spoken with William since the dinner?" she asked.

"Alex called him after . . ." Instead of finishing his thought, the man broke down in a fit of sobs.

Crap. Moorely hunched forward, looking down. She waited a few moments before trying to probe again, but he just sat there, folded over himself. Ree sat up as straight as she could, armoring herself with the role of the FBI agent, immune to the raw human emotion of a man broken by grief.

"Mr. Moorely, are you all right?"

He made another short choking sound, then breathed deep. He sat up and wiped his eyes. "I'm sorry."

The investigative questions had come easily, popping up in her mind like she was being fed a script. This time the words were her own. "No need to apologize. It's the only sane thing to do." He nodded, so she continued. "Can I see her room?"

Probably eager to do anything other than talk, the bedraggled man stood and led her upstairs to a room decorated in posters and signs that read *Parents Keep Out* and *Twihards Only*. Ree opened the door and took in the room all at once, like a panorama photo in 1080p plastered in her mind as she unleashed the Sherlock Brain.

Slightly messy. Pastel colors. Layers of blankets and colorful sheets on a simple wooden bed frame. White faux-wood desk with shelves built in. A flat-panel screen and desktop below. Speakers flanking the screen.

The pop-up text returned: *Average media consumption.*

Small TV on a dresser. Guitar in the corner on a stand. Posters of sparkling vampires, androgynous boys, and famous divas lined the walls in equal proportions.

Sexually inexperienced.

Everything was as it should be for a normal teenage girl.

Except for, that is, the bloodstain on the floor beside the bed. It was two feet wide, slightly oval-shaped.

For a moment, Ree saw Angela's body on the ground, in photo-realistic detail, the blood pooling beneath.

Ree closed her eyes, forcing the sight out of her mind. She opened them again, and the body was gone.

Died here. Wasn't moved, popped up in Sherlock text.

Ree scanned the room for another few seconds, taking in data. Nothing was relevant.

No signs of struggle.

More Sherlock text: No secondary pool from a bloodied weapon.

Ree returned to her own thought processes, holding back the Sherlock Brain.

Where was the weapon? How quickly had the parents found her—what had she done that would let her bleed out without anyone hearing? Eastwood had said there was a trace of magic on the death, but what kind, to what effect?

She was floundering in deep water here. She felt her Sherlock-ness receding, and looked around the room one more time, her eyes passing over a silver locket she hadn't noted as relevant before. A bit of text popped into shape above the dresser, reading *Locket,* fading out as soon as it appeared.

Ree gave the locket a once-over. It contained an old picture of a woman who could have been Angela's mother or grandmother. Ree briefly searched for connections, then filed the image away for later.

With the Sherlock Brain gone, she was left with exhaustion and the sense of needing to smoke. Which, since she hadn't smoked since college, she blamed on the detective. Use the effects, get the needs. Made sense, if in a disturbing way.

Eastwood damn well better teach her every single trick and give her a pony for this.

She stepped around the room, taking extra care to avoid the stain on the carpet. Moorely stayed at the door, like he couldn't bring himself to cross the threshold.

With all the magic gone, Ree was left on her own. Pulling the door partly closed, she tried to assemble her thoughts, figure out how to put the pieces together.

What did she need? Emails and other online messages, maybe lists of friends to talk to for a third-party perspective.

Ree opened the door a crack, seeing Mr. Moorely standing outside, his eyes unfocused.

"If possible, I'd like to get access to her computer, check to see if there were some hidden factors." *Hidden factors? The hell was that? This is going to fall apart fast without the magic. Less talking, more snooping.*

Moorely didn't respond at first, so Ree opened the door all the way, blocking the blood as best as she could with her body, and stepped out into the hall.

That broke him out of whatever reverie had been holding him. He shook his head, then nodded. "Sure. Her passwords probably have something to do with Justin Bieber, or maybe Tyra Banks."

Ree nodded and opened the bedroom door again. "I'll work here until your wife arrives. Thank you for your help, Mr. Moorely."

She closed the door, sealing herself in again. Ree heard steps in a slow descent. A shiver ran over her body at the thought of losing a child. She didn't even want kids, but the idea of losing them was far worse. To have the ghost of a person who was part you, part the person you love, haunting you for the rest of your life.

Shit. Ghosts. Were they real, too? Was Angela's spectre hanging around in the room? Ree looked over her shoulder, realizing that while she didn't have a clue about how to deal with spirits, she still didn't want to be surprised by one.

Uncertain, she spoke aloud to the room. "Angela, if you're here, I'm doing what I can to understand what happened to you, so you can move on . . . or whatever the ghosts of suicides do."

She waited but received no response.

"And don't ask me for answers. I'm new at this."

She turned her attention to the desk and the girl's computer and started the creepy process of learning about someone's life from the inside, scrolling through status updates and friends lists.

Note to self: Better passwords so that people can't snoop through my life when I die.

While the creepy-intruder feeling didn't go away, Ree did manage to pull up some information that gave her leads on Angela's emotional state. She'd seemed fairly happy and teenager-in-super-mega-greatest-love-ever, though "teenager" automatically indicated "hot mess." The hormonal soup of adolescence was vicious, viscous crap, and even skimming it through someone else's perspective was enough to give Ree flashbacks to being the skinny nerdy girl with the big glasses and no friends except a circle of a half-dozen geeky boys. Every last one of whom wanted to date her and would eventually reveal that in their own marvelously clumsy ways.

Ah, memories.

Reaching her digital-voyeur limit, Ree left the computer behind and took another look through the room, making sure she hadn't missed anything. She treaded lightly through the house, returning to the main floor, as if it were 2 AM and she was returning from a late party.

Fuck, this place is depressing.

She promised herself a solid evening of goofing off once this was done, which would have to come at some imagined future after laundry, cooking, cleaning, and paying bills (which was its own kind of magic, trying to stretch a tiny wage across all those bills each month without letting her life collapse while simultaneously walking the tightrope of Sandra's goodwill). At times she felt like the lost member of the Flying Graysons—and then wondered whether that story line had already been done.

Chewing on that bone of Bat-trivia, she found Angela's father at a desk, hunched over a computer. Still no sign of Alexandra.

Her smooth-talking magic was failing her, and it was rapidly becoming food-o'-clock, as Ree's blood sugar was plummeting. Her stomach grumbled in agreement in a most unprofessional fashion. She waited for another half hour, her stomach protesting all the while, but eventually, Alexandra Moorely returned.

Alexandra's telling of the story took several minutes, as she broke down into sobbing repeatedly—she'd tried to keep the sight from her husband and failed, though the police had come quickly when called. Alexandra gave William's phone number to Ree, and Ree took the opportunity to excuse herself and try not to look too obvious in fleeing from the downtrodden site of tremendous emotional anguish.

Outside, she made the first turn available and then stopped to sit on a bench and clear her head, shivering for every reason except the cold. *The blood, gods, the blood. And her parents.*

Caught in a gut-wrenching thought loop, Ree popped in her earbuds to mainline happy-bouncy music until she could close her eyes and *not* imagine Angela on the floor of the room amid a pool of blood.

Rocking to Florence + the Machine, Ree walked back home to change and call Eastwood to figure out the next step. Could she quit now—would that even be allowed? This shit was too real by half. But it never worked that way in the movies, did it? At least that's how it was in the (Narrative) World According to Joseph Campbell. But why her? She didn't have to do this. There were real cops and feds, and she was thoroughly out of her depth.

Trying to keep herself in a loop of pleasant thoughts as insulation from the nasty reality, she reflected on the fact that there was no case of sad in the world that could stand up to a pint of ice cream and a few hours of *Super Mario Bros.* She'd once made a pie chart to prove it. And by pie chart, she meant a pie. Which she'd eaten.

Perhaps another pie was in order. *Pumpkin. No, maybe apple.* Bit by bit, she shook off the feeling of the Moorelys' house.

As Ree walked down the empty street pondering what pie to make, she was, as a result of such pleasant thoughts, left woefully unprepared to make a Perception Check and thus avoid surprise.

As a result, she was completely blindsided by the furry paw that slammed into her shoulder, sending her crashing to the ground. She heard the mystery thing howl as it leaped after her, blocking out the early-evening vestiges of twilight.

Just what I wanted, was all she had time to think, *an ambush.*

CHAPTER FIVE

Blood and Cocoa

Ree hit the ground hard but then rolled with the shot as her training kicked in. Pain flashed up her arm like a grease fire, and her vision clouded.

She wished she'd kept Eastwood's lightsaber, realizing that the closest thing she had to a weapon was a pen in her pocket.

Turning to face her attacker, Ree was instantly split between an impulse to scream and one to burst out laughing.

Her attacker was a werewolf. But not a CGI werewolf or a good-FX werewolf. This was a crappy-body-suit-with-a-super-fake-headpiece werewolf.

For all its ridiculousness, the damned thing managed to climb a brick wall to about ten feet up and then jump at her, which put some more fuel into the scream impulse.

Instead, she pushed off with one foot and leaped to the side, throwing a jumping roundhouse kick as the Hammer reject landed.

Ree expected a yelp, maybe a snarl or a growl. Instead, she got an *oof. Huh?*

Ree hopped back when she heard the all-too-human sound, and asked, "Who the hell are you?"

The response began as a guy's impression of a growl, but a moment into the sound, an animalistic voice joined the human one, then drowned it out as the wolfman charged her again, its jaw opening wide.

Okay, not funny anymore. She snapped out a front kick that caught the werewolf in the jaw but sent the left shoe of her Respectable Person outfit flying up and out of her line of vision. *Where are the witnesses? Fuck the Doubt, right in its ear.*

If she weren't alone, it wouldn't be jumping her. Going with that totally shaky but reassuring logic, she decided to try shouting.

"Fire! Fire! Fire in the alley!" She'd read that shouting "Fire!" was more likely to get a response than anything else, though that was a while ago, and maybe "Terrorist!" would do the job just as well.

Looking back out of the alley into the street, she saw a frustrating lack of passersby and turned her attention to the decreasingly laughable werewolf as it swiped at her with claws that Ree could have sworn looked more fake a second ago. It was tall, tall enough that she didn't have a reach advantage with her kicks. Infighting was out, since, y'know, claws and teeth. To prove her point, the weresuit's claws tore at her blouse, leaving three gashes just under the bust.

Eastwood better pay to have this shit replaced.

Ree circled back and around, trying to get clear enough to make a break for it. The beast's next dive was telegraphed Western Union, so she was able to grab its left arm with both hands, step aside, and swing it into the side of a Dumpster, headfirst. There was a most gratifying thud, but no *crack* or *crunch* that would have signaled a serious blow.

In fact, her attacker pushed the Dumpster aside with ease—disconcerting, given the fact that it was full and should have weighed the better portion of a ton.

When the weresuit howled this time, the sound was pure wolfman. Ree's skin broke out in goose bumps, riding a wave of real fear. The thing snapped at her, jaws throwing more spittle than her retriever. Also, Booster never tried to bite her head off, though he did occasionally seem to be trying to lick her face to the bone.

She caught the weresuit across the temple with an elbow as she zigged, then wrapped up its near arm, trying for an arm bar while guiding the creature's forward momentum into a downward spin; she needed to end the fight or get herself the lead time to run. The weresuit pawed at her, but with her leverage on its arm, she didn't take anything more than a few shallow scratches.

"Down, boy!" she said through gritted teeth, adjusting the hold as the furry beast squirmed and huffed. She cranked the arm even farther and heard a satisfying crack. There. The weresuit yowled in pain, and Ree slammed it into the ground to compound said pain, then sprang up to run.

Sweet Muppety Hermes, please grant me speed so I can run the hell away.

In the third of the five long paces it took to get out of the alley, Ree lost her other shoe, but she turned to head home, banking that the calluses on her feet from martial arts would protect her enough from the nasty street detritus and any potential tetanus. If she were lucky, a broken arm would be enough of a deterrent to make Weresuit-man-thing reconsider its ambush.

The *Firefly* line echoed in her mind. *I'm smelling a lotta "if" coming off this plan.*

Not now, Jayne, she told the voice.

Not that she knew why it had attacked her to begin with, or how exactly a guy in a wolfman outfit could climb walls or make a rubber suit strong enough to cut through silk. It had looked more real at the end of the fight than the start, not the other way around. What the hell kind of magic would do that? *This being-in-the-dark thing is getting tired really fast.*

Ree bolted down the street, thankful now for the sparseness of the traffic, fewer people to slow her down.

Would the wolfsuit follow her if she ducked into a store? An apartment? She wracked her brain trying to remember what exactly Eastwood had said about the Doubt, what she'd need to do to be safe. Ree didn't hear anything chasing her, so she ducked her head back to check.

No one on the street, on the walls, or atop roofs—as far as she could tell.

She kept running.

She ran until her side threatened to secede and start its own sovereign abdominal nation. Checking over her shoulder again—and satisfied with the lack of weresuits—she slowed and ducked into the nearest store, which turned out to be McDonald's.

She went straight for the bathroom to get a sense of how preposterous she looked. Her shirt hadn't frayed any more, thanks to the tight weave of the silk. She had scrapes and cuts over her torso and arms but nothing on the face. And she didn't have any bite marks, which was a relief in case the world was so beyond that getting bitten by a guy in a wolfman suit could spread Lycanthrubbery.

Ree did what she could to fix her hair, then found a stall and called Eastwood. He didn't pick up, so she left a stream-of-scared-consciousness message on his voicemail.

"This is Ree I was just attacked by some guy in a rubber wolfman suit but as the fight went on he looked more like a real wolfman and I lost my only good businessy shoes and this is all bullshit and on top of that but before it so underneath that but on top of it the Moorelys were so depressing I want to take a shower for a week and you seriously need to tell me more about how this all works because I am seriously freaking out—okay?"

Ree took a breath, then said, "I'm going home now for that shower. Call me." She hung up and just focused on her breathing, trying to calm down.

Then she walked out of McDonald's as if having claw

gashes in your shirt and no shoes were the most fashionable thing one could possibly do.

Taking stock at the next intersection, Ree saw that she was only a few blocks from home. She walked the rest of the way, frequently checking over her shoulder and doing her best to ignore the strange looks people gave her for her barefootedness. It was way late in the day for a walk of shame, and she didn't even have the shoes to carry in-hand to pull off that look. At least if the cops came, she could probably wave them off with the psychic paper. She checked her coat and sighed; it, at least, was still there.

As she approached the U-District, the streets got more crowded, the city more lively. People dashed here and there to their fabulous Friday nights, and Ree felt strangely apart from them, the reality of the Strange like a one-way glass that kept her separated from the normal world while allowing her to see in.

Crap, too much emo.

When she reached her building, it was all she could do to drag herself up the stairs and stumble inside, praying that Sandra would miraculously be out and she wouldn't have to explain things. Thankfully, she was greeted by an empty apartment and no keys on the table. Ree closed the door behind her, and after securing each of the five locks, she allowed herself a moment of stillness.

It could still come after me, she thought, time to get ready.

Ree went to the kitchen and pulled out the biggest knife she could find. Then she went to the fridge and pulled out a beer, taking them both to the shower. She set the knife in the far back lip of the tub and listened. *No way in hell am I going down like Marion Crane. I have the knife this time.*

×✗×⊗×✗×

Naturally, the hot-water heater gave out before she was

done calming down, so Ree finished her shower and headed for her room, peeking out from the bathroom to check the apartment first.

She took Eastwood's advice and popped in an episode of *Buffy* as she changed into a fresh set of clothes. She would have gone with "Once More, with Feeling," like she usually did to cheer up, but since she didn't want her life to become a musical right then, she settled on "Band Candy."

Ree quoted lines to get in the groove as she watched, settling into a comfortable (and defensible!) position on her bed, the knife beside her. She felt an energy buzzing in her head, like she'd downed a Red Bull made out of quippiness.

A few minutes after the episode ended, Eastwood called.

Ree picked up and launched right in, the nervousness back in force with the ringing. "Thanks for calling me back. Have you seen that thing? What do I do to fight it? Will it track me?"

"First, calm down. Keeping your head is the best way to stay safe."

Ree nodded to herself. "Got it. Easier said than done, of course."

"Tell me what happened, all of it."

Ree replayed the episode, the details scary-clear in her brain. The scratches itched as she talked. "Are they contagious?"

Eastwood huffed. "Never that I've seen. And you didn't get bitten, did you?"

"No . . ." Ree said, uncertain.

"Oh, that's good. Did you watch something invincible-y?" he asked.

"I watched some *Buffy*."

Eastwood murmured something that sounded affirmative. "Good. I can buzz by the neighborhood and try to run it off. Best thing you can do come nightfall is be in public, with several people, and carrying a weapon. When they're in hunting mode, Furrymancers avoid crowds, pick on lone prey. Make sure you're powered up when you leave home, stay in public, and I'll shadow you on the way home, in case he's persistent."

"Wait. Furrymancers?" Ree asked, her chuckle like warm water melting the ice-cold fear.

Eastwood hrmed. "That's what most everyone else calls them. Officially, they're Atavists. They can usually only channel their beast for a short time each day, like 3rd ed. D&D Barbarian Rage. If it can't find you or any other prey, it'll go back to being someone in a suit."

"So it really was a killer furry?"

"Ish. Furrymancers are weird ones. Pretty rare, thankfully. But if it couldn't run you down and gut you, it wasn't that strong."

Ree wasn't sure whether to be offended or relieved. "Um, good?" she volunteered.

"Oh. What did you find at the Moorelys'?" he asked.

Ree laughed to herself. *He's really got the absentminded-professor vibe going.*

A shiver went down her body as she recounted the scene and her conversations with the Moorelys. The cops on TV were always so calm; they could maintain distance from the dead while empathizing with the living. Ree wondered if they taught that in the police academy and if she could audit. It hadn't been too bad when she was there, with the Sherlock magic on, but afterward . . . Ree shuddered again as she finished up.

"Does that help?" she asked, hoping for answers.

Eastwood murmured in the affirmative again. She heard typing through the phone.

"I'll add this to the files I have and see if anything shakes out. Then I'll swing by to deal with the Atavist. Go out with friends, maybe those friends from yesterday. And bring a weapon, but nothing conspicuous. Unless you watch *Highlander* so you can hide it in a trench coat." Eastwood started another sentence, then cut himself off. ". . . sorry, rambling."

Ree smiled. "No prob. My *Highlander* tapes are worn to nothing. Methos was my TV boyfriend for several years."

"Yeah, right. Just keep your eyes open. And you don't have to keep doing this, you know."

Ree took a breath, a bit of her mind tugging on her to take the out. She shook her head. "To hell with that. I'm not going anywhere. You're stuck with me, buddy."

"It's only going to get more dangerous," he said.

"Good thing I'm not going to be alone, then."

Eastwood started to say something, then hung up.

Ree looked at the phone. "Weird."

She searched her bedroom, trying to decide what she could bring, since a butcher's knife didn't go with dinner wear, at least not at any restaurant she'd want to visit.

Ree turned out her closet and found a pair of dusty arnis canes, a training sword from her dalliance with tai chi, some boffer weapons, and the super-tacky Fantasy Sword that she'd bought on a lark at a ren faire three years ago. Her bedside table held a switchblade, which at least was a real weapon.

However, she looked at the Force FX lightsaber she'd placed on her bed and regarded it like a puzzle.

I did the genre thing; does that mean I can use you? And if I can, do I have to cart the whole thing around, or can I just take the hilt?

She replaced the leaning tower of miscellany in her closet, mulling over the lightsaber.

"Can't hurt to bring," she said, unscrewing the plastic blade and slipping the hilt into her coat, keeping an eye on the activation button to make sure she didn't accidentally turn it on. Ree thought it'd take more than an errant bump to make the thing get all glowy, but she wasn't willing to risk a foot on her shaky understanding of Geekomancy. She could feel the quippy energy of Buffy in the back of her brain, fainter than Sherlock had been.

Maybe it's stronger, the more of it I watch?

Ree walked out to the living room and saw Sandra lounging on the couch in her work clothes.

"Hey," Ree said. "Didn't hear you come in."

"Mrr," Sandra responded.

"You okay?"

"I don't wanna cook." Sandra rolled her head back around her shoulders, cracking her neck.

Ree walked around the couch, gathering her energy. "Then we go out. Priya is free tonight, and Anya doesn't have rehearsal." Ree grabbed Sandra's hand, trying to pull the tall woman to her feet. Luckily, Sandra relented and did most of the standing herself.

"Do you have a master plan?" Sandra asked, stretching the day out.

Ree raised an eyebrow and squinched up her mouth, thinking. "What's the tapas place on Wilco called now?"

"Oh. It's . . . Bites."

Bites was, by Ree's counting, at least the fourth incarnation of a tapas bar at that one location, each folding after about six months. Inevitably, it would be reopened by another brave and/or foolish entrepreneur who came along and gave the place yet another makeover and slight thematic twist. Then they'd try once again to hit the critical mass of patronage that would let them stay afloat atop the astronomical rent of the U-District. There were other tapas joints in Pearson, but Bites and its predecessors had been the only ones in the area.

Ree nodded. "Sound good? I can make with the wrangling, if you want to shower or change or sacrifice a goat or whatever."

"Fresh out of goats, sadly. They make such good cheese." Sandra walked toward her bedroom, saying, "Mmm, goat cheese. Add almond shavings, dried cranberries, some herby greens . . ."

"We're *going out*! They'll have goat cheese salads, love."

Sandra made "yeah, yeah" sounds from her room, and Ree's smile widened.

Just what the doctor ordered. Girl time, with a side of sword. *The sommelier recommends a pinot grigio from the Mariposa Valley with the emerald-crystal lightsaber* . . . Ree's mind trailed off merrily into daydreaming, and when Sandra emerged in jeans and a sweater, Ree remembered to text the rest of the crew.

Bite's version of a restaurant embodied the approach of New York simplicity-chic with an industrial design and East Asian/Spanish fusion cuisine, complemented by a kick-ass wine selection and art by the new owner's husband, a painter in the tradition of Anselm Kiefer meets Gustav Klimt. Since it was on the far side of the U-District, Anya and Priya were already there when Sandra and Ree arrived. As she and Sandra walked inside, Ree felt the Buffy magic fade.

All right, so now I have to hope the furry doesn't feel like tapas as an appetizer before chowing down on some broke screenwriter.

She kept her coat beside her when she sat down, just in case. A bottle of merlot stood on the table, already one third empty. Priya Tharakan (Strength 8, Dexterity 13, Stamina 12, IQ 17, Will 14, and Charisma 15—Geek 5 / Professional 3 / Seamstress 4 / Steampunk 2) had light brown skin, warm brown eyes, and an easy smile. Priya was five-feet-nothing on a good day, leading her to favor four-inch heels, which she managed with grace. The four of them walking somewhere together made quite a sight, with Sandra towering over the three of them like an elf among hobbits.

Ree's seat gave her a commanding view of the bar. Several scenes played out between various couples: from the old and comfortable to the middle-aged and tense to, best of all, the young and hilariously transparent.

Anya poured Ree a glass of wine, which she downed in one long swig.

"Whoa. Rough day?"

Ree hrmed and poured herself more wine, then stopped. "How much was this bottle?"

"Half-off $45," Anya said, chuckling.

Oh, my poor, poor credit card, Ree thought, remembering her expenses over this last week of flailing.

"Oops." Priya and Sandra traded a look.

"Rough day. Sushi?" Ree asked.

Priya curled her nose. "I had sushi for lunch."

"Empanadas?" Ree quirked an eyebrow, hands out, to say, *How about it?*

Anya nodded, and Sandra shrugged. The sharply dressed server came around, a slim red tie over his crisp white shirt. 2–1 said local actor or acting student.

Pearson had been attracting more and more TV work in the last couple of years, following a move by the mayor that offered massive tax breaks, ridiculous amounts of civic support, and leniency for things like closing downtown to film a scene including an exploding car (for instance). Which had led a lot of would-be actors to flock to the city as well, hoping that standing out in Pearson would be easier than in L.A., Vancouver, or NYC. Ree sent her scripts around Pearson first now, hoping that she could get in with a local producer or catch a company when they were in town filming pilots. She had met several PAs and a couple of other crew here and there, but nothing had really jelled so far.

Ree ordered a pitcher of Urban Ale-ian, which would make for far more thrifty slammable drink.

"My box of awesome junk arrived today," Priya said, her eyes bright.

Ree raised her glass in toast. "Fantastic! What are you going to make?"

"I've got a commission for a brass gear case mod to a netbook, and I think I'll use the rest to go on the Ghostbusters backpack."

"Can you finish in time for Halloween?" Anya asked.

Priya shook her head. "Probably not. I have to do the commission first so I can pay for that underbust corset from Jeanine."

Ree raised an eyebrow, conspiratorial. "Think you can make three more by next year? We would totally sweep the contest at Trollope's with Steampunk Ghostbusters."

Priya chuckled. "Not unless you all get your asses over to my place and help me with the grunt work." She looked to Ree. "You're the one who told me I needed to start charging for these things."

"I didn't mean for *us*," Ree said.

Priya scrunched up her eyebrows in mock frustration.

"I'm totally up for some sewing parties—*Lord of the Rings* marathon?" Ree asked.

Anya piped up, "I vote *Harry Potter*."

Sandra shook her head. "*Community*. You two need to watch this show." She beamed, her voice getting faster as she talked excitedly. "Ree showed me the first episode last month, and I can't get enough. Then they did a paintball episode, a zombie episode, and a gangster episode with fried chicken—"

Ree added, "And the greatest D&D episode ever."

Priya put her hands up, surrendering. "We can figure the media later. Ask me again after New Year's, and we'll get started. But if one of you wanted to help me out with my projects this weekend . . ."

Ree, Sandra, and Anya conspicuously looked away.

Priya sighed. "That's what I thought."

"I tell you guys, *Community* is the smartest sitcom. It takes everything bad about the genre and makes it amazing."

Ree nodded. "It has genre emulation and fourth-wall breaking so good, it's a wonder the show ever got renewed. I bought three DVD sets for Christmas last year." One for her, one for her dad, and one to loan out. She'd started the practice with *Firefly* after finding that she was constantly loaning out her set and still wanted to watch the episodes at will.

The empanadas arrived, at which point all talking ceased as they worshipped at the temple of deliciousness.

Ree had gotten some food in her stomach before the wine and beer hit, which kept her from dive-bombing off the ledge of sobriety. Instead, she proceeded to slalom down into intoxication with diligent self-destructiveness.

This was the third straight night of heavy drinking. This time she couldn't tell anyone what else was getting to her. History had taught her that getting a good drunk on was excellent therapy, and less expensive than actual therapy.

Current prescription: more beer and a change of subject. Thankfully, Sandra brought up Darren's impending birthday and her grandmaster plans to have a big surprise party at The Shithole, despite his expressed request to not have a party.

Ree and the Rhyming Ladies dove into planning, assisted by the alcohol, until it was decided that they'd host their own private *Rocky Horror Picture Show*, with Ree as Frank-N-Furter and Sandra as The Creature, Priya and Anya fighting over who was Magenta and who was Columbia. Assuming Darren didn't run off screaming, they'd get him into the golden Speedo and could change around the roles or not, depending. Darren was a bit of a stick in the mud, but Ree hadn't met a likes-girls-sexual alive who could resist the Amazonian Sandra in a shiny gold swimsuit and pasties.

Just after 11, they packed it in, deciding to go to Anya's place for bad movies until sleep o'clock, which on such nights could range from 1 AM to 8 AM, depending on the number of rounds of AMFs consumed.

As the four women walked through the streets, chatting loudly, four vessels and at least twelve sheets to the wind, Ree's phone rang.

It was Eastwood.

Ree realized that in all the fun, she had successfully put him out of her mind. Go, team booze!

Screw him, I'll call back tomorrow, after the hangover is gone. So, maybe Sunday, before work.

She let the call go to voicemail, and two minutes later, he called again. She waved off her friends' questions, saying that it was her student loan office. After that she got a text, then another. She didn't even bother reading them.

Five minutes later, a block from Anya's apartment, her phone rang again. She held the button to turn it off, but it kept ringing. When she looked up from the phone, she saw Eastwood across the street, giving her a *What the hell are you doing?* look. He waved for her to come over.

Wow. She wasn't going to be able to shake him. Rather than having to subject the ladies to Eastwood, she decided to peel off. "Guys, I've got a headache, I think I'm going to call it early." She got a few raised eyebrows, but they didn't object.

"Good night, Blitz," Anya said as she walked across the street. And now, on top of it all, she was the Blitz.

Damn you, Jorge Garcia, she thought as her friends walked on. She waited until they rounded the corner, then walked over to Eastwood.

Stepping up onto the sidewalk, she asked, "So, what now?"

Eastwood's seemingly-customary dourness melted into something that could, if you looked at it right, be interpreted as compassion. "I threw you right into the deep end, and it can be nasty. But we need to talk about this case."

"Joke's on you, I'm hammered," Ree said, wavering to the side and catching herself on a light pole. In a moment of microsobriety, Ree realized that she was perhaps not taking this whole thing very well. Her recent track record of adult decisions wasn't exactly stellar. Ree blinked a couple of times and straightened herself out, walking deliberately.

Eastwood didn't move. "I can deal with that. Let's go."

"You aren't much for small talk," Ree said.

"All of my problems are big problems. No time to talk about menial *go-se*. Let's go."

"All right, then. To the Dorkcave!" Ree pumped her right hand in the air, rallying.

"How'd you know what it was called?" Eastwood asked.

Instead of answering, Ree just laughed.

Maniacally, for several blocks.

CHAPTER SIX

Plato in the Dorkcave

When Ree and Eastwood returned to the Dorkcave, they were greeted by John Williams's "Binary Sunset" playing on the PA. She looked back and gave him the *Really?* look, and Eastwood shrugged.

"I put Williams on loop when I need to think."

"Fair enough. So here's what you need to know . . ." Ree ran through an account of her visit to the Moorelys', punctuated by her questions, which Eastwood waved off until she was done. She got to the breathless voicemail and sighed. The episode with the weresuit seemed more bizarre in retrospect, albeit more funny and less terrifying.

Eastwood nodded. "So, like I said, the guy in the fur suit was an Atavist. They channel the power of a primal spirit, and for the truly hard-core Furrymancers, it means suits like that. The more they give in to the spirit, the more real their powers become."

"Freaky. And what about ghosts? Could Angela's spirit still be there somewhere in the house?"

Eastwood looked down and away, pacing without making eye contact. "Not likely. If she follows the pattern of the last two suicides, her soul is absent from the scene."

"So then there *are* ghosts."

"Yes."

Ree nodded, processing. "And werewolves, sort of? What about the rest? Vamps, mummies, changelings, succubi, demons?"

"Most everything is around in one form or another. Vampires used to be the Dracula types, but in the last ten years most of them have become weak, brooding androgynes that only go after teenagers. A friend of mine took the opportunity to rid his whole city of them after the fourth Mormon Vamps book hit and the sparkle meme was at its strongest."

"So does that make Ms. Mormon Sparkle Vamp a hero?"

"Of a sort. Before they started to sparkle, there were a lot of vamps who were tortured antiheroes, thanks to Rice and Whedon."

Ree grimaced. "Do you know if she was clued in?"

Eastwood shrugged. "She's very secretive, no one in the Underground has been able to say for sure. It's all rumor. My guess is she lost someone to a vampire and decided the greatest revenge she could inflict was to turn them into a laughing stock."

Ree blinked a few times, her head still foggy from the booze. "So, what do we do next? If I keep going investigator on this, the interview list is getting CVS-receipt-long, and I have a job."

Eastwood stopped a couple of paces from Ree and looked at her. "Next I teach you more about genre emulation."

Ree shrugged. "I did the Sherlock thing just fine."

"But with more control, you can use more power, longer, and with better effect. I knew a Geekomancer who channeled *Star Wars* so well she called herself a Jedi and no one questioned her."

Ree raised an eyebrow, thinking, *Now, that would be cool.* She imagined herself in Jedi robes, wielding a real lightsaber,

"Duel of the Fates" playing in the background as she faced down Darth Maul.

Ree shook off the daydream and saw Eastwood smile at her. "Cool, right? Channeling genres takes a lot out of you, and you'll get better with practice. It'll also be easier to switch when you need to. For now, you should stick to watching a whole movie or episode, preferably things you already know and love. Your emotional attachment to the material determines how much you can get out of it."

"So *Die Hard* is a better choice for action-fu than *Ballistic: Ecks vs. Sever.*"

Eastwood snarled at the mention of the second film. "I hated that movie so much, I got my ninety-one minutes back."

"Huh?"

"Not relevant." Eastwood waved his hand, dismissing the thought. He turned to his wall of screens, typing a few things in on one of a half-dozen keyboards. "I'll handle the witness investigations, but to do that, we need to pick up some things. Ready for a field trip?"

Ree pulled out her pockets. "I forgot my permission slip. Does this mean we get to raid the stacks?" she asked, eager to dig into his Willy Wonka–level stash. In the short time she'd spent in the Dorkcave, she'd already decided that she could spend a solid month rummaging through all of his loot. *You could practically run Gen Con out of this place,* she mused.

"Are you still channeling anything?"

Ree shook her head. "Not unless Drunkomancy is a thing."

Without missing a beat, Eastwood said, "Dipsomancy is very real, but it takes more than just getting hammered to do anything useful."

"I was joking," Ree said, half apologetic and half amused.

Eastwood shrugged. "Get yourself some water." He indicated a watercooler off to one side of his mega-desk. "Then find something useful to watch on my computer while I sort out our supplies for the trip. It won't be particularly safe, but it should be hella instructive."

Ree raised an eyebrow. "Hella?"

"I spent about a decade in NorCal. Deal with it."

Ree sat down at Eastwood's computer and found the Media folder. It popped up to full screen, and she saw what must have been thousands of files. "What were you doing in NorCal?"

Eastwood had disappeared down an aisle that was mostly boxes marked with D&D module titles, but he'd apparently heard her. "Saving the world."

She looked away from the screen and shouted, "Can you expand that a little, Captain Cryptic?"

Eastwood harrumphed. "My nickname comes from my time there, fighting over the Wild Wild Web, when W-W-W was new. A bunch of techie practitioners discovered how to astrally project into the Internet. Poof: digital cowboys, spiritual boom towns, and then turf wars to decide the Web's ontological disposition."

Ree blinked and stopped for a second. "Are you shitting me?" She looked back at the computers, with several screens open to various webpages. She remembered early Internet browsing, BBSes, Usenet, and the Didn't Seem So Bad at the Time horror that was AOL.

"Not in the least. This monster-hunting stuff is my retirement plan, young padawan."

Ree followed Eastwood down the row, intrigued. "Forget movies, I want to hear that story right now."

"No time. You can borrow my friend's memoir, though—it covers most of the good stuff. Now pick a movie—we don't have time for you to watch something through, but I refuse to take you to the market without something awesome kicking around your mind."

"Market?" Ree asked.

"We need stuff. I said that already." There was impatience in his voice.

Someone's grumpy, Ree thought. She let it go and returned to the Media Database from Heaven. He had *Six-String Samurai, Trolls 2,* the Remastered (but not Special Edition) *Star Wars,* and the complete works of Roger Corman—all on just one column of one page. What kind of organization structure that was, Ree couldn't say, but it was impressive. She browsed for five minutes until Eastwood emerged from the stacks and told her to hurry up and pick something.

"What would I get from *Hellboy II*?" she asked.

"Invincible Hand, probably."

Meh.

Seeing an old favorite, she asked, "Do you have a rapier I can use?"

"Sure."

The Princess Bride *it is.* She double-clicked and sat back as the film started to play on Eastwood's 3x3 cluster of monitors. Her reverie was occasionally interrupted by a clunk or thud as Eastwood stomped through the stacks. By the time Buttercup went out on her ride, Eastwood had finished assembling his bag and taken a seat beside her, sorting a bag and half-watching the film. He handed her a disturbingly familiar prop rapier that she couldn't place, which she balanced on her lap while watching. *The Princess Bride* was, by many rubrics, a near-perfect film. Adventure, romance, fencing, monsters, miracles, pirates, torture, everything. She must have watched it a hundred times as a kid, sitting on her mom's lap.

As soon as the duel at the cliffs was done, Eastwood stood up. "Okay, that's enough. We need to go."

"But . . . Fezzik! The poison!" She felt approximately five years old, complaining like that, but when Eastwood narrowed his eyes, she merely sighed, standing up. "Do you have a belt for this?" she asked, holding up the rapier.

Eastwood fished something else out of the bag and presented her with a slim black belt, complete with a black-leather-and-crushed-red-velvet sword hanger.

"Schweet," Ree said in her Cartman voice as she pushed the sheathed rapier through the loops of the hanger, then put on the belt, tightening it a few notches past its most worn point.

"Yes, so don't lose it. Now follow me, and don't talk unless I'm talking." Eastwood punched a code into a keypad on the wall, which produced the "secret door opens" sound from Zelda. A door swung open where Ree was sure there hadn't been a door before. It revealed a dingy, dimly lit hall that reminded her of far too many slasher flicks.

Eastwood gestured to the hall. "First stop, Grognard's."

×✕ˣ✖ˣ✕×

The tunnel was dank, moist, and dim. It was lit only by dust-covered incandescent bulbs in cages spaced every fifty feet. Eastwood and Ree each had a flashlight, but Eastwood had told her they'd save them for if the lightbulbs went out, which wasn't at all ominous.

The weight of the rapier tugged at her waist, but she felt comforted when she put her hands on the cool, oiled handle. It just felt . . . right. Like she was doing what she was meant to do. A fantastic mélange of genres and wit rolled around in her mind, and she kept herself entertained by choreographing fight scenes as they walked.

Eastwood broke the uneasy silence. "There are more critters down here than bedbugs in a Queens apartment, and most of them are attracted to light. They're used to the lightbulbs, but if we give them more to go by . . ."

"Got it. Just how much time do you spend tromping through tunnels?"

Eastwood quirked an eyebrow. "I never really thought about it. This is the safest way to get to Grognard's."

"Through the tunnels that are infested with monsters?" Ree asked.

"Monsters I can handle. The gangbangers who pretty much run the neighborhood above us, not so much. I have a handful of things that can stop a bullet, but they're damned hard to come by." Eastwood held up his lightsaber. "Weapons like these things have a nostalgia battery, and when it's used up, you have to wait until the people's investment in the object recharges the psychic energy. It has a daily limit, more or less, like the Furrymancers. Lightsabers would recharge almost instantly, except there are so many of them around, the energy gets divided up."

"And then I woke up and went back to having a normal life." Ree pinched herself, shrugging when nothing changed. She let her mind slip back to *The Princess Bride*, keeping the energy moving, hoping it would stay with her longer if she kept excited.

"You're going all the way down the rabbit hole, *chica*. It's time to get over the shock and start following the Eat Me and Drink Me labels."

Ree tapped Eastwood on the shoulder with her flashlight. He stopped and turned to face her. She said, "Call me *chica* again, and I will beat you into a bloody pulp and sell your blood on the Internet as mana potions. Got it?"

Eastwood gave her a predatory smile, then closed in, crowding her back against the wall. "I've faced down things so terrifying that if you looked at them through a TV, you'd lose all of your hair. If you heard their voices echoed down an endless hollow, you'd claw out your own ears. A single touch from some of these things can sap every ounce of youth and vitality from your skinny body, and it wouldn't be more than a crumb of sustenance for them."

He leaned forward into the light, which washed out his face even more. "I've faced down horrors older than time itself, creatures that, were they to wake fully, would drag the world down into a cold sea of tormenting ab-existence to be slowly digested, body and soul. I've faced these things and

I'm still here. I could have retired a decade ago, but instead I'm on the front line of the war to keep this frakked-up world running so you and your friends can fritter away your lives."

Eastwood stuck a finger in front of Ree's face. "Understand that you are an ally at best, an amusement in practice, and cannon fodder at worst. If you raise a hand against me, I will put you down so fast, you won't even have time to consider whether your death is more Jango Fett or Red Shirt #2. Get it?"

Daaaamn. Ree felt the musty and rough concrete wall behind her and Eastwood inches from her face, his pupils narrowed and eyebrows hard-set. Until that moment, she'd believed he couldn't possibly deserve the name he used. Not anymore. Ree raised her hands in surrender. "Got it."

Eastwood stepped back and smiled, the Rar-Face gone. "Good. You'll need to toughen up, *chica.* That was too easy." He turned back and continued walking, the shadows shifting around him from the various light sources. "Plus, I don't kill people. People who are people, that is. And you're still people."

"What kind of people aren't people?" she asked after a second to shake out the fear. *I can't tell if I was actually threatened or if I was just To the Pain—ed.*

"The ones who've traded their souls to demons, or anyone who delves so deep into magic that they lose track of their humanity, go off the deep end, and become monsters themselves. Those are the things to look out for." Eastwood shuddered. "Luckily, they're pretty rare, since folks in the Underground are good about self-policing. Anyone gets too close to the edge, we have an intervention. And if that doesn't work, we have to put them down."

Wow. This guy needs to get out even more than I do. "You've had to do that?"

"Sadly, yes." Eastwood's voice was soft, sad, far weaker than it had been a minute ago with his threat.

"Like the fur-suit guy?"

"Maybe. I picked up his scent earlier but never caught up with him. I think he figured out he had a tail aside from the rubber one and beat it."

Eastwood stopped at a door Ree hadn't noticed, and she walked up beside him. It had been red at some point but was now faded and stained, and a third of the paint had flaked off to reveal coarse wood below.

"Here we are. Don't talk back if anyone gives you flak. Let me handle it. These are mean old bastards, and Grognard is the meanest of them all."

Ree raised an eyebrow but nodded when Eastwood stared at her. He opened the door, and they walked up a flight of stairs to another door. Eastwood opened the second door to reveal . . .

A game store. No, wait, a bar. Somehow it was both. Someone had crossbred a pub and a game store and succeeded. It was a split-level arrangement, the bar a short flight down from the game-store section. The upper seating consisted of metal folding chairs around game tables that had undershelves loaded with terrain and figures. The lower seating was sturdy wooden chairs around cherry and walnut circular tables. Ree saw game books and miniatures packs lining the walls.

The patrons were mostly older men, complete with grizzled gamer beards and paunches. There were also men with Gamer Body Type 2: tall and lanky, trench-coat-enabled. There were ponytails and faces pocked with acne scars, ancient black T-shirts sporting the logos of obscure games from the '60s and '70s, only half of which Ree could identify. It was Gamer *Cheers*.

"How have I not heard of this place?" Ree stage-whispered to Eastwood. She had to restrain herself from skipping up the aisles to fondle the merch.

"You can only get here if Grognard wants you to. This place is as much social club as bar or store."

"How does he stay in business?"

Eastwood walked toward the bar, beckoning Ree to follow. "His customers are very, very loyal."

Even hunched over, the man behind the bar was more than six feet tall. He had a full beard showing more salt than pepper, but his head was bald. He wore a leather jacket that was so worn in, it might as well have been his skin.

The bartender huffed approvingly and grabbed a lean glass to pour a pint of dark beer. "Good to see you, Eastwood. How'd the *oni* gig go?"

"Done and done. I had to get Morrison on him, though. Speaking of which, this is Ree. She's new. I'm invoking my guest privilege."

Grognard rolled his eyes. "You remember what happened last time you brought someone here?"

Eastwood settled his weight onto one hip. "I do. And *she's* not that rash," he said, turning to look at Ree.

Not knowing and not wanting to know what incident they referred to, Ree smiled. "This place is amazing."

In response, Grognard huffed.

Eastwood smiled. "You are twenty-one, right?"

Ree stepped up to the bar and looked at the liquor selection. She spent several seconds appraising, then said, "Macallan 15, just a drop of water."

Eastwood nodded approvingly, and Ree hoped she wasn't imagining Grognard's near-twinge of a smile. The older man turned, plucked a bottle off the wall, and poured the Scotch with deliberate grace, taking up the well tap and kissing the water button, pouring enough into the drink to release the taste of the Scotch. It was a trick she'd picked up long enough ago that she'd forgotten who'd taught it to her.

Grognard slid the drink down the bar to her. Ree picked up the glass, took a sniff, then a sip. As good as ever. She flashed Grognard a smile, and this time he grinned in earnest.

Eastwood pulled out a tablet computer and spun it around

to show to Grognard. "I've got a shopping list. Hope you can help me out."

Grognard picked up the tablet and rubbed his face, thoughtful. The big man led Eastwood away from the bar and into a back room.

Eastwood turned at the door and said to Ree, "Don't touch anything."

To hell with that. The interdiction nearly compelled her to mess something up, but instead she downed the rest of the Scotch and walked into the store section of the lair. She found the vintage RPG section and lost herself in D&D supplements from the '80s.

Looking up from a *Rules Cyclopedia* (which was technically a '90s supplement, but Ree had played *Cyclopedia* with her first gaming group, and they all used their older brothers' books from the '80s), she caught a glimpse of something that made her double-take. Amid the middle-aged and unimpressively shaped customers, there was something of an oddity.

He wore the Gamer Standard-Issue Trench Coat™, in brown instead of black. He was shorter but not round, therefore defying both of the Stereotypical Gamer-Boy Body Types. His dirty-blond hair was cut in a professional style, and he wore jeans, brown boots, a vest over a white collared shirt, and, incongruously, goggles. They were strung loose around his neck but looked like they belonged on the 1st-place podium in a Steampunk costume contest.

Priya would shiv a nun to see those, Ree thought, taking mental notes to relay to her friend, if she could figure out a way to do so without revealing too much else of what she was involved in.

The man caught her staring and strode over. He wore well-oiled brown leather gloves, removing one as he extended his hand to her.

"Greetings, mademoiselle. I do not believe I have seen you at this fine establishment before."

Is he for real? Ree met his hand and shook while giving him another look.

He gave a formal bow. "Drake Winters, at your service."

With a name like that, he did belong in the D&D section.

She found herself dropping into a curtsy to match his bow. *William Goldman, you punk.*

"Rhiannon Anna Maria Reyes." She added, "Call me Ree."

Drake spoke with all the bombasticity of a cast-off from Marvel's Asgard. "It is always a pleasure to make the acquaintance of a beautiful woman, Ms. Reyes. What brings you to Grognard's? Tomes of knowledge, figures of power, or merely a chance to let down your hair and mingle with fellow keepers of the light?"

Ree laughed. She had to think actively when speaking, since what was coming into her mind was all *Princess Bride*–flavored. "You can drop the LARPer act, man. I haven't played since college."

Drake straightened up. "It is no act, Ms. Reyes. I am . . . displaced, you might say, from my original context."

Ree narrowed her eyes. "Run that by me again?"

Drake took a breath, then said, "I was born in the Year of Our Lord 1864, and while I was battling the Kadel torture-ships across the skies of great Avalon, my Aetheric Rifle had an unforeseen effect upon the Kadel gravitic drive, catapulting the ship into the deepest reaches of Faerie. After years of adventures with My Mistress, the Contessa of the Lapis Galleon, I found myself in the twenty-first century, far from home."

Ree knew her eyes couldn't get any narrower and take in light, but it wasn't enough to convey her doubt. Still, he didn't *look* like he was lying. "Are you serious?"

Drake leveled a severe look at her. "One must always be serious when speaking of the beautiful dangers of Faerie."

Ree shifted her weight, continuing to work on the puzzle that was this man before her. "And what do you do these days?"

Drake smiled. "I do what I've always done. Protect the innocent, punish the wicked, seek to find the light of truth amid the dark cloud of ignorance."

"So, super hero?" Ree asked.

His expression seemed to say *not quite*. "I have read the exploits of some of these super heroes." He thumbed through a bin of back issues and pulled out a *Batman* comic. "I find the Dark Knight to be quite compelling—one man pitting his cunning and determination against the forces of corruption. Very inspiring."

Ree nodded, finding it easier to speak in her own voice now that she was conscious of the *Princess Bride* energy pushing her to act differently. "I've always been more of a Spider-Man girl, myself. Do you know Eastwood?"

He nodded. "A stalwart if somewhat morose figure. Are you his apprentice?"

"No. Well, maybe. Has he had apprentices before?"

"None that I know of."

Drake was charming in the same way that a Cinnabon roll was sweet. A little goes a long damn way, and a lot quickly becomes too much to stomach. "Do you know anything about the recent string of suicides in town?"

That eyebrow quirk said *no*. "I had not heard of such a thing. I admit I am not good at using thinking machines for news. I prefer the texture of the daily paper."

Fair enough. "Well, that's what we're working on. If you hear anything, can you drop me a line?" Ree fished a business card out of her purse—it was her "Rhiannon Reyes— Screenwriter" card, because why in the nine hells would someone ever make a business card that said "Barista"?

"I certainly will—I have acquired a mobile telephone, thanks to the infinite kindness of our dear host." Drake produced a flip phone at least four years out-of-date, though she supposed that for a nineteenth-century throwback, it would be slightly less of a Future Shock while still being totally alien.

"So, what do you think of the twenty-first century?" she asked.

Drake paced back and forth, talking with his hands. "Everything is very clean here, except in certain neighborhoods which are rather more like the streets in Avalon. Technology has advanced in so many directions and fashions I would have never imagined. However, I find the everyday approach to technology rather impersonal."

Drake threw back his coat, revealing a collection of gadgets on his belt and strapped to the inside of his coat, like a fake-watch-salesman-turned-vigilante.

"I made every piece of my gear by hand and know it inside and out." He closed his coat and held up the phone. "But this phone. I couldn't start to tell you how it works, where it was made, or how to repair it, and I feel that I am not far behind the average citizen in that regard."

Ree shrugged. "Clarke's Third Law."

"Beg pardon?" he asked.

Right, Ree thought. "Arthur C. Clarke was a writer of scientifically based fiction. His Third Law states, 'Any sufficiently advanced technology is indistinguishable from magic.' I.e., for most people, technology might as well be magic, since they understand it so poorly."

Drake nodded approvingly. "So it would seem, and it was much the same way in my day for those not among the privileged. I cannot say I am comfortable knowing that little about the technology I use, but adequately covering more than a hundred years of technological advances to bridge the gap of knowledge has proved difficult."

Ree shifted her weight, taking in the sight of Drake Winters and his aggressive oddity. "I bet."

"No wager necessary," Drake said. "But I'm afraid I've waylaid you long enough. I shall take my leave and allow you to resume your mission."

Drake gave a graceful bow and reached down to kiss her hand. Instead of making contact, he merely brought his lips to within an inch of her hand. She felt the warmth of his breath and ignored the small shiver that went down her back, blaming that, too, on William Goldman. Then the walking anachronism rose, spun on the balls of his feet, and walked away.

"Huh." Ree considered the oddity for a moment, then went back to browsing. She had just found a well-loved copy of *Underground* when Eastwood emerged from the back room, a burlap sack thrown over one shoulder.

"Ready?" he asked.

Ree walked with Eastwood back toward the bar section. "I could spend a week in here."

Eastwood huffed. "I've done that. Wasn't very fun. But that was more due to the Yu-Gi-Oh! zombies."

"Metaphorical or literal zombies?"

Grognard joined in from behind the bar, where he had returned to the Most Archetypal Bartender Thing Ever: cleaning glasses. "That time it was literal," the big man said. "I stopped carrying that crack afterward. The profit wasn't worth dealing with the junkies."

"Does every part of the geekverse have a weirdo supernatural aspect?" Ree asked.

Eastwood nodded several times. "Just about. The trick is learning which what goes where and does what."

"That was some Tennant-level vaguebabble."

"Thanks, I've been practicing." Eastwood swung the bag out for her. She caught it with a huff. It was somewhere between really heavy and really f—ing heavy. "And on that thought, *allons-y!*" Somehow he'd acquired a crook-handled umbrella, which he used to gesture as a cane.

"I've got a bad feeling about this," Ree whispered as she swung the bag over her shoulder and followed Eastwood out the door and back down into the sewer.

CHAPTER SEVEN

Nostalgia Consignments

The sewers had spectacularly failed at getting less drab and gross during their visit to Grognard's, but after a couple of miles of walking, Ree decided to study the various types of grates, concretes, and doors. Who knew when a taxonomy of sewers would come in handy.

"What exactly is this place we're going?" Ree asked.

"It's the Midnight Market. Think of something between a town council meeting and a monthly convention."

"Well, that's not the least bit confusing."

"You can say that again." Ree was about to reply when Eastwood cut her off. "But please don't. The Market's the best place to acquire oddities, and we all check in to resolve issues, make plans, and, usually, get drunk and tell stories about the old times."

"It sounds like I'll have a blast."

"You'll get plenty of attention." Eastwood led them down another stairwell. Ree was surprised that there was more down to be had, since they were already in the sewers. But given the week she'd had, it was barely worth a twitch on her WTF-o-meter.

On this level, even Ree had to squat to avoid the low ceiling. Eastwood and her steps synced up, making moaning chords in aged wood over concrete. "That's the problem. I get hit on or ogled enough at work," she said.

Eastwood chuckled as he reached the bottom of the stairs and opened another door. "But this will be ogling dangerous enough that you worry for your soul. Far superior, grade-A-plus major-league ogling."

Ree made *ooh I'm scared* hands, which resembled spirit fingers, but with a fake-scared expression.

Eastwood gave her a hard look. "Seriously, there are some not-nice people involved. Market is neutral territory, but it doesn't always stop people when they get in a murdering mood."

Ree pulled the rapier a foot out of the scabbard. "Hence the sword?"

"Hence." And with that, Eastwood stopped at another door. "This is it. The doorman is going to ask a bunch of questions—let me answer, and don't talk unless directly addressed. Once we get inside to the social mixing part, it'll be less anal-retentive, don't worry." Eastwood's stern default broke, letting out a little bit of warmth.

He knocked fast four times, break, another four, break, and a third set of four. Ree recognized the pattern from *Doctor Who* and smiled. The familiar trappings of geekdom went a long way toward making the "magic and monsters are real and want to eat you alive" thing less stressful, if only just.

A slat opened in the door, and brown eyes appeared under furrowed brows. "How many antennae on an Imperial probe droid?" a voice asked.

"Two," Eastwood said without missing a beat.

"First appearance of Ambush Bug?" the voice asked.

Eastwood cocked his head to the side, thinking. "*DC Comics Presents #52.*"

"How many times does Inigo Montoya repeat his mantra in the duel with Count Rugen?"

Eastwood scrunched his eyebrows and looked somewhat lost. He turned to Ree, who smiled. "Five," she said.

"Wrong," the man said. "It was four."

Eastwood's face dropped.

Ree leaned in at the slot and said, "Bullshit. He says it once in the hall, then four times in the basement after he takes the knife to the belly. I can recite the whole scene, if you'd like."

There was a moment of silence. Ree looked to Eastwood with wide eyes. Eastwood looked at her with a *what the hell are you thinking?* expression.

Crap. But I was right!

Ree heard a chuckle from within, and then the door swung open with a groaning creak. Ree exhaled, the momentary panic leaving with her breath.

They passed a skinny man with a shaved head and a tattoo of a Warhammer Chaos symbol on his skull, then walked down a dank hallway. Thirty feet later, they emerged into a vast room.

Ree stopped and took in this Midnight Market. The ceiling was at least fifty feet up, the whole room as wide as a football field and nearly as deep. It looked for all the world like a Tim Burtonized version of the exhibitor hall at Gen Con. There were rows of stalls set up with signs, assorted books on ancient shelves, corsets and leather coats and gossamery blouses on dummies, and racks upon racks of increasingly ridiculous-looking swords.

Food carts were parked along the edges of the floor, including one kind of cart that Ree was glad pretty much never made it into the exhibitor hall at Cons—a bar. The sign above the cart said *Grognard's,* and Ree recognized the beers on tap.

"You guys drink here, too?"

"Not all of Grognard's beers are for getting drunk. Where most wizards have potions, he has beer."

"Magic beer?" she exclaimed. "That's the best impossible thing yet this week!"

"You're going to need a big pad of paper for that list," Eastwood said as he led her down an aisle.

They passed a set of triplets in red, yellow, and blue jumpsuits, arguing in a C-minor chord with a plump woman wearing a tie-dyed shimmery dress. Across the aisle, a living manga teen with spiky purple hair and more hardware on his body than an early Borg poked through dusty old digests. He said something unintelligible as Ree passed, and an honest-to-goodness 3-D speech bubble appeared over his head, showing a paragraph of handwritten Japanese.

Ree let her head track over her shoulder as she passed, continuing to watch the speech bubble. Another one popped up as the kid kept talking.

Eastwood dodged through the moving crowd, sidetracking through an open booth area with pewter miniatures. They passed another dozen stalls, carts, shelves, and thirty more attendees. Ree didn't recognize a single one of them except as archetypes, variations on people she'd known or characters she'd seen. These were her people, if maybe the awesomely weird end of that set. For every twenty well-adjusted geeks who punched the clock, doing his or her time in the real world, there might be one of this sort.

She'd had the "all geeks are freaks" fight more than once with Jay, who did his best to see only the maladjusted side of geekdom. His own interest in *Sandman,* Hammer horror flicks, and everything Nintendo didn't make *him* a geek, of course.

Dick.

But were these folks the actual fringe, or were they an even more obscure subsection that she'd never known before? Did that really matter? Eyes wide, she continued to follow Eastwood across the floor to a space with a hundred or so seats set out in rows like at a discussion panel or an auction house. More than twenty seats were already filled. Some folks were chatting in low voices, others sat alone.

"This is what we're here for." Eastwood took a seat a quarter of the way up the aisle, near no one in particular. Ree sat down beside him, continuing to scan the audience. Eastwood leaned over to her and spoke softly. "They're auctioning off a Claddagh ring, and I need at least one for rituals."

"What rituals?" Ree asked, but just then a bell rang out three times, echoing through the hall. The shoppers and vendors picked up the pace, the overall din in the room ramping up a notch.

Eastwood leaned in and spoke in a soft voice. "The three suicides in this string have all been virgins, and all recently brokenhearted. That's a lot of emotional energy, and with a specific accent to it. And a Claddagh ring has the appropriate semiotic resonance. I need to find out who is next and if there are going to be more."

The bell rang again, and more people filtered into the auction area. A woman in a black three-piece suit and slate-gray hair under a top hat walked up to the dais at the front of the auction area, followed by a small legion of whatever the auction equivalent to roadies were called, who carted, hefted, and hauled various boxed and bagged items up into rows and stacks.

"Anything weird that I need to know about how this works?" Ree asked.

"Bidding goes by barter, not cash, and is adjudicated by the auctioneer. Here it's possible to bid memories as materiel, though I don't recommend it. Don't raise your hand or draw attention, and you'll be fine."

"Why did I even come if I don't get to do anything?"

"Do you want to learn about this world or not?" Eastwood snapped, his voice raising a tad. Heads turned, and Ree shrank into herself.

"I want answers, not a handholding, look-but-don't-touch tour of Magic Con. And to stop the suicides." Ree shivered, the pool of blood on the carpeted floor superimposed on her vision.

The seated crowd had grown to nearly a hundred by the time the third set of bells rang. The auctioneer scaled a step up and looked out from her podium.

"Greetings, and welcome to the Midnight Market. We have a full docket tonight, so I will dispose of most of the pleasantries. Each of you should already have a voting card. If you are new to the auction, please see one of the attendants in the back." She gestured down the aisle, and Ree saw a pair of nondescript men at the entrance to the auction area, each wearing a top hat with a card in the brim that read *Staff*.

No one stood, so the woman continued. "As is custom, we will begin with something to whet your appetite." The auctioneer pulled a large disc out of a folder and held it up to the audience. "We have for your interest the very first LaserDisc produced of the remastered *Star Wars*. What am I bid?"

A mountain of a man with blond hair raised his card and boomed out, "I bid an unopened pack of *Magic: The Gathering, Arabian Nights*."

Ree nodded in appreciation. A woman in Elegant Gothic Lolita gear called, "Ten hours of instruction in the art of divination."

The auctioneer considered for a moment, then called, "I have a bid of ten hours of instruction from Lady Lucretia. Any other bidders?"

Ree whispered to Eastwood, "What would you do with that? Aside from treasure it forever?" Ree's mother had owned a set of the LaserDiscs, but they'd disappeared when she left.

"The primacy is the most important thing, but it's both rare and untampered by Lucas's later revisionist hard-on. For a purist practitioner, it'd be an essential ritual tool."

"Do you have one?" Ree asked.

"Mine were . . . inherited." Again, the note of sadness in Eastwood's voice. Ree wondered what story had left him with that scar. If her math was right, he'd been active in the magic world since she was six or so. A lot of time in which to get bitter.

No one else bid, and the blond man didn't add to his offer, so the disc went to the Lolita diviner. During the shuffle, Eastwood gave Ree the lowdown. "The giant blond guy is Sven Carlssen, badass for hire, makes most of his money bodyguarding. The Goth queen is Lady Lucretia, fortune-teller and rorikon expert."

Ree regretted not having brought a notebook, so she typed as fast as her thumbs could go on her phone. The next item was a letter from John Lennon to Yoko Ono from April 1968, which went to a Buddy Holly look-alike with Reed Richards gray sideburns.

A nineteenth-century typewriter went to an aging ex-fratboy with double-popped collars, followed by a *kukri* that was traced to the first commander of the Royal Nepalese Army, which went to Carlssen in exchange for a World War II Japanese officer's *katana*.

One hour and a dozen lots into the auction, Eastwood pulled out a tablet and called up some kind of app. He leaned in to Ree and said, "Put on your earbuds and refresh your connection. We may have trouble on the way out." He handed her the tablet, which was queued up to *The Princess Bride*.

She nodded, since the buzzing feeling of swashbuckling and wittiness had faded long ago. She attached her earbuds and hunkered down to watch, shielding the light from the crowd with her arms.

Ree had watched back through the duel at the cliffs when Eastwood nudged her with his elbow. "It's up."

Ree sat up straight and removed her earbuds, the film's energy buzzing in her head again, as strong as when they'd left the Dorkcave.

The auctioneer held up a golden ring. "This is the original golden Claddagh ring given to Jim Morrison by Patricia Kennealy, lost in the early nineties and replaced by another. What am I bid?"

Eastwood raised his card and called, "I bid an original White Box Edition Dungeons & Dragons, signed by Gygax and Arneson—well loved and oft used."

Murmurs spread across the crowd like a wave. Ree knew that normally, collectors would want something mint. But if artifacts and memorabilia ran on nostalgia, maybe the well-loved aspect was a selling point. *Something else to ask, Ree noted.*

A voice from across the room called, "I bid a playbill from the original run of *RENT,* signed by all principals."

Ree rose up in her seat to look at the bidder, a tall, gaunt man with unnaturally long fingers.

The auctioneer considered, then shook her head. "Insufficient. Do I have another bid?"

Lucretia's card went up. "I bid a marker for one month's blessing by Lady Fate."

The auctioneer nodded. "Accepted. Eastwood, do you wish to add to your bid?"

Eastwood considered for a moment. "I will add the first Chaos Orb ever shredded in a tournament."

A wave of "ooh" and "aah" rippled through the crowd. The Chaos Orb was a famous card from *Magic: The Gathering.* Dropped from a height above the play area, it destroyed every card it touched. It was an early legend of the Magic community that people had started taking Chaos Orbs, tearing them into dozens of pieces, and trying to scatter them over the entirety of the opponent's play area like confetti. It was a move filled equally with brilliance and jackassery, though of course it was a onetime ploy. As a result, Chaos Orbs were damned rare anymore.

Lady Lucretia immediately countered, "I will add a marker for a custom-made Lucretia original gown of the holder's choosing, inlaid with my most powerful blessings and protections."

Eastwood cursed under his breath, "Witch." He fidgeted, biting his lower lip.

Either he's taking this item pretty personally, really hates Lucretia, or is a sore loser.

The auctioneer looked to Eastwood again, asking for another bid. He gritted his teeth, then said, "I will add a first-edition Obi-Wan Kenobi FX lightsaber, once wielded by Branwen nic Catrin, the late Jedi of Pearson."

A dozen gasps erupted from within the audience.

Sven Carlssen turned in his chair and flashed a nasty look at Eastwood. "Don't you dare."

"Silence!" called the auctioneer, her voice somehow filling the room from all directions. The room fell silent save for the echoes of her voice. "Lady Lucretia, do you wish to add to your bid?"

Lucretia shook her head. "If Eastwood is willing to part with so dear a thing, his need for this ring must be greater than my own. I withdraw my bid."

The auctioneer looked around. "Do I have any other bids?" There was no response except more murmurs and shuffling. It was as if anyone else were scared to go for the item. *She must have been hot shit around here,* Ree mused.

"Going once, twice . . . sold to Eastwood for a signed white-box Dungeons & Dragons set, the original confetti Chaos Orb, and the lightsaber of Branwen nic Catrin."

The auctioneer clapped her gavel and the crowd applauded.

Eastwood sighed a deep sigh. "This had better work."

The auction moved on with several more lots, but Eastwood stepped out a few minutes later, Ree following.

"Who was Branwen? Is that the Jedi you were talking about?" she asked.

"Yes. She was a . . . close friend." Eastwood said it in a way that made it clear she had been much more than just a friend. "When she passed, I inherited her implements and collections, according to her will."

"Not that I don't appreciate you wanting to save people's lives, but why is that Claddagh so important that you'd trade off her weapon?"

"It's what she'd want. She was the most selfless person I ever met. She'd approve." Eastwood sounded like he was trying to convince himself that what he said was true.

"Let's take a walk. Want a drink?" Ree said, jumping into her Take Care of a Friend in Crisis mode without even realizing it.

"I shouldn't, but thanks." Eastwood's walls went back up, and Ree backed off. They wandered the floor until the auction was over. Ree continued to take mental and digital notes about the stalls, the merchants, and the buyers.

Next month I come with a plan, a bag of swag to trade, and a shopping list.

Another set of bells rang out, and Eastwood turned back to the auction area. "Time to settle up."

Ree swung the bag of goods onto her other shoulder, feeling the burn in her forearms. The ring would be a hell of a lot lighter than all the crap she was lugging around now, though she suspected the bag contained more than his bids.

Back in the auction area, there was a short line of bidders in front of the auctioneer and her sharp-dressed staff. Lucretia and Sven had made up enough to be chatting amicably ahead of them. A half-dozen auction winners collected their goods, walking away with knives, discs, tomes, and more before Eastwood approached the stage.

Ree opened the bag, and Eastwood produced his bids. First, the beat-to-hell D&D box, cardboard worn through at the corners. He held it for a moment, sighed, then handed it to one of the attendants. He pulled out a small clear plastic box filled with shredded paper, the confetti Chaos Orb. He handed that over as well, then reached into the bag and pulled out the lightsaber. This was a different model from the one he'd used to save Ree from the troll, but even from a few feet away, she felt the energy contained in the prop.

It called out to her, and she had to restrain herself from reaching out for a touch. Eastwood held the prop like a baby, and Ree saw a tear bead up in the corner of his eye before he handed the lightsaber to the auctioneer directly, stepping past the assistants.

"Remember the legacy she left. I hope you will honor her memory as I have," Eastwood said.

The auctioneer took the lightsaber and admired it, running her hands over the handle. "I will do with it as I see fit, Eastwood, but I will remember your words. Branwen was well known to me." More support for Ree's not-just-a-friend suspicions.

The auctioneer produced a small velvet-covered jewelry box and popped it open to reveal the ring, gilt and gorgeous. Eastwood exhaled upon seeing the ring and accepted it like it was as delicate as a Fabergé egg.

He slipped the box into a pocket of his coat and shook the auctioneer's hand. Ree failed her save vs. curiosity and looked into the bag. There wasn't much light, but she saw a cast-iron teakettle, a sheathed *tanto* knife, and the real culprit of weight, a white half-longbox, which would explain the boxy chunk o' heavy she'd felt digging into her back.

"So, what now?" Ree asked.

"Now it's time for a drink." Eastwood looped around the stalls and made straight for Grognard's stall, moving at a "walking crosstown in Manhattan" clip. Ree kept pace as best she could with the sack.

Eastwood already had a drink in hand when Ree caught up to the stall. He downed it in a single go.

"Okay, let's go. I've had my fill of this place," he said, tossing the empty cup into the nearby trash can.

Without so much as a glance in Ree's direction, Eastwood delved into the crowd, geeks parting to make way as he passed.

They were deep in the tunnels and halfway back to Grognard's proper when Eastwood stopped to sniff the air. "We're being followed."

Ree looked over her shoulder, trying to listen. "How do you smell anything down here?"

"Experience. I need you to get the *tanto* and the blaster."

Ree set down the bag and rummaged through it, trying to identify things by touch.

"Faster. They're closing."

"Who's closing? Can't we run?" Ree asked, panicking.

"No good. They're cutting us off at this juncture. If we go back now, we get trapped into a set of downward paths toward bad-nasty's territory. Get that sword ready, it's time to test your steel."

Ree found the *tanto*'s hilt and kept feeling for the blaster. She found something vaguely gun-shaped and pulled it out. Eastwood took both weapons, stuffing the *tanto* into his belt and drawing the lightsaber she'd seen earlier. Ree drew her rapier and scanned the darkness for movement.

She heard the laughter first, a throaty laugh in a deep but feminine register. Lady Lucretia stepped out of the shadows, followed shortly by Sven Carlssen, his hair brushing the ceiling of the sewer passageway. He hefted a bat'leth in both hands, the Klingon weapon that seemed a whole hell of a lot scarier in person than on TV.

Lucretia smiled, locking them in her gaze. "I've come for the ring, Eastwood."

CHAPTER EIGHT

With This Ring, I Thee Pwn

"**F**rak off." Eastwood held the lightsaber in a low guard out and to his right, not yet activated.

Lucretia's painted lips drew up into a terse smile. "This is not a negotiation. This is a trade. I take the ring, and you keep your life and that of your apprentice."

Sven curled his hands around the bat'leth, a caged tiger waiting to be released to the hunt.

Ree started to protest, "I'm not his—"

"She's not my apprentice." Eastwood cut her off, his voice raised and laced with anger and frustration.

"Whoever she is, she dies unless you give me the ring. You can fend off one of us, but do you think you're Geek enough to take us both?" Lucretia looked straight into Eastwood's eyes, smirking. "You're no Branwen." She spat the woman's name at him like a weapon.

Eastwood raised the blaster, pointing it at Lucretia. "How about you leave, and I refrain from disintegrating you and cutting off Swedish Chef's balls to serve to his wailing children?"

Sven shifted his weight side-to-side, clearly antsy. Lucretia was photo-still, her breathing imperceptible. Eastwood, Sven, and Lucretia maintained a stare-down for most of a minute, while Ree did her best to seem intimidating. She grabbed on to the magical energy in her mind with white-hot mental knuckles.

All right, William Goldman, don't fail me now.

Sven broke first, lunging forward with a huge pace. He moved far faster than anyone his size had a right to, cutting up toward Eastwood's neck with a swipe of the bat'leth. As Eastwood's lightsaber fired up, the tunnel filled with green light. Eastwood faded back and under the cut, dodging by inches and counter-attacking with his own upward slash. Sven reversed the blade and parried the lightsaber with the back side of his blade.

Inconceivable! Ree thought. *Or not.* She focused, using the *Princess Bride* brain to try to predict what would happen next in the fight.

Lucretia raised a hand and said something under her breath. A jagged pattern flashed in front of her hand, and the hair on Ree's arms stood straight up. Something cracked in the air, and Eastwood lost grip of his lightsaber. The blade reverted to prop form as it dropped into the sludge at the center of the tunnel.

"Frell!" Eastwood said in a panicked voice, ducking under Sven's horizontal cut and firing a point-blank shot with the blaster. When it went wide, he dived to the sludge, trying to fish out the saber.

Sven carried his cut through, on track to take Ree's torso off at the rib cage. She responded automatically, pushing off one foot to jump back and parry into the cut. Her blade was pushed out of the way by Sven's powerful strike, but the blow was deflected enough to miss her by inches.

Ree moved with the rapier's momentum from the parry, circled it over her head to cut at Sven's shoulder. The blond man backed off, raising the bat'leth at an angle to stop the cut. The tip of his blade bounced off the ceiling, but the parry held.

Oh, this is awesome, Ree thought as she let the magic guide her though the fight. She skipped back another pace, watching Eastwood sweep a hand through the muck while rapid-firing at Lucretia, who somehow danced around the shots, dodging them time and time again.

Eastwood pulled the lightsaber out of the muck and fired it up again, the iridescent green blade lighting up the tunnel once more. He fired a couple of shots at Sven as the blond man turned away from Ree. Sven took the blasts, which singed his coat but seemed to do little to stop him as he charged.

Ree pushed her weight off her back foot and launched forward, leaning into the lunge to align her whole body with the strike. The shot landed around the side of Sven's rib cage, but the blade skipped off his coat.

She cursed at his somehow-armored coat, but instead of "Fucker!" it came out as "Cowardly sod!"

Eastwood took a wide stance in the muck, meeting Sven's downward cut. Sven pushed Eastwood back, trying to tangle the lightsaber up with the blaster. Ree slashed at the back of Sven's head, figuring that it'd be harder to armorize one's neck. Without looking, Sven leaned forward, dodging the cut. Ree felt her feet slip on the muck-covered concrete and had to flail to keep from falling into a forward split.

Ree felt the magical energy fading as she fought, the buzz dimming. *Not just yet,* she pleaded with herself. *Keep going . . .*

As Ree recovered from the slip, she saw Lucretia backing up, the woman's long fingers dancing in a pattern. The air in the tunnel crackled with energy again, and the next time Eastwood's blaster fired, it made a pathetic *wooom* sound of powering down. Sven pressed the attack, pushing Eastwood's blade aside and clocking him across the temple with an elbow.

Eastwood collapsed into the several-inches-thick sewage, and Ree leaped to intervene, her blade whirling in a tornado of slashes and thrusts.

Sven parried each attack, taking one, two, then three steps

back. As she pushed forward with a double-disengage thrust to the shoulder, Sven leaned into her attack, knocking the sword out of her hand and slamming her into a sidewall.

Red and black covered her vision, and the world faded away.

⋅✕ˣ⟨12⟩ˣ✕⋅

Upon waking, Ree's first thought was: *What a hangover.* Except she hadn't been drinking.

Her next: Where am I?

Right. In a sewer, fighting Petticoat Strega and the Swedish Cuisinart.

She opened her eyes, regretting it when the light came into her eyes like hot-blasted sand. She closed them, trying to feel out her surroundings.

The ground below her was something squishy, and the room smelled like old paper, the air stiff. Her neck was cramped like she'd slept upright. She tried rolling her neck, feeling more than hearing the cracking and popping.

She brought a hand up to her face and tried opening her eyes again. The light still stung, but she managed to take in the room. She was flanked by bookshelves and a desk with stacks of old computer equipment. The squishy floor turned out to be a smelly futon. Ree looked around the room and heard someone whinging just before she spotted Eastwood behind the top of a shelf. His shirt was off, and he was wrapping a bandage around his chest, covering a nasty wound in his side.

She lurched up to a sitting position, and her head lagged several seconds behind. "Eastwood?"

He managed a weak smile. "Good. Can you give me a hand?"

"Why aren't we dead?"

"Nightcrawler trading card in my pocket. Instant BAMF."

Ree gave him the stink-eye. "So why didn't you do that when they showed up?"

Eastwood looked down. "I thought we could take them. Plus, Lucretia was loaded for bear, and she'd have been able to stop the effect at the start of the fight, but I thought maybe I could wind her first . . . Anyhow, she got the ring before I could get to you and teleport out, and Sven left me with this." He indicated the wound in his side. Blood was already seeping through the bandage.

Ree wobbled over to Eastwood, her head still tracking behind her body, and held the roll of gauze while Eastwood spun, wrapping himself in.

"I'm no doctor, and I think you need one," she said.

Eastwood shook his head. "I have no interest in explaining myself to the police. I've been around the block, and hospitals lead to complications. That concussion of yours, however, you can take care of without too much trouble."

That explained the wobbling and the lag. *Great, just what my weekend needed.*

"What do we do now? Try to get the ring back?"

"Right now, you go home and I convalesce for a while until my healing potion finishes brewing."

Ree quirked an eyebrow at *healing potion* but let it go. "Is there something else you can use to predict the potential suicides?"

"That's what I get to figure out today. It's 3 AM, so be careful on your way home. If I saved your life twice just to have you get shanked by a meth-head for spare change, it'd be a *gorram* shame."

Ree put her hands over her heart. "I'm touched. You'll call when you have something?"

Eastwood nodded. "Go have a life, and see if you can take the next couple of days off so you don't get fired when things heat up again and you have to start pulling all-nighters."

Lovely.

Ree looked around, seeing the rapier propped up against a shelf along with the bag-o'-stuff. She took a minute to make sure she wasn't forgetting anything, and when her head had cleared a little more, she started home, leaving Eastwood to his wincing and whinging.

There was a chill in the air, and the moon was bright in the sky. She kept her hands out of her jacket pockets, ready to respond to muggers or monsters or whatever might come along applying for the job of Fail Cherry on top of the Sundae of Suck that was her night.

Thankfully, there were no takers, and she spent the walk home alone with her thoughts, somewhat jumbled by the continuing ache in her head and neck.

She slinked up the stairs as quietly as she could, unlocked the four locks slowly, then crept inside, since she was supposed to be "asleep." She tiptoed to the bathroom to take some naproxen and then escaped to her room, tossing her coat on the floor and collapsing onto her bed. She stared at the ceiling until the drugs dulled her pain and she drifted off into long-overdue sleep.

This time Ree woke without questions, to the sounds of Sandra rattling around the kitchen. She heard Darren's voice as well, the couple's talking cutting through the paper-thin walls. She ambled out to the living room and then the kitchen, seeing Sandra and Darren in their Saturday-morning domestic bliss. Darren was supposed to be buried in work. Apparently, he'd made time. Ree smiled to herself.

The two slid past each other in the small kitchen, whisking batter in bowls, cracking eggs into a pan, and generally being disgustingly cute. A memory flashed across her vision for a second—Ree and Jay in the same kitchen, making dinner several months ago, when they still saw each other regularly.

"Good morning," Sandra said, an *I got laid last night* grin plastered on her face.

"Coffee?" was all that Ree could manage, her voice gravelly.

Sandra spun in place and placed a half-full French press on the table next to Ree. Darren handed her a mug, and Ree inhaled deeply as she poured, savoring the smell of Bryan's Morning Maniac blend. She took a sip, ignoring the scalding heat. She was still, savoring the smell until the first kick of caffeine hit her system and life filtered back into her limbs. She sipped again, popping her neck. Her head ached, but clarity rode in on the heroic tide of java.

This, this is my real life. Not that shit, she said to herself, forcing down the memories of the last couple of days.

"And now she's rebooted." Sandra dolloped some batter onto a pan, which sizzled immediately. Darren layered several strips of bacon onto another pan.

This is why I put up with the cute. Ree leaned against the wall, wrapping herself in the comfort of normalcy and familiarity.

A few minutes later, there was a feast—blueberry pancakes, bacon, fresh fruit, and coffee. Ree set the table and happily played third wheel while the couple chatted over breakfast. Her downtime would end soon enough, but she had the closing shift today, so she didn't need to be there until two.

"How's your head?" Sandra asked.

Conveniently, Ree had acquired a real reason for a headache. *Small blessings.* "A bit fuzzy, but doing better. I'll be fine."

Darren shook his head. "Just as long as you aren't getting sick. I can't handle another end-of-semester with the flu. That nearly killed me last year."

Ree shrugged. "Hey, if you're dead, no term paper."

"I'd have a problem with that, even if he doesn't." Sandra ran her hand over Darren's short hair, a familiar caress.

"Just for you, I'll soldier on. After this, it's back to the mines." Darren picked up a strip of bacon and ate it a centimeter at a time, making happy grunts.

Ree believed that even the most refined of men would be reduced to caveman sounds when being fed bacon, and she had borne up that belief with more than a little experiential data (aka anecdotes).

"What have you got on for today?" Ree asked Sandra, who was chewing a bite of pancake.

Her roommate wiped her mouth with a napkin and said, "Laundry, groceries, and then downtown for a cooking class. Beef bourguignon."

"Save me some?" Ree asked.

"Of course."

Ree would probably be twenty pounds heavier if not for Sandra. On her own, Ree could subsist on café leftovers and whatever she could barter with pastries from her network of restaurateur friends. Sandra made real, fresh food, specifically for herself and Ree, not repurposed or traded away because it was marred or about to expire. Ree had taken a while to get used to the idea, but she wouldn't give it up for the world now.

How am I going to keep this life while living a Bizarre Urban Fantasy existence? Those chicks are always single and lonely.

But she was a badass, she could make it work.

Ree helped herself to another serving of fruit, munching on slices of honeydew while Darren polished off a third giant pancake. "If I fall asleep and miss my train stop, I'm blaming you." Darren leveled his fork at Sandra, who demurred.

"You could always blow off the paper until next week and come with me to the cla-ass . . ."

Darren leaned back in his chair and looked at the ceiling. "Lord, give me strength to resist this gorgeous woman."

Sandra frowned.

". . . long enough to finish my papers," he added with a smile.

Ree quirked an eyebrow. "Do you think God would rather you coop yourself up finding new ways to cite Lacan or go out and live?"

Darren dropped his gaze back to the table and met Ree's eyes. "Sadly, I can't just cite Jesus and be done with it. That only works in seminary."

Sandra, who had gone to seminary for a semester, gave Darren a playful scowl, then sipped some more coffee. Which reminded Ree to drink more coffee. So she did.

Yep, still amazing.

Ree finished her cup and went for another as Darren and Sandra finished their meals. Ree volunteered to do the dishes, then went through the rest of her morning routine: shower, café clothes, and packing up her bag for a day of work.

She put the essentials on her bed to take stock. Keys, wallet, laptop (to write during break, theoretically), phone, and from her bedside table, the psychic paper wallet she'd gotten from Eastwood. Like as not, it'd be another long night, and she might not have time to come home and change.

Anticipating that, she laid out an extra shirt and gathered some makeup. She pulled out her Mace, along with the Swiss Army knife and her butterfly knife. Her arnis canes and *jian* wouldn't fit, so she'd have to rely on Eastwood's toy-aisle armory.

Looking at the weapons, tools, and essentials spread out over her bed, she thought, *This, ladies and gentlemen, is my new life.*

Right on cue, her phone alarm went off at the time she'd set last night.

She'd switched it back to the ringtone Jay had called the air-raid siren. But since Jay was history, back it came. She packed the bag, slipped the laptop into its case, and then set up in the living room to make an attempt at writing before work.

She popped in *Sahara* (the perfectly competent 2005 version) in case the night led to any action-adventure, and fired up Final Cut Pro and her file of notes. She looked through her idea seeds, trying to find something that could spark, an idea that could flourish and let her get past the creative drought.

And . . . nothing.

Her attention continually drifted up to the movie, so she gave in, shutting down her laptop and curling up to enjoy.

She was tuning in on Steve Zahn playing a genre-defyingly competent sidekick in the climax when her phone rang. It was Eastwood. *Joy.*

"This is Ree," she answered.

Eastwood sounded rushed, out of breath. "Did you call in to work? We've got a big problem, and I need some backup."

"What's up?" she asked.

"I've got a lead on Lucretia's location, but she'll only be exposed for about an hour, starting at three."

"I didn't call off work today, I was going to check with people to see if they could take some shifts later this week. I have rent to pay, you know."

Eastwood switched into his impatient paternal-figure voice. "Right now you need to call off work so you can help me take that witch down a notch and get back the ring."

Ree sighed. "I'll see what I can do. Call you back in ten."

"Make it five." Eastwood hung up.

Ree looked at the phone and said in a mocking snippy voice, " 'Make it five.' "

She hated to dip into her "my boss adores me" cache with Bryan, but then she thought of Angela Moorely and dialed Zombie Cafe.

Bryan picked up after three rings. "Zombie Cafe, this is Bryan."

"Bry, it's Ree. Any chance you can do without me today? Something's come up with a friend."

She waited while Bryan considered, answered a customer, or whatever it was that he was doing.

A snarl of guilt started twisting around in her stomach until he answered. "Yeah. Charlie's been asking for more hours, I'll bring him in to close. Good luck with the friend."

"Thanks, and thanks for the bailout. Best Boss Ever."

"Flattery will get you in trouble with my wife," Bryan said with a chuckle.

"I'm no homewrecker. Crusher of customers' hearts, maybe, but I don't do breakups."

Bryan's laugh told her she had escaped with her cache mostly intact. "Take care."

Bank of Blin
Adoration Account Summary
Reyes, Rhiannon—823527

Starting balance = Loved Like a Daughter
Deductions = No Questions Asked re: Last-Second Bailout
Final balance = Massive love

She continued enjoying the movie for another minute, soaking up the energetic fun of it all, then called Eastwood back, the buzz of magic in the back of her head.

He picked up on the first ring. "You good?"

"Yeah, but you're comping my pay."

"Good luck. We're going to Carmine Wharf. I'll pick you up in fifteen minutes."

"Why do you know where I live?"

"I cracked the CIA's blackout files when you were still in diapers, kiddo." Eastwood hung up before she could respond.

Why am I calling off work to go risk my life for no money? Damn you, conscience.

She put on her shoes and coat and then rewarded herself with another ten minutes of movie, finishing out the flick before her scruffy grump of a mentor arrived to cart her off to mortal danger. At least she wouldn't have to clean the bathroom.

CHAPTER NINE

The Precious

Carmine Wharf was one of Pearson's worst neighborhoods. This was where the actual hard-core dealers lived and worked, where the real shit went down, where murders were covered up with concrete shoes and various other nastinesses.

Understandably, Ree hadn't spent much time in the area. Fortunately for her, Eastwood seemed to know it like his backyard. Which, as an apartment dweller, he didn't have and had apparently compensated for by learning the lay of the land in the city of Pearson's best effort at aping Crime Alley. They passed an abandoned lot housing a crude tent city for a dozen, replete with jagged nylon tents and lean-tos made out of aluminum siding and cardboard.

Ree had spent a few afternoons in the Occupy Pearson camp over in Jackson Park, across from the courthouse. It was a bit of a shock to contrast that encampment of protesters with this one composed of the truly homeless.

Ree was glad she'd chosen something contemporary for her genre magic; there was no filter to break through, so she could easily speak in her normal voice.

"Here's a question: Why don't magicians do something about homelessness?" she asked Eastwood.

"If we got involved in one issue, we'd get involved in every issue. There's no magicians' union; we're all independent, if occasionally interreliant. There are places where the rules work differently, though. More than a few smaller towns are basically run by practitioners, Town Elders–style." Eastwood shook his head. "Pearson is too big for us to do that without drawing scary kinds of attention."

"What about the Doubt?" Ree asked.

"That only goes so far when you start digging up fraud and conspiracy. Authorities might think you hacked in or stole documents, instead of copying them magically, but you'll end up in jail just as fast. Plus, there are powerful factions of magicians who like the status quo right where it is."

"But what if you just Batman-ed it up a bit down here?" She saw a pair of men in an alley on the opposite end of the street, probably selling drugs.

"Some say that's how Branwen got herself disappeared."

That stopped Ree cold. *Crap. If she was that powerful and got taken down . . .* Ree reconsidered her small inclination to sideline as a vigilante, no matter how much time she'd spent daydreaming about it when she was fourteen. "Where exactly are we going?" she asked, noticing that they'd garnered several people's attention. She felt their gazes and found herself calculating sight lines, looking for cover, and figuring out what she'd do if someone opened fire at any given point. *Thank you, Sahara.*

"She's supposed to be meeting someone in a warehouse in Pier 7, which is down this street. Don't worry about the people. Though maybe you should have dressed more shadily."

Ree gestured to her outfit. "I would have thought 'broke-ass twentysomething' would pass muster."

" 'Broke-ass twentysomething *artist*' makes you stand out. Next time, wear a hoodie."

They turned a corner to face an A-frame long warehouse that extended all the way out to a pier. The rusted sign above the entrance read #7.

"Gotcha. And what is our plan?" she asked.

Ducking behind a smaller building, Eastwood pulled out a pair of rings, holding them out to Ree. "These will only work for a few minutes, so we need to delay use as long as possible. Get in, lift the Claddagh, and get out. No stopping, no fighting, and if we can swing it, no noticing. I did a bit of my own divination to figure out in which of her million pockets she's stowing the Claddagh, so we should be good to go. Any other questions?"

Ree held out the golden ring. "Will this ring make me go evil and lose all my hair?"

"Not if you use it for ten minutes, like we're supposed to."

"And if I keep it on?"

Eastwood shook his head, his face gone grave. He cracked a smile. "It'll stop working."

Ree matched his smile, stowing the ring in her pocket. She peeked around the corner and saw several dockworkers milling around fifty yards away. "Bystanders. Rings now?"

Eastwood nodded. Ree slipped on her ring, and at first, she thought it hadn't worked. She could see herself fine.

But then Eastwood disappeared.

"Did it work?" she asked, waving her hand where she thought Eastwood could see it.

"Yep. Let's go."

They approached the warehouse, halting in front of the #7 door. Ree heard a rustling with the lock, then some sort of sci-fi gadget sound. The lock clicked open, and they moved inside.

The interior was vast, with a high ceiling, big piles of boxes, more boxes, and for a change of pace, in the far corner, there were some boxes. The space was sparsely lit, with high-wattage bulbs suspended twenty feet from the ceiling.

Ree scanned the room, trying to figure out where Lucretia was or would be. *If I were a prissy Goth queen who makes Nabokov turn in his grave, where would I be?*

Eastwood led her along one wall, and they stopped at the end of a row of boxes. At the other end of the room, Ree saw a trio of muscle-bound fratboys in their early to mid-twenties enter like they owned the place. Maybe they did. Or maybe they'd just drunk deeply of the Jersey Shore Kool-Aid.

A few seconds later, Lucretia emerged from a side row and nodded to the men. Feeling a tug on her arm, Ree moved forward, closing with the two groups. Several steps later, she realized she was holding her breath. She exhaled slowly, trying to slow her racing heart. They could be in a four-on-two fight if the invisibility gave out or if someone had a way to see through the enchantment or if fate decided to find any other way to take a dump on their heads.

Ree took a long breath to steady herself, trying not to overwhelmed by the hyper-vigilance the magic was giving her. *Keep it together. Use the magic; don't get used by it. Or something.*

Ree wondered if Carlssen was around or supposed to be around. *If I were bodyguarding, I'd be in the rafters, covering with a rifle,* she found herself thinking.

Ree scanned the rafters, but didn't see anyone. So he was either not there, really good, or also invisible. *Damnit, now I have to worry about invisible people. It's like fighting freaking Geth Hunters all over again.*

Eastwood continued to tug her along until they got within twenty feet of the group, which meant she could make out the conversation.

Only the center fratboy had been speaking to Lucretia. He wore a pink polo and a Yankees baseball cap over his clipped-short black hair. His skin was bronzed, but it looked like he'd earned it the natural way instead of buying spray-on orange (poor Charlize Theron at the '04 Oscars). His eyes were a too brilliant blue, probably colored contacts.

Ree made out " . . . it before I'll talk prices . . ." as their words settled into sensibility.

Lucretia smiled. "Of course, Antonio." She reached into her skirts and produced the ring, holding it up for the boys to see. "The price stands at ten thousand, which you must agree is a pittance for gentlemen of your means."

"Shit, ten G's?" one of the other fratboys said. He was a meathead, no hair to be seen anywhere on his head or bulging arms.

"I've got this, Nic," said the leader. "I said five, and don't you try to gyp me."

Lucretia drew herself up to her full height, leaning into the somewhat confused Antonio. "The Roma are an ancient and proud people, boy. To reduce them singularly to thieves and misers does as much disservice to you as it does to them."

Ree felt another tug, and they closed to within almost arm's reach of Lucretia. The annoying hair at the back of her neck that grew far too fast and always made her want to take a razor to it stood up on end. She continually scanned back and forth between the fratboys and Lucretia.

The ring disappeared from Lucretia's hand, and her eyes went wide. She snapped her fingers, calling out, "Hireke!"

In an instant, Eastwood appeared in front of her, holding the ring pinched between his fingers. Seeing that he was exposed, Eastwood hustled to the side, putting Lucretia between himself and the fratboys.

"The fuck?" cried Antonio, looking between Ree and Eastwood.

Shit—mine, too? Ree thought, realizing her cover had been blown.

Antonio reached behind him to pull a chunky gun from the band of his pants. The bald meathead pulled out a set of knuckle-dusters large enough to fit his Vienna-sausage fingers. The third guy, who looked like a throwback to the greaser era, drew and pointed a knife in Ree's general direction.

Antonio and the bald meathead did a chest bump, which Ree thought was kind of excessive.

Then Ree saw mostly translucent blue-silver armor plates shimmer into focus around Antonio. Beside him, ghostly fists the same shade of blue appeared around the meathead's brass-knuckled fist.

Well, shit.

Ree circled opposite of Eastwood, trying to draw the attention of all three. *And now I'm running interference in the grandest tradition of the sidekick.*

"Get out of here, and watch for the Bromancy!" shouted Eastwood, who was chewing pavement down an aisle. Lucretia flipped her hand, the air popped, and Ree heard him shout, "Frak!" just before the wet-slap sound of him hitting the floor.

He wasn't kidding about Bromancy, Ree thought as she continued to circle around, putting the meathead and the slick-haired third mook between her and Antonio's gun. Her life just kept getting weirder, and it was showing absolutely no signs of stopping.

Pay attention, she told herself as the meathead came at her with a confident cross. With her martial arts skills enhanced by the talents of *Sahara's* Al Giordino, she hopped out of the way of the enlarged fist, watching Eastwood scramble to his feet. Ree exploded forward when the meathead twitched again, punching his bicep to stop his swing. She pressed forward, shooting under his exposed arm, then wrapped her arm up around his neck to prepare a hip toss.

She felt him yield an inch, but then he settled back down onto his feet. Even her magically enhanced kung fu wasn't enough to topple the three-times-her-size thug. She struggled with it, trying to take his balance, but he was too well planted. And here came his bro.

The greaser dove at her with the knife, and she pulled on the meathead to get out of the way, trying to keep him between her and the knife.

All right, you've bought enough time—get the hell out.

Ree kicked the meathead in the nose the next time he closed, giving herself some breathing room. She turned and jumped through an empty spot in the stacks of boxes, hearing the crack of gunfire as she went. Shots hit boxes with the sound of exploding shards, but nothing caught fire or *felt* shot, so she kept going. Ree rolled to her feet and made for the door they'd used coming in, hoping that she could catch Eastwood on the outside without the fratboys.

As she ran past a break in the row of shelves, the greaser slammed into her, knife-first. He caught her in the side, and she felt the blade skip off a rib, which was far more painful than "skipping" anything would normally imply. They rolled to the ground, Ree reaching for the knife on instinct as she screamed. She tried to shove back the wave of pain, but that was about as effective as pushing against an actual wave. She felt her genre magic starting to fizzle.

No, screw that. I have to use the pain. Use it, she thought, *digging in.*

Ree found the greaser's wrist and dug her nails into his veins. She drew blood, and the greaser snarled at her in a string of creative, if lowbrow, curses. Hoping she could remember them later for a script, Ree waited until she was on her back and kneed the greaser in the groin.

His strength vanished, and Ree socked him across the jaw and then pushed him off of her. She pulled on a shelf to haul herself out from under his well-tanned body, her side roaring with pain. The door was thirty feet away, so she ran full out, wishing she'd kept up with her Wii Fit this year.

There was another pop in the air, and she felt a lava-hot tear in her shoulder—*Ow ow ow ow! Damnit, keep going,* she told herself.

Still sprinting, she ran into the door without opening it. She fumbled with the handle, hearing bullets ricochet off the cement wall but, thankfully, not off her. She nearly fell through the entryway, barely catching her feet as she continued to bust ass back to where she and Eastwood had put on the rings.

She saw Eastwood twenty yards away, waving his hands frantically. It would have been funny except for the burning pain that was doing its best to crowd out every single other thought or sensation.

The only thing that occurred to her was another letter to her dad.

Dear Dad,

When you said that getting shot sucked, I believed you, don't get me wrong. However, I now realize how painfully right you were.

Love, your bullet-dodging daughter.

P.S. Can I borrow your Clive Cussler novels sometime? No reason.

She reached Eastwood as the firing resumed, someone (presumably Antonio) emptying his clip into the open air of the pier.

Will even gunfire get the cops to come down here?

"What in Crom's name were you *thinking*?" Eastwood yelled at her as she dashed to the smaller building they'd hidden behind. He started running to keep pace, unfairly unimpeded by a gunshot wound. Ree imagined that without the *Sahara* action-hero magic, she'd have gone into shock by now, which meant that when the power gave out in a minute or so, she'd be well and properly fucked.

"I had to buy you some time to get away," Ree said, her pace slowing as everything in her body started hurting. "No way you'd have made it out if the thugs were coming after you as well as Lucretia throwing her curses."

They reached the chain-link fence that blocked off the pier, ducking under the same hole they'd used to enter. "Maybe, but you're not in a position to make that call."

"You're welcome." Ree scraped her wounded shoulder on the rough edge of the fence, and the pain spiked again. "Goddamnedmonkeyfuck that hurts."

Eastwood shook his head as they ran across the street. "We need to stop so I can wrap up that shoulder."

"Are we safe?" she asked.

Eastwood slowed to a jog and leaned over a manhole cover. "Not yet. Time for a shortcut."

Ree sighed. "Sewers again?"

"Come on, unless you want to find out whether Tony had a backup clip." He made a grand sweep of his hand, inviting her down the hole.

"What could possibly go wrong?" Ree asked, looking down the manhole. No ladder. She hopped down, bracing her legs to land wide and sink into the impact in the muck. *I foresee a gigantic laundry bill in my near future.*

⨯✖⬡✖⨯

Here's a recipe for a crappy time: Take a knife across the ribs, get shot in the shoulder, run into a wall, then run another half-mile so you can take a stroll through a sewer, where your shoulder wound totally won't get infected at all. I recommend it for everyone, as long as your name is Jay, Lucretia, or you are a brother of the most ignoble Busta Kappa Nu fraternity.

Eastwood power-walked through the sewer, and Ree struggled to follow, her adrenaline fading fast along with the confidence that had accompanied the action hero–ness. This section of sewer had a light every fifty feet or so, leaving patches of darkness between each.

"Where are we going now?" Ree asked.

"Dr. Wells's. She's good, don't worry. Saved my life more than a few times. Five, to be exact. Though one of them might not count, since saving my life also saved hers. Spell thing. Point is, she's trustworthy and won't gouge me like some people. We just have to go through gnome territory first."

"Gnome? As in David the?"

Eastwood shook his head, which Ree could see only from the shadows it threw on the wall. "Not hardly. They're about three feet tall and are more like hyenas than people. They're the scavengers of the undercity, hang around the outskirts of beasties' territories, and live off the scraps. But if someone wounded comes through the area, they'll come looking for a bite."

Eastwood stopped, raised a finger to his lips, then peered around the corner. He faced her again, whispering. "This is where we start being quiet. They're most active at night, in sync with the creatures, but that isn't a guarantee."

Ree said, "Seriously, gnomes?" Eastwood shushed her, and she continued softly. "They sound more like ghouls."

"I didn't make up the name. They started as earth elementals in Greece, became legend in the sewers of Rome, and they've been worldwide since the age of sail. Stay close, be ready to run—and this time I mean actually *run*."

Ree nodded emphatically. "Oh, don't you worry, I've used up my hero quota for the day."

Seemingly satisfied, Eastwood drew his blaster and stepped around the corner. Ree followed, left shoulder cocked back to shield it from whatever the sewers might reveal. She focused on listening to the sounds of the sewer and watched for the movement of shadows, all the while trying to get over the idea that "gnomes" were something dangerous rather than being tiny bearded heroes who rode foxes and tussled with trolls. She looked over her shoulder and thought she saw a shadow twitch. She stopped, took a step back, and saw that it was just a change in the angle of light from an overhead manhole.

A minute later, Ree thought she heard the sound of scuttling from down an adjacent hall, but Eastwood didn't stop. Ree found her thoughts drifting to *Alien* and was grateful she was wearing more than her underwear, even if Ripley had a flamethrower to make up for it.

They turned a corner, and Ree felt air flow in from the tunnel they'd just left. She stopped to listen again but didn't hear anything. She took three quick steps to catch up with Eastwood, who held out his hands to stop her, spreading them wide to take up the whole walkway.

Ree dug her toes in to stop herself before running into Eastwood's hand breast-first. Having spared herself the embarrassment of a groping, she looked over his arm and saw black moving on black, shadows overlapping twenty feet away. The lightbulb ahead of them was burned out, broken or otherwise, not making light.

"Ready to run?" Eastwood asked.

"I don't know where we're going." Ree heard chittering, like the sound cats made when they saw birds. It was one voice to start, then an echo from the other side of the tunnel. More voices joined them, all chittering back and forth until the sound was a continual buzz.

Okay, starting to get the gnome = creepy part.

Her shoulder decided to take that moment to kick up the throbbing a notch, dulling everything she felt below the socket. *Thanks, body.*

"Right at the next junction, then past three junctions, there'll be a gray door on the left. Tell her I sent you, and take this." Eastwood handed back the *tanto* he'd used in the last sewer fight. She hadn't trained with a *tanto*, but it was a damn sight better than going in bare-handed, and was better in-close than a rapier.

Eastwood reached into his coat and pulled out a gel tube. *How many random things does he have in there?* Ree supposed it made sense that a Geekomancer's equivalent of a utility belt would be a trench coat. He cracked the thing, and reddish light washed over the tunnel.

There were at least a dozen three-foot-tall creatures standing across the width of the tunnel less than ten yards away. They looked like wizened children with gore-and-spittle-stained beards. They wore filthy rags or nothing at all; one wore a Pokémon shirt that had probably once been white but was now soot-gray. They recoiled from the light but regrouped quickly, climbing over one another, fighting to get to the front of the group.

What I wouldn't give for a good fireball spell right now.

"Got any handy tricks up your sleeve?" Ree asked.

"These things are mostly immune to magic, 's why they're so damned resilient."

Ree's shoulders slumped. "Awesome. Can we go around?"

"There's about fifteen behind us, maybe forty feet back."

Ree thought, *How do you know that?* but instead said, "Fantastic. So Butch and Sundance time?"

"Pretty much."

And then Eastwood yelled. It wasn't a nerdy-guy-trying-to-be-scary yell or an I'm-scared-but-trying-to-hide-it yell. No, it was a how-the-hell-does-a-guy-that-size-make-a-sound-so-big? yell. If the gnomes were as scared as Ree, the two of them would be fine.

Eastwood charged forward, blasting away at the group. Ree lurched after him, holding the *tanto* in a low guard and trying to find a gap in the minifiends' line.

Eastwood punted one of the gnomes, smacked another with the closed fist of his flare hand, and blasted a third at point-blank range. The blasted gnome launched backward and smashed into the wall. As soon as it hit the ground, it charged him again. The gnome in the Pokémon shirt leaped at Ree as she closed in. Ree slashed at it with the *tanto,* and the blade cut through one of its arms and into the other hand. It crashed into her, and she swatted it off while another one scratched at her legs. She lashed out with her boot, met the tough resistance of muscled flesh, and felt the sting of claws biting into her ankle. She jumped, trying to clear the crowd, and several more claws tore at her legs and feet. The entire shock of the landing went straight to her wounded shoulder, and she dropped to one knee.

Oh, this is bad, she thought.

Eastwood hauled her to her feet and proceeded to drag her as he busted ass down the tunnel. The chittering resumed, along with the scratching and clicking of claws on concrete that indicated the gnomes' pursuit. She felt dampness from her shoulder running down her back and front, seeping into her shirt and the strap of her bra.

Now would be a really great time for a miracle. Ree gave the universe a second to respond, half-expecting something to come along to help, but for lack of divine or celestial intervention, good old Doctor Who–style running through hallways would have to suffice. Her shoulder burned with a hateful intensity, worse than the time she'd cooked bacon in her underwear.

In her defense, she had been kite-high on weed. *Ah, college.*

They had passed the second of the three junctions when one of the gnomes caught up to her, kitten-sharp claws raking across her calf. She kept running—

And her leg gave out. She half-rolled to the floor, taking the fall as best as she could. Concrete scraped her knee and forearms hard, and she called out to Eastwood, "Help!"

The older geek grabbed an overhanging pipe and swung around it, parkour-style, charging back to fire into the crowd of chittering scrapes behind her. Ree tried to flip over to her back to face the gnome that had bitten into the back of her thigh.

"If I go out this way, I'm so haunting you," she said to the little fiend. Up close, she saw it had sunken eyes, wrinkled skin mottled by liver spots, and small flecks of skin and muscle in a stringy bloodstained beard. All positive associations of gnomes were irrevocably thrown out the window, a facet of her childhood retroactively pwned.

With defenestration on her mind, Ree grabbed the gnome by the shoulders and kicked it over and behind her. She pulled herself up with her good arm to stand on her good leg. Eastwood supported her, laying down covering fire with the blaster.

"It's not far, come on."

She hobbled on, feeling faint from lack of blood. *So that's what it feels like,* she thought as her eyes got heavier, her thoughts more clouded.

"Stay with me, kid!" Eastwood shouted, shaking her. One foot in front of the other, she dragged herself along. The chittering was a constant drone in the background, drowned out only by the crash of blaster bolt on concrete and flesh.

"We're here, hold on to this." Eastwood draped her good arm over a pipe, and she held herself up while Eastwood pounded on the door. "Wells, it's Eastwood! Open up, now!"

A few seconds later, Ree heard the croak of hydraulics, and the door opened. Eastwood half-threw her through the opening. She heard a final triplet of blaster shots, then a powering-down sound. Eastwood muttered a string of curses in Klingon as he dove through. The door slammed shut behind him, crushing several small clawed hands. Gasping for breath, Ree looked up to see their savior.

The presumptive Dr. Wells was a black woman who stood about five-five in black stilettos. She wore her thickly curled black hair cut short and the obligatory lab coat over a fine purple blouse, with flared black slacks rounding out her look. She was somewhere between thirty and forty-five, either youthful or well preserved. She had a heart-shaped face and amber-brown eyes behind red plastic-rimmed glasses.

Pounding continued at the door as Ree looked around the room. It looked more like what she'd seen of morgues from TV shows than an actual doctor's office. Everything was metal or slate-gray concrete, with several examining beds spaced across the room and various indescribable accoutrements that probably added up to cost more than the doctor's degree.

Ree blacked out for a second, and when she opened her eyes, she was prone, her back to a cold slate of metal. Dr. Wells was above her, latex gloves and scalpel in hand. "This will be easier if you're unconscious, dear. Just lie back and close your eyes."

Ree intended to resist long enough to get a word in edgewise, but her head found metal, and she drifted away.

CHAPTER TEN

Suck It, Crystal Ball

When Ree came to, the first thing she saw was a derby girl on the ceiling. Derby girl had impossible features, exaggerated waist-to-hip ratio and too-big eyes. Derby girl was hunched over in ready-to-skate position, winking down at her.

Ree blinked, but derby girl was still there. As her eyes continued to focus, she saw it was a painting, one of many on the ceiling, which she hadn't noticed when she first arrived.

Dear Derby Girl,
Why do I have to fall unconscious so much? I appreciate the sleep, but I imagine there are better ways to get some Z's. Speak to me, O painted muse.

Big fan of your sport,
Ree

Her shoulder and leg felt numb, but numb was a damn sight better than "burning hotter than the flames of Mount Doom." She scanned left and right, looking for Eastwood or the doctor. Eastwood was standing in the corner, leaned up against the wall and fiddling with a smartphone. He looked up and caught her gaze. "Good morning."

"Morning?"

"It's 7 AM, Sunday."

Crap. Ree was on the schedule to be at work approximately now. With the look of panic on her face apparently clear as daylight, Eastwood raised his hand. "It's fine. I called your roommate and told her you'd gotten into a small fender bender, nothing serious, but that she could call off for you."

"Invasive much?"

"It means you get to keep your job for another day."

"Does anyone in this world hold down a regular job?" Ree asked, trying very slowly to sit up. Her sight lagged behind her head, but one inch at a time, she righted herself.

Eastwood walked to a coffee mug on a table and poured a cup, then walked to Ree. He offered the Styrofoam cup, which Ree took with reverence. "Not many. Those who do are their own bosses."

"So what am I supposed to do?" Ree took a whiff of the coffee, regretted it, then sipped some anyway. Caffeine was a mistress cruel enough to shame the most aggressive dominatrix in Amsterdam. Colors brightened, and her head cleared slightly, despite the terrible smell and taste.

"Where's the doc?" Ree asked.

"Sleeping. She said you'd be free to go when you woke up."

Ree pulled the sheet back enough to make sure she was wearing clothes. A hospital gown could barely be called clothes, but it covered enough for her to pull the sheet back more and check her legs. They were bandaged, but when she tried moving her feet, they seemed to work fine. "Is she magic, too? Aesclepomancy or something?"

Eastwood cracked a smile. "She doesn't call it that, but yeah. The rituals of medical science are more than enough to charge up her magic. We need to get back to the Dorkcave and put this"—he held up the Claddagh ring—"to work."

Ree held up two fingers. "Two things. One, where are my clothes? And two, how are we getting out through the gnomes? The rings again?"

"The rings will take a while longer to recharge, plus I won't know if Lucretia permanently broke the enchantment until I do a study at my lab." Eastwood reached under an adjacent examination table and pulled out a bag. "These are your clothes, and I spent the last three hours working up a ritual that will keep us safe from the gnomes long enough to get out."

"Why couldn't you—"

Eastwood cut her off. "—have done that earlier? I didn't know we'd be going through gnome territory, since I expected a quick in-and-out, not your 'heroics.' Anything else?" He was more terse than usual, each new word jumping in at the end of the last, leapfrogging in a race to finish.

Ree took another sip of coffee, then set it down to rummage through the bag. The pants had been shredded but might be salvageable as jean shorts. The rest were dirty but intact. "Changing room?"

Eastwood shook his head and turned around, walking toward the corner.

Fair enough. Ree slid down from the table, cautious about putting weight on her legs. They supported her well enough, though all the sensations were fresh, heightened, like the just-shaved-your-legs closeness. She pulled off the gown and started dressing. *Something will need to change if I'm going to keep doing this weird stuff and not lose my job. It's not like Eastwood is paying me. Well, maybe.*

"You make your money with the memorabilia and props, right?" she asked.

"Yes. Can I turn around?" he asked.

"Not yet." She ripped off the bloody scraps of the jeans, making a rough approximation of cutoffs. *Geek tested, Punk approved.*

She checked to make sure everything was in place, then said, "Go ahead." Eastwood turned around as she continued, "There's no way I can keep regular hours at Zombie Cafe and be a magic super hero or whatever you put in the Career box. So I need another job. Could you use another hand around the shop, help move lots, maybe drum up some buzz?"

Eastwood narrowed his eyes. "I'm doing fine as is."

"If I lose my job and get evicted, I won't be able to help you. No more snappy Sherpa, no more ground-pounding kung fu investigator. Sandra doesn't make enough to float me for rent more than once a year, and my dad the hairstylist isn't exactly swimming in cash."

"I'll take that under advisement. Now here's how this is going to work." Eastwood pulled out a makeup kit from his vast trench coat. "Ever play in the Camarilla?"

"I was One World all the way."

"Same difference. We're going to obfuscate our way out of here." Eastwood pulled a folded paper from the kit. "Here's your character sheet. I've already taken the liberty of doing the makeup."

Ree took a hand mirror from the kit and saw what Eastwood had done. Her face was dusted white, eyebrows accented, and she had a general pallor that screamed Nosferatu, the clan of horrifically ugly vampires who, in the game, were masters of the arts of disguise and stealth.

"Okay, so with this makeup, we can obfuscate our way out?"

"That's the idea," Eastwood said.

Ree raised an eyebrow. *I smell a* but.

Eastwood shrugged. "But I've never actually tried this. Symbolically, it matches up with things I've done before. Now I need you to do mine. I always screw up if I do it myself."

Ree sighed and took the makeup kit. *Shot in the shoulder, trudged through sewers, attacked by cannibal gnomes, and now I'm doing some guy's makeup. At least one part of my day makes sense.*

Flashing back to her One World by Night days, she put on foundation, applied a white base, and did detail work around the eyes to make Eastwood look at least good enough to be a Boris Karloff cosplayer at Gen Con.

When she was done, Eastwood evaluated her work with the hand mirror, nodding. "If somehow this doesn't work, I'll hold them off, and you bust a move to the nearest manhole."

She didn't argue. He handed her a chicken-scratched character sheet with dots for Obfuscate, her skills and stats. Her name was Ignatia. Eastwood showed her his own sheet, folded it, and replaced it in his breast pocket, then said, "Cross your arms and think ugly."

Trying hard not to think of how ridiculous she felt for using live-action role-playing sign language as stealth magic, Ree followed Eastwood out of the doctor's bolt-hole, arms crossed in front of her, hands on opposite shoulders. She stayed a single pace behind him, repeating in her head, *Please let this work, please let this work.*

She continued the mantra as she saw the first gnome ahead. Another two appeared behind the first. Nestled in an alcove left by a collapsed wall, they fought halfheartedly over a bloody bone. As they passed, Ree watched for any indication of their presence being detected, but there was none. One of the gnomes slammed a concrete chunk onto another's head and grabbed the bone, sucking at it like a kid would a straw in an empty glass.

They hustled another couple hundred yards before Eastwood stopped her and gestured up to a manhole. "This is our exit. Should dump out near Wilkerson, and we can hop a cab."

He hustled up the ladder and moved the manhole cover, letting in a swath of cloud-dimmed sunlight. The alley was empty except for graffiti and a stencil of the starfleet symbol.

"Was that you?" Ree asked, trying to wipe off the assorted muck from the sewer.

After a quick sidelong glance to check, Eastwood shook his head, walking toward the street. "I use a different color of spray paint. Don't know who did this one. Might not even be someone in the know."

Daydreaming of the empty-the-hot-water-heater shower she was planning to take, Ree scanned Wilkerson for a cab. "How long will the Claddagh thing take?"

"Several hours, at least. I have to gather the other materials, pop in some Mists of Avalon to set the mood, and go through some books to refresh myself on the ritual. It'll go faster with you to help me fetch things. We should know the likely next candidate by dinner."

At the mention of food, her stomach reminded her of the cruel neglect she'd heaped upon it. Eastwood flagged a cab, and that hunger stayed with Ree all the way across town to the Dorkcave.

Step 1: Food. Steps 2 & 3, shower. Step 4, Claddagh-ring-magic thing. Step 5, stop suicides. No biggie.

⬧×⬢×⬧

All Eastwood had to eat were protein bars, chips, and a week-old pizza. The protein bar proved very tough, so Ree gnawed determinedly while stripping down for the shower. It was very much a stereotypical dude shower: more than a bit dirty, with only bar soap and an off-brand shampoo in the white plastic rack that hung from the neck of the showerhead. Eastwood had one ragged black towel and a far more pristine sky-blue towel. The blue one was a bit dusty but smelled clean.

Branwen's, perhaps?

Stepping into the shower, Ree wondered who this woman was, where she'd gone, and what her relationship with Eastwood had been like. She had a reputation in the area as a badass, but when she'd disappeared, what had the locals done? Nothing? That didn't sound like much of a community. Or maybe it went to show how much trouble she'd gotten herself into.

Ree didn't believe that Eastwood would have simply sat by, so wherever Branwen had disappeared to, they must have covered their tracks damned well.

From Branwen, Ree's thoughts turned to the Moorelys. Was there some secret connection between the three victims? If the ring didn't give them any information, how could they even *attempt* to search the whole city for the next person likely to commit suicide? She wondered how many people in a city this size committed suicide anyway, and how had Eastwood figured out or decided that this was a pattern?

She was riding damn close to blind, always playing catch-up or second fiddle or something else frustrating.

The shower worked nearly as well as a cappuccino in helping her wake up. She'd expected soreness, tenderness in her shoulder or legs, but they just felt tender, like new skin. Either Dr. Wells's magic was damn good, or Ree was on some kind of painkiller. *Something else to ask.*

She didn't have anything to change into, but she felt far more human after the shower. If she was lucky, Eastwood would decide to put together materials for the ritual on his own so she could go home to change. If she was *really* lucky, the ritual would determine that there weren't going to be any more suicides and they could console the families of the dead and move on. Ree wasn't betting on either.

Now cleaner and less starving, she made her way back through the stacks and found Eastwood flipping between several books. Behind him, there was a cauldron sitting on top of a space heater.

Eastwood spun in his chair. "Great. I need you to find these books. They'll be two rows over, on the top shelf. There's a ladder in the corner," he said, gesturing to the opposite corner of the Dorkcave with a paper in his hand.

Ree grabbed the paper as he spun back to resume poring through the books.

Scanning the list of books, she sighed. *Innocently Irresistible: Love Spells and Emotional Magic in the 19th Century, Sympathetic Magic, Empathetic Efforts,* and *The Oxford Shakespeare: Complete Sonnets and Poems. Huh.*

She found a ladder on rails and dragged it behind her, scanning the stacks for the appropriate section. She'd already seen that Eastwood's categorization system was more associative than alphabetical, so she searched for the Love section.

She walked past the sections of Jokes, Practical; Joker, The; and Keyzer Soze, as well as King, Stephen, a section sporting an impressive hardcover collection as well as several boxes of props labeled Pet Sematary, Carrie, and The Mist.

She abandoned the ladder and moved to the next row over. There, she found Love, which had boxes labeled for various romantic comedies, a big stack of books, a half-dozen DVD cases for *Love Actually,* and finally, the three books on the list.

Which were, of course, on a shelf too high to reach from the ground.

This row of stacks didn't have its own ladder, so Ree found a folding number in a corner and brought it back to the section. She stared at the ladder, her breathing getting away from her.

This is no big deal, Ree. The ladder is sturdy, it's not a long fall, and you have more important things to freak out about.

Ree wasn't as afraid of heights as she'd been as a kid, but she still had a healthy respect for what falling damage could do to a body, and she occasionally freaked out about it. She exhaled but started to climb. The ladder obligingly stayed underneath her, making only one small terror-inducing creak.

She pulled the books out one by one, setting them a shelf down. Then she descended two rungs, moved the books, and repeated the process until the books were reachable from the floor. She stepped down to the concrete and exhaled again, snapping the ladder closed and returning it to its corner.

Ree picked up the books on her way back, and when she cleared the stacks, she saw Eastwood standing over the cauldron holding a wooden spoon to his mouth. He took a sip and then wrinkled his face.

Not tasty, then. I wouldn't imagine a Who Is Going to Commit Suicide? recipe would be.

"Have books, will divine," she said.

Eastwood nodded. "Put them over there, then turn to Sonnet 116. I think it's that one. Starts with 'Let me not to the marriage of true minds.'"

Ree set down the books and flipped through the book to find the sonnet, which was in fact #116. "Now what?"

Still looking at the cauldron, Eastwood beckoned her over. "Come over here, then recite it at the solution."

"Why, exactly?"

Eastwood shook his head. "It'll take longer to explain than to do. I need to keep adding ingredients at the right intervals, so you get to recite."

Ree cleared her throat and started reciting the sonnet. She'd read them all back in school but hadn't touched them since. #116 turned Shakespeare's epic writing chops to the subject of qualifying true love. True love is beyond time, it's unchanging, so on and so forth. Ree was reminded of the passage from 1 Corinthians that was used in every single wedding she'd been to as a kid.

Eastwood hurried back and forth between the nearest shelf on the racks, looking half like a cooking show host and half like one of the "more scared of you than you are of them" customers at Zombie Cafe: head down, seemingly shut off from the world. And to top it all off, still smelly, as he'd forgone the shower that Ree had deemed necessary.

Though maybe he'd showered at Dr. Wells's and smelled of only *one* sewer expedition. Ree prayed that she'd never spend enough time in sewers to be able to tell the difference. The thought almost cost her her spot in the sonnet, but after a pause, she finished the second line of the final rhyming couplet.

Eastwood scurried back with the last ingredient—the Claddagh ring—and cast it into the cauldron. The ring made more of an explosion than a splash, and Ree leaned back to avoid whatever magical colorful wooj the rising plume was made of. When the plume dissolved, Eastwood leaned over the cauldron and squinted. He pulled on Ree to lean in beside him. "Keep your eyes open, and don't freak out."

"Huh?" Ree didn't have time to freak out when the liquid in the cauldron bubbled up, flashing colors more brilliant than a soap commercial, washing over her and sucking her into . . . something?

It started with flashes of light. Bells, then drums, then an electric-guitar riff. She felt dropped into a liquid mass, a pool or an ocean. Sensation rolled over her—sight, sound, taste, touch, and smell all at once. It was overwhelming at first, but after what felt like an eternal moment, she surfaced, got her head above water. The world settled into a hazy outline, sepia-toned, and she found herself in a bedroom. The edges of her vision were wispy, dreamlike, and when she tracked her head, the side of the room she focused on became clear while everything else became hazy.

A door opened, and a young man walked in, spiky hair in a Mohawk and a half-dozen piercings in his left ear. He slammed the door and locked it, tossing a bag on his bed. The room's decoration suggested a Millennial Goth Punk— here a Ramones poster, there a computer tower modded with skulls. As he walked across the room, Ree saw a ghostly outline of Eastwood beside her, also watching. She opened her mouth to speak, but he put a finger over his lips in the unmistakable sign of *Shhhhhh*.

The boy sat down in front of a computer and opened an email folder. Though it was across the room, Ree could read it clearly. It was a Dear John letter from someone named Jeanine to a Tomas. The words of the letter didn't stay with her, just the feelings of dread, betrayal, and loss. There were no last names, the email addresses reading Autumn Razor and Winter Knife—notable for their teenage affected coolness but not much else.

A bitter cold rushed over Ree, and she saw a phantom shadow play across the wall, reaching out to Tomas. As she tried to process the sight of the darkness wrapping itself around the boy, Tomas pulled a pair of pliers out from a stack of tools, beginning to cry.

And then he shoved it toward his eye.

The vision shattered, and Ree felt an intense pain in her eye. When the pain faded, Tomas's body was on the floor. His body flickered in and out of place, switching with Angela's body and two others she didn't recognize. Then the rooms, too, changed with the bodies, visual whiplash nearly overloading her eyes. She squinted and focused, trying to isolate one room at a time. Her vision settled back into Tomas's. It was night, where it had been daytime.

The window opened, and a strange figure's head peeked inside, checking the room. The silhouette scampered through the window, making no sound when it landed. It stayed half crouched and shuffled over to the boy's corpse. Still in shadow, the figure reached into itself and produced a red-and-white sphere, generating a light that swirled and folded in on itself rather than illuminating anything around it.

Ree hunched down to get a better look, maybe catch the face of whoever this shadowed figure was.

The murderer returned? Some scavenger?

As she looked the figure eye to eye, she saw no light, no

shadow of black on black, just a mask of darkness. She reached into her coat, hoping to find a flashlight, a lighter, anything. When she brought her hands back out, she had nothing.

She looked sideways to the dream-Eastwood, who stood frozen as he watched the interloper.

The figure waved its hand over Tomas's body, the body that Ree saw but refused to register, wouldn't analyze or examine. She took it as a gestalt, keeping it distant so that the pain couldn't pour through the cracks in her emotional armor that had been left by the sympathetic pain in her eye, the memory of Angela, and a hundred other emotional scars from her life.

An attenuated string of light seeped out of Tomas's mouth and nose, a dead ringer for every TV show or movie she'd seen in which a creature took someone's soul out of their body. The light floated up and began swirling around the stranger's sphere, seeping in and joining the captured light. Ree lunged forward, trying to stop the process, half-knowing she couldn't affect anything in the vision and half not giving a crap because she had to do *something* or yield to the pain that was peeling away at the edge of her vision.

Let go, said the pain in a sharp, gravelly voice. Let us in, and we'll take it all away. You don't have to hurt. We can take it away from you, leave you in peace.

Instead of pain, a warm dullness started to enfold her, wrap her up in nothingness. The vision faded away, the sepia tones fading to black and white, shifting grayscale.

"Aw, hell no." Ree shook off the blanket of numbness, grabbed the edge of the pain, and yanked hard. It hit her like electricity, and the sepia vision rushed back in on a tide of pain. Still holding on to the pain, she tried to focus it into light, blasting the energy at the shadowed figure.

The light cast on the figure, illuminating the features of a middle-aged man with dark hair in a fedora and long coat, and a set of surprised eyes. The dream-Eastwood tackled her, shouting something incoherent. In another scattershot avalanche of sensation, she was torn out of the vision and dumped onto the floor of the Dorkcave.

✗✗⬡✗✗

She came to with a start, as if woken from a bad dream, that is, with a scream. She was back in the Dorkcave, her hands on the edge of the cauldron. But this time she felt like she was going to vomit.

Good gods, let's not do that again.

"Are you all right?" Eastwood asked, looking green around the gills.

"What the hell was all that? Who was that guy, and did you see the shadow on the wall just before he—? Was it something that could be making these kids take their lives?" Questions popped up in her mind and spilled out of her faster than she could check them through the internal censor in her brain.

Eastwood held up his hands to stop her, then rubbed at his temples. "Hold on for a sec. Prophetic hangover sucks Bantha pudu."

The room continued to spin, though she was standing still, and her ears were hot. She felt like she'd just slammed three doubles of tequila and needed a fistfight chaser. She paced back and forth, looking for something she could kick without consequence. Instead, she grabbed the lip of the cauldron and squeezed as hard as she could, digging her nails into the wrought iron until they scratched along the surface, biting into her palms.

Ree turned back to Eastwood. "We need to go now. I have his email address. You can track that and a given name to an address, right?"

"Theoretically, but that depends on the ISP, email provider, a lot. Hold on a minute, okay? This hasn't happened, and it may not ever happen, or at least not like you saw. The ritual gave us a look at what *might* happen."

Ree closed on Eastwood. "Or it could happen just that way, could be happening now, right? Who were those figures, the phantom and the shadowed figure? Is this some kind of magical serial killer or what?"

Eastwood backed up a step. "Give me a minute to sort things out."

Something was wrong. Not just the situation. Eastwood. *Something in his eyes. Those eyes.*

Ree's nostrils flared, and she felt lava-hot anger pour through her veins. "It was *you* I saw in there—the shadow with the sphere!"

Eastwood's eyes went wide for a moment, then cast to the side. "No, no, no, of course not. Let me look up that address, you say you remembered it." He turned his back on her, headed for the computer.

Oh, hell no.

"It sure looked like you, unless you have an evil twin—and I don't think you have an evil twin. So if you do have an evil twin, you better let me know, because it really seems to me that you're involved with this somehow and you're trying to change the subject."

He turned around again quickly, an argument playing out on his face. He changed his mind several times, almost starting to speak twice and stopping himself.

Ree continued to press forward, stepping to within a hand's span. She had to look up to lock eyes, but she felt for all the world like she was looking down on him.

"You better sit down," he said.

Ree gave him the stink-eye and he stepped back again, gesturing to a desk chair. Not one time in her life had someone prefaced good news with "you better sit down." She'd been told to sit down when Mom left, when Grandpa died, when Dad got fired by the state of California (both times), and if there had been a chair available when Jay was dumping her, he'd have asked her to sit down.

She took a seat. Channeling her inner petulant child, she crossed her arms and leaned back, eyes locked on the man who she was *certain* was the same as the stranger she'd seen in the dream vision. But what had he been doing there that he felt guilt about it now, buckling under the barrage of her indiscriminate rage?

"It all starts with a girl," Eastwood began.

CHAPTER ELEVEN

Revelation Station

"**B**ranwen nic Catrin was the most powerful genre specialist I'd ever seen. We met around ten years ago, when she was new to the city. The dot-com bubble was bursting, and I was getting out of the computer business, burning my bridges with the EFF, and setting up shop here." Eastwood gestured to the Dorkcave, then took to pacing. "She was good then and was even better by the end. When she vanished two years ago, I turned over the whole rutting magical Underground looking for her. I called in markers, knocked heads, and padded wallets. But she was gone."

He made the universal magical sign of *poof.* "No one could place her anywhere later than Howard Park on October 31st. I kept digging, turned up more and more sources."

Ree shifted in her chair, arms crossed, hackles still up.

Eastwood stopped and took a moment. "And then the Duke showed up."

"Duke? Of what, Windsor?" Ree asked, thick with sarcasm.

Eastwood narrowed his eyes, disapproval clear. "Hardly. Not only are demons real, there are lots of kinds. The fallen angel who plagued Jesus in the desert, the daemon that haunted Plato, *oni, rakshasa, manitou, shen,* and more. As we've changed, demons have kept pace, developed specialties to match ours.

"The 'Duke' is properly His Brilliant Marvelousness, the Thrice-Retconned Duke of Pwn, Chief of the Dork Lords of Hell."

Ree burst into a most unladylike bout of laughter. The rage and frustration that had been at a rolling boil found the hole of the laughter and rushed out. She cackled so hard that her very proper Puerto Rican Catholic godmother would have chided her in Mach 3 Spanish had she seen Ree act in such a way.

Eastwood let her finish laughing, waiting to resume his story like a politician letting an audience play out its applause during a speech.

"I'd heard of the Duke through Branwen—he'd had a major hate-on for her because of some history I still don't know. I figured that if no one on earth knew where she was, he'd be the one being off earth who would."

Ree wrapped her arms around herself, holding tight.

"And he did. The Duke taunted me with her, promised to bring her back, for a price. I tried everything I could to get to her on my own: rituals, summonings, divinations. None of it worked. And last full moon, he showed his face. Or at least the face he shows to the world. Exacts on demons are sketchy, since they're each as different as we are—individual eccentricity trumps general description. He appeared to me during one of my divinations, offering a bargain."

Ree let her arms drop to her lap. "And I'm assuming that bargaining with demons is as bad an idea in reality as it always is in fucking every single story ever?"

"Almost certainly. But for Branwen . . ." He trailed off, then blinked and continued. "He gave me an offer. If I delivered— in full and on time—he'd return Branwen to me, unharmed, alive, and renounce all claim on her."

Ree stood into a fighting stance, her cheeks hot. "Delivered *what?*" already thinking she knew the answer. *I want to hear you say it.*

"Demons run off of emotional energy. They breathe it like we do air. The anguish of a widower, the triumphant joy of a world-cup winner, the sadness of a broken heart. But to get it, they have to use intermediaries, since they can't touch our plane without being summoned. Their lackeys here on earth do their dirty work, but they can't harvest the emotion directly. No, that job falls to schmucks like me who've gotten themselves in over their heads."

"Deliver *what?*" Ree asked again, her heart pounding like a jackhammer.

Eastwood shook his head, chagrined. "Everyone has a price. You don't believe it until you're the one crouched over a body harvesting its emotional by-product like some hippie vegan saving her afterbirth to freeze and cook into a casserole."

As Ree was about to yell her question at his sad little face, Eastwood stopped, looked her in the eye, and said, "I have to bring him the souls of five virgin suicides with broken hearts before the full moon on All Hallows' Eve, or I'll never get her back. That *oni* I was chasing broke my last ritual focus, so I needed the Claddagh to get back on track."

Ree moved in on Eastwood again, nostrils flaring. "You knew the suicides were happening early enough to break into their houses and steal their souls."

"Yes." Eastwood narrowed his eyes at her. "Ree, she'll spend eternity suffering at his hands. I can't fail her. Not again . . ."

Ree's ears started burning. "And you came in like some cowardly hyena ghoul jackass, took their souls, all to pawn them off to get one woman back, a woman who probably got herself into whatever it was that killed her?"

Eastwood narrowed his eyes but looked away from her.

"And now you're willing to trade five deaths for one life?"

Eastwood's eyes were bloodshot, puffy. But his voice was clear. "Yes."

Ree punched him. She used the single-mindedness of purpose, the smoothness and certainty of action she'd cultivated to pass her black-belt Taekwondo breaks, and she punched him in the nose. It broke, and he reeled back, collapsed into his chair.

His hand went up to his nose and was quickly covered by blood. He didn't stand up, didn't retaliate, just looked at her through ever-more-teary eyes, and said, "I'm sorry. It was the only way."

Ree shook the impact out of her hand, stepping back. "Seriously? That's what villains say, Eastwood, not heroes. You're the grand-high Geekomancer narratological magical badass, you should know that better than me."

Ree gave him the nastiest glare she could muster, then picked up her pack and walked out the door.

⋅✕ˣ◈ˣ✕⋅

She walked straight home, up the stairs, and into her room at The Shithole, where she turned on her stereo and queued up VNV Nation as loud as she possibly could and collapsed into a heap of crying and shouting.

What in the fucking fuck am I supposed to do now?

Ree went to her computer and tried to recall the email addresses she'd seen in the vision. The memory was foggy, like a dream. It had been so vivid, so visceral, but now it was barely a rough impression, aside from the pain. She pieced together what she thought Tomas's email address must be, and started drafting a message.

What do you say to someone who might commit suicide? Who might not have even gotten the final impetus to go through with it?

Tomas must have already been unstable or depressed, for a breakup to push him over the edge. But that was in a normal, no-monsters paradigm. She had no idea what the phantom shadow she'd seen was, or what amount of influence it could have over someone. But who would know? Who of the people she'd met would help her even if Eastwood told them not to? The list was damn short.

Not Grognard, who barely knew her, and certainly not Lucretia or Carlssen, since Ree was as likely to shiv them as ask them for help.

If she wanted help from someone who was clued in, it came down to Drake Winters, the temporally displaced bombastic Victorian would-be hero. Who might actually just be some random whacko whom Grognard permitted in the store. Ree tried to remember the sewers, what Eastwood had said, tried to piece together whether there was any way to get to Grognard's that wouldn't require going through the Dorkcave or another run-in with gnomes.

Her phone rang with the Unknown Number ringtone she'd set. The number wasn't familiar, though it bore a local area code. She picked up. "Hello?"

"Is this Ms. Reyes?" said the voice from the other line, proper but uncertain.

She stood up. "Drake?" *The hell?*

A sigh of relief came from the other side of the line. "Indeed, Ms. Reyes. The pull of Providence urged me to my phone and to produce your calling card. May I be of assistance?"

Woah.

"Providence? How does that work? Some faerie magic, or some Steampunk probability matrix?" *Or are you also a stalker? Are you in on it with Eastwood, maybe through Grognard?*

"Since my time in Faerie, I have been gifted with a strong sense of Providence, a call to adventure so that I might be in the right place at the right time."

"Are you sure you're not stalking me?" she asked. "You could be working with Eastwood."

"Eastwood? Is he not your mentor? Miss Ree, I have only the noblest of intentions. Are you truly in need of service?"

Ree ran her hands through her hair, sighing. "Like how. This will work better in person. Can you get to the U-District?"

"I was enjoying a constitutional in Washington Park. With advantageous traffic, I can reach the University District within one half hour."

"Great. Meet me at Turbo's Pizza in half an hour. It's on University and Wilson."

"Of course, mademoiselle. Shall I bring my arsenal?"

"Whatever you can conceal. Turbo's is not a part of . . ." Ree struggled to find the words. "They're not in the know, as far as I know, you know?"

"No."

Ree laughed at the inadvertent wordplay. It was nervous laughter but better than nothing. "Then concealed it is."

⊗

Turbo's Pizza, on a Sunday afternoon in the fall, when the air outside was just cold enough that the idea of hot food became marvelously appealing, filling the same sense aesthetic as mulled cider in the winter or cold beer in the summer, was awesome.

Ree was early for the meeting with Drake but had wanted to arrive first. Her internal oddsmaker had Drake Will Sell You Out/Kill You at 5–1 against him being creepy or evil, but she decided to hedge her bets. *Plus, pizza. The greatest of comfort foods, especially when combined with beer.*

Turbo was not actually a person but a dog. He was the owner's retriever-chow mix, a dopey but lovable mutt that was as much like his name as Robin Hood's buddy Little John. Local health code meant that Turbo's presence in the restaurant was symbolic only, but the pizzeria's logo showed Turbo wearing a jet pack, holding a white pizza box in his mouth.

And while Turbo himself wasn't fast, the pizza was—the fastest in Pearson. The owner, Cole Lutz, followed the NYC model of slices, keeping a continual flow of business while also offering sit-down meals for the less hurried customers.

The front of the restaurant was devoted to the by-the-slice crowd, with three different types of pizza available at any time: cheese, meat, and veggie. Today slices were Cheese, Italian Sausage, and Spinach.

She knew triangular portions would not satisfy her, and she had the time. Ree walked past the by-the-slice counter and the seven-people-deep carryout line. She nodded to Joni, the tiny-spunky part-time-actress hostess, and walked straight down the aisle between filled tables to one of "her" booths.

The fire-hydrant-red cushions looked a little worse for the wear; maybe they hadn't been cleaned in a while, or maybe someone had spilled something that even Cole's hippie-industrial-grade cleaners couldn't get out. The table had the requisite white-and-red-checkerboard pattern and an upside-down lampshade of green glass in a turtle-shell pattern.

She slid into the three-sides-of-a-square booth and faced the door, putting her back to a wall. It'd be harder to get out, but the place was busy enough that she didn't expect anything untoward would risk that much exposure.

One minute before the appointed time, Drake Winters pushed open the door. He was wearing his big brown coat, but there were no obvious signs of weaponry on him. He looked around the restaurant, walked past the amorphous line, and scanned the restaurant section. Joni greeted him, and he responded with a big smile and a nod, then gestured in Ree's direction. Joni waved him through, and Drake strode through the restaurant like he was the cavalry coming over the hill.

Which, in a way, he was. But damned if he wasn't self-satisfied about it.

Stay good, Ree. This guy might be your only chance of pulling this out.

Drake stopped at her table, gave a quick bow, and waited. *What's he waiting for? Oh.* "Take a seat," she said, gesturing beside her.

Drake nodded, then slid into the booth next to her.

Old-fashioned is the name of the game, Reyes.

"So, Ms. Reyes, how may I be of assistance?" he asked.

Ree shook her head. "First, call me Ree. Or Ms. Ree, if you must be formal. And before we talk, I need food, unless you have a way of doing a reverse-lookup on someone based on an email address and we can cut right to the chase."

Drake's blank stare told her all she needed to know.

"Food it is. What do you say to a deep-dish with spinach, feta, and sausage?"

This time Drake's expression wasn't nearly as lost, so she took that as a yes.

With the timing that had helped him build his pizza kingdom, Cole Lutz appeared around the corner, exclaming, "Ree!" He wrapped both hands around her shoulders and squeezed.

Cole Lutz was on the far side of fifty, but the only ways to tell were the shock of white hair and the permanent laugh lines. He had the energy of a twenty-year-old and was as fit as the grandpas in spandex Ree saw running at 7 AM on days when she opened the café.

Look as good when 50 years old am I, I will not.

"Cole, this is my friend Drake." Ree gestured toward the Victorian refugee, who stood and offered his hand. The men shook, and Drake took his seat again.

"I'm feeling Chicago-style today, Cole. Can I get a spinach, feta, and sausage?" Ree asked.

The man nodded. "Start with hero fries?"

Ree leaned back and grinned. "Only always."

Cole had stolen the hero fries recipe from a localvore restaurant in southern Indiana, though since he'd done it with the express permission of the chef, the "stealing" descriptor was mostly for effect. They were spiced with garlic, lemon, and a few other tweaks that Cole had made. They came in a bowl the size of one's head and were impossible to stop eating.

Would binge eating make the problems go away? No. Would it be delicious and distracting? Yes.

"And a bottle of the chianti Ruffino, to come out with the pie, please."

Cole cracked his half-smile. "You I know, but I have to card this gentleman." Ree's smile dropped as she realized that Drake might not have an ID.

Drake pulled a leather billfold out of his coat and showed it to Cole. Ree was somewhat disappointed to see that it was a standard state-issue identification card. In the picture, Drake looked somewhat annoyed, staring off-center.

The pizza master scanned the ID and nodded. "Hero fries coming right up."

Ree rolled her shoulders, shrugging, and when she looked back, the dough-slinging sprite was gone.

"Okay. Here goes." Ree launched into a retelling of her misadventures with Eastwood, focusing on the suicides and the cauldron-borne vision, ending with Eastwood's confession and her storming off. Drake listened politely, stifling several questions she saw grow on his face and get set aside.

Her story finished, she leaned back, sipping on the water that Joni had apparated onto the table while Ree was talking about getting attacked by gnomes.

Drake took a drink of his own, furrowed his eyebrows, and gave a thoughtful "Hmm. Several thoughts."

Ree nodded. "Please."

"Eastwood is a noted member of the local magical community. His reputation since Ms. Catrin's disappearance has slid more toward that of the curmudgeon, but he is universally regarded as being on the side of the angels."

"Literal or figurative?"

"Figurative," Drake responded without missing a beat. "I think. I've not encountered any angels myself, but I would not rule them out. I've seen beings as strange, terrifying, and wonderful in my travels through Faerie."

"So—can you help? I need to find this Tomas, figure out a way to protect him from whatever that thing was."

"If my suspicions are correct, it was most likely an Aberrant Muse."

"It inspired the White Wolf Iron Age Superhero RPG?" she asked.

Drake cocked his head to the side, regarding her for a second, then shook his head and resumed. "There are many varieties of muses. We mostly know the Greek muses, who inspired artists and philosophers. They were the more positive muses, nine singular entities that governed art. The Aberrant Muses were their dark reflections: numerous, cruel, and persistent. Far darker than even Melpomene, who governed tragedy, the Aberrant Muses inspire sorrow, hatred, jealousy, and so on. If I am correct, this phantom would be a muse of despair."

Ree asked, "And it could be responsible for the string of suicides?"

"Easily. I would surmise that this Muse was part of a colony under the control of, or at least the influence of, the Duke, sent to Pearson to create the opportunities for young Master Eastwood. The Muse pushes the poor youths into the deepest despair, then Eastwood arrives to collect the souls and condemn himself as part of his desire to rescue his True Love."

Undercutting the somberness of the conversation, Cole appeared around the corner with the bowl of hero fries. Ree took a long smell, letting the spices and heat and cheese hit her senses, prompting an eat-your-heart-out-Pavlov's-dog response.

Ree started to tear in, then stopped herself. "You first. Otherwise they'll all be gone before you get the chance to join the cult of the hero fries."

Drake raised an eyebrow. "Cult?"

Ree waved a hand reassuringly. "Joke. They're delicious, try them."

Eyebrow still up, Drake ate a fry. He chewed thoughtfully. The suspicion dropped, and then so did his hand, reaching for more. "These are marvelous! I've not had a treat its equal since the Mistress and I were guests in the grand hall of Count Dabbalio."

They feasted on fries while Ree considered implications, happy to have the food take her mind partially off the depth of what they were discussing. "Can you locate Aberrant Muses, track them at all? Maybe we could follow this one and cut it off before it reaches Tomas."

Drake wiped crack spices from his mouth and took a drink of water. "I could attempt to isolate its aetheric signature based on Dr. Woolenstein's inferences on the residual frequencies of post-living entities."

Ree asked, "Is that a yes?"

"It's a maybe, mademoiselle. But if your fears are correct, then time is of the essence." Drake took another handful of fries and stood up, munching. It was hard to look dashing and intrepid while chowing down on french fries, but he made a valiant effort.

"We haven't even had the pizza yet," Ree protested.

"Ask for a canine box. If we are to save this young man's life, then we must let science be our guide, lest we arrive too late. We shall not leave him to your former mentor and condemnation in the torture tournaments of the Duke of Pwn!"

People were staring. Ree laughed and flagged down Joni to ask for the pizza in a carryout box and to cancel the wine. She unfolded a twenty and a ten, doing the mental math based on a hundred visits and dozens of order combinations. *Fifteen for the pizza, eight for the fries, generous tip including tipping on the bottle of wine we're not actually going to drink just in case they already popped the cork. This heroing is expensive. Okay, I should have skipped the wine.*

Ree and Drake waited for three minutes, then he said, "I will go ahead and make preparations. When you have the pizza, reach me on the cellular telephone and I will provide directions."

With that, he turned, jacket flaring. He strode out with the determination of a hundred action-movie heroes.

Ree distracted herself with fries and a lap around the Internet on her phone until the pizza came out fifteen minutes later. She smelled the gloriousness and resisted the urge to open it up and have a slice as she walked.

Drake's phone rang three times before he picked up. "Hello?"

"It's Ree. Have pizza, will travel."

"I assume so."

He rattled off directions, but she stopped him. "Is it an actual address or something weird?"

"Weird?" he asked.

"Do I have to go down a set of stairs that shouldn't exist, knock three times, and then close my left eye as I open the door?"

Beat. "No, none of that nonsense. It's Apartment 7E. Master Grognard located the apartment for me and assisted in its acquisition. I did not, however, inform the landlady of my scientific endeavors. Fortunately, I have constructed sophisticated ventilation systems and have evaded notice thus far."

Ree chuckled, balancing the pizza box in one arm as she held the phone to her ear. The streets were getting busier as people wrapped up their errands, preparing for party night. *While* my *plans are shaping up to preventing a suicide or picking a fight with my magical mentor. Awesome.*

"Got it. See you soon." Ree hung up, then reset her armful of pizza, dodging through the crowds, trying to stay positive instead of wondering with every step whether she was too late, if Eastwood was one soul closer to going all Robert

Johnson and the Crossroads. Even worse, since Eastwood would be using stolen chips.

Jackass.

CHAPTER TWELVE

Marconi's Nerdy Granddaughter

Ree reached the building after a short train ride and was happy to find a buzzer intercom. Pleasantly normal. She set the pizza on the flat top of the concrete railing and buzzed 7E. No answer. She waited a few seconds, then buzzed again.

The voice was scrambled by static, but she still recognized Drake on the other end. "Yes?"

"It's Ree."

"Entre-vous, mademoiselle." The door opened. Ree retrieved the pizza and made her way up the stairs, through hallways with cracked paint and worn wooden rails to a poorly lit hallway with dirty tiled floor, all the way to 7E. Arms still full, she knocked with her elbow.

She heard three locks click, slide, and unhinge, and then the door opened, revealing Drake Winters, who, in addition to the outfit he'd been wearing when they met—leather jacket over a fine shirt and sturdy britches, brass-tastic goggles on the forehead—now had a rifle slung over his shoulder and an impressive laboratory behind him.

The lab took up the entire living room. Beakers, boilers, racks of herbs and ingredients, tubes and wires plugged into everything. And on the ceiling: fans, filters, and unnameable ridiculous devices that shouldn't work and therefore probably were the most important. She'd been to a Steamcon, and they had pretty good decorations. Drake's laboratory put them all to shame. With an ear-to-ear smile of wonder, she walked inside, taking it all in.

"This is awesome!" Ree said, looking for a place to put the pizza box where it wouldn't be melted, electrified, or otherwise rendered less tasty.

Seeing her look around, Drake beckoned her to follow as he walked through the room. "We best take the food to the kitchen."

For all that the living room was overfull, the kitchen was nearly empty. *Not a chef, then.*

Drake opened a cupboard, revealing a stack of paper plates and several plastic cups from Pizza U, the best of the local delivery joints.

She sliced up the pizza and ripped a still-steaming piece from the pie. She introduced the slice to a paper plate with about as much brevity and intent as a sorority girl introducing the black-sheep sister at a party, then started devouring it.

She bit through juicy chunks of tomato, chewed on succulent spinach, and crunched on the perfectly baked crust. The world went away for the third time in the day, but in the happy I-love-food-screw-the-world kind of way rather than the significantly less awesome here-comes-or-goes-a-dream-premonition kind of way.

Ree hoped not to add to her index of Ways That the World Falls Away to a Pure World of Sensation. The existing three on the index were mostly positive (the third being good sex, naturally), and she'd rather keep it that way.

Her first slice was gone before Drake could get his piece extricated from the pie and onto the plate. Half of his slice had slid off and slopped onto the table. Drake applied a spatula and attempted to re-dress the slice. "Rather problematic," he said, his nose curled up in a face that was both cute and ridiculous.

"If you need to use a fork, I won't think you less of a man," she said.

Drake gave an unself-conscious smile and retrieved a fork and knife from a drawer.

Ree walked with her second slice back out into the living room, tiptoeing her way through the maze of lab equipment. With pizza in hand, she was far less tempted to reach out and touch things, so she just took a mental inventory, speculating to herself what various devices could or would do. She turned and saw Drake cut a large bite and pop it into his mouth.

"What do we have to do to track the Muses?" she asked, smiling at her successful timing.

Drake's eyebrows scrunched up, possibly in annoyance over having been questioned with food in his mouth. Ree kept a round of cackling on the inside and waited for Drake to finish chewing.

"I understand now why you were insistent on acquiring this supper, Ms. Ree. It is quite phenomenal. It reminds me of the grand feast put out by the Pirate King of Barkeria, who ruled over an archipelago of bizarre islands, each stranger than the last."

Ree beamed. "We don't know each other so well, but let me give you some advice. Always trust me when it comes to three things." She held up a finger for each point. "1) Obscure trivia of post-crisis DC Comics continuity; 2) my gaydar; and 3) where to find the best pizza in every neighborhood I've ever lived or worked."

Drake cocked his head to the side. "Gaydar?"

Ree shook her head. "Never mind. Muses?"

Drake crossed in front of her to set his greasy plate down next to a burner. *That won't become a problem, nope. No risk of grease fires here.*

"It's a question of frequencies, so I will need to use my

aetheric goggles to create the proper filter. I will then attach the filter in one of the goggles' settings, and we should be able to detect any traces of Aberrant Muses."

Drake crouched down and started rummaging through a box of parts, still talking. "Do you know anything else about where this young Tomas may live? There may be several Aberrant Muses in a city this size, though given the particularity of this Muse's taste, and following with Spengler's theory of niche distinction in post-living entities, we may be able to distinguish between different signatures across the emotional spectrum. Do you have access to any radio or satellite arrays?"

"You know about satellites?"

"I made communication technology a priority in my acculturation, given my technological predispositions."

"Okay. I don't have any radio hookups. A friend of mine on the north side has satellite Internet through work. Wait, would satellite radio work?"

"XM?" he asked.

Ree nodded, taking another bite.

"That should be sufficient, depending on the signal."

She stumbled upon a burst of excitement, immediately balanced by annoyance and a little dab of shame. "Now all we have to do is go back to Zombie Cafe and explain why I'm running around playing scavenger hunt but couldn't come in to work."

Drake shook his head. "We would only need to be within ten yards or so to allow me to utilize the satellite connection."

Ree didn't know much about satellites, but that seemed unlikely. "Really?"

"The joys of a worldview that conflates magic and technology. At the moment, contemporary understanding of science has as much bearing on my work as I wish it to."

"So you get to cheat?"

Drake smiled. "I rather prefer to think of it as a creative

reinterpretation of rules that I never agreed to in the first place."

"Then why do you need to bother learning about modern tech if you can just cheat?"

"As with many pursuits, one must know the rules in order to confidently break them."

"Fair enough. What can I do to help?" Ree asked.

Drake set a box of beakers on the table before him and stopped a moment to consider. "How would you evaluate your knowledge of physical chemistry?"

"I got an A-minus in AP Chem in high school, but that was about a decade ago. I'm pretty sure I can still operate a Bunsen burner without hurting myself."

"Brilliant. If you don't mind, I will have you perform some simple procedures while I work on adjusting the aetheric goggles. I can talk you through the steps. Please interrupt me if I am spouting nonsense or if you have problems. Especially if something explodes."

Drake talked her through several reactions that sparked vague shadows of memory from her time in AP Chem, back when she'd been carrying a torch for Andy Ritcher, who was not only a point guard on the basketball team but the captain of the Academic Decathalon team. He'd been beloved by girls throughout the school. But when he showed up one cold Friday morning and stripped his sweater to reveal a Kingdom Come Superman T-shirt, Ree was doomed.

Musing on Andy Ritcher's shoulders, she almost added too much phosphorus and spilled some on the table, prompting a string of cursing and some rapid towel application.

"What's wrong?"

"Nothing!" Ree sputtered and continued to wipe down the counter with all the desperate speed of a backed-up Monday-morning rush. Her cleaning done, she returned to the procedures, resisting the urge to put on a pair of safety goggles and give her best Evil Scientist laugh. Instead, she played it out in her head and channeled the glee.

Several minutes of mixing and measuring and heating and one small explosion later, Ree had prepared the necessary supplements, and Drake had done whatever calibration he had to do on his big honking goggles.

Drake Winters

*Victorian Pulp Adventurer, Steampunk Scientist,
and Neighborhood Quixotic Curiosity.*

Ree wondered if she could fit that on a business card, blocking out the text in her mind while trying to fit an artsy brass gear on an oiled but burnished background.

"Done!" she said, pulling the thermometer out of the last solution upon seeing it settle at 175 degrees.

Drake whirled into action, plucking up beakers and tubes of solution and assorted chemicals. He mixed and applied and coated the ingredients with the deftness of a ballet dancer and the deliberation of a painter. Ree stood back in amused awe as he worked and then clicked the filters into place and declared, "Huzzah!"

"Huzzah?" Ree asked. "Isn't that a little old-school even for you?"

Drake gave a rakish smile. "I've always been fond of 'huzzah' as a triumphant declarative."

Ree nodded. *Fair enough.* "So, are we good to go?"

"Indeed. Our first step will take us to the satellite signal, and from there we should be able to pick up the trail of our Aberrant Muse, presuming it *is* an Aberrant Muse. I'd feel rather foolish if we've spent all this time only to discover that the fiend in question was a Boggard or a Brer Ghast."

Boggard she knew, but the other . . . "Brer Ghast?" She returned to the kitchen and stared longingly at the pizza.

"A localized breed of post-living psychophage."

"Gesundheit," Ree said.

Drake looked around discreetly, as if there were actually

someone who had sneezed. *Such hilarious manners. Today's adventure brought to you by* Kate and Leopold.

"Sorry?" Drake asked as he cleaned up the workspace. On their way out, he picked up his rifle again and strapped a bag to his belt.

"Joke. So, do you just walk around town with that thing?" Ree had gotten away with some weird costumes for Halloween or cons, but that gun was far too, well, gunlike for him to be able to walk around town.

She'd hate to drop $30 on what amounted to three slices eaten, but she couldn't exactly carry a pizza box around while hunting a supernatural entity that pushed the depressed into suicide. Or could she? *No, that's ridiculous.* Instead, Ree pulled out a slice and fished a freezer bag from her purse while Drake talked. *Hu-mothereffing-zzah.* Now to make sure the bag didn't get smashed to bursting in a fight.

Drake locked the door to the apartment as he explained. "The rifle, being primarily supernal in nature, tends to be ignored by those who are affected by the Doubt. I'm told they view it as a rather unconvincing prop by an Arab craftsman by the name of Neruf?"

Ree chuckled as they walked down the stairs.

The sun was slouching behind the tops of the skyscrapers and was well on its way to the coastal horizon by the time Ree and Drake reached the alley beside Zombie Cafe.

Ree had suggested that they round the block to approach from the alleyside, to make absolutely sure no one saw her. She would have to figure out how to keep her job, but this wasn't that time.

Had it been daytime in her vision? Thinking back, she couldn't clearly remember. The room had been lit, but whether that was via sunlight or boy-cave lamps, she couldn't tell.

Drake prowled through the alley, trying to find the best sliver of signal, holding up a brass-and-copper box with antennae that danced as he moved, twitching their frequency until Drake stopped in place, fiddling with the box and his goggles at the same time. A minute later, he bounced in place with a small "Huzzah" and strode out of the alley, saying, "Follow me."

"You don't need to stay in range of the XM?" Ree asked, still confused.

"Negative. I needed only use the satellite signal to scan the entire city. Now that I have pinpointed the appropriate signal, this device can accurately track relative direction and distance."

Ree nodded. "If you say so. You don't happen to have an extra pair of those goggles?" she asked as they wandered through the U-District. A block away from the café, Drake crossed against traffic and was nearly run over by a Suburban.

Great. I've traded the socially ignorant silicon cowboy for an absentminded professor. Note to self, schedule self-reflection time with the theme: "Why do I always end up playing second fiddle to bizarre and variously broken men?" Reference abandonment issues and Elektra complex. Tomorrow on Dr. Phil.

The oil baron's wet dream of a car missed Drake by slamming on the brakes. It slowed enough so that Ree could push Drake out of the way, shouting at him to move. The driver stopped, leaning out of his car to spout profanities at Drake, then at Ree, every third word referring to one or another of their orifices and what he was angrily going to do to them.

Ree desperately wanted to stop and chew this asshole out for several minutes, but they had better things to do. So she just led Drake across the street, hurrying to get out of view of the jackass in the Suburban. Drake ground his feet, boots skidding on the sidewalk.

"Not quite so fast," he said. "The goggles are incapable at calibrating at this speed."

Ree took a long breath and let Drake proceed, fiddling with the top button on her jacket as the man in the Suburban gave up and drove away.

They continued for another half-dozen blocks, Drake following the trail while Ree stalked like a panther on a leash. The sun continued to drift westward, the sky shifting toward orange-red. If she were someone to believe in omens, she'd take this as a bad one. She never used to believe in that shit, but who the hell knew how things worked anymore? *Not me, not Leftenant Anachronism here, for all his quixotic chivalry. Captain Hubris knows, but now that I know he's* Empire Strikes Back *Lando instead of* Return of the Jedi *Lando, screw him and his Dorkcave that smells like feet and old booster packs.*

As the orange bled into rose-red, they reached a residential neighborhood, and Drake's pace quickened. "The trail has strengthened. We must needs hurry now, I believe. Have you weaponry of your own?"

She'd left the *tanto* behind at the Dorkcave and hadn't brought anything from home. *And* her media battery was long-empty. This was why Batman had a TiVo. She wasn't Batman, but she did have a smartphone with streaming video.

"Ha!" she said.

"Is that an affirmative?" Drake asked.

Fortunately, there was almost no one around them on the sidewalk, but Ree imagined they were still about the most ridiculous thing anyone in Queensland had seen in at least a week. She pulled out her phone and started to load a video.

"Not right now, but I'm about to get way more badass." *Thank Asimov* The Matrix *is on streaming this month.*

She followed Drake around several corners as they spiraled in toward the Muses' target, though she feared they'd need to speed up to beat her. Him. It? (*Do Aberrant Muses have gender? The Greek ones were female . . .*)

She hoped that whatever fight they found wouldn't take long, because by the time she reached the part of the film where Trinity and Smith raced for the telephone booth, Drake had stopped in front of a two-story midcentury house. It was blue with white trim, looking purple and pink in the fading light.

"This is it?" she asked, seeing the world in a slightly greener hue à la *The Matrix* applying its color filter to her vision.

Woah, she thought in her best Keanu Reeves voice.

"By my best estimation, the trail ends inside the house."

There were lights on both upstairs and on the ground level. Ree checked her purse, mind racing. *C'mon, c'mon, please . . .*

She still had the psychic paper folder. *Sweet.*

All she really wanted was to bust down the door and run upstairs. How do you talk your way into a house that has a potential suicide?

Ree looked to Drake. "Do you have an idea of how we should approach this?"

"My preference would be to smash down the door and charge up the stairs, but I imagine that the directness of my former adventures in Faerie may be inappropriate in this regard."

"Sadly," Ree agreed.

A hundred possibilities played out in her head, but none of them seemed actually "good," so she walked up the stairs and knocked. She tried to remember the carriage she'd used when she visited the Moorelys, but instead of channeling Sherlock, she tapped into her inner Agent Smith.

Answering the door was an older woman, probably somewhere in her sixties, with silver hair cut short and swept above her left eye. If not for the tears and puffy eyes, she'd probably be lovely.

Shit. Shitdamnfuckpleaseno.

The woman sniffed back a sob. "Hello?"

Ree produced the psychic paper, and the woman nodded. "You're earlier than expected. The dispatcher said it'd be an hour or more."

Ree's brain filled with a constant stream of curses, like a half-static radio station that wouldn't slide into a real signal but neither would it fade out. She leaned against the curses with the methodical magic from emulating *The Matrix* and found her balance.

"I'm Agent Reyes. This is Agent Winters." She gestured to Drake, hoping whatever magic it was that hid his weapons applied to his outfit as well. "May we come in?" *Shit, I never got their last name.*

The woman nodded and opened the door for them.

"We'd like to see him, if that's all right."

At Ree's request, the woman looked like she'd taken a hammer to the spine, visibly shaken. She curled her lips inward, and her eyes darkened. "Yes."

If the woman had time to call the police, Ree worried they'd be too late to intercept Eastwood. Even if she couldn't save the boy, she didn't want him left to whatever fate Eastwood would condemn him to. But if she did catch up with Eastwood, what would he do? What would she do?

Ree was getting used to flying by the seat of her pants, but that didn't mean it didn't blow goat chunks.

The woman moved without urgency, scaling the stairs at a slow, resigned pace. Ree saw the house and its decorations but didn't take them in. The house was a shell, holding a husk that was probably already robbed of whatever spark Eastwood needed for his deal.

As they ascended, she focused on the door to Tomas's room, or what she imagined was Tomas's room. She had an ever more vague memory of his face but was sure beyond doubt that she'd recognize him.

Shuffling across the hallway, the woman, Tomas's grandmother or aunt or whoever she was—the bereaved—opened the door. The woman stood to the side, not looking in. Ree nodded to the woman and stepped inside.

The torrent of curses in Ree's head spiked in volume, popping the internal speakers of her mind and threatening to drop her to the floor. She steadied herself with a hand on the doorframe as she took in the sight.

The room was different from Angela's, in small, innocuous ways like the posters on the wall, the arrangement of the bed and dressers, the computer tower covered in skull designs.

And also in one horrible, unforgettable way: The body was still there.

Tomas had fallen from the desk, like in the vision. And she could see the pliers on the floor, stained past all memory of their original metallic color. Ree felt the pizza threaten to come back up all at once, so she stopped in place, focusing on breathing.

As she looked, she saw a shadow move outside the window. That window, the same as in her dream.

Oh, no you don't, fucker. Even if she was too late for Tomas, it didn't matter.

"Winters—downstairs. Head him off!" Ree ran across the room in a second, pushing herself with *Matrix* speed. She heard the pounding of Drake's boots on the stairs as she reached the window and threw it open.

The shadowed figure was sliding down the roof over the garage. Ree took two steps back, then charged forward and dove through the window, trusting the magic. She flipped in midair with perfect form, hitting the person's torso with both feet.

"Oof," it said as they both flew through the air.

Thank you, Trinity. The magical buzz in Ree's mind faded as they fell, and Ree hoped it was enough to take the fall.

The two of them tumbled down the roof and off into the space between the garage and the next house. Ree softened the fall as best as she could, folding her legs as she landed and dropping to her side. Her adversary took the impact hard on the left side, and lungs emptying with a pained "oofh." As she rolled to her feet, she confirmed her suspicion.

No mistaking, this was Eastwood.

Pain stabbed through her leg as she stood, but she bit her lip and continued. "Did you take it—did you? You found him and you just waited for him to kill himself?"

Eastwood scrambled back, pulling himself up on the white

fence between the houses. He produced the blaster out of his jacket, training it on Ree as he stood. "It was already done. I came as soon as I could, and he was gone. It's a horrible loss, but it doesn't have to be pointless."

"You could have done something," she snarled.

She heard the click of a hammer being pulled back. Drake appeared in the corner of her vision, his rifle trained on Eastwood. "Even if you could not help the boy, Mr. Eastwood, you have stolen the most sacred of personal property, and I cannot in good conscience allow you to continue in your endeavors."

Eastwood shot Drake a nasty look. "Winters, you should have learned enough to do your research before sticking your cravat out for someone. If I recall correctly, your mistress did far worse out in Faerie, so where did you get a leg to stand on?"

"My two legs are more than sufficient."

Neither Ree nor Eastwood corrected Drake on the missed reference.

"So what now?" Eastwood asked, gun still trained on Ree. The *Matrix* magic was gone, and without it, trying to close the distance and disarm him was a big bet, one that involved going against a guy named Eastwood in a gunfight.

So Ree stood still, poised to move. *You've got to do something,* she thought.

Ree flipped through ideas like the Rolodex her dad still kept despite the fact that everyone's info was in the phone she'd gotten him.

Tangent. Not. Helping. Focus.

"You blast me, Drake kills you, and then no one brings Branwen back and you've condemned four souls for no reason," Ree said.

"Don't expect me to back down." Eastwood was talking to Ree, but his eyes were on Drake.

Would he pull the trigger? Could he? This was the problem with being the new kid on the block. *If this were my tenth Mexican standoff with these guys, I'd have a better clue.*

Eastwood slipped his hand inside his jacket and sighed. "I'm sorry, Ree."

She heard the sound of glass cracking, and Eastwood vanished in a plume of black smoke. Charging forward, diving through the smoke, she slammed into the fence, thereby proving to herself that he hadn't just gone invisible.

Ree resisted the urge to kick the fence, instead turning to Drake. The displaced adventurer's face matched hers, frustrated and surprised.

"What now?" she asked, of the world as much as of Drake. Her track record as lead hero was leaving something to be desired.

CHAPTER THIRTEEN

Downtown Dogfight

Drake looked back at the house. "I imagine that we'll either want to extricate ourselves from the situation to avoid notice, or return to speak with the distraught woman inside and explain ourselves. Somewhat explain ourselves, that is. I don't imagine she could handle the full truth at this moment, nor would I wish to inflict it upon her."

Ree made a *hrm* sound, thinking. "Do you have some kind of 'forget I was here' magic you can use? We should really just follow the Muse if we can."

Drake nodded. "I should be able to push our visit out of her mind, but regardless, I'll need to go back into the bedroom to reset the goggles and see if I can pick up the trail. Perhaps the shade lingered out of sight during our skirmish."

Better you than me, Ree thought, shuddering.

Drake shouldered his rifle and walked back to the front door, leaving Ree with her thoughts. They were constant company, if not always the most pleasant. A wind curled across the alley, and she pulled her jacket tighter, wishing she could go home, make herself a latte, and snuggle up with her laptop for the rest of the day.

Writing was comfort and therapy both, and she needed either that or something to drink. She'd long ago chosen booze as her Writerly Vice of Choice, pretending that caffeine didn't count. She occasionally subbed in media marathons and self-destructive behavior, just to mix things up.

If we find the Muse, we kill the hell out of it, with optional interrogation if said Aberrant Muse can talk, and assuming we can subdue it and convince it to spill its spectral beans. Just tracking it again won't be fast enough. It was already the 30th, so there wasn't much time left for Eastwood's deadline.

Ree thought back to the last Halloween, when she and Jay had gone as Johnny and Lisa from *The Room*, which had displaced *Manos: The Hands of Fate* at the top of The Shithole's official pantheon of Worst Movies Ever. They'd had to explain the costumes to almost everyone at the party, but after that, they'd won Best Duo and a gift card to the Illyrian Theatre, which played classics and foreign films.

She had taken Jay to the Illyrian on their second date, to see *Black Orpheus*. It was, in retrospect, a crap choice for a date movie, one that Jay teased her about for the entirety of their relationship. The old emotions came up like a looming exit sign that read MEMORY LANE—DEPRESSING RELATIONSHIP THOUGHTS, ½ MILE.

She stopped herself before taking the off-ramp. *Not helping, kiddo.*

Hell, I'd rather watch The Room again, without being able to make fun, than keep dealing with this shit.

Another voice answered in her head, sounding half like her father. *Then why don't you?*

She could give up, technically. She wasn't a cop, wasn't a social worker. Why didn't she go home and live her life? It wasn't like she was made of free time, not like her imagination wasn't already well trained enough for her to be a writer. Maybe someone in the city would commit suicide before the 31st, even without being pushed by a post-living entity or whatever it was. She didn't have to do any of this. She could still quit.

But that's not how you tick, love. Her dad's voice again.

Her dad—she could try telling him everything, and he might believe her. Or he might call Sandra and ask her to force Ree to go back to therapy, which would be great except Bryan couldn't afford health care that good for the café monkeys. And then her dad would insist on paying, and it'd wipe him out for another year.

The person she *could* tell, maybe, possibly, without getting committed, was Bryan. He could fire her for it, but he'd been a devoted Pagan since he was eighteen and was about the most enlightened person this side of wherever the Dalai Lama lived these days. If she brought it up the right way, it might even make her double life something resembling workable. No other super heroes explained their secret lives to their bosses, but then again, she didn't work for J. Jonah Jameson. Who said her life had to suck as much as Peter Parker's?

Drake rejoined her, goggles in place.

"Do you have a trail?" she asked.

"Yes, but it's fading fast. We'll need to take particular measures to follow. Can you help me unfold?" Drake reached into his coat and pulled out a fist-sized bundle of metallic something.

"Say what?"

Drake set the bundle on the ground and started unfolding little pipes. "At this moment, we have a great need for alacrity, Ms. Ree, so we will be taking my aerothopter. If you would, please help me unfold it so it can return to its proper size."

Ree squatted down, looking at the jumble of tiny pipes. She leaned over and tried to pick things apart, pulling a spoke here and there, but Drake did most of the work, revealing a one-foot-long mix between an ornithopter and a helicopter. She only knew what an ornithopter looked like because of *Magic: The Gathering.*

After she pulled out one last pipe, Drake said, "I would recommend standing back, Ms. Ree."

He pulled back his glove and twisted a dial on a bracer, and the tiny contraption started to shake, squeak, clank, and hop around, growing in fits and spurts, first one part and then another. It popped out to twice, four times, eventually ten times its original size. Full-grown, it had a brass-and-copper frame, some kind of boiler, twin propellers helicopter-style, and a two-seat cockpit, with levers and a steering wheel in one seat.

"Devices of Faerie are tremendously adaptable, if occasionally unreliable. But this aerothopter hasn't given out on me in years. In we go." He patted the side of the cockpit as he stepped into the front seat.

Ree looked around and saw people dodging around the vehicle without even looking at or noticing it. A car was idling just beyond the tail, the driver fiddling with his phone.

Drake pulled levers and pushed buttons with the same efficiency and grace he brought to everything else, despite the goofiness of the gigantic goggles he wore. "We haven't much time, Ms. Ree."

"Is this a good time to tell you that I hate flying?"

Drake smiled. "No, I think this a rather inopportune moment. I would prefer if you informed me of that once we have already completed our voyage, at which point I will be properly accommodating." Drake dropped his smile. "The Muse is getting away, we must depart." He reached into his coat and pulled out a pair of silver goggles, handing them to her. "You best wear these as well."

"Here goes nothing," Ree said, stepping into the copilot's seat, trying not to dwell on all the laws of physics that they were about to break. Magic was one thing, but this was Ridiculous Steam-Powered Faerie Magic that was going to make her fly around Pearson.

The hot mug of coffee and her laptop were sounding more appealing by the minute.

The aerothopter lurched, and several things popped into or out of place, and she felt heat peeling off from the boiler behind her. She strapped on the goggles and fiddled with them until they approached comfortable.

"Ms. Ree, please take the rifle and keep an eye out for the Muse. And please try not to lean over too far, I haven't had the chance to install seat belts." Without notice, the aerothopter popped off the ground, wobbling slightly before ambling up and forward.

Oh shit oh shit oh shit. The several-times-a-year trips to LAX had been daunting when she started, but she'd gotten used to the routine, the airline psychopomps, gate agents, security, flight attendants, and pilots all protecting her, assuring her. But this, this was too much. There was nothing but air around her, she didn't have a seat belt, and the whole thing could drop out of the air at any moment like any other capricious bit of Faerie magic.

She didn't know how it worked in real life (how's that for a thought), but in folktales, Faerie gold would turn back to leaves and rocks within hours of being taken for real. However, Changelings could go unnoticed for years. Cold iron would undo Faerie magic, but Drake had a metal boiler. The contradictions piled up and were actually comforting. *I have no idea what's going to happen, and I have no way of controlling it. So there, panic.* They climbed higher and higher, cresting the horizon of the houses and buildings around them, and emerged into the Pearson sky at twilight. She hoped the Doubt had covered their ascent and that people would continue to discount the aerothopter. *I am not explaining this contraption to the police.*

Trying to focus, she kept her eyes open for the Muse. She pulled the rifle up and over Drake's head, trying to move slowly and leave him time to unloop his left arm from the strap. She took the rifle in both hands, tested its heft. She'd been to a shooting range only a handful of times, back when she was dating Jo the Libertarian. But while she'd shot real weapons a few times, Ree's local arcade proudly displayed her initials (RAR) as the #1 high scorer in *Time Crisis 2* and *House of the Dead.*

She wondered if there'd be time to queue up something on her phone to buff her skills, but decided against it both because she had to be on lookout and because if she dropped her phone from a couple hundred feet up, its last act would be to clobber some poor pedestrian.

She raised the rifle to her shoulder, trying to remember the best way to brace, and tested the scope. There were several filters, and she clicked through three until she found one that gave her a high contrast, distinguishing the clouds more clearly.

"Did you treat any of the filters on the scope to track the Muse?"

"I'm terribly sorry, but I did not. I'm on the trail, however, and we're not far behind the fiend."

She lowered the rifle to rest on the lip of the copilot seat and started scanning, deliberately keeping herself from looking down. *You're going to have to look down to shoot this thing, Ree. Think FPS, think FPS.* But even the best first-person shooter or flight sim didn't give you the wind cutting at your face, the chill of the air, the lurch of a make-believe airship, or your own personal issues with heights.

They continued to climb, then banked right to take a wide arc around an office building. She let her gaze dip down, a death grip on the polished wooden stock of the rifle.

Drake brought them around and started heading north. "Getting close now. It'll be somewhere above us, most like."

"Do they usually travel this far off the ground?"

"Not to my knowledge, but I do believe this one has caught our scent."

"Wait—what—"

It knows we're coming, Ree realized, more than a little concerned. *Sweet.* She brought up the rifle again, looking over the scope. To brace herself in the aerothopter, she pushed her feet against a pair of pipes that might have been the landing gear. She saw a scrap of shadow in the corner of her eye, scanned to track it, rifle crossing to the left. *No, just a cloud.*

"The trail is crossing over itself, Ms. Ree. We are in the vicinity, so I will loop around to give you a chance to spot."

They banked left, and Ree pushed into the pipes again. But the turn was sharp enough that she had to drop a hand from the rifle to the ship and steady herself.

"Next time, seat belts!" she said over the wind.

"Understood, Ms. Ree."

"Drake—I think we're probably at the point where you can call me Ree, okay? Just keep her steady!"

"Affirmative," Drake said, fighting the chop.

She leveled the rifle again, tracking another shadow. This one raced up and to the left, dodging behind a building.

"Nine o'clock, bearing to our left and climbing!" she said, recalling jargon from the last time she'd played a multiplayer flight game. *Crimson Skies,* a few years ago, one of her failed attempts to get Sandra into video games other than *Guitar Hero.*

Drake started to climb, banking left once more. She picked up the shadow, which was growing larger, its spindly form taking shape. She put her right goggled eye to the scope and sighted the creature. Magnified, she saw its jagged limbs and diamond-shaped head. Below the waist, it faded off into a whispy Casper-esque trail, no legs to speak of.

"Here goes nothing!" Ree shouted over the wind, and pulled the trigger. A burst of light shot out from the rifle in brilliant emerald.

Awesome.

However, the shadow faded to the side, and the burst flew past. The Muse banked and crossed from Ree's left to her right. She had to pull the rifle up and rebrace on her right. By the time she was set up, the Muse was bearing down on them, no more than a hundred feet out.

"Incoming!" Drake said, sending the aerothopter into a dive.

"Will the blades stop it?" she said as she aimed another shot. It went wide, the Muse just twenty feet away.

"That is a capital question, Ms. Ree," Drake said, his voice strained.

"I said, call me Ree!" she shouted over the wind. The nervousness and Drake's insistence on formality made her crack up as she tried to sight the Muse again, spoiling her aim.

"Apologies . . . *Ree*. Look out!"

The Muse passed over the aerothopter and through the blades without effect and took a swipe at Drake. He ducked, pushing the machine into a deeper bank. Ree leaned against the turn, her shoulder landing hard on the metallic frame. *Shitfuckow*. She aimed the rifle again, taking a parting shot as they pulled away.

"Bastard is fast."

"Coming around. I will do my best to give you a dead-on shot."

"Let me cross the *T*, and we'll be in business."

Drake laughed a full-bellied laugh, the kind you almost never heard in real life. "Now that, my dear, is a colloquialism with which I am familiar. Brace yourself."

Wondering which part of the flight she *hadn't* needed to brace herself for, she reset her straddled position and tracked the Muse across the sky. They were into downtown, with tall buildings forming a metal maze around them.

"How's your maneuverability?" she asked.

"Not good, I'm afraid."

Damn. If they could use the skyscrapers as terrain, it'd narrow the lanes of attack. Instead, the Muse came screaming up from below and to the left. Ree caught it early enough to squeeze off two shots in quick succession before it got close enough that the machine or Drake would block her shot. The Muse dodged the first, but she'd guessed the dodge and tracked left, clipping the thing's left arm with the second shot.

"Take it!" she shouted.

The Muse spun, dove, and regrouped for another run. Drake banked to the right, and she pushed hard into the pipe below, turning as far as she could in the seat to get the Muse in her sights. She led the shot and fired, trying to get in as many as she could before it crashed into them.

The Muse dodged the first shot, and she overcorrected for the second. The third blast clipped the Muse's right arm. Spinning as it came in, it swiped an arm through her chest. Heat and cold hit her with a double whammy, like she'd been in a sauna for two hours and then decided to go for a bout of Polar Bear diving in the Arctic Circle.

A hundred images crashed in on her at once: Jay as he explained that he was dumping her; Dad, telling her that Mom wasn't coming back; Tomas's body on the floor; every rejection letter, unreturned phone call, and lonely night mixed together into a 151-proof angst cocktail and forced down her throat.

Her heart stopped for a moment, and she had to gasp to find her breath. The rifle dropped half out of the aerothopter, hanging only by the finger loop.

Mother. Fucker! I am not going down like this, you hear me?

Ree latched on to the sensation of the rifle amid the emotional hurricane. Pushing the pain out with an angry scream, she held tight to the rifle and pulled it back up as her lungs remembered how to work.

"Are you all right?" Drake shouted over the din.

Ree took another gasping breath, then said, "Hell no! I don't think I could take another one of those!"

"It's far more maneuverable than we are. I can either follow it or dodge it."

"If we let it go, can we track it again?"

"Not in time to prevent its next attack."

Fucksticks. The Muse climbed toward them, its right arm fuzzy, out of focus. Ree fired and the Muse dodged left, looping around to come at them head-on. Drake banked right, turning tightly to avoid a radio tower. She lost the Muse behind the tower only to pick it up again as it soared down at them. She waited, hoping to draw it in for a clearer shot, keep it from dodging.

Just a little closer. Stay on target . . .

The Muse grew large in her vision, a shifting mass of jagged angles made of shadow, and still Ree waited. When she couldn't see anything but the Muse, she fired. The world flashed in green and she ducked, hoping to miss the Muse's swipe. She gritted her teeth, anticipating the hit, but none came. She poked her head up and saw the Muse, which looked like the T2 after Schwarzenegger had taken a shotgun to it, a big chunk missing out of the middle and right side. She felt more than heard its scream, and saw it retreat, fading through a building.

"Drake, Drake—turn here! We have to finish it off!"

Drake sighed. "That will not avail us this time. It has phased out of our world to recover. I'm coming down for a landing, please hold on."

The aerothopter's tip dipped as Drake guided them down to the top of the Western Bank Tower.

"When will it come back?"

"Difficult to say. I suspect it will spend at least a day recuperating before it tries to strike again."

"That means Eastwood will be cutting it damned close."

"And we may yet have time to discern a solution." Ree thanked the gods of Steampunk that Drake's whacky invention wasn't a biplane, since rooftop landing strips weren't terribly common, even in a techie town like Pearson.

They coasted down toward the open roof, then dropped the last two feet and landed with a crunch. Ree tucked her neck, but the impact was hard on her butt. "Ow!"

"My apologies. The landings are always the trickiest bit. The aerothopter's dorsal sensor is sometimes off by a few feet."

Ree took a long breath, trying to slow her machine-gun heartbeat. "Hey, any dogfight with an immortal spirit of depression you walk away from, right?"

Drake pushed forward a lever and climbed out of the aerothopter. "You best evacuate quickly."

"Why's that?" she asked as she swung a foot over the side. The seat beneath her shrank in a spurt, and the bars that had framed her seat started to fold in on themselves. She jumped and crumbled onto the roof with an "Eep."

Real graceful, Ree.

The aerothopter continued to fold in upon itself until it returned to its pocket-ready size. Drake picked up the cube, tossed it up, and caught it with a grin, then slipped it back into his duster.

"Did you pick a building where the roof door is unlocked?" Ree asked, crossing to check.

"Sorry?"

Panic drove up Ree's pulse, and it spiked when she tried unsuccessfully to turn the handle. Ree rolled her eyes and groaned. "Can you pick locks, or do I have to do it?"

"If you return my rifle, I could blow the door off."

"I'll take that as a no." Ree knelt down in front of the door and pulled a hairpin out of her hair, thankful she'd decided to wear it up. *Now we see if the lock-picking kit Dad gave me for my twentieth birthday will pay off.* She felt around in the lock, trying to figure out what type it was. Anything too sophisticated, and she'd be SOL without the professional tools.

"Could we just turn the aerothopter back on and land on the street?"

"It won't function for at least six hours, I'm afraid."

"Then why didn't we land on the street?" Ree said, trying not to let too much annoyance show in her voice.

"The charm that assisted the Doubt in keeping us from notice has expired. This was the only way to land without causing a scene," Drake said, apologetic.

Her day just kept getting better. At this rate, she'd get home and discover that Anya and Jay had hooked up and had secretly been in love and were now super-happy together. "Do you have a pin, a needle, or something like that?"

"That, I can supply." Drake walked up, took the rifle, and half-disassembled it, handing her a pin.

She could pull up a video and use genre magic, but Ree wanted to see if she could to it herself. For once, they weren't in a mortal-danger level of rush.

Ree hunkered back down and played with the lock for another minute before it clicked. When the door opened, she played the *Final Fantasy* victory music in her brain.

Having skittered down and escaped the Western Bank Building without notice, Ree and Drake returned to Drake's apartment for more planning. And pizza. Drake put on some water for tea.

"I have an herbal tisane that does wonders for the spirit. It should be most beneficial," Drake said. "I first learned of this mixture when my Mistress led us through the hills of the Worry-Wargs."

Ree half-listened to Drake retelling the tale, the other half of her attention put to the task of devouring a piece of pizza. She could officially add "Dogfight with a malevolent spirit" to her rapidly growing list entitled:

Shit I Never Thought I'd Have to Do But Somehow Have Anyway.

1) Justify my video game habit to a boyfriend.

2) Listen to a drunken asshole talk about all the places he wants to grope me just for the tip so I can make rent and not get thrown out of my apartment.

3) Write a response to a letter suggesting I rewrite my Lovecraft Roller Derby short film into a children's cartoon.

4) Dodge the wild swipes of a troll.

5) Seriously consider the various superpowers I could gain by mimicking different narrative genres.

6) Aerothopter dogfight with a malevolent spirit through downtown Pearson.

"How would you like to proceed?" Drake asked as he pulled ingredients from his jars and bottles.

"The hell if I know. When we tracked it, we were always a step behind." She arced her back and twisted left and right to pop a couple of vertebrae. "You said it goes somewhere to recover? Where is that? Can we follow it there and take it out?"

Drake's eyes went wide. "That would be highly inadvisable. When spirits are wounded, they retreat beyond the Veil to recover their strength in the aether."

"So, how bad of an idea is it to go there? On a scale of cooking-without-a-shirt to being-an-evil-priest-in-an-Alexandre-Dumas-book?"

Drake raised an eyebrow, pausing in his apothecary-ing to consider. "I imagine it is rather the equivalent of attending a Victorian grand ball wearing nothing but your unmentionables and trying to woo the stuffy archduke so you can cement a marriage that will save your country from certain destruction."

Ree smiled. "Great, when do we start?"

Drake had apparently ignored her last comment, going back to mixing ingredients. The teakettle whistled, and he deftly snatched it from the burner and poured hot water into the bowl. With calm efficiency, he produced a wooden spoon from a drawer and stirred.

"Piercing the Veil is difficult enough to do on its own, but what lies beyond is far worse. In my journeys, I was accompanied by a being of incredible power, and even I nearly lost my way a number of times. It may be far easier to pierce the Veil now, given the imminence of All Hallows' Eve, but that will mean the denizens of Spirit will be all the more agitated."

Ree took another bite and chewed thoughtfully. "Do you have a better idea? I'd be happy to not go anywhere near uppity spirits if I can avoid it." An echo of the Muses' emotional gut punch rippled through her like a shudder mixed with a cold burn.

Drake poured part of the concoction into a mug and offered it to Ree. "This should help."

This will probably taste nasty as hell, so I might as well go for it. "Bottoms up," she said, and took a big swig.

Guh. It tasted like crusty socks, sunflower seeds, and spoiled milk. She set the mug down and tried to scrape the sensation off her tongue with her teeth and rolled her shoulders in distaste. But after a few seconds, the aftertaste mellowed, and her whole body felt warmer, like she had been basking in the sun.

"Wow. That's good stuff. Tastes horrible."

"So it goes. Pastries are marvelous yet terrible for you. However, your people make them so sweet these days. And salty. I nearly retched the first time I had a donut."

Ree narrowed her eyes at Drake. "We're in a fight now. Donuts are amazing."

Drake held up his hands, yielding. "Only the first time. I've become rather fond of their decadence since then. I once subsisted on nothing more than donuts and root beer for a week. It ended rather poorly."

Ree quirked a half-smile and nodded. "You'd have to at least throw in some cheeseburgers to make that diet work." She took another sip of the tisane, grimaced, and relaxed as a second wave of warmth ran through her body. She took a deep breath, then chugged the rest of the mug.

"Eaucch." Ree stamped her feet in a flamenco-esque burst, then exhaled slowly. The immediacy and closeness of the pain brought on by the Muse's touch receded, like it had happened a month ago instead of an hour. "That's good stuff. Needs honey."

Drake shook his head. "Sadly, the taste is part of the effect. If you were to change the taste, the tisane would become just a foul drink with a touch of honey."

"So, can we get into spirit-land or not?"

Drake sighed. "Yes. But I cannot stress enough how dangerous it would be."

"I get it. But I'm already neck-deep in ridiculous danger, and if I sit by, someone else dies, and then Eastwood will get eaten by demons or start an eternal rain of fire or something. If there's no better way to stop it than by going through the Veil, I have to try."

Drake crossed the room and took a slice of the pizza. "I can show you how to pierce the Veil. I can even go with you. But once we cross the threshold, I cannot guarantee anything."

Uncertain doom versus almost total failure? Fantastic choice. Maybe he has a time machine and can go back to change things so I never meet Eastwood in the first place.

Not like it would help.

Wishing herself back into ignorance wouldn't matter. The suicides would still be dead, and Eastwood would still be on a collision course with damnation or whatever it was that happened when someone Fausted themselves out in the real world. He'd said that people could become not-people, but she didn't know what that really meant. Maybe he was just being melodramatic.

"If it's that dangerous, why would you go with me?"

Drake's face hardened. "No one should face Spirit alone, and your mission is righteous." His smile returned. "Also, I have on several occasions been rightly accused of possessing a lack of common sense. I *am* an adventurer, after all."

"When can we leave?"

"It will take some time to make the preparations. Midnight, at the earliest, barely before dawn if things go poorly. You should get some rest, one way or another."

"I could help."

Drake took a step toward her and put a hand on her shoulder. "Help me by getting some sleep. You'll need to be well rested. Make your spirit as healthy as you can before testing it again. Spend time with friends, loved ones. Stoke the fires of your heart as best you can, because they will be cooled to embers by the trials of the Otherworld."

Ree smiled up at the man from another time. "You're a little much sometimes. But you know that, right?"

"I've been told that as well. I will telephone you when the moment is come."

Ree reached up and squeezed Drake's hand, then collected her things.

CHAPTER FOURTEEN

Wait for It . . .

Ree caught the train home and plodded her way up the stairs. The elevator was, of course, broken. Either the universe conspired to have the elevator out of service only when it was particularly annoying, or she never noticed when it didn't matter. Either way, she tried not to take personal offense and decided to make herself some coffee when she reached The Shithole.

Sandra wasn't home. *Probably out with Darren.* Ree mulled over possibilities. Sleep, TV, beer, sleep, video games, call Anya or Priya, sleep.

Sleep was the leading contender, but it was contraindicated with coffee, which was already in process. And wasting good coffee was against her religion. She poured the water into her French press, taking in the steam and the wafting nutty aroma of Bryan's Dark Dungeons Roast.

She fired up her console and loaded *Portal*. She'd played the game through a half-dozen times, but the idea of solvable puzzles sounded amazing. *Something I can beat, something I'm actually good at, unlike this carnival of kooks.*

Zapping doorways into walls and platforms, she did her

best to relax, let the caffeine fill the chill from the dogfight and the Muse's touch. The world fell away, and there was only the cheerful sadism of GLaDOS.

Two hours later, she noticed the apartment was dark save for the glow off the TV. She turned on a couple of lights and fetched her phone to call Anya.

"What's the word?" Anya asked when she picked up.

"Cabin fever. You free?" Ree paced around the apartment, walking heel to toe like a tightrope walker. It was one of the many things she did to occupy her mind while on the phone.

"Sure thing. Where should we go?"

"Trollope's?" Ree suggested.

Anya made an *mmh-hh* sound. "Sounds good. Meet you there?"

"Say nine?"

"Got it. I'll bring my hollow leg."

Ree hung up and went to change. She emerged five minutes later in tights, a dark red skirt, and a loose black top cinched with a wide belt. She grabbed her corduroy blazer out of the closet and checked her phone on the way out the door. No messages.

Commence drinking!

Trollope's Trollops was packed with students and townies eager to catch the 9:30 burlesque show. Anya was already there, sitting on a stool at the corner of the bar area. She had a pint of cider in front of her; it was her drink of choice for long nights of talking.

Ree weaved her way through the crowd, dodging waitresses with full trays of drinks, shiny shot girls in short skirts and glitter, and beefy barbacks with buckets full of dishes. The tables were full, between college students fueling up to finish the drinking weekend, Woo Girls worshipping at the altar of shots, and a few unassuming regulars drinking quietly at the bar.

Anya stood from her stool, and Ree gave her a hug. Seeing that there weren't any other stools free, she scanned the room for two open seats together. "Do you see anything?" she asked.

"You're the tall one here. I've got nothing."

Ree continued to scan. Finding nothing, she turned around and caught Andrew's attention. Andrew was one of the few males charming and efficient enough to get weekend shifts. Most places in the U-District had 100 percent female bartenders Thursday through Sunday, but Andrew was so good, he might have been a magician. He was six-two and had the muscles of a former barback who never let himself go soft, along with the black T-shirt and shaved head that seemed part of the "male booze enabler" uniform code.

Ree leaned in to the bar, and Andrew appeared in front of her. He grabbed four bottles, scooped up some ice in a glass, and poured the liquor for a Long Island. "Hi, Ree. What'll you have?"

"Grey Goose martini with a twist, thanks." She had been ruined on well liquor before she was eighteen, sadly, leaving it along with any possibility of being a cheap date.

Andrew grabbed the well tap and topped off the drink while he reached down and pulled out the lemon. He vanished for a second to deliver the drink and returned, pouring and shaking with speedy ease.

"I say we camp here and wait for a table," Ree said to Anya.

Anya raised her glass in salute and took a drink.

Andrew set Ree's martini in front of her with a smile, then vanished again. *It's good to be known.* She'd been coming to Trollope's for years, and that kind of loyalty bought you a certain amount of trust from the staff. Sometimes the leeway included free drinks. Mostly, she enjoyed being known, being in her comfort zone.

"So what's up? You haven't been at the café much this week," Anya said.

Ree sighed. *Divulging my new secret Urban Fantasy life is probably not advised.* "Stuff has come up, and I was hella-sick for a day. What about you?"

Anya shrugged. "Still banging my head against my theory essay, but at least I got to show *Chasing Amy* in section. That was a riot."

"Actual riot?"

"Close. I've got three students who should probably drop the class but seem like they've decided to dig in and start arguments instead. One guy asked how a lesbian could fall for a guy, and then one of my lesbians started tearing into the movie, talking about how it was crap because bisexuality was a lie, and then this bi guy jumped in to rage against her . . ."

Ree raised an eyebrow. "Sounds like a great time."

"Once I got them calmed down a bit, it *was* great. The next unit is on bisexuality, and this opened things up in a big way. Though I do miss the beginning of the semester, when I got to blow poor freshmen's minds." Anya gave a wicked smile, and Ree toasted her friend's evil.

Anya had to fight tooth and nail to get her teaching appointment, stealing it away from an English-department grad student by sheer force of awesomeness. And lots of recommendation letters. She deserved to enjoy it.

Ah, to be in college again. College, when Ree had a Mohawk and went to Goth clubs, wrote epic amounts of fanfic, and spent two years dating girls to tragically drama-ridden results.

It wasn't that she'd lost interest in girls; more like after three messy breakups in a row, she'd decided to take a break from the ladies. Not that going back to guys had served her terribly well of late.

Ree shook her head, banishing the thought. "You know what Priya is up to tonight? I remember her saying something."

"I think she had a date on the east side."

"Same guy as last time, or is this Climber Guy?" Ree asked.

"Climber Guy, I think. He invited her to try the wall and then wanted to go to some underground bistro."

"Literally underground?" Ree thought of all the time she'd spent in the sewers over the last week.

Anya shrugged. Ree heard the sound of shattering and a flash of movement across the room, and her heartbeat raced. When she saw that it was just a server jumping away from a broken glass, she breathed out slowly.

"Are you all right?" Anya asked.

Ree took a long sip of her martini, savoring Andrew's fantastic pour. "It's been a hell of a week."

Anya gave her the eye of suspicion.

"Just a lot of things piling up." *That sounds so pathetic. I could tell Anya everything. She probably wouldn't believe me, but maybe she would.* Ree needed to tell someone, someone who wasn't already tied up in all of this. *Buffy has the Scoobies, why shouldn't I?*

But Anya didn't need anyone unloading a huge pile of drama on her. Neither did Priya, Sandra, or anyone. *Who ever needs angst unloaded on them? We do it anyway, when we need to, but do I really need to?*

Ree stayed through the martini and another one, cutting herself off before she could get too far into drunk-and-depressed-because-life-had-gone-mad.

⌖✕⬡✕⌖

Once she was back home, Ree made herself some tea to sober up (peppermint, with local honey) and stared at her phone, trying to figure out how to start a conversation with her dad.

She'd always been close with her dad, and after her mom left, she and her dad had moved around even more, so it was the two of them against the world. Now that the world was kind of against her, there should be no one she could trust more.

Except that he was thousands of miles away and had no reason to believe what she was planning to tell him. And she wasn't entirely certain she hadn't cracked and created herself a geeky version of *A Beautiful Mind.*

A calmer part of her brain spoke up. *Just call.*

Ree closed her eyes and pressed the dial button. She listened for the rings, still not looking.

Ring.

Come on, Dad, please.

Ring.

Maybe he won't pick up. That might be better. This is all too much.

Ring.

What if he's not home? Do I call Priya, Anya? Just deal?

Ring.

Is he okay?

"Hello?" her dad answered.

Ree exhaled a breath she hadn't realized she had been holding. "Dad, thanks for picking up."

"What's happening, Ree-bee?"

Ree asked, "Can you get a secure line?"

After a beat, "What?"

"Can you get a secure line? There's some weird stuff going down, Dad."

"I could call you back from a proxied VoIP line, I guess," he said, his voice uncertain.

"Could you, please?" Her voice was strained by the emotional hurricane rampaging inside her.

Her dad's voice settled, hardening. "I'll call back in a minute. Just stay put."

She sat down on her bed and focused intently on her tea, trying not to think anymore, to just be in the moment, calm. Failing that, she downed the entire mug of tea and got up to pour herself some more.

Her phone rang as she was pouring. She looked at the phone long enough to see the number listed as [Blocked] before she picked up. "Hello?"

"It's me," her dad said. "Are you okay?"

Ree walked back into her room, setting the mug down on her bedside plastic crate. "I'm fine. But this is going to sound ridiculous, and it'll probably go better if I just give you the whole story and then we talk about how wild it is after. Is that okay?"

"Yes, ma'am." Ah, marine voice. He was taking her seriously. *I love you, Dad.*

And so she told him the whole story, starting with Eastwood bursting into the comic shop, then the troll, the Dorkcave, her first attempt at Geekomancy, her visit to the Moorelys', the rubber-suit Atavist, everything, including realizing Eastwood's real game and her current conundrum: how to chase down the Muse.

The story took another two mugs' worth of tea and a bathroom break, but when it was all done, she stopped and waited to see what her dad would say.

A part of her wanted him to swoop in and fix it, to take care of her as he had for so much of her life growing up. She knew she'd have to face it herself, and maybe she could do it, but there was a small part of her that just wanted the problem to disappear as if it had never occurred.

"Well, if you're pulling my leg, this story definitely needs to be your next screenplay," he said with a chuckle.

"Cross my heart and hope to die, Dad. It all happened. I may have missed some of the details, but that's only because I really have no clue what I'm doing."

Her dad waited a second. "I believe you. I'd rather believe that things I thought were impossible are happening than you're actively lying. Plus, as far as I can tell, there's no reason for you to be lying."

Ree sighed. "It's all real. Or if it isn't, I'm going to make some therapist famous."

Her dad chuffed, not seeming to confirm or deny what she'd said. "I don't know what I can do for you, but Ree, it means a lot to me that you trusted me with something this important. It seems like you've taken on a very dangerous task and stayed with it when it would be very easy to walk away."

A weight sloughed off of Ree's shoulders, and she smiled. *He better not forget this as soon as we hang up. He can't. He's my dad, and that's its own magic, Doubt-be-damned.*

"Thanks, Dad. I've been thinking about you the whole time. I wanted to tell you about the weird things, the cool things. It's like everything we watched growing up really matters now, like it was secretly training for this whole new life."

Ree could hear her dad's smile through the phone. "I guess it was. I think you're on the right track. You've got someone helping you, and you know what this Eastwood is trying to do. You're doing the right thing, attacking his asset, this spirit." His marine was showing again.

Ree paced around the room, running her bare feet over the carpet she'd put down. "I sure hope so. Drake is working on some ritual to go into the spirit world, and, well, that sounds scary as hell."

"Aren't you the girl who drove herself across the country to go to a college in a town she'd never heard of and got a double major while working the whole time? The girl who saved up for a year, then flew down to L.A. with no contacts and no connections to pound the pavement for a week to start making her writing career happen? The girl who passed her first-degree black belt test with flying side-kick colors?"

"I wish you were here so I could hug you, Dad . . ."

"Me, too, Ree-bee. I'm proud of you. I can't pretend I understand what you're going through. It's so different than anything I did in or out of the military that all I can do is pray for you and offer encouragement every way and place I can. Do you need money? It sounds like you've had to skip some shifts."

Hell, yes, I need money. "No, I'm fine. It'll be fine."

"Ree . . ." her dad said. He knew she was bullshitting him.

"I'll be fine. If things get much worse, then maybe, maybe I will consider it. But the last time I asked for money, you had to sell one of your guns."

"So? This is a much better reason than last time."

"Fair enough," Ree said. "I guess that's one benefit. No more distracting boyfriends."

"What about this Drake? He sounds pretty dashing," her dad said, a hint of the mischievous in his voice.

"*My* romantic efforts are focused on getting *you* a girlfriend first, and that's going to have to wait until this whole monster thing is under control, so hold your horses."

Her dad laughed, a deep-belly laugh. Ree closed her eyes and listened, imagining her dad was right beside her.

"Thanks, Dad."

"Anytime. Is there anything else I can do?"

"I don't think so." Ree's eyes snapped open as a thought hit her. "Actually, yeah. They might not get here in time, but could you pull a few boxes of my stuff out of storage?"

She had left most of her teenage detritus behind when she went off to college, thinking she'd pick it up eventually or sell it off. But now . . . those old toys and cards and books were worth their weight in Adamantium.

Her dad chuckled. "Sure thing. Want me to look for something in particular?"

"Toy guns, swords. Anything that inflicts imaginary violence, really. And take your allergy meds beforehand."

"Who's the parent again?" he asked, still in good humor.

"You are. But that doesn't make me wrong."

"It doesn't. I promise. And in exchange, you promise to be safe."

Ree nodded to herself. "Yes, sir."

"All right. Now go get them, hon."

"I love you, Dad," Ree said, tearing up.

"I love you, too."

Ree wiped her eyes and hung up. She felt energized, tired, scared, relieved, but mostly, she felt relieved.

Okay. That could have gone much, much worse.

It felt amazingly, reassuringly good to have her dad's

support. But he was far away, and who knew how much time she had to kill until Drake's which-what-ever magic was ready. *So, what next?*

She could try to go back to Eastwood's, make him see reason. But she didn't have much confidence in that working, not while he was on a roll. Maybe if they took out the Muse before it could strike again, he'd be willing to listen to reason. Or, if not reason, impressive amounts of yelling and browbeating. If she had Drake's help, could they take Eastwood in a fight, or would he pull another ninja vanish?

She looked at the clock on her phone and rolled her head. Though the tea had calmed her through the talk with her dad, she was still sore. Sleep would be the smart thing. But unless she wanted to down some NyQuil, she wasn't settling into that anytime soon.

Instead, she dialed Drake, hoping he'd have something for her, anything.

He picked up on the third ring. "Ahoy."

"This is Ree. Any news on the Doors Dimensional Method?"

"Excuse me?" Drake asked.

My pop-culture-reference Rolodex is useless! Ree thought in a Rainer Wolfcastle "The goggles do nothing!" voice.

"Never mind. How's the magic going?"

"Beautifully. We will be able to depart presently. But before you arrive, you'll want to have something to eat."

"Why's that?"

"I have the unfortunate fortune of knowing from experience. The fattier, the better. A colleague of mine told me that lipids facilitate the reuptake of several neurotransmitters that are inhibited by aetherial travel. Regardless, a meal would be advisable."

Ree could see Drake shaking his head as he recognized that he was on a tangent. It was cute. *Too bad half of the things I say make no sense to him.*

"Fatty is good. Got it. I'll grab something on the way and be there by quarter till."

"Very good. Have you any weapons with you?"

"I have a training *jian*, but that's it right now. Care to loan a girl a sword?"

"I'll see what I can do. Winters out." With that, he hung up.

Winters out? I guess he's caught up on some action movies, at least.

Ree pocketed her phone and grabbed her jacket. *Fatty, eh? This calls for a Garbage Shake.*

⋅✕ˣ◈ˣ✕⋅

Ree thanked the fates that the Burger Bin was open late even on Sundays. She managed to sneak through waves of tipsy folk indulging their munchies and grabbed two Garbage Shakes, arriving at Drake's apartment-of-safety-code-violations at 11:43.

Drake opened the door, his goggles down and his face covered in soot. He smiled, wiped his face on his jacket, and said, "Good evening. You're just in time."

"Hey. I brought you a shake. It's super-fatty and made of delicious."

Drake raised an eyebrow at the cups, then stood aside to let her in. Ree handed the full shake over, and Drake regarded it for a moment. "What is in here?" he asked.

"Just about everything, which is why they call it the Garbage Shake. Like a garbage burger, but liquidier. Banana, chocolate, peanut butter, vanilla ice cream, almond and walnut shavings, caramel, and some secret stuff they won't tell anyone. I suspect blood of the innocent."

"That last part is a jest!"

Ree smiled. "He can be taught! Give it a try."

Drake sipped at the straw, failed to get any shake, then tried again. He considered, then said, "That is very rich. Far more robust a flavor than we had in Avalon. But quite delicious. My thanks"—he started to say "Ms.," then corrected himself—"Ree. But we haven't much time if we're to cross in the vicinity of midnight. Please feel free to take something from the armory."

Ree began to speak, but Drake quickly followed up. "My apologies. The armory is the second left, past the water closet."

She turned right and walked down a dimly lit hallway, finding the doorknob and twisting it open. As the door opened, the lights came on, revealing a small room completely filled with weapons and armor.

"Holy Frank Castle's Wet Dream, Batman!" she exclaimed, overwhelmed. She scanned the sword section and found a *jian* with a rippled green pattern in the steel. It wasn't rust, was more like . . . jade?

She stood on tiptoes and pulled down the sword, feeling it move easy in her hands. *Damn, that's a nice balance.*

Ree wandered over to a closet that held a half-dozen types of armor inside. She picked out a buff jacket that looked like it belonged on the set of a wuxia movie and tried it on. It was too big at first, leaving big gaps at her armpits, but a few seconds later, she heard the sound of fabric on fabric, and it tightened to fit her perfectly.

Satisfied, Ree returned to the living room, saying, "Who is your armorer? I want to marry them and have their baby hauberks."

"It was not inexpensive to find someone so talented in this era, but it turns out that there is quite the demand for what you call 'Steampunk technology.' All thanks to the wonders of the Internet. If only Babbage and Lovelace had known what their efforts would lead to."

Ree held up a hand for a high five. Drake looked at her hand, then nodded and slapped it.

"Are you sufficiently appointed?"

"Yeah, but how does this armor work?"

Drake walked around the living room, where he'd set up six small engines in a circle. He walked the circle, tweaking a knob on each machine. "It was constructed by one of the locals in the Underground. I will be sure to introduce you if we manage to survive this odyssey."

"Sounds great. I could use some more friends in the know, especially friends who can make armor this awesome."

Drake continued as Ree talked. At the fifth machine, the knob stuck, so he produced a wrench from his jacket and gave it a tweak. Then he squinted at the machine and kicked it once.

Ree shrugged. "So . . . what do I do?"

Drake knelt at the sixth device, slightly larger than the others, and looked at meters on a panel. "Stand in the center of the circle. I need to calibrate the device to your spiritual signature. Mine is of course already on record."

Ree stepped into the circle and held the sword at her side. "Like this?"

Drake looked up, then nodded. "That will be sufficient. Now if you would be so kind as to hold your breath for a moment."

"What?" Ree tried to hold her breath, but thinking about holding her breath made her very aware of the fact that she was holding her breath, which made it even harder. She tried to imagine she was swimming, back when she'd been on the junior high swim team for an entire six weeks. That is, until Janice Egan had to go and recover from her twisted ankle instead of being out for the whole season. Rather than going back to JV, Ree quit and spent more time at the dojang.

"That will be sufficient—" Drake paused again, finishing with "Ree."

Ree exhaled, her shoulders collapsing forward. *Nothing like a trip on the way-back machine to pass the time.* "So what exactly does this do?" she asked.

Drake stood and crossed to take up his rifle from its resting place in the corner. "This device, the Aetheric Breakthrough Actuator, once calibrated to an individual's bioaetheric signature, creates an electrical current that will momentarily unify our world and Spirit. This will allow you to exist in both dimensions concurrently for a moment and step through into Spirit, bypassing the Veil. Since the machine has your individual signature, it maintains a tether while you are on the other side, not unlike the string Ariadne gifted young Theseus in his journey into the Labyrinth."

Returning to the larger box at the head of the circle, he held up a box that looked like a remote control made by Nikola Tesla. It reminded Ree of the Farnsworth communicator from *Warehouse 13*. "This will allow me to pull us back along that tether to return, but it is more dangerous to use, the farther away we are from our point of entry."

Ree shifted back and forth in the circle, holding her borrowed weapon over her shoulder. "All right, I don't need to know any more. Just push the big red button, and let's get this show on the road."

"Very well. We go!" Drake called like a battle cry. He raised his finger, waved it in the air, and then slammed it down on the red button.

CHAPTER FIFTEEN

Aetheric Boogie

The world lit up, and for a moment Ree thought the passing-through would be like the cauldron-induced vision at the Dorkcave. Instead of an overload of images and sensations, it was like one huge static-electricity shock.

When she opened her eyes, she was still in Drake's apartment, but it was like someone had put the whole world through the graphics-filter love child of *Tron* and *The Matrix*. Lines of light coursed through the walls and the various gadgets in the room. She looked down and saw that she looked normal, except for a faint veinlike light skeleton.

Are you what a bioaetheric signature looks like when it's at home? Her borrowed sword glowed with a faint green light, the tip and edges crackling with little licks of electricity. *Cool.*

Ree took a couple of steps toward the entrance hall, then saw crackling in the air, the six connected engines lighting up like a techno-magic Christmas tree. With a crack, the air popped and Drake appeared, goggles down and holding the remote in one hand, rifle resting on the other shoulder. He looked back, saw Ree, and smiled. "Excellent. No transference errors."

Ree enacted a classic double take. "What? You didn't say anything about transference errors."

Drake shrugged. "You said you did not need to know any more. There was only a small chance of an error, and it is irrelevant now. Let us endeavor to ascertain if we can catch a Muse!"

Ree laughed, working the nerves out. "You are one gutsy bastard. Let's go."

She stepped out onto the street to take in the view. The sky was purple, with streams of aurora borealis–esque lights streaking across the sky. They combined and broke off like a giant river system, with streams feeding into buildings and through the street. The pavement below shimmered like water, and as she stepped onto the street, she saw a ripple form from her step, bounce into other ripples, and fade ten feet out.

All around her, clusters of light whipped around—not the streams but larger chunks that flickered between several shapes. One moment they were a circuit board of lights, the next a rolling cloud, and then a half-human outline with the same electrical skeleton.

Awesome! Ree thought. *This place may be dangerous, but it's wicked-cool-looking, at least.*

Drake stepped beside her and gestured up to the watercolor sky. "Those aetheric streams are known to some as ley lines. Our best chance of tracking the Aberrant Muse is to follow the ley lines to the places where they cluster. The intersections form large pools of spiritual energy, where spirits congregate to rest and recover."

"Magic watering hole?"

"Something along those lines."

"How far down the rabbit hole are we here? Can I fly if I want to, imagine where I want to go and step right there, or is this more a straight-up shadow world, where a ten-minute walk in real life is ten minutes here?"

"Time passes in a 1:1 ratio, but there can be some perceptual differences in chronal flow. Fortunately, my chronometer keeps perfect time even in this domain. However, flight and point-to-point apparation are not possible, to my knowledge."

"You're just an endless utility belt of oddly named gizmos, aren't you?"

Drake gave a bow. "As charged."

Ree scanned the horizon, trying to make sense of the flows. "All right. Lead on, Friday."

Smiling, Drake said, "You have found a cultural reference that I actually know. Brava." He adjusted a dial on his goggles, then turned a 360. "We head north-northwest. Keep your blade at the ready. There's a hint of doom in the air."

"Awesome. Just what my evening needs."

⋅✕⋅⬡⋅✕⋅

A half hour later, Ree and Drake stood in a park on the edge of Pearson's shipping and warehouse district while Drake recalibrated his goggles. They were in a clearing around a small pond that was also the nexus for dozens of streams of aether, which Ree couldn't help but think of as mana.

Thank you, Magic: The Gathering.

Standing watch, Ree tried not to jump at the incongruous sounds and lights. *Though you can't blame me for getting twitchy when trees pulse with light or pop out fruit-energy bulbs every thirty seconds. What upside-down logic does this spirit world follow, anyway?*

Drake grumbled incoherently, and Ree took another cycle around the pond, still trying to sort out the literalization of the metaphors and all the other stuff that reading Jung made more confusing instead of less. Was it all first-level symbolism, or would she have to dig for weird metaphors? Or was it all in her head? She had to filter the sensory inputs, so maybe this was her brain's way of rendering things and she should trust her first interpretations. Or not.

Pushing aside the headache, she leaned over to check behind a tree.

From the other side of the clearing, she heard a crash. In the ten minutes they'd spent at the pool, she'd heard plops, thuds, chirps, whirrings, whispering willowings, but no crashes. She spun on her heels and squinted, scanning for the source of the noise.

Oh, that'd probably be the gigantic snake that just dropped out of the tree and is coming right for me. Awesome.

Ree charged back toward Drake, calling "Snake!"

"What?"

Pointing with the sword, she repeated, "Snake!"

The serpent was at least twenty feet long, with yellow-green scales, a head as broad as a linebacker's, and teeth the length of her forearm. Drake grabbed his rifle off the ground and took a potshot at the snake, which coiled out of the way and kept coming for Ree.

"Why did it have to be snakes?" she asked, waiting for the moment to move. The snake lunged forward to bite, and Ree pivoted on her right foot, reaching out to stab while she pushed off to her right. Her blow glanced off the snake's scales, but likewise, its bite missed her. What didn't miss was its head slamming her back into a tree. The impact knocked the wind out of her faster than freshmen left a college party that had run out of food.

Drake fired again, his next shot going low to hit the snake along its trunk. The blast sizzled into the scales, leaving a melted-metal texture. The snake hissed and coiled itself up to protect the wound.

A moment later, it lashed out for Ree, a strike that she dodged by hopping back as she cut at the snake's face. But its strike was a feint; the snake turned and slithered by Ree, diving for Drake. The gadgeteer rolled to the side, and the snake curled around to chase him. Ree spun her blade into a reverse grip and plunged it down with both hands into the center of the snake's length.

A hiss of pain hit her eardrums like a jackhammer, and she pulled her hands up to her ears to blunt the sound. As the snake rolled away, she grabbed at the sword, trying to twist it free. The snake flipped over itself to snap at her, and she jumped over its trunk into a perfect shoulder roll.

Thank you, Ms. Young, she thought, thinking of the founder of the Taekwondo dojang who had made her practice shoulder rolls until she could do them without thinking, without notice, and without failure. She came up with the sword in hand and drew the snake's attention, seeing Drake recover and draw a bead on the thing's head.

"Anytime now would be good," Ree called across the clearing while backpedaling. She kept the sword high and in front of her as she retreated, the tip of the blade tracking the snake's head.

Drake's voice was level, formal. "I am aiming as quickly as I can, Ms. Ree, but also endeavoring not to hit you in addition to—"

The snake lunged, and Ree dodged to the side, counter-thrusting at its eye. The serpent shrugged around the blow, and her sword skipped off the side of its head, taking a scale with it. "Then go for the tail!"

"Very well," Drake said, and Ree zigged to her right, drawing the snake's attention, then pushed off and zagged left, putting extra distance between her and the *very* persistent reptile.

"Now!" Ree called, and she heard the *vraahm* of the rifle's blast. The green blast hit the snake just above the tip of its tail, and the beast coiled back in on itself. Drake fired again, and the snake recoiled, slithering toward the shimmering pool.

Ree raised the sword up high, shouting her best *kiai* as she brought it down, chopping off the tail right above the glowing wound. The snake became nothing more than a trail of iridescent ichor that drained into the pool.

Ree backed up, blade dripping and heart pounding. She took conscious control of her breathing until she felt a flash of pain across her back when her lungs were full. *Right, not so much on that.* She watched the pool, but nothing came back out.

"Frak me, that was close," she said.

Drake trained his rifle on the pond as he approached. "Are you struck?"

"I didn't get bit, but my back got painfully friendly with a stump on that tree." She stretched out her back, finding where the hurt started. "Where the hell did that thing come from, and why?"

"A fine question, and not one I am currently able to answer. I would, however, suggest that we vacate the premises, lest we find ourselves drawing the attention of any denizens of Spirit that might investigate the reptile's cries."

"Got it. Which way, navigator?"

Drake paused to look up at the ley lines arcing across the sky. He turned in place, looking in all directions. He stopped and pointed. "North. Or rather, the direction corresponding to north in our world. The poles in Spirit are foci of elemental rather than electromagnetic forces. Regardless, north shall suffice."

He really can't help it, can he? she thought, finding the overexplaining more amusing each time, rather than less, which was a blessing. "If you say so. Let's blow this snakesicle stand." Ree checked the moon and started walking the way that matched north in the real park.

Following her, Drake chuckled. "Mademoiselle, if you ever had the opportunity to visit Avalon, I would pay all the gold in the world to see people react to your mannerisms and vernacular."

"I'll take that as a compliment."

"I'm not sure—"

Ree cut Drake off. "I'll take it as a compliment. How about we leave it there, and we both get to feel good about ourselves?"

"As you wish."

Emerging from the park woods, Ree saw a pack of half-mouse, half-cockroach beasties scuttling and scrabbling across the street, and she quickly did her best to sandblast the image from her brain lest it haunt her dreams for all eternity and then some.

Another hour here, and I'll have enough wild-ass images to last me through a hundred screenplays.

Ree looked up at the north side of the city, where the hills dropped down to the bay. A cluster of ley lines converged into a tower in the industrial district. Others arced away, out of town or out into the ocean.

"Where now?" Ree asked.

Drake reached a gloved hand to his chin and pondered. "This will take a moment." He pulled several tools from his coat and took off his goggles. Ree paced back and forth, trying to stay awake and aware while he fiddled with his gadgets.

Drake donned his goggles again, then looked to the tower. "It's as I feared. The trail seems to lead this way, though not to a glen but to a nexus! It appears that the spirit is attempting to quit the city!"

"So the Muse is skipping town?" she asked.

Drake nodded. "Spirit parallels our world, ports serving as their nexus points as well as connecting distant realms."

Ree scanned the towering pillars that lined the aetheric port. Each had a beacon at its top, with energy streaming in from all around. "Are those the portals, then?"

"Indeed. Though it may not be leaving. It may be calling in assistance."

Ree shuddered. "Let's say it's skipping town. That way's less terrifying."

"Either way, it will be among a myriad of other spirits. We will have to tread lightly, Ree. Perhaps some sort of cloaking method would be appropriate."

Ree waited a second as Drake looked at her expectantly. "What, me?"

"Indeed. My capabilities are limited here without the rest of my devices. Whereas your talents are more flexible."

Ree scratched her head, thinking. "Since when? All I've done is the emulation trick, and I'm fresh out of genre. Are you saying I'm going to get cell reception in the spirit world?"

"I don't know, do you?" Drake asked.

Ree looked at her phone. No bars. She wandered around the street, feeling foolish all the while. Streaming was out of the question, so she tapped through to her video library to see if any of it could help. *What I really need is a whole weekend of downloading, indexing, and making playlists to build up an arsenal.*

Flipping through video podcasts, short skits, and the two episodes of her abortive webseries, she stopped on a film clip she'd ripped a while back. *Hey, that might actually do something.* She tapped on a video excerpt from the seventh Harry Potter movie, where she'd cut out the fantastic animated short to show off to people. "I think I've got something. Have you seen this?"

She played the video for Drake, focusing on the feelings the video evoked, the implications in the story world, the cool of being a spell-slinging badass like Tonks or Hermione.

As the video clip reached its conclusion, with the third brother greeting death, Ree felt the Geekomancy open a door in her mind, energy crackling through her consciousness.

"If only I'd brought my wand," she mused to herself when the video was done. She rummaged through her pockets and pulled out a fountain pen, one of the nice ones she practiced signing her autograph with when she needed a pick-me-up.

I can do this. Your focus determines your reality, right? I can do this.

She stared at the fountain pen, thought wizardly thoughts, and tried to come up with the right fake Latin for the occasion. "*Obfuscari,*" she said, crossing her arms over her chest as she remembered Eastwood's trick in the tunnels. A second passed, and she didn't feel any different. Ree sighed.

"Hullo?"

"Did it work?" she asked.

"I believe so; I cannot see you at all," he said.

Ree fist-pumped in the air, and Drake's smile dropped. "I can see you again."

Ree slumped at the fail. "Balls. Okay, here's what you do."

She told the inventor her idea, and Drake obliged, pulling off his belt and offering one end to Ree so they wouldn't lose each other in the crowd. After Ree had worked a cloak to cover both of them this time, they made their way into the dock area, dodging spirits of all shapes and sizes.

It's like Grand Central Station by way of Hayao Miyazaki.

Some of the spirits were small, bouncing, flitting things that sparkled, making swooshing sounds as they zipped by. Others lumbered on the ground, each footfall striking a deep bass chord. Countless more were in-between, spiraling through the traffic, shuffling like busy commuters, or meandering like sullen teens in packs. Ree wended her way through the crowds, glad that getting jostled here and there didn't bring down the cloaking spell.

They reached the base of one of the immense towers, and Ree felt a tug on the belt, leading her inside. *If our cover breaks in here, we're toast. Worse than toast, we're the crappy crumbs of carbon left at the bottom of a toaster oven that I haven't cleaned out in three months.*

The interior of the tower looked like an airport. Spirits stood in a series of lines with eight-feet-tall sentinels that looked like they were nothing but suits of armor prowling around between them, inspecting each being before waving it through.

Wishing she could just text Drake to coordinate, Ree scanned the room and followed his tugs, weaving around and through people, trying to stay as close as possible to keep some spirit from clotheslining itself on the belt, breaking the spell, and getting the two of them killed.

Through one round of security, she followed the belt into what must have been a large supply closet of some sort. The room was about twenty feet long and maybe eight feet wide. The shelves inside were lined with squishy-looking eggs that glowed like the Easter Bunny's overstock. They were the only source of light in the room aside from the faint crack at the bottom of the door.

Ree let her hands drop, and the outline Drake appeared in front of her, his arms still crossed. She slumped into the shelf, which shook, eggs glorping into one another. Ree grimaced, hoping the sound wouldn't escape the closet. Speaking in a whisper, she said, "Three things. One, this was a bad idea. Because two, we need a way to communicate while we're cloaking it up. Three, what the hell is this room?"

Drake nodded, responding in a stage whisper. "First, you were the one who suggested we follow the Muse. Second, I do not know of a way for us to be able to signal each other besides the belt, lest we spoil our disguise. Third, this room contains the coordinate icons for a variety of locations. When spirits need to travel to nonstandard locations, one of the minor functionaries will retrieve the appropriate icon from such a room as this."

"And how often does that happen?" she asked.

Ree heard a thrumming at the door, the same noise it had made when Drake opened it.

"More often than one might think, it appears."

Ree scrambled toward the back of the room, hiding behind a two-high stack of crates. Half-forced by their belt, Drake joined her, huddled under a dozen meter-long metallic rods that leaned against the wall. He unclasped the belt and looped it around his waist again.

More light flooded into the room, then chirping. Some birdlike voice moved into the room. Ree heard the click of nails on tile, the steps getting closer.

There was the glorp of shuffling icons, then a chirrup that sounded like a question. The clicking got closer, and she heard short chirps and the sounds of the bird-thing's footfalls. Then the sounds receded until she heard the door close again.

Ree peeked out from her hiding spot to check on Drake. "Did it see you?" she asked.

"I suppose not. The transport gates will be upstairs, so if the Muse is attempting to leave or summon assistance, we will find it there."

"So we can get it?"

Drake slid out from under the rods and stood. "Yes. Assuming we can find a way to corner it alone, or care to fight through an entire waiting room of aggravated spirits, yes."

Ree stood and looked at the shelves. "Is there anything we can do with these icons? Power spells, ransom them, or the like? We have to even the odds somehow."

Drake's eyes lit up. "Actually, I may be able to do something quite incredible." He grabbed one of the icons off the shelf, pulled up his goggles, and held the icon to his nose. "Yes, indeed. Rather brilliant. Should have thought of it the last time I was in a conundrum like this. I would still have that fine cummerbund and would not have had to go shopping before last market—"

"I'm sorry, I'm shaky on my rambling Avalonian. What are you going to do?"

"With the correct adjustments, I should be able to set my rifle with the coordinates in the icon and use it to teleport the other spirits in the room, or the Muse itself."

"I don't want to teleport the Muse, I want to kill it."

Drake removed a cylinder from his rifle and turned the icon in his hand, looking back and forth to the rifle. "Yes, just so. But if we can transport the other spirits in the room, we will be able to deal with the Muse directly." He studied the icon with a serious expression. "Now, how are you going to fit into the focusing chamber, my dear little thing?"

Ree quirked an eyebrow. "You are a piece of work."

"I am as the creator made me, I suppose, though on my own terms." Drake winked and thumbed down a lever with a click. "That should suffice for now. I do not imagine I will get much more than one minute of functionality with this modification, so we will need another exit strategy."

Ree scanned the shelves. "Can't we just hop the tower-portal-whatever with one of these?" She waved at the icons. "Preferably not the same place we've just sent a bunch of spirits?"

Drake nodded, considering. "Perhaps, but it would be highly dangerous. The portals are not designed for mortal transport, and I will have to see if there is an icon here whose destination is close enough to our exit to be workable." He started a slow walk down the aisle, checking the icons.

Ree sighed, looking down. She saw a faint glint of silver, and scooped up the lifeline that had followed her since they entered Spirit. It was far fainter than when they'd first arrived in the otherworld. "Or could we just tug real hard on our escape threads?" Ree scooped up her silver cord and held it. Given that she couldn't see Drake's, she imagined they were an Only You Can See Yours thing.

"That, sadly, is not an option. We are far too distant to pull the rip cord." Drake picked up an icon, examined it, then clucked his tongue and set it down again, the slight downturn in his lips deepening.

"What are you looking for?" she asked, staying close so she could whisper.

Drake held up two icons. "We need one that has this sigil next to that one, but with three lines above them at a forty-five-degree downward slope."

Ree looked at the icons, then started scanning the other line of shelves for a match. She held the image in her head and was thankful for countless hours of puzzle games.

After several more abortive hopeful sounds from Drake that ended in grumbling, Ree found what she thought was the one. Pulling it down, she took the thing to Drake, its semisolid goopiness cold in her hands.

Drake looked it over, and his eyes lit up. "This will transport us to the park just south of the university campus. Brilliant." He pocketed the icon and walked for the door. "It's time to get out of the closet."

Ree covered her mouth to keep from snickering. "It's 'come out of the closet,' my dear," she said with a huge grin.

"I do believe you are having a laugh at my expense. What have I said?"

"'Come out of the closet' is a euphemism for telling people you're gay."

"But I am usually quite gay— Oh. Not in the contemporary parlance. Though I did get to meet Oscar Wilde once. Quite a witty fellow. He asked if I wanted to see his scripts, which I rather imagine now was an invitation to examine his briefs."

Ree reached for the wall as she tried to keep the laughter in. She put her other hand on Drake's face to shut him up—*Damn, his skin is soft. No, focus! No time for mushy thoughts!*

She gathered herself as she let go of Drake's surprised mug. *All right, once more with feeling.* She played the Harry Potter short for herself. Feeling the same energy build in her mind, she pushed it into the magic, using her pen as a makeshift wand.

The obfuscation back in place, Ree opened the door.

CHAPTER SIXTEEN

Blue Stone Express

Up a flight of stairs, they found the waiting room, filled with hundreds of seats of varying sizes and shapes. There was something for all of Spirit's creatures. There were seats for spirits whose lower halves kind of faded out, seats for spirits who had octopi for tails, for those that were ten feet tall, and for many more configurations of bodies. At the center was a terminal with a team of busy spirits that checked the travelers' shimmering-energy boarding passes and calibrated their machines accordingly, switching out the various icons and repeating rituals that activated a portal a few feet away.

The portal itself looked like a cross between a Stargate and Stonehenge, covered in runes that didn't match any language Ree recognized, real or imaginary, and with a large empty circle that stretched to the roof of the room.

Ree was sure the runes weren't any normal-people-known language, since she killed at fictional-language Trivial Pursuit. She ought to, since she made up the fifty questions for Fictional Languages back in college when she and the folks of the SF Club made a Far-from-Trivial Pursuit for their year-end party. *All that work, and I still didn't make president senior year.*

Ree continued to puzzle out how spirit-world travel worked. It seemed that a spirit would step into the center of the circle, and as the adminstrators' rituals finished, a blue cloud of energy would wrap itself around the spirit, then collapse in on itself, leaving an empty space and a *pop!* sound. She was disappointed that it sounded nothing like *BAMF.*

That's just not right.

Drake pulled on the belt, and she felt him put a hand on her shoulder. "On three," he said in a whisper.

He tapped once, twice, three times.

The room turned into an action movie. Drake appeared in front of her, dropping to one knee and firing into the crowd. He'd done something to make his rifle shoot on full automatic. Instead of bursts of energy, his rifle hurled dozens of crackling blue blobs across the room. When they hit, each blob wrapped itself around the spirit like they had done in the ritual and pulled its target through makeshift vorteci, almost seeming to wink them out of existence entirely. The pops from Drake's gun came fast enough that Ree had flashbacks to the Chinese New Year when she and her dad had lived in Oakland and spent the night on the roof wrapped in blankets.

As the field narrowed out, Ree saw the Muse, all jagged edges and gaping maw. It stood out more on this side, like someone had run it through Photoshop and scaled up the contrast to distinguish its shades of gray and black. Ree closed on the Muse, large steps chewing up the space between them, and dropped the veil so that Drake didn't accidentally port her to Botswana or wherever all those things were headed. She circled toward its flank, and the spirit surged forward to meet her.

"Hey there, fucker. Remember me?" She rolled left, taking a swipe at the Muse with the sword. Her slash missed, but she avoided the thing's charge.

"When I'm done with you, you're never going to hurt a single person ever again." She came up to a kneeling position, blade out in front of her. All around, the room was in chaos, screams and shouts of stampeding spirits rapidly getting swallowed up by Drake's machine-gun relocation program.

She pulled the pen out of her coat, the wizardy fu faint at the edges of her mind. She leveled the pen at the Muse as it advanced, dug in her feet, and loudly proclaimed, "This is my boom stick!"

She willed out as big a haymaker as she could, pouring into it her anger, her fear, and the memory of the pain it had heaped on her. She imagined the Muse getting ripped to shreds by pure energy, obliterated by her blast.

The spell lashed out as a semitransparent wave with an orange tint. It hit the Muse and knocked it back into the side of the ritual circle. But as she moved forward and took a breath to shoot another blast, her grasp on the Potter energy dissipated and her pen was just a pen again.

No time for a video break now. Just me and ol' stabby.

"Yo, Drake, wanna give me a hand here?" Ree asked as she chased the Muse. It float-limped away from the circle, trying to put distance between itself and Ree. *I've got you now, fucker.*

"I'm rather indisposed, sadly," Drake shouted back. "Security has arrived."

Ree glanced over her shoulder and saw a dozen of the all-armor guards storming up the spiral stairs. Drake laid down fire to cover the stairs, but the brutes had taken to climbing across the walls and flying around.

"Then you're all mine," Ree said to the Muse as she dashed across the room. The Muse scaled up the wall to the ceiling, and Ree slowed, staring up to the corner. *Well, crap. I didn't think about that. Screw you, high ceilings.*

Ree shouted at the Muse, "You've got to come down sometime, you predatory piece of slime. I've got all day, and this sword is itching to rip you to shreds." She stalked below the spirit, trying to keep it as close as she could manage while it probed the walls and ceiling like a frustrated fly.

"Can't just fade away here, can you?" She checked over her shoulder again and saw Drake run-and-gunning from cover to cover. *Shit, no time for taunting. How can I get to you?*

Under the ceiling was a lattice of rafters, a honeycomb dome. Ree imagined it had something to do with the portal, but what it really meant was that if she could get up to the ceiling, she could swing around and chase the Muse monkey-style.

Ree plotted jumping paths from kiosks and chairs, but the only way for her to get to the ceiling was the transport circle. She ran for the standing circle, jumped onto a chair, bounded up to a kiosk, and finally hurled herself up and at the structure. Wrapping her arms and legs around the cool granite-esque surface, she held strong to it. Reaching up with her sword hand, she tried to pull her body high enough to loop a foot over the lattice. Her first effort failed, so she sliced upward and got her sword stuck in the ceiling.

Well, that works. She hauled herself up by the sword and grabbed hold of the narrow stone bars. She wrenched the sword free as she plotted a path across the ceiling toward the Muse. She swung back and forth several times, then looped one foot up into the lattice. She rested her other foot beside it and reached out with her sword arm to get another handhold.

She got the hang of the process, thankful for her countless hours on jungle gyms and for her finger strength from video games and martial arts.

"I'm coming for you now, bucko." She crawled toward the Muse, which bounced around a corner. She heard a louder commotion where she imagined Drake to be.

"I am afraid time is running short, my sarcastic friend!" came his call. There was urgency in his voice, cracking through the normal bombasticity.

"Working on it!" She sped up the swinging, but two rungs later, she flubbed the grab, her hand slipping off the loop. She tucked one foot in and splayed the other one out, stopping herself in a not-cool upside-down position. The pressure on her leg and foot was unbelievable, and she hoped she hadn't sprained anything.

Wishing she'd kept up with her crunches, she hauled herself back up with her core, reaching for the lattice. Her lungs ran dry and her stomach clenched, but her fingers reached the stone, and she was upright again. In the meantime, the Muse had switched corners, so she had to move faster.

"Get your ass over here, you low-rent nightmare machine. I've seen scarier shit on old reruns of *Goosebumps*, you grayscale leftover boggart. What does it say that all I wanted after our last fight was a warm mug of milk and more weapons? Maybe you were scary back in the BCEs, but these days, you're about as terrifying as day-old espresso grinds, you spindly sack of shit. I bet you get frightened by Ugly Dolls!"

Okay, that last part probably went over his head. Hey, wait!

In an instant, the Muse was charging her, jaw opening to reveal a darker-than-black maw.

Bring it. She unlooped her sword arm from the lattice and prepared to swing.

Don't screw up, don't screw up, don't screw up.

The mantra ran on repeat, and as the Muse flew within distance, Ree swung the sword with as much of her body strength as she could muster, twisting in the air. Seeing it cut through the Muse's jaw, she let go with her left arm and reached for another handhold. She dropped her feet out of the lattice and swung with all her strength, biting a cut into her lip as she hauled herself over to grab on again.

Ree leaned back and saw the Muse looping around, bleeding ink-black somethingplasm as it swiped for her.

Come on, one more pass.

Hoping she had the thing properly enraged, she swung

again, so forcefully that she let go with her arm. She dropped, hanging by her feet, but she kept on swinging. *Die, already!* The Muse's claw tore at her arm, and it took a big bite of her shoulder.

Ree rammed the sword into the creature's chest with a scream of pain and rage, and she felt the thrust pierce deep. As the cold closed around her, squeezing on her heart, she twisted the blade and kicked out of the lattice, somersaulting in the air.

She hit the ground hard, the impact knocking the wind out of her like a cartoon anvil.

Above her, the Muse, cracked from the cuts, poured out somethingplasm and lit up with dark-dark-blue light. With a scream that poured fire on the cold burn around Ree's heart, the beast exploded.

Ree tried to shout in victory, but no breath came. Every bit of her ached or burned or stung, and blackness knocked on the door to her mind. It was so inviting. She could just let go, close her eyes, and be done.

The Muse was gone, and what were the chances there'd be another suicide that fit the bill before midnight tomorrow? She'd saved at least one life, maybe another soul, and had done some awesome hero shit. Wasn't that enough?

The air wasn't coming, only the black and the burning cold. The cold ate up her pain, the ache, and the sting in her lungs. It wouldn't be that bad after all. All she had to do was let go . . .

The black closed in on her, offering the easy way out. But Ree pulled herself up, gritting her teeth. She had no air, no voice, so she took the pommel of the sword and slammed it into her solar plexus.

The rest of the air in her lungs came out with a *puh*, then she inhaled one sharp breath. It hurt like hell, but after the first breath came the second, then another. She looked around, the edges of her vision blurry. Drake stood by the gate, firing the rifle one-handed while his hands played over some kind of panel.

"Get up, Ms. Ree. We must escape while the opportunity remains!"

Ree dragged herself over to the portal, her legs flopping uselessly to the ground when she tried to get onto her feet. *Come the fuck on, girl. It'd be pretty damn ironic to fall over and die after pushing back the* easy *death, right? Move your ass.*

Drake reached down and helped her pull herself into the ritual circle. He fired his rifle several times more into the oncoming crowd of spirits.

"As they say, here goes nothing!" Drake stepped into the circle and swung the butt of his rifle down on the panel.

Liquid blue smoke wrapped itself around her, and the world went—

BLINK.

When Ree opened her eyes, her vision was cast in blue tones, like she was looking through sunglasses. She saw the rough outline of a street, car-esque blobs, and lines of windows. She blinked a couple of times, and the tint faded. She was splayed across the middle of a street, probably Lincoln, judging by the poshness of the buildings and the coffee shop on the corner of the cross street to her right.

Ree looked around and saw Drake kneeling next to her. She pulled herself up on her arms, and another wave of pain crashed over her. She dropped to the ground, tucking her head to the side to avoid a face-plant.

She took several long breaths, trying to push the pain aside. *Get it together. Keep going. There's shit to be done, people to be saved.*

She rolled over to her back and sat up, focusing on Drake. He reached out a hand and helped her limp her way out of the street and into an alley as the spirits wound their way through the street, apparently with better things to do than harass some humans.

Drake produced a roll of bandages from somewhere, which he used to bind a sopping wound on his left arm. His sleeve was stained with blood just below the elbow.

"Are you all right?" she asked.

Drake grimaced through bloodied teeth. "I rather think that I had the easier time of it. Can you walk? It is not too far to the maximum safe distance and a quick return."

Ree grunted as she planted the sword on the pavement and tried to use it to help haul herself up. Pain crashed in again, but she held it back, creaking to her feet. The cold fire was still licking at her, numbing everything except the pain.

"I'm good. Just how about no more fight scenes for a while, 'kay?" Ree asked.

"Fates grant that will be the case. We need not travel far, and if I am correct, the ritual circle should be overtaxed and nonfunctional for several minutes yet. We best be on our way, though."

"Got it." Ree hobbled forward, using the sword as a cane, the tip biting into the ground, making blue digital ripples in the ground as they hurried. This was even worse than when the Muse first wounded her; she'd started out more tired, taxed herself more using magic she didn't know she could do until she did it, and taken two hits from a desperate monster in its own territory. She needed to get out of Spirit fast, then drink a two-liter of Drake's nasty soul goop like it was Mountain Dew at an all-day game-a-thon.

Ree was thankful for the lack of traffic, with just a few spirits walking and flying by. Apparently, there was no aetheric equivalent to Twitter or APBs, since they passed by without notice, not even caring that two humans were in their realm. Ree limped along, her arm over Drake's shoulder, and they leaned on each other, trying to stay upright. They stopped once so she could catch her breath, then again so Drake could replace his already-soaked bandage.

Three blocks later, Drake stopped to check the cross street, then looked behind him. "We should be within range."

Ree looked over her shoulder and saw that her silver cord had brightened, shining like it had when they first crossed over.

"So we just yank?" she asked.

"Thankfully, yes. I can wait to make sure you get through."

Ree cracked a half-smile, thankful for Drake's help. *You don't meet many genuinely good square-jawed heroes anymore. Good people, sure, brave people, but not too frequently together.*

Ree reached behind her back, closed her eyes, and yanked.

When she saw she was back in Drake's living room, Ree collapsed in relief. She dropped the sword, flopped on the floor outside of the ritual circle, rolled onto her back, and breathed. A few seconds later, Drake appeared to her left. His shoulders sagged in relief, and he set down his rifle.

"Thank the Mistress," he said.

"Mistress nothing. That was all you, Drakey."

Drake raised an eyebrow, restraining a smile. "Drakey?"

"Yeah . . . That didn't work at all," she said, breathing heavily. Drake gave her a tired smile. "Do you have more of that soul-sludge?" Ree ran her hands over her arms, cold from the Muse's touch. *If I never have to do that again, I'll still say it was too much. This better work.*

Drake walked around to the kitchen, and she heard rattling in the fridge.

Ree pulled out her phone and checked the time. 6:30 AM. *Damn timey-wimey crap. Do I have to work today? Yes, just about now. Do I (A) call in again and risk my job, (B) drag-ass my way through the day, or (C) none of the above?*

Drake returned to the living room and mixed up another batch of tincture. Ree stumbled into the bathroom and checked herself in the mirror to assess how unprepared for work she was.

Ree tried to blink the tired out, to no avail. She had bags under her eyes, scrapes and cuts on her arms and face, and her shirt was trashed. She might be able to make it home and throw on new clothes if she left now and chugged the soul goop on the way. But with that much gunk, there was no way she could stay awake. And Steve Jobs only knew what Eastwood would be able to do in that time.

Ree leaned out of the bathroom and asked, "So what are you going to do next?"

Drake looked up from his mortar and pestle. "What would you ask me to do?"

Ree tried to clean off her face, wincing as she dabbed her face with a damp cloth. "All I can think of now is try to find Eastwood again, stay on him like white on rice, and try to persuade, intimidate, or face-beat him into dropping the devil's bargain."

"Technically, the Duke is a demon rather than a devil."

"Is this a Chaotic Evil/Lawful Evil thing?"

Drake blinked, waited a second, then continued. "Demons are administrators and executives, where devils are functionaries and field agents. Devils report to demons."

"How the hell does that work if all the Christians complain about the Devil?"

"The Devil, Lucifer, and Satan are all different entities that overlap to different degrees at different times, changing with human conception. It is rather like the pantheism of the Hindus."

"Thanks, Dr. Exposition," she said with more bite in her voice than she intended. She saw hurt flash across Drake's face and ducked back in the bathroom, flushing with embarrassment.

"Sorry, that was out of line," Ree yelled through the wall. "I have to get to work, double time, or I'll lose my job, but I haven't slept, I look like shit and feel worse, and none of that helps me keep Eastwood from doing something monumentally unwise."

Emerging from the bathroom, she checked her phone again and looked up to see Drake in front of her. He wrapped his arms around her and squeezed her into a hug.

"You've done more than anyone could have reasonably expected, and you're willing to do more. If you need assistance in obtaining leave from work, I will try my best to assist. But nothing binds you to this mission other than your will. It is your right to step away from it if you do not wish to continue."

What I want is to sleep for a day. Ree soaked in the feeling of envelopment and safety. Then she pulled herself out of the hug and met his eyes. "I've got to go. See if you can track down Eastwood, then let me know."

"Of course. I have prepared more of the tincture. Take this to speed things along." Drake walked back, grabbed the French press, and handed it to Ree. "You're welcome to take the sword along as well, should you wish it."

"I'm not that paranoid. It's a ten-block walk."

Drake nodded. "Of course. I will send word when I have it."

Without thinking, Ree stood on her toes and kissed Drake on the cheek. She turned toward the door, blushing.

Why did I do that? Damnit. Bone-tired is worse than drunk. Get going. She opened the door and hurried down the stairs, trying to jolt herself into wakefulness.

I do not need more complications right now. Step one, job. Step two, find Eastwood. Step three, save lives. Step four, sleep for a week. And . . . go.

The first rays of orange sunlight crept in from the east, lighting one side of the sky as she hustled home to grab a fresh shirt.

She ran everything over in her head, trying to keep her brain going so she didn't get groggy. She sipped on the scalding-hot tincture, and each bit warmed her inside and, well, disgusted her on the outside. If she could explain things to Bryan, things would be so much easier.

He's a Pagan, after all, maybe he already knows? Or has some idea?

When Ree got home, the apartment was empty. Sandra had apparently stayed over at Darren's, since she was usually puttering around in the kitchen by ten till seven on Monday mornings. Ree tore through her laundry pile and found a not-that-dirty black top, wrapped her blue-and-purple-and-pink scarf around her neck, grabbed a pair of chopsticks for her hair, and thanked her luck that the elevator was still there to take her back down.

Even so, she reached the door of Zombie Cafe at 6:59, according to her phone. Looking through the windows, she saw Bryan inside, looking distracted. Ree waved to him as she entered, going straight to the back to drop off her bag.

Bryan stopped in front of the coffee grinder and asked, "Are you all right?"

"Long night. Drama."

Bryan gave her the *you can confide in me* look, but Ree wanted to get into the rhythm of the day before she unloaded.

"I'll explain in a bit. I need to get those scones in the oven." Ree sneaked around him and started working on the baking for the day.

Cinnamon raisin, cranberry orange, and apple walnut scones, banana bread and pumpkin cream cheese muffins, pumpkin butterscotch cookie clouds (her specialty), and the requisite tray of cinnamon rolls, the most disgustingly deliciously decadent dessert she'd ever had the self-hating pleasure of making. Each one of those monsters clocked in at nearly a thousand calories, nearly none of them any sort that you'd call good.

The scents and sounds helped her calm down, let her slip back into her comfort zone. She'd gotten only half of the baking started, since she hadn't been around to pre-prep the last few days, but she emerged from the baking meditation at 7:30, when the shop opened.

When she unlocked the door, there was a line of four polo-wearing young geek professionals, three regulars, and a girl she'd never seen before—artsy-looking, with dyed-purple hair and a tie for a belt.

Ree and Bryan welcomed the early risers, serving the three regulars and shuttling them back into the world with the awesome efficiency that had made Bryan famous. They banged out two cappuccinos and a mocha in three minutes flat, bringing the purple-haired new girl to the front of the line with two more people behind her. Another hour and a half of Zen barista action, and the crowd settled down.

Being back in the café reminded Ree of her "real life." She asked Bryan, "Any word for Aidan and his ladylove from Stanford?"

Bryan looked up from cleaning the tables. "Nothing yet, but it could just be late. The October 31st deadline for response is one they made up, so they can break it if they want." He shook his head with a chagrined smile. "I tried to get him to put it out of his mind, try to have fun with the day, but he's been more twitchy than ever."

Ree continued wiping down the coffee bar and mentally ticked off her still-to-do list for baking. *He has his own crap to deal with. I can handle my own,* she told herself.

Best boss ever, remember? she countered. He may be able to help. Plus, you're going to have to come up with some understanding if you plan on skipping more shifts.

Ree put down the cleaning rag and leaned on the counter. She took a deep breath, then said, "Hey, boss?"

Bryan looked up again. "Yeah?"

"This is going to make me sound like an absolute weirdo. If you don't want to hear it, let me know and we'll pretend this conversation didn't happen. Actually, chances are you won't remember it even if it does happen." She hadn't talked to her dad since cluing him in, so she had no clue how the Doubt really worked.

"Is this a writing thing?" he asked, giving her his circumspect look.

"I wish. It's a 'my life has gone through the looking glass' thing." Ree wandered into the back, checking the freezer that held their fruit. *The more time I spend thinking about scones, the less I have to think about teen suicide and a Darth Vader showdown with Eastwood. Happy, happy café drone.*

Bryan was still wearing the concerned face when she walked back into the main room. *Yeah, that's not going to work.*

"Bryan, what kinds of magic do you know about?"

Bryan shifted his weight and leaned back, looking unsure where she was going but relieved that it was a topic he knew something about. "Well, Ritual magic is what I know best. It has two main camps: white magic, which creates and preserves; and black magic, which corrupts and destroys. Other people believe in different types, but for my purposes, it comes down to those. Why do you ask?"

"I've gotten into some wild shit, and you're the only person around that I know whose worldview doesn't think magic is bunk."

Bryan considered Ree's face, then checked his watch. He walked around the counter and flipped the sign on the door to *Closed.* "Okay, why don't you start at the beginning," he said.

Ree smiled and dropped into her Inigo Montoya voice. "There is too much, let me sum up."

She focused this telling on the magic bits, the Geekomancy and the nostalgia-fueled props, the midnight market and the ritual with the crucible. And, of course, Eastwood's bargain. When she was done, she realized that she'd burned through two full cups of coffee; maybe they would help her see through time and predict the future.

Bryan poured himself another mug of tea and breathed in the steam. "You should have come to me about this sooner."

What, so he's in on the secret? Who else knew about this without telling me?

"Are you in on the Occult Underground thing, too?"

"Not so much in as adjacent to. I have some friends who are deeper in than I am. I've heard of Eastwood. He was a legend during the border disputes over the Wild Wild Web."

"Did you know Branwen?" Ree asked.

Bryan shook his head. "I only ever heard bits and pieces." He set down his mug and walked behind the counter. He pulled up the traction mat that they kept on the drain, flopped it over to the side, and reached down to fiddle with the grate.

"What are you doing?" Ree asked.

"Those friends I told you about? They're more paranoid than I am, so I let them put in a panic room for me. It has some things you might be able to use."

I've got to hit the bottom of this weird-ass rabbit hole anytime now, right?

Bryan hopped down, and a few seconds later, a light came on. Bryan stood flush against one side, with a trough for the waste going off to one side. "Come on down, just watch the sludge."

Ree sat down into the pit, grabbed the ledge, and dropped off, slowing her fall so she could land on the side. The light showed a narrow tunnel toward the street, which Bryan climbed through. Patently avoiding checking out her boss's ass, she followed him into a larger space. He clicked on another lightbulb to illuminate the room.

Compared to Eastwood's Dorkcave, it wasn't much, but it was a helluva lot more than she expected her mild-mannered nerdy Pagan boss to have stored away right underneath her feet.

The room held several beat-up old chests, a bookshelf that took up one whole wall, a small fridge, and a travel-sized weapon rack.

"Whatcha got?" Ree asked.

"If you're going up against Eastwood, you'll want protection from all of those props of his."

"I have some armor I'm borrowing from a friend." The words sounded strange coming out of her mouth. A smile slipped across her lips. *A lifetime of video games and RPGs, and it's all still weird.*

"Yeah, but this should be better for going up against a Geekomancer." Bryan pulled out a T-shirt-shaped quilt with four-inch-square blocks. When he held it up, she leaned in and took a closer look. There was screen-printed type on each block, bits of dates and locations. As far as she could tell, the dates were mostly in the '6os and '7os.

"What are the blocks?" she asked.

Bryan smiled. "This is made from the T-shirts of the first year of ten major science fiction conventions, including the first Worldcon, the first World Fantasy, and first Gen Con. The collected geek cred of these shirts is strong enough to shrug off most anything that's powered by nerdstalgia."

Ree chuckled, then cackled, then doubled over with laughter, thinking of all the proud gamers and geeks walking around game and sci-fi conventions with their T-shirts. She'd never been one for convention shirts. Nor band shirts, for that matter. But she did have a proud collection of Nintendo shirts locked up in her dad's storage unit, and if things like that kept her safe, they'd be worth the strange looks.

Something else to have Dad send. Assuming I survive this whole thing.

"Has this been washed?" she asked with a smile.

Bryan rolled his eyes. "Wear that over whatever armor you've got for real stuff, and you should be able to stand up to whatever magic he's throwing around. But what are you going to do then?"

Ree leaned against the corner of the hallway, her head grazing the ceiling. "Still working on that. I know that I don't want the deal to go down. I don't know what Dork Lords of Hell do with souls, but I bet it's not good."

Bryan was absently flipping through a box of comics as she talked. "And Eastwood?"

Ree waved a hand, dismissive. "He's in over his head. But I owe him my life at least once over. Best case is I pull his ass out of the fire and keep the demon from getting more soul Pokémon. Worst case, I get flayed alive and have incubi hump me to death."

Disgust flashed across Bryan's face. "You're pretty nonchalant about all of this."

Ree shrugged. "I'm overtaxed, outclassed, and exhausted. I came here half-expecting that you'd call the cops on me, and my troubles would get narrowed to a ten-by-ten padded room with room service. This is way better already."

Bryan looked her up and down like they'd just met. Or like he was reevaluating her, maybe starting to consider her as more than just Ree—27, worked for me for two years, can drop a shot of espresso in 20 seconds on the dot every time, and knows more about the oeuvre of Marv Wolfman than anyone this side of the Rockies.

But what then? Ree—27, in over her head and six hours from dead, or Ree—27 and more of a badass than expected?

"What's that look for?" she asked.

Bryan smiled. "You're more than I pegged you for, Ree."

Ree beamed that her boss had gone with the badass evaluation and struck a pose. "Call me Optimus."

"Opti*mistic*, for sure." Bryan pulled out a backboarded issue, chuckled to himself, and set it aside.

Ree leaned into the room, scanning the shelves and stacks. "What else is up for grabs?"

"Just about everything. My friends donated a lot, but I can't use much in here, it's all over my head or out of my paradigm. The broomstick is my quick-escape plan, and the longbox at the bottom is set aside for the kids' college tuition, but other than that . . ."

Ree looked around the room, starting to sort items by how useful she thought they'd be in the upcoming likely fight. When she'd finished, she realized she had something else she needed to talk with him about. "You know that if I survive, I'll probably be stuck doing this hero crap some more. Will I have a job waiting for me?"

Bryan clucked his tongue on the back of his teeth. Ree had worked for him long enough to know that was a bad sound. "I don't want trouble coming through my door, Ree. The store barely makes ends meet, and my insurance isn't good enough to handle it if something does break bad.

"And if I play favorites, cut you slack, everyone else will start asking for it, too. If you can't hack the schedule . . ." He put his hands out in a *what can you do?* gesture.

"That's it?" Ree found herself getting angry, not at Eastwood or the Duke or any of the dozen beasts and bullies whose paths she'd crossed, but at her boss, whom she'd considered one of her best friends. This hero shit was all the less fun if you couldn't leave it behind at the tabletop or the laptop.

"I'm sorry," he said, passing her on the way to the tunnel. "I just don't have the wiggle room. Take what you like and get going. I have to open up the shop."

"I can stay until my shift's up," she offered, her voice wavering.

Bryan smiled. "I'm fine, Ree. Go do what you have to do. We can talk again after." With that, he slipped out of sight, carrying the sleeved issue he'd pulled out.

Well, that didn't go as expected. Ree had made up a short list of possible results, including: call sanatorium, uncomfortable firing, an outside chance of being totally okay with it somehow. "Here's my arsenal" had not been on that list, for some strange reason. *In the future, assume everyone knows about magic until proven otherwise.*

Ree poked around the room, flipped through some old comics, and started loading stuff into her bag. She grabbed the T-shirt quilt-mail, slipped several dozen Magic cards into her purse, and reverently arranged a few late-'70s comics in board-backed sleeves, putting them away while a shudder went up her arm.

Don't make me have to use these, please. If we have to destroy stuff every time we use it, sooner or later there will be no Star Wars laser discs, no Chaos Orbs, no Action Comics #15.

It was a lot more than she'd had an hour ago. Bryan may not be able to pay her for work she didn't do, but the gear might end up saving her life.

She held the bag to her chest, looked around the room again, and slipped another couple of things into the bag, noting every single thing she took in case she needed to repay Bryan for the swag. Or at least, that spendy Ethiopian blend that his wife got him for his birthday every year. Fifty bucks a pound and worth every penny.

Well, I've got myself some weapons, an impressive if ridiculous ally, and I know what my opponent needs to succeed. Not much left to it but to do it.

Next stop, the Dorkcave.

CHAPTER SEVENTEEN

Revelation Redux

When Ree met up with Drake a block from the Dorkcave's basement entrance, the gadgeteer was casting glances over his shoulders, looking up and down the street suspiciously. "What are you watching for?" she asked.

He closed his eyes and rubbed the bridge of his nose. "I am not certain, but I imagine I will know if I see it. My adventurer's senses tell me that things are coming to a head, my dear, and in such times, vigilance is a given."

He looked about as bad as she felt. "Are you all right?" Ree asked.

"I believe I may be in need of some tea."

Ree shook her head. "Silly Brits. You need to cop to your mortality and start pounding cappuccinos like the Italians and the rest of the overstimulated world."

"Perhaps you are right."

"Okay, let me take the lead here. I need to clear things up before we can start talking sense into him anyway. And from what I can tell, he holds grudges."

Drake took a deep breath. "For now—we have a greater purpose. But if the situation goes awry, do not hesitate to summon me."

"All right, but it'll be by text, not girlie scream. I don't play damsel in distress. I don't even like dresses. Except the slinky ones."

She blinked a couple of times, trying to shake the sleep-deprived loopiness. No such luck. *Yeah, I should have taken a nap before tackling the bad guy.*

Walking down the stairs, she shouted over her shoulder, "Watch your phone, and try to act casual."

Drake crossed his arms and leaned against the railing above the basement steps. Even that bit of casual managed to look awkward on him.

At the bottom of the stairs, Ree knocked on the door and leaned on the bell for several moments. She waited, arms crossed. *Come on, come on.*

She knocked again, then leaned up against the door to listen. The surface was as cold as it had been yesterday and yielded no more sound.

A half-minute later, Ree kicked the door, then instantly regretted it, having not worn her steel-toed boots to work.

She bit her lip and knocked again. *A voice in her mind said, He's not home, or he knows it's you and he's not answering. Just go home and go to bed.*

Oh, bed. How she longed to creep under her sheets, pile blanket on top of blanket, and curl up with her hot pad to pass the hell out and play *Skyrim* from bed forever.

Instead, she knocked on the door again. She turned over thoughts in her mind, trying to think if there was a genre-fu move she hadn't thought of that would get Eastwood to show. She wouldn't do any kind of Mind whammy, reach into his mind and force him to abandon his plan. That would be Left-handed, Dark Side, and worse karma than kicking a three-legged puppy in the rain.

Footsteps. Ree put her ear to the door and heard them coming toward her. She threw Drake a thumbs-up, and he walked toward the corner, leaving her alone as the steps grew close.

Ree stepped back and smiled, then dropped to a neutral expression. *How do I play this? Happy to see him, angry at his continued jackassery? Compassionate and empathetic for his obviously intense situation?*

The door creaked open, swinging on the when-were-you-last-oiled? hinges.

Standing in the doorway, Eastwood looked tired, even worse than Drake. His hair was mussed, his shirt was stained by what might have been sweet-and-sour sauce but was probably blood, his pants were rumpled, and his face was mottled with purple and blue bruises. The way he held himself made Ree think he might have other bruises elsewhere. *What put him through the wringer?*

"Thanks for answering the door."

Eastwood sighed. "What do you want?"

"I think we owe it to each other to sit down and talk like vaguely adult-type people."

"I'm busy," Eastwood said.

"No, really?" *Snark not helping now, girlie.* "Sorry. Ten minutes?"

Still holding the door, Eastwood settled his weight onto his right leg. He curled his lip, considering, then stepped back, leaving the door open for her. He turned and walked back inside slowly. Which was when Ree saw the blaster he carried in his right hand. *He'd probably been ready to blow me away, or was that for someone or something else?*

Ree walked down the stacks and stopped in front of Eastwood's wall of screens. She turned and saw him put the blaster down and pick up a thermos of something that she hoped was caffeine and not booze.

"Do you have the fifth soul?" she asked. No reason to beat around the bush. Well, there were plenty of reasons, but if he'd already done the deal, then what was the point?

"No."

"Do you have a lead?"

"Are you here to stop me?" Eastwood asked, crossing his arms and sitting on the desk, his back to the dozen screens that showed *Star Trek* reruns, CNN, and on one screen, a live-updating RSS feed that included Pearson PD, what looked like voice-to-text transcripts of a suicide hotline, and several other emergency services.

Ree waved at the screens. "I killed the Muse. Your chances of a natural suicide that fits the bill today are what, a million to one?"

Eastwood's nostrils flared, and with the puffiness around his eyes, it looked like he could start to cry. "If I don't deliver, Branwen will be tortured for eternity."

Ree stepped toward Eastwood. Even sitting on the desk, he was taller, but she did her best to up the menace factor. "So you'll condemn five innocents to take her place?"

Eastwood exhaled, his brow set as he waited a second. "Yes."

"And when she gets back, what will she do when she finds out what you did?"

Eastwood looked like a petulant child. The same look Ree had used a hundred times on her father and saw little kids use every day to get a cookie from their parents at the café.

"It'll be too late then. No one would willingly go back. She'll learn to forgive me," he said.

He's just another hurt lover missing the one who got away. Shit, who of us doesn't?

"I don't know. You make her out to be pretty saint-tacular. Why do you get to make this choice for her, to say that her life is worth more than five children?"

Eastwood's mouth flexed like he was about to say something but swallowed it instead. "I don't have to explain myself. Are you here to help or to lecture me?"

"Are you going to be a petulant selfish ass, or are you going to listen to reason?" Ree regretted the harshness as soon as she finished, but damnit, she was in the right. *Moral high ground, population = me.* Ree didn't want to live in a world where sacrificing a bunch of kids was something the good guys did. "Why did you even get me involved if you were dealing in crap like this? Did you think I wouldn't find out what you were up to?"

Eastwood shook his head. "I could tell in the alley that you weren't going to walk away without an explanation. I sent you to the Moorelys' to put the fear of God in you, but you had the bad luck to get jumped by that Atavist and ended up pissed off instead. By then I knew you were too dug in. And I thought maybe you'd want to help me even after finding out."

"What the hell makes you think I would ever—" Ree paused to fume. "Ever help you do that to those kids?"

Eastwood's eyes lit up with anger, and he growled, launching off the desk and walking away from her. "She told me not to do this, but if you're not going to listen, then I don't give a flying frak."

Hey, what the who now? What's he talking about?

He took another few steps, then turned back to face her. "Branwen nic Catrin was her name here, in the magical underground. But she was born Sionnan Casey."

By Lucas's Force Ghost . . .

Mom?

Ree crash-landed through a dozen emotions, skidding across surprise, disbelief, anger, relief, guilt, and settling again on anger.

"What? *What? Are you fucking kidding me?* You knew my mother, were trying to bring her back, and you waited until now to tell me?" Ree took a step toward Eastwood, her ears hot. "Why would she tell you not to say anything? And while we're at it, why the hell did she leave the first time? My dad nearly died when she left. He put his life together piece-by-LEGO-sized piece after she walked out on us, and for what? So she could play Jedi with a hacker burnout?"

Eastwood backed up onto the desk, hands up to placate her. "Slow down. I can't answer eight questions all at once."

"Then get started."

"I can do you one step better." Eastwood picked through a pile of papers and hardware on the desk and handed her a cube.

"What's this, a holocron?" she asked, turning the cube over in her hands.

"Not quite. This has a USB port." Eastwood plugged the cube in and ran his fingers over one of the desk's many keyboards. Ree sat in one of Eastwood's cushy chairs, dead tired but with a strange energy running through her.

The wall of monitors all went black. A moment later, they showed her mother against a blue background. She was older than Ree remembered, maybe mid-forties. Her brown hair was pulled back in a complicated braid. She wore simple cloth-spun clothes and a leather vest. Her face was pale, her eyes bloodshot.

This could be a fake, Ree thought.

"Hello, Ree. I've tried to record this message, I swear, a hundred times, but I can't get the words right. I should have sent cards, presents; I should have been there for you, and I miss you every day. I miss you and Julio both, but I couldn't stay.

"I stopped doing magic when your father and I settled down. I knew I couldn't risk anything happening to Julio and then to you. But I couldn't stop being who I was. Every TV show, every commercial, every book and song pulled at me, begged me to fall into it. And when I did, the next show called. I kept shifting, my mind rearranging with each new input. Some Geekomancers can handle the changes, but not me. I was too much a specialist, I couldn't keep up."

Ree's doubt fell away like the years, and she felt like a kid again. She wanted to reach out, to touch her, to have her mother gather her up in her arms and make the hurt go away. But she was gone, and the only way to get her back was unthinkable.

Her mother looked away from the camera, wiping her eyes. "A friend called it genre-schizophrenia, and it nearly drove me mad. I couldn't cut you off from the world, couldn't tell Julio that the stories that had brought us together were making me unhinged. I couldn't . . . I did my best, tried to fend off the barrage, but I couldn't stand it anymore."

"That's crap!" Ree said, turning to Eastwood. "Isn't it? I've been doing this for a week, and none of that has happened."

"Keep listening, Ree," was all he said.

". . . working to protect people here, and I hope you will forgive me. I told Eastwood to help me stay away, because I don't want your life to go off the rails like mine did. Once you get into this world, it's nearly impossible to get out without losing everything about yourself.

"But if you're listening to this, something went wrong, either that or I need to kick Eastwood's ass. And he knows I can." Ree's mother smiled at that, and looking over, Ree saw Eastwood's cheeks flush.

"He'll help you as much as he can, but the best thing he can do is to help you stay out of this messed-up marvel of an occult underground. Everyone has screwed-up relationships, short life expectancies, and a crap insurance plan. So there you go, the completely unromanticized, no-shit-it's-scary introduction to the world of magic and Geekomancy. I'm sorry it isn't like *Star Wars* or *Princess Bride* or anything where the good guys always win in the end and the girl gets to ride off or fly off with the handsome rogue in the great vest."

"Wow, Mom. Bummer much?" Ree said, trying to keep her cool.

Sionnan continued. "Bummer, I know."

Ree laughed. *I really am your kid.* She hugged the cube to her chest and remembered the way her mother smelled. Lavender and rosemary, from the shampoo and soap.

"I can't tell you what to do or how to live your life. I just hope that whatever you choose, you trust in yourself and bring all of your energy to it like you've done with everything so far. I wish I were here with you right now, that I never had to leave."

A tear beaded at the corner of her eye, then trickled down to her mouth. "Please tell your father that I love him and that I'm sorry."

Sionnan touched something underneath the camera, and the video feed cut off.

Ree sniffed, her nose snotting up worse than when she'd first seen the end of *Star Trek II: The Wrath of Khan*. She'd been six, lying across the laps of her parents.

Well, crap. What am I supposed to do with that?

"I'm not going to stop, Ree." A quiver worked its way into Eastwood's voice, his steadiness faltering.

He doesn't want to do it, Ree thought. She stood, moving in at an angle, trying to get a bead on the man. She threw back her shoulders, drew herself up to her full height. *I can talk him out of this.*

"What do you think my mom will say when she hears what you did to get her back? Do you think she'll give you a big kiss and say thanks? I know my mom, maybe not as well as you, but all of those shows and movies you shared, the ones that I never knew tore her apart, they were all about the heroic few fighting for the many, not *fucking over the little guy to win.*"

Ree wiped a tear out of her eye as she stared down Eastwood. "You do this, and you're the bad guy, twirly mustache and all. And I'll have to stop you."

Eastwood stood, defensive. His own eyes were teary. His nostrils flared, and he stepped forward. "I've shown you what you needed to see. I could blast where you stand. Or you could join me. And when it's done, you'll have your mother back. And *then* she can judge me however she likes."

Ree stood and closed on Eastwood. "Screw that. If I knock your ass out and tie you up to your stacks, you miss the deadline, and the Duke gets nothing."

"You're going to take me on here, in my own home?" Eastwood laughed.

"This stuff works for me as well as you. And you can't afford to waste me—how would you explain that to my mom? So, you're going to back the fuck down, and we're going to figure out a different way to get her back." Ree gestured to the stacks, drawing his attention to the shelves as she pushed a button on the smartphone in her pocket, dialing Drake.

Anger flashed across Eastwood's eyes, and he straightened his posture to loom over Ree. "Don't you think I've already been down this path? I didn't exactly jump directly to this bargain, kid. I spent the last two years of my life looking for a way to get her back." His voice broke. "One of those attempts nearly got me killed. Every time I got close, the Duke showed up and handed me my ass. And when I was beaten and broken, he'd offer this bargain or that bargain. The only way I can get her back is on the Duke's terms. This is my last chance, Ree."

Ree reached for her knife and Eastwood grabbed her hand.

It's on now. Ree shot her left hand under Eastwood's right and wrapped him up into an arm-bar, pushing down to knock the larger man off balance. Eastwood spun and ripped the knife out of her hand as he broke distance.

Ree pulled out her cell and shouted, "Get in here now!"

She ducked behind one of the stacks and pulled out an oft-reused prop gun. It looked like it dated all the way back to *Aliens*. She flipped off the safety and clicked the gun over to three-round bursts.

She turned, looking for Eastwood, then aimed down, firing a burst at his feet. The geek held up a handful of gaming cards, and her shots ricocheted off of a dome that flashed with their impacts and disappeared. One of the cards shredded in his hand, but he still held a dozen.

Eastwood raised his blaster in his other hand, and Ree ducked behind the stacks and resumed running.

Well, crap. She grabbed the first thing off the shelf, hoping it would serve her better. It was a plush dragon with green fur and a red felt tongue. Ree had no idea what it did outside of being cute.

Yeah, no. She tossed the dragon over her shoulder and circled around toward the door, praying that her backup would show up and *soon*. Behind her, a plume of flame shot ten feet in the air.

Too late now. Ree kept running.

Eastwood's voice echoed through the room. "If you stop now, I'll let you stay here while I finish, Ree. It doesn't have to go down this way."

"Can you hear yourself? You're one step away from monologuing while holding me over a pit of sharks."

She saw Eastwood halfway down a row of stacks as she dashed by. He had the blaster in one hand, his cards in the other. And he looked pissed.

He fired down the row at her, the shot hitting the wall behind her. She kept running down two more aisles, then stopped and ducked, crawling along looking for another weapon. She crawled past a large box marked BOWLING BALLS—MARVEL and another one labeled CABBAGE PATCH DOLLS and DANGEROUS. Then she found a mannequin with a Wonder Woman outfit, complete with lasso and bracelets.

Score. Ree grabbed the lasso and looped it over her shoulder before pulling the bracelets off the mannequin. She crab-walked on her knees down the row as she slipped on the bracelets. She thought a prayer to her favorite Wonder Woman as she checked over her shoulder to look for Eastwood.

Dear Lynda Carter,
Please be with me in my hour of need. Especially if I don't have to twirl around to get my powers.

Big fan,
Ree

She felt the power hum in the bracelets and lasso in response. Ree rose to her feet at the end of the row and threw her voice to the other side of the room. "Come and get it!"

She listened and looked for Drake, but all she heard was the clomping of Eastwood's boots a row to her left. She pulled the lasso free and gave herself a couple of yards of slack, her left arm up to deflect shots with the bracelet.

Eastwood appeared around the corner of the stacks, and Ree threw the lasso, trying to loop it around his head or at least one of his hands. Eastwood saw the golden lariat coming and dove into a roll, firing as he went.

The bracelets moved on their own on Ree's wrists, intercepting the blaster bolts, which deflected up and away to scorch the concrete walls. Ree jumped forward, lashing out with a roundhouse kick to where Eastwood's head would be as he came out of the roll. Eastwood brought the knife up to cover his face, and Ree twisted on her planted foot, turning the roundhouse into a sidekick, striking him on the side of the head. Eastwood's roll continued, and he caught himself on the wall.

Ree whipped the lasso out again, and it looped loose around Eastwood's knife hand. Ree stepped back and tightened the rope, shouting, "Got you!"

Eastwood didn't stop. He raised his blaster and shot Ree point-blank in the chest. The bracelets twisted her hands, trying to stop the blast, but they were too slow.

The red blast hit the quilt-mail T-shirt she'd forgotten she was even wearing . . . but didn't pierce it.

Still, Ree felt like she'd been hit by a battering ram. She crashed to the ground, hard, and dropped the lasso. Her lungs were empty, and she gasped for air, instinctively curling into a ball.

Owfuckshitowgoddamnbraceletsow.

The quilted shirt-mail had saved her from becoming a geekabob, but her chest still hurt like a mother. When she opened her eyes, Eastwood stood above her, blaster aimed at her head.

"Nice shirt. I've got a trick of my own for these artifacts." Eastwood held up a green lantern power ring. "It's Rayner's, not Jordan's." He shook his head. "Weakness to yellow. How silly. You stay in here until I'm done, and you'll thank me when I bring your mother back to you. If you try to get up and fight, the deal is off."

Eastwood was huffing, and his hand shook as he held the blaster. His power ring let off a green trail of energy, buzzing. At this distance, it wouldn't matter if the ring could negate her shirt. He could take a head shot and he'd never miss, even as fast as she could dodge.

"Get it?" he asked.

By way of response, Ree groaned in pain.

"Good."

Eastwood twisted a knob on the blaster, and the last thing Ree saw were blue rings of light accompanied by a familiar sound.

CHAPTER EIGHTEEN

Did You Get The Name of That Truck?

Ree woke to a swimming, foggy feeling wrapped around her head and set to Shake.

Ow. She risked opening her eyes and saw that she was still in Eastwood's Dorkcave. She tried to sit up and met resistance. She looked down and saw that she'd been tied to one of the shelves with the Wonder Woman lasso. The bracelets were gone. As was her quilted shirt.

Ree twisted in place to feel for her cell phone. The fog kept rumbling around her head, but she squinted and saw her phone on Eastwood's desk.

Ree mumbled to herself, "Okay, what now?" And then realized that talking hurt, hearing hurt, and everything in between hurt.

I need something, something to cut with. And where's Drake?

Ree turned her head slowly and looked around the room.

She saw that the stacks were on lockdown. She hadn't known they *could* lock down. The shelves were covered by metal panels that she assumed collapsed up or down when Eastwood wasn't keeping former protégés from foiling his plans.

Ree blinked a few times, trying to push the fog out of her mind. The screens on Eastwood's wall were off, so there was no chance of emulating anything to get her out of the ties.

Okay, Ree, what are you going to do now? If Drake hasn't shown up by now, then you can't assume he will.

She tried to work her fingers up to the bindings and feel what Eastwood was using. It wasn't cold, so she guessed it was a zip tie instead of a cuff.

Zip ties I can do. She knew from TV that zip ties were never meant for long-term containment. They'd zip-tie you, then throw you in a squad car and cuff you or lock you in. It was the same thing they did with the folks at the various Occupy encampments. But with no one to stop her, Ree had time to bust them.

First she tried to Hulk them off, pulling her wrists apart and flexing her arms. The ties bit into her wrists, and she felt the ties flex, but not enough. She growled as she pulled, but the ties didn't budge, so she gave up, exhaling.

Ow.

Wincing, she wriggled her right hand around to feel the other side of the tie. If she remembered right, they worked like the ties for trash bags. Which meant there was some mechanism that grabbed the ridges on the tie itself, keeping it from sliding out.

She stuck out her tongue and shifted her shoulders, changing the angles until she caught part of the tie on a nail. She exhaled and pushed her wrists open. The ties moved, and when the ridged bar of the tie clicked again, she pulled her left arm out, then shook the zip tie to the ground. She undid the tie at her feet with ease, reaching around and pulling the same trick with the pressure bar, much simpler since this time she could see what she was doing.

"TV, motherfuckers," she said to no one in particular. "Rot your brain, eh?"

Ree pushed herself up and walked over to Eastwood's desk,

rubbing her tender wrists. She had ten missed calls. Nine from Drake and one from Anya. And it was already five-thirty.

Sorry, Anya. Love you, but I don't even have time to catch my breath right now.

She massaged her head as she hit redial to call Drake, hoping he wasn't far away.

"Ahoy?" Drake answered.

"Where are you?"

"Ree?" Drake asked. "By the heavens, what happened?"

Ree walked toward the main door leading outside. "Tons. Where were you?"

"Are you quite all right? It's been hours. I attempted to join you upon your call, but the doors had been barred by some renewed enchantment. I lingered and pursued Mr. Eastwood when he departed. I believe he has noticed me, since we've spent the last hour on a fine bout of cat and mouse. But one doesn't travel with the Mistress for seasons upon seasons without learning that game at the level of champions."

Ree tried the door and saw that it was locked from the outside. *Crap.* "Where are you now?"

"Bearing east, approaching Miner Park."

Ree walked to the side entrance, the one that led up to Eastwood's apartment. "All right. Stay with him, and I'll call you when I'm closer. Assuming I can get out of this place."

The side door was locked, too. Ree circled the room again, trying to pick out other exits from her memory, fighting through the cottony dullness that persisted in her head.

Okay. Inventory. Ree pulled everything out of her pockets as she walked the room, checking her assets. Wallet, money, key cards, credit cards, including one she never used that could work to jimmy a simple lock. Hair ties and the pair of bobby pins she always kept in her hair for weird occasions. *Now we're getting somewhere.*

She tried her jankety lock-picking kit out on the side door, then the front door, and gave up when the credit card broke on the door. *Next time, bring the good kit.*

"Okay, what now?" she said, scanning the room.

She saw a glint of fading sunlight and tracked it across the room to a window, peeking out above a row of shelves. Only the very top of the window was visible behind the closed-off shelves, and it was fifteen feet up. So, all she had to do was climb up the shelf, break the window, and avoid cutting herself open as she crawled out. The window would open out to the side street, so she'd have to make that landing, too.

John McClane never had it easy, either.

Ree scanned the closed-up shelves and ran her hands along the nesting plates, trying them for handholds. *Not going to happen.* She hadn't even thought of rock climbing since middle school, when she was invited to a "leadership" program. She'd since realized it was a "get the shy kids some confidence" program, with team-building exercises and ropes courses.

The program hadn't made her any new friends, but it had helped some with her fear of heights. After those ten weeks, being twenty feet off the ground didn't make her seize up with terror anymore. She'd never gotten great at the ropes, but she was an expert fort-builder.

Ree went back to Eastwood's desk and grabbed his trash can, fan, and a multi-tool from the top of one of his towers. Then she pulled the bungee cords out from where he'd used them to tie down computer cables or suspend a footrest under his desk. She'd thought it was a great idea when she checked out his work desk the first time, and now she was doubly thankful for his ingenuity. Especially since he used the high-grade ones that were rated for industrial use.

She piled everything in the chair and wheeled it over to the corner at the end of the shelf. She took a couple of slow breaths to clear her head, then started stacking. She put the trash can upside down on the chair, then set the multi-tool to its knife and took the bungees in her left hand. She locked the chair wheels in place and started to climb.

Ree stepped up to the top of the chair, one foot on the trash can. She scanned the wall and stepped up to a foothold. Then she stuck the knife into one of the joints between the metal plates, trying to work it open. She grabbed the knife with both hands, twisting back and forth to open a slot where she could stick a bungee hook in.

After a few more seconds of twisting, she tried to slot the end of a bungee into the hole. Not quite. She used the hook as a lever, trying to open the hole wider. Her legs wobbled a bit, and her head spun, and suddenly, she dropped to the chair and all of her tools clattered to the ground.

Come on. Ree picked everything up and tried again. She climbed up, set her foothold on the wall, and tried the plate. She opened it enough to slide in the hook, letting out a "Woot!" when it locked.

One more. She repeated the process thirty inches to the right, and after dropping back to the chair twice, she set the other hook. Then Ree took the footrest and hooked it back into the bungee cords. They'd stretch a fair amount with her weight, but all she needed was one solid push and she'd pull some *Assassin's Creed* parkour fu to get to the top of the shelf.

Ree grabbed the top of the shelves with both hands and tried to pull herself up. She faltered, and her chin slammed on the corner, making her bite her tongue.

Focus.

Holding on with one hand, Ree tried to curse, stopped because it hurt to talk, and just grunted as she tried to get her other hand back on top of the ledge.

Come the fuck on, Ree thought as she pulled. She kicked out her legs, trying to push off the wall or the stack, anything to get her body up onto the shelf and avoid falling face-first onto the concrete floor.

Her left leg found the wall and she pushed, pulling with her arms. She got her left shoulder on the shelf and pushed again with a foot until her belly slid up over the cold metal.

She huffed there for a few seconds, shaking with adrenaline.

Thank you, Mrs. Haines and company—how's that for leadership?

Ree shimmied on her stomach toward the window, then took off her coat and wrapped it around her left hand. She closed her eyes and turned her face away from the window, breaking through the window with a hammerfist. The glass gave on the first blow, and Ree carefully pulled her hand back through.

Clearing out the rest of the window, she flexed her hand to feel for cuts, then pulled off the coat and checked again. There were several scrapes and little marks, but nothing worth stopping for. She poked her head outside and saw that the drop was only about five feet to the alley.

Rock.

Ree slipped on her jacket again and spun around to stick her legs out the window. She jumped out and took the fall, kneeling into the impact and dropping to her side. She dusted herself off, looked back up at the window, and smiled at her own awesomeness.

After making the executive decision that a triple cappuccino was essential for morale and a functioning brain, Ree made her way across town to Miner Park, sipping her drink.

The little-kid trick-or-treaters were already out as she rode the bus north. Smiling, cautious, or consternated parents followed kids by ones or in packs, bright orange plastic pumpkins already getting full. A kid in a cowboy costume held his pumpkin in both hands, filled to the brim.

Ree thought about what her plans for Halloween had been. Without this ridiculousness, she'd have thrown together a costume for Trollope's Trollops' holiday burlesque. Trollope's Halloween bash was the best of the year, with costume contests, epic decor, and specials on the local pumpkin beer. Sandra would be performing, and Ree would have been watching alongside the Rhyming Ladies and Darren. At one point they'd discussed going as gender-swapped supers: Plastic Woman, Kraven the Huntress, Booster Goldette, and Iron Woman.

Ree had called dibs on Booster Goldette, in honor of the family dog. She ground her teeth at the lost chance, but the sight of children enjoying themselves as they kicked their way through piles of leaves undercut her angst enough that she got her focus back.

Ree took a long sip of her cappuccino.

Eastwood is at least pretending like he knows what to do. So either he's already gotten the fifth soul and didn't tell me, or he has a hunch about where to go for it. She'd been decently armed at Eastwood's, but now all she had was the multi-tool. Drake would have his gear, but no doubt Eastwood had loaded up. Which meant that a head-on confrontation would be dangerous, even with 2–1 odds.

Ree rocked lazily with the motion of the bus, holding a handrail as she zoned out, facing the window. *So we can wait until he starts to do whatever it'll take to make the deal, or we can try to stop him before.*

Option one would involve demon lord danger, which seemed like a terrible idea. But Eastwood would be distracted then, whereas he wouldn't be while on the hunt.

Damnit, Mom. Ree spent the rest of the ride spinning her wheels.

Ree hopped off the bus at the corner of Miner Park, near the edge of the city that used to be a rough part of town but had since made its way up in the world. Bryan's family lived a few blocks away, and she'd been to a few big parties not far from here thanks to Priya's connections. The park itself was several square blocks, large enough to hide in but not so big that you could stay hidden.

She dumped the empty cappuccino in a trash can at the edge of the park and called Drake.

The call rang through to voicemail. As Ree started talking,

her phone buzzed with another call. It wasn't from Drake, it was from Bryan's cell.

"Hello?" she said as she picked up.

"Ree? It's Bryan. Aidan's gone." Bryan's voice was thick with worry. "Amy called and said he left the house in a hurry, with a bag."

Ree's heart sank. She had a solid guess where this was going, and that was Nowhere Good. "Where'd he go?"

Bryan was rushed, far more panicky than his normal mellow self. "I don't know. But with the mission you mentioned, and the time you've spent with him, I figured . . . The police won't do anything yet, Amy's home with the kids, and I can't close the store."

"I've got a lead, Bryan, it's a wicked-bad time."

"Please, Ree. I called my other friends, but they're up to their neck, saying the spirit world is gonzo with All Hallows' Eve and some explosion at a transport nexus."

Ooops.

"Find him, Ree. You're my only hope."

And . . . the trump card. Ree sighed. "Of course, Bryan. I'll do everything I can."

CHAPTER NINETEEN

Be Vewy Vewy Quiet, We're Hunting Cowboys

Miner Park was already dim, lit only by the intermittent lampposts and the wan light of the full moon. Ree had stomped through most of the grounds, and she was getting worried. First she had jogged through the clearing where Aidan and his friends played boffer LARPs during the summer. Then she'd wound her way through the path that he'd mentioned taking Diana along for their second date. She passed several bundled-up couples and a few joggers, but no Aidan. She walked through the basketball court and the playground, scanning the small stands of trees around the edge of the court.

Nothing. Where the hell are you, Aidan? Where else would you go to be alone?

Ree pushed through the loose brush in the thickest wooded area, looking into the trees and pulling apart the bushes. She already had scratches on her hands, legs, and face, even with her gloves, boots, and scarf.

He might not even be in the park—but where else would he go?

Ree stopped to fire off yet another text message to Aidan. She'd called ten times and texted fifteen. She wished that

Eastwood were on her side, that he could ping cell-phone towers and track Aidan with Big Brother hacker fu, while all she had were her feet and an out-of-time dandy tracking the man who should be helping her.

Ree pushed a sparsely leaved branch out of the way and saw something black moving in the distance. She made her way past several more branches and saw the image: someone in a black trench, head down, making their way through the trees, bound for the pond in the corner of the park.

Either that's Eastwood, or another member of the trench-coat mafia has decided to take a very coincidental stroll. Ree scanned the branches for Drake but saw only the one figure making its way. She quickened her pace, pulling her scarf up to cover her face as she moved through nettles and bushes.

Ree closed distance on Eastwood, then saw him turn and notice her. She heard him say something along the lines of "frell," and he began running, swatting branches out of his way.

Eastwood broke through the edge of the woods, and his shape faded quickly in the distance. Ree heard the sound of the river that fed out of the pond, bubbling out to the east, and started huffing as she took huge steps through the brush. She pushed aside branches and stepped over bushes, thankful for her stompy boots.

"Eastwood, stop!" she shouted as she broke through the tree line and took a look around.

The pond was twenty feet across, dotted with fallen leaves in orange, brown, and red. The river flowed down from it for twenty yards or so before emptying out into a drain that took the water beneath the eastern edge of the park.

On the opposite side of the pond, sitting on a bench with an orange prescription bottle in his hands, was Aidan Blin.

Eastwood was standing beside him, speaking in a low voice.

Even twenty feet away, Ree could feel Capital-M magic rolling off of the prescription bottle. It hit her like an echo of the cold burn she'd felt when the Muse had taken a chunk out of her soul.

Oh, no you don't. Not him, not now, and sure as hell not while I'm around. "Get the hell away from him!" Ree shouted at the top of her lungs. She ran around the pond, hoping that Drake would hear all of the commotion and come in the nick of time.

I've got to get Eastwood away from Aidan, or at least get rid of that bottle, she thought.

That won't be hard at all, replied the sarcasm dripping out of her mind.

Eastwood lifted a blaster in her direction while leaning in to Aidan. "Go home, Ree. This is his choice."

Aidan looked up at Ree, tears in his eyes, before turning back to Eastwood. "She's my friend. I don't know you." Aidan's voice was strange, distorted. *Is that the bottle, too? Does it have some kind of lock on him?*

"I'm trying to help you, Aidan." Eastwood's own eyes were bloodred, his movements jerky. He looked like he'd either pounded a six-pack of energy drinks or just come through a fight with a jackalope. *Maybe that's Drake's doing—but where is he?*

Ree took two more steps along the edge of the pond, and Eastwood's gun moved to track her.

She stopped in place and put her hands up by her shoulders. "Put the gun down, Eastwood. Let's talk like civilized nerds." She'd charged up with *The Matrix* on her way to the park, but since the fates were kicking her ass, it had faded by the time she saw Eastwood, and it wasn't like he was going to wait for her to refresh.

Eastwood waited for Aidan. "Put the gun down," the boy said. Eastwood holstered the blaster and knelt beside Aidan, speaking sotto voce. Ree hurried around the pond and took a seat on the bench next to Aidan.

"What can I do to help?" she asked. *And sit still long enough for me to get that bottle.*

Aidan doubled over, sobbing. Ree heard a muffled word that she guessed was "nothing."

Ree moved slowly at first, reaching down for the bottle. Eastwood slapped her hand away. Ree shot Eastwood the nastiest look she could manage. He met her gaze, his bloodshot eyes unyielding. He showed the blaster again. She didn't trust him to have it set on stun.

Ree wrapped an arm around Aidan, hoping that physical connection would let her break through whatever the bottle was doing. "Did he tell you why he's here, Aidan?" she asked. "He's let four kids be pushed to kill themselves, and he wants you to be the fifth, all so he can cheat death himself."

A cold wind howled through the trees behind her and into the clearing, blowing leaves up into a spiral around the three of them.

Aidan shook with the cold, and a moment later, he pulled himself up and looked at Ree, holding the bottle with white knuckles.

His voice broke as he said, "Diana dumped me when I told her I didn't get into Stanford. She said I was a waste of space—she dumped me to go to Stanford with some guy she's only met once—she knew it for six months and never told me. I screwed it all up."

The air went out of Ree's lungs. She'd guessed Diana would break it off, but the girl didn't have to be a punk about it. And Ree couldn't exactly comfort him with Eastwood hanging around like the fucking Grim Reaper and that bottle pushing Aidan to the edge.

Eastwood leaned in. His eyes were sad, but his face was hard-set, determined. "I promise I can help you take the pain away, Aidan. And you'll be helping someone who was loved, a hero who died too soon."

Ree nearly hissed at Eastwood, balking at the stalemate. Eastwood was loaded for bear, so Ree knew she couldn't take him straight up, especially with Aidan in the line of fire. And yet if he thought he could get away with gunning her down or knocking her out, he would have done it by now. Which meant that he'd lose credibility with Aidan.

Which meant her best play was trying to talk Aidan down.

"Plenty of people love you, Aidan. Your parents love you, the twins love you, your friends love you. If you give up now, your story will be unfinished, and even if it brought back Gary Gygax, Steve Jobs, and Mahatma Gandhi, it wouldn't be worth throwing your life away."

"I don't care," Aidan said. "I don't want to feel anything." He fingered the prescription bottle, hands shaking.

Shit shit shit. Ree's mind flailed. She had to pick every word exactly right, say it exactly the way he needed to hear it, and beat out a shoulder devil. *How can Eastwood honestly push a sixteen-year-old boy to suicide? Is he that broken? Or is he just honest about it?*

Ree said, "Breakups suck. They always suck. They suck if you're the one doing the breaking up. They suck even if you've only been going out for three weeks. I've dumped, I've been dumped, and I've had relationships stop before they started. No matter how it happens, it sucks for a while. But it always gets better, because there's plenty more to live for. If you quit now, it'll never get better. Just worse." She jabbed a finger at Eastwood. "He's trading these souls to a *demon*, Aidan, a real honest-to-goodness demon, the deal-making, soul-taking kind, not the flappy-skin Clem kind. You think you'll just blink out like a light when you go?"

Ree reached out a hand and pulled Aidan's chin up to face her. "The way you're feeling now will be a happy fucking memory compared to when that demon gets its hands on you. Who are you going to trust here? I've known you for three years, and this asshole rolled up five minutes ago offering you the coward's way out."

Aidan's eyes went wide, and Ree prayed she was cutting through all the pain to get him to wake up.

Eastwood intruded on the moment. "I can guarantee that the Duke won't do anything to you, Aidan. He wants your energy, not your soul." He was unable to fit himself into the intimate moment, uncomfortably shifting between kneeling and standing, trying to cover Ree without getting close enough that she could jump him.

"That sounds pretty damn fishy to me," Ree said. "What do you think?"

Aidan stood and pushed them away. "Leave me alone, both of you."

Ree snatched at the bottle, but the teen had a death grip on it. Eastwood fired a shot into the ground by her feet, and Ree backed off, cursing under her breath.

Aidan started on a path down to the pond and knelt, looking into the broken mirror of the water.

Ree followed him. "I'm not leaving you, Aidan. You need to hear that you are important. You're not a waste of space, you never have been. Diana is a callous ass who was trying to justify her terrible decision."

Eastwood took a step toward Aidan, hands open. "I'll leave, Aidan, but Ree has to leave, too. It's your decision, not hers. You have the power here."

Ree took a couple of wide steps to get into Aidan's peripheral vision. "If you have choice, then you have hope. Eastwood is desperate. If he doesn't get his way, he'll pull out his blaster and try to blow me away like he did when I confronted him earlier today. Do you see the burn marks on my shirt? He tried to kill me for getting in his way."

Aidan looked back toward Eastwood. "Is that true?"

Ree heard anger in his voice and gave a silent cheer. *Anger is good.* She felt the aura from the bottle dim and recede, and she jumped in. "Good. Be pissed. You have every right to be pissed—at Diana, at Eastwood, hell, at your parents for not being rich graduates of Stanford. Anger means that things matter, that life matters."

Eastwood pointed at Ree. "She threatened me, and I defended myself. And the woman I'm saving? It's Ree's mother. The one who left and broke her. I'm trying to rescue her mom from hell, and I asked her to help me, but she's afraid to get her hands dirty to do it."

Ree snapped back at Eastwood. "I think convincing kids to kill themselves gets more than just your *hands* dirty, you son of a bastich."

Aidan pursed his lips, thinking.

Come on, Aidan. I can't take him in a fight when he's loaded up, especially since Drake is who-knows-where. He should be here by now, which means he's probably hurt or dead. Ree searched Eastwood's face for answers, trying to find catches of guilt or worry that would give him away.

Aidan stood to his full height, looked at the bottle, and dropped it in the pond. He turned, pointing to Eastwood. "You. Leave." His voice was his own again.

Ree barely restrained a shout of joy.

Eastwood's face darkened. He turned the blaster on Aidan. "Sorry, kid. Not going to happen."

"See?" Ree said, pushing forward to interpose herself between Eastwood and Aidan, who stumbled back, holding her wrist tightly. *If he needs them to be suicides, how is he going to force it? Or maybe the Duke doesn't give a shit about what kinds of souls he gets.*

Ree leveled her best I Am Intimidating glower at Eastwood and spoke with determination. "You're going to have to finish the job with me before I'll let you touch him. And if you kill me when you swore to protect me, do you think my mom will give you a chance to explain yourself?"

Another gust blew through the clearing, flipping leaves in spinning routes between her and her adversary. The wind rolled over the pond and whooshed out the other side.

I have to end this fast and get Aidan home.

Ree said, "Drop the gun and back off. And then maybe I

won't come after you. But if you try anything, or if you come after me or any of my friends again, all of the revenge movies in the world will pale next to the shit I'll do to you."

"That won't help Aidan," Eastwood said, advancing on her.

Ree inched forward. "Nothing is going to help Aidan. Except me." *That's right, get closer. Let me within range of that blaster.*

"May I play as well?" came a voice from Ree's left. *That better be who I think it is.*

Drake Winters stepped through the tree line, brushing leaves and brambles out of his coat. His left eye was swollen with a bruise, and his coat was burned just above the hip.

"I apologize for my tardiness, Ms. Ree. This ruffian bushwhacked me as I was tailing him." He hefted his Aetheric Rifle and leveled it at Eastwood. "I am rather inclined to return the favor, if you do not terribly mind."

Eastwood turned his blaster on Drake and circled around toward Ree, trying not to be flanked.

"Now I feel left out. Where's *my* phallus?" Ree asked.

Aidan laughed, and Ree smiled. "You're done, Eastwood. Beat it," she said.

"Just saying that doesn't make it true. The fop can try me, and you'll have another body to handle." Eastwood turned to Aidan. "You can end this now, Aidan. With those pills, you can make the whole situation go away. Everyone else goes home, Ree gets her mother, and I get my life back."

"Go to hell," Ree said.

"I've been there, kid. I fought my way to the obsidian gates and tore through a dozen demons, and it got me frak-all. You're in way over your head, and yet you think you know everything."

"Go away, all of you!" Aidan shouted, twitching nervously.

"No." Eastwood fired off a shot at Drake, who dove to one side. The blast blew off a tree limb.

Ree jumped forward, hoping to tackle Eastwood before he could fire another shot. "Get into cover!" she shouted to Aidan.

Eastwood strafed away from Ree, tracking on Drake and firing again as the gadgeteer came up to his knees. Drake aimed his rifle as Eastwood's shot bounced off of a shimmering field that was visible for a split second in front of the adventurer. An amulet around Drake's neck shimmered the same color, and then he returned fire.

Now, that's what I'm talking about.

Ree leaned back and dropped her pace as the shot came in, and Eastwood pivoted in place with *Matrix*-level speed. The shot went past Eastwood's shoulder and flew off into the distance.

Ree leaned forward and jumped at Eastwood with a roundhouse to the shoulders. Without Geekomancy, she was stuck with her own skill set, which she hoped was better kung fu than what Eastwood had. *As long as I can get that gun out of his hands.*

Eastwood ducked forward under her kick, but not at Matrix speed. *His tricks are all one-offs, and I can fight like this all day.*

Ree flew over him, turning through her kick so as to land facing the older geek. Eastwood came up with a flashing knife, which she caught on the thick wrist cuff of her buff jacket as she landed. She felt a small bite from the cut but ignored it as she wrapped her hand around Eastwood's wrist, trying to lock him in a chicken wing and make him drop the knife.

Eastwood spiraled with the hold and continued to cut, piercing her coat to draw blood inside her wrist. Ree let go and threw her arm out, away from the knife. Eastwood dropped from her sight as she winced with pain, and she saw him on the ground, Drake beside him.

The older geek kicked for Drake's head, which Drake blocked by ducking behind his forearms. Eastwood scrambled back as Ree followed, trying to land a quick low kick. But Eastwood scrambled with grace that belied his potbellied form and found his feet, firing a blaster bolt at Drake and slashing up and to his left to tear through Ree's jeans and slice open her shin. Ree fell to the ground, holding her leg, and she heard Drake hit the ground as well.

Ree looked through pain-lidded eyes for Eastwood. The geek leveled the blaster at Drake, but when he pulled the trigger, the gun made a whining sound instead of firing. Ree smiled through the pain. *Ha! Out of juice.* As Eastwood pistol-whipped Drake in the head, his eyes glazed with rage. Drake slumped to the ground, limp.

Eastwood tossed away the blaster, saying, "Pudu."

Watching Drake loll on the ground, Ree's cheeks flushed, ears getting hotter. *I didn't need any more reasons to kick your ass, but you have to keep giving them to me.*

Looking up at Eastwood, she saw nothing but cold fury in his eyes. "I gave you more than enough chances to leave me alone, Ree. Branwen will never know what happened to you."

Ree lashed out with her good leg and caught Eastwood behind the knee, sending him stumbling. *I have to get to Aidan, but I can't leave Eastwood alone with Drake. He's still got the knife and who knows what else.*

Ree didn't know how much time Eastwood needed for the ritual or where he needed to be. She didn't have the time or the information, just a desperate man chasing her with a blade.

Ree crawled over to Drake and picked up his rifle, hoping that it had some juice left after all the use of the past day.

As she sighted the rifle on Eastwood, he threw the knife at her. She ducked under the flash of silver, which hit wrong and bounced off the hard bark of the tree instead of sticking. Realigning her shot down the barrel of the rifle, she saw only a puff of smoke where Darth Geek had been.

"Ninja vanish? Fucking hell." Ree looked around the clearing for Aidan. *Gone. Thanks, universe. I needed that salt on my wound.*

"Drake?" she called as she crawled over to him. He moaned in response, curling up into a ball.

"Get up, we've got to follow him."

Drake's voice was dreamy, distant. "No, Mistress, I cannot."

Sounds like a concussion or worse. Shit, shit. The longer I leave Eastwood alone with Aidan, the more likely it is that everything will go straight-to-the-pole south.

"Come on, Drake. Your *Mistress* needs you."

After a moment, Drake grunted and uncurled himself, his eyes blinking open. A wave of realization hit, and he exhaled. "By stars, that hurt." He spoke haltingly, his focus somewhere else.

"Looks bad, and you probably have a concussion. But Eastwood's gone, and so is Aidan, so we've gotta go." Ree stood and tried to help Drake up. But with one leg for balance and no help from Drake, she pulled him up only to sitting.

Adrenaline won't last long, girl. Vamos, rápido.

"You've got a first-aid kit in here somewhere, right?" Ree asked, gesturing to Drake's coat.

"Kit. Yes. It's . . ." Drake fumbled at his coat, and Ree waited for a second before pawing through it herself.

"I'll buy you dinner when we've made it through this."

Drake stared up to the darkening sky. "We dined with the crown princess of Jupiter."

Ree cupped his chin with one hand. "Oh, boy. You are way out of it. I can't leave you like this."

She had to follow Eastwood, protect Aidan, and get Drake to a hospital, none of which went together with any ease. She could call an ambulance for Drake, but he probably didn't have insurance and might get himself sent to the psych ward if the concussion made it hard for him to remember he wasn't in the 19th century anymore.

She found a canvas bag with bandages, glass bottles of pills labeled in scrawling longhand, as well as tweezers and a scalpel. She took out some acetaminophen and got Drake to dry-swallow it, since she wagered the crap in the pond water would be worse for him than the blow to the head. Then she took some bandages for herself. She pulled up her pants leg and slathered some antiseptic over the cut, restraining a scream. She bound the wound with some gauze, wincing all the while.

Tick-tock, Ree, she thought. *But you can't just leave him like this.*

Ree pulled out her phone and hoped that the little red sliver of battery would hold on awhile longer. She dialed Bryan's cell. After three rings, he picked up.

"Bryan? It's Ree. Big shit's going down. I was just with Aidan, but so was Eastwood. They're both gone, but I can't leave Drake. He's hurt, probably a concussion."

"Wait, what?" Bryan said.

"Drive now, questions later. Get to Miner Park right now."

Bryan said, "I'm on my way home. I was going to help look for Aidan."

"Help by coming and getting my friend. We're at the pond in the northeast corner of the park. Got it?"

"I don't know how to handle a concussion, Ree," Bryan admitted.

"He's a tough guy, but you need to go to a hospital—he needs someone to go with him, or they'll think he's totally jacked or a psych case. I have to follow Eastwood now, Bryan, so get over here ASAP."

Bryan sputtered, and Ree could imagine him on the other end of the line, scratching his head.

She spoke in the calmest voice she could manage. "I'm going after your son, like you asked, but to do so, I need you to come and handle my friend. There's no time."

"Okay, I'm on my way," Bryan said.

"Great. Now I get to do more impossible things. Wish me luck."

"Good—"

Ree hung up the phone before she could hear the end of Bryan's response. Her phone beeped at her, begging to be charged. She dropped the phone back into her jacket, then grabbed Drake to haul him up against a tree.

She produced a flashlight from Drake's bag and flicked it in his eyes; both pupils were wide but about equal. She squeezed his hand as she popped some painkillers for herself and stood, wincing when she put weight on her bad leg.

She limped around the clearing, looking for any trace of Aidan or Eastwood. She tried to talk herself up, get her adrenaline racing again: "Bruce Willis time, all right? Go Linda Hamilton on this shit. Think action hero. Come on."

She left the flashlight on, illuminating Drake, then scanned the tree line and tried to make out shapes in the woods. She heard the crashing of hurried bodies to her left, and turned to see what looked like Eastwood's trench coat flapping through the distant brush.

"There's one. But would Aidan go that way?" Ree's mind raced down her best-guess list of Aidan's favorite hangouts. Other than the park and the café, she knew he went to the library. *No good, not enough privacy. Maybe the Burger Bin?* She remembered him talking about role-playing there a few times before the owners "kindly" asked him and his friends to find another place to game. And Aidan had a Burger Bin soda cup at least half the times he came to the café.

If I'm wrong, I'm screwed. Better not be wrong, then.

She flailed for hope, dialing Aidan's number and repeating "Come on, come on" to the phone as she walked to the edge of the park. Ree scanned the street as the phone rang. No answer. But it rang through instead of going straight to voicemail.

The phone was on.

For all that meant.

She could think of as many bad possibilities as good, so she discarded the lot of them and talked to Aidan's voicemail.

Her voice caught in her throat as the pressure fell on her again to say just the right thing. "It's Ree. Call me back. Your family is worried sick, and so am I. I want to help. Please call me."

The street held scattered packs of teenage trick-or-treaters; the little kids were all home now that the sun was down and the cold of night was rolling in. Some looked older, likely college kids heading to parties. But no Aidan. No Eastwood.

Ree started down the street, pushing past the wall of pain that slammed into her each time she put weight on her injured leg. She got to the corner and turned left on instinct, deciding without knowing why that she was going to Burger Bin. Chances were she was wrong, but it was a damn sight better than doing nothing, and if she stopped now, she would collapse.

She kept hobbling down the street, promising herself she'd get an absurdly overloaded milkshake if she could make it to the restaurant, Aidan or no. Unless there was a line, which there would be. *Damnit. But he will be there, and there will be a milkshake. Magical thinking will actually work for me this time. There will be a milkshake. Or at least a soda. And Aidan, yes.*

Ree had always been ravenous after sparring classes at her Taekwondo studio, and she was finding that real fights left her feeling pretty much the same. Only with more accompanying nausea. Strangely, the nausea and hunger didn't cancel each other out; they just kind of sat there, coexisting and making her feel like she'd be sorry if she didn't eat and maybe worse if she did.

People passed her on the street, but none of them looked at her twice. People let a lot slide on Halloween, and she'd looked more bedraggled and torn up from drinking in previous years without anyone asking questions.

The irony of a life-and-death soul-bargaining, demon-dealing event going down without so much notice as a police cruiser was not lost on Ree. *If only the real ghouls took the day off, like they did in* Buffy.

When Ree rounded the corner leading to the Burger Bin, she saw that the line was out the door and most of the way down the sidewalk. Nearly everyone who was in line was also in costume, and Ree realized she must have been so caught up in the case that she'd uncharacteristically missed whatever Halloween promo the chain had put out.

Her phone beeped, and for a desperate second, she hoped it was Aidan calling back, but when she looked down, she realized it was her OMG You Are Running Out of Battery 4 Realz OK? sound instead of the Pavlovian life-validation of the Someone Is Calling You sound.

Ree sneaked around the line, scanning faces and bodies as she made her way through the costumed crowd. She didn't think Aidan would stop long enough to wait in line, but she was going to be as thorough as she could possibly manage. She passed vampires wearing glitter, bespectacled brunette boys with lightning-bolt makeup, sexy nurses, sexy witches, and sexy firewomen (the last one earned an extra-raised eyebrow and rolled eyes), but no Depressed Teenage Sons of Gamer Café Owners.

She squeezed her way inside to scan the rest of the line as well as the crowded tables and booths.

The restaurant was loud, filled with dozens of conversations between excited kids, harried parents, scenester kids, and overworked Burger Bin employees, who put up an impressive front of professionalism behind their purple hats and aprons.

Ree walked down the narrow side room, peeking into each booth and ignoring the suspicious stares she got in return. She reached the end with no success and turned about-face.

As her vision tracked across the full-length windows and through them to the outside, she saw a familiar mop of hair. She stopped, looked again, and saw Aidan weaving his way through the crowd on the far side of the street.

Thank you, Jeebus, Ree thought, then pushed her way through the crowd to get toward the one and only door.

She said "excuse me" and "sorry" on a constant loop as she went, trying to keep her eyes on Aidan and to look out for Eastwood.

Ree slid between two Power Rangers and broke out of the waiting crowd, her stomach pining for a milkshake or for any kind of food to keep her going.

She checked the traffic and dashed across the street, calling, "Aidan!"

Aidan's head shot up, startled, and he turned to watch Ree as she sprinted across the street.

Ree slowed to shimmy between two cars parked far closer than was comfortable, and swung around a parking meter to face the younger geek. She wrapped Aidan up in as fierce a hug as she could manage. Her forehead rested against his cheek with a flash of cognitive dissonance as she remembered meeting a four-ten Aidan during her first week of work at the café.

"I'm so glad you're all right. Let's get you home, okay? Your family is worried sick."

Aidan pulled away from Ree, but she held tight.

"Lo siento, mi amigo." Ree used the affected bad Spanish of their in-jokes, then returned to English, saying "no can do."

Aidan chuckled despite himself. "You suck."

Ree squeezed Aidan. "No," she said, then continued in her actual Spanish, telling him she was his friend and that he will always appreciate her terrible humor.

They were the quiet island in a river of motion as a crowd of people flowed by, coming up from a subway station.

"Ready to go home?" Ree asked.

"Only if you sneak me some whiskey."

"Just steal some of your dad's. He already knows you do it. And I think he'll understand."

Aidan laughed grudgingly. "Okay."

Ree exhaled fifty pounds of worry. *Hey, Mom. I did it. But what will Eastwood do now?*

CHAPTER TWENTY

Freytag's Shotgun

At the Blin house, there were no monsters. Nor were there any crazed bereaved geeky antiquarians. There were just two tremendously relieved parents and a pair of four-year-old twins who were entirely confused as to why everyone was so worried and why no one had chased them back to bed.

The living room told the story of a boy who never quite left Neverland. He had, however, gotten organized with some help. The long dinner table spent a great deal of time serving as the play surface for role-playing adventures, miniatures battles, and board-game nights, but it spent even more time with tablecloths stained by cereal, pizza sauce, and whatever else the twins consumed with all of the gusto of preschool Wookiees.

The wall was as filled with bookshelves as it could have been without folding space, and Ree still wondered on occasion if Bryan's wife hadn't figured out some way to fit paperbacks inside of hardcovers when arranging the library.

The kitchen was Amy's domain, everything expertly arranged down to the enviable hanging organizer, which held pans, spatulas, and dozens of other tools. Bryan's business was struggling, but Amy's company was chugging along fine, selling supplies to the endless tide of restaurants that flowed through Pearson.

Amy and Bryan were wrapped around their oldest son, both crying. Aidan was a standing lump held up by his parents. On the way home, Ree nearly had to drag the heartbroken boy, but she was pretty sure the danger had passed.

When they arrived, Bryan had told her that Drake had woken up on the way to the hospital and hadn't wanted to go. Bryan had forced him to check in, with strict orders to stay put and avoid violent movement.

So it's just me, Ree thought as she sat with the twins. The kids played halfheartedly, watching their parents and brother.

"Is that a LEGO X-wing?" Ree asked Luke, who sat on her left.

He nodded, and Leia picked up the LEGO Han and Chewie, doing her best Wookiee voice.

Ree was impressed. *That's better than mine.* She breathed deeply, trying to bleed off the tension, pain, and general angst of her last weeks before she dashed back out into the night to find Eastwood and keep him from getting himself killed.

Why should I even bother? asked a voice in her head.

She was taken aback at the thought. *He's grief-stricken. He needs more friends, not fewer.* In the time she'd spent with him, she'd seen him with plenty of acquaintances and associates but no friends. Not even Grognard or Dr. Wells.

But how? He could be back at the Dorkcave, or he could be between two statues on top of an apartment building. *Where did one go to summon a Dork Lord of Hell?*

Ree looked up from the LEGOs, where Luke and Leia were making Wookiee and spaceship sounds to the Blins' wall of media.

She ran through her mental media Rolodex to try to figure out if she could emulate something that would help her find Eastwood.

She could read a book from *Changeling: The Dreaming*, the Eshu kithbook, and try to copy their ability to be in the right place at the right time, but she'd never tried genre emulation off of a book, and a role-playing book at that. *Does the magic require a narrative, or just the concept?*

Too risky. Try that sometime when there aren't lives on the line.

Star Wars could give her a clairvoyant Hail Mary, and a Marauder's Map could tell her where Eastwood was, but for that, she'd need a prop. A replica might not even work. She scanned the DVD racks: *LOST, Indiana Jones, Monty Python, Angel, Buffy, Babylon 5, Star Trek,* and nothing came to mind. She checked her watch, glad that she kept wearing one as a fashion piece even though her smartphone told the time.

10:17. That didn't leave much time for any kind of media power-up.

Ree got to her feet, seeing that the Blins were moving to their big couch. Bryan went to the kitchen and looked like he was preparing hot chocolate, firing up the restaurant-grade espresso machine that took up a good third of their counter space. *Benefit of family in the restaurant biz.*

"I should get going," Ree said, though no one was looking at her. Bryan turned from the machine and waved her over. The twins kept playing, and Aidan slowly sobbed on the couch.

"We're going to be fine now. What about you?" Bryan asked when she got into the kitchen, just loud enough to be audible over the sound of steaming milk.

"I have to go after Eastwood. He's . . ." Ree sighed. "He's not really a bad guy, he's just gone off the deep end for this woman. He's got himself convinced that he *has* to do it."

Bryan put a hand on Ree's shoulder. "Do what you feel *you* have to, Ree. Your instincts have served you pretty damned well today, from where I'm standing."

Ree hugged Bryan delicately, leaving his hands free to deal with the machine. She squeezed Aidan's shoulder and collected a round of hugs from the twins on her way out, nodding to a thankful Amy.

"You'll come over for dinner soon?" Amy asked.

Ree nodded. "Of course. Got to go, sorry."

All right. First stop, Dorkcave. Maybe my luck will hold out after all.

With her phone partially charged thanks to fifteen minutes at the Blins', Ree watched fifteen minutes of *X2* on the bus back to the U-District, hoping for some mutant powers, though she skipped past the Cyclops-centric scenes, as she was fresh out of ruby quartz to contain optic blasts.

> *Dear Legba and the League of Liminal Holiday Gods,*
>
> *Please give me a mutant healing factor and rad claws, minus the pain and the wonky haircut. I will accept a cigar-chomping habit in return.*
>
> *Love,*
> *Ree*

She stepped off of the bus in the U-District just after 11:10, watching her phone wavering at 5% charge when she stopped the video and booked it for Eastwood's as fast as her beat-ass leg could handle.

She felt the tingle of a genre emulation but wasn't sure what it meant. She found herself checking out only women as she walked for a block; then she turned her head at the gorgeously lanky African-American boy in the Michael Jackson *Thriller* outfit.

I get it. Metaphor. Thanks, Stan.

Ree still felt the tingle of power when she reached the stairs heading down to Eastwood's lair.

All right. I might have to power up to open this door, if he's put up the moat.

Ree tried the door. Locked. *Duh.*

She could go around the side and see if the window she busted was open, but she'd be completely compromised as she entered, and she'd either have to climb down the stacks or jump down if they were sealed. *No good.*

"Okay, so how do I do this?" Ree asked herself. She threw her hands open and to the sides, but no claws popped out. She raised a hand to her temple and took off her glasses, staring at the door. No blast.

She closed her eyes and tried to see inside the door, hoping for some telepathy so she could lock on to Eastwood's thoughts and see what was happening—*think* what was happening?

Again nothing.

Ree stepped back onto the bottom step, took a breath, then ran forward two steps to shoulder into the door, hoping for superstrength.

THUD. Ow. Well, that was a terrible idea.

"Next time, I watch *Superman*," she promised herself.

She slumped forward against the door, catching her breath. As she exhaled, she heard a familiarly odd sound.

BAMF!

And with a noseful of sulfur, she found herself inside the Dorkcave, a blue-black cloud dissipating around her.

"Sweet," Ree said in a whisper. She stood still for a moment, watching and listening.

The stacks were open, a panoply of merchandise, memorabilia, and various libraries open to the air. The room was lit by the side runners along the walls and the LEDs Eastwood had rigged along the edges of the shelves. At the other end of the room, there was a circle of lights around Eastwood's big-ass cauldron.

"Oh, man." He was going through with it, or doing something to avoid the deal, or something else. Whatever it was, it was big. The last time she'd seen the cauldron active, she'd almost died of psychic shock and then nearly killed a man who she thought was her friend. *Not great associations, overall.*

Ree stepped down the metal stairs as softly as she could, thinking, *Ninja, ninja, ninja.* Teleporting again wouldn't help except for surprise, and she wasn't sure she wanted to startle Eastwood right now. Her wealth of fictional experience told her that startling magicians during demon summonings didn't tend to yield positive results for *anyone.*

She tiptoed up to the edge of one of the lines of shelves. Peeking around the side to look at the cauldron, she saw Eastwood standing opposite, his hands up and out to the ceiling. He was chanting in some language distinctly not English. Ree stepped to the far side of the shelf and crept across the room, feeling the tingling in her mind fade.

No more BAMF. Time to go shopping, Supermarket Sweep–style.

Ree picked out a Glaive from *Krull,* a replica of Sting from *The Lord of the Rings,* and a Captain America shield that looked like it had been on the shelf since the 1990 film. Well armed with nerd artifacts, she reached the edge of the stack as the older geek's chanting approached a climax.

There was light emitting from the cauldron in a dark luminescent purple. Bubbles popped up and out, and Ree felt the ground start to shake. *That can't be good,* she thought.

Holding the shield strapped to her left arm and Sting slung at her belt, Ree lifted the Glaive and stepped out into the open, facing Eastwood. "Stop this!"

For a moment, Eastwood didn't even register her. It took a beat, and then he turned to face her, eyes wide.

"I can't! It's too late." Eastwood's arms dropped, and Ree noticed a foldout table behind him, with five Pokéballs in a tidy row.

The souls? she wondered. And if they are, what has he got in the fifth?

The earth shook again, and the bubbling in the cauldron reached a violent boil.

"What does that mean?" she asked.

"It means he's coming and that you should run. There are a million things that could go wrong now."

"Then why did you do it?" Ree asked.

Eastwood's face dropped. "I had to. This deal was my last chance. Not just to get Branwen back but for me. It was more than a trade. This was supposed to be me settling my debt. Unless he takes the offering, he's going to take me with him."

Ree took a sharp breath. *Jackass.* "Why didn't you tell me this earlier?"

Eastwood stepped back and behind the table, a lightsaber at his side and the quilted T-shirt under his jacket. "This is my mess, not yours, Ree. Go now, while there's a chance."

The earth shook again, and Ree heard the rumbles of laughter coming from everywhere and nowhere. Her arms broke out in gooseflesh as she steadied herself on the shelf.

"I can help," she said, but her voice broke.

A purple cloud exploded out of the cauldron, and the laughing crescendoed until Ree dropped her head and covered her ears.

After the cloud had faded, she saw a seven-foot-tall figure in a suit standing beside the cauldron, arms crossed. The Thrice-Retconned Duke of Pwn wore a trench coat over an expensive brand-name-she-was-too-poor-to-identify suit, and he had long, thin hair slicked back into a ponytail. He was pale, wan, but his skin had a red cast. When he smiled, his teeth were yellow, stained, and cracked.

When he spoke, his voice was smooth but booming, like that of a lounge singer talking into a mike rigged for a metal concert. "Good evening, Eastwood." The Duke turned to Ree, holding out one hand, fingers tipped with long and jagged nails. "Who is this lovely young thing?"

Eastwood took a step forward and waved his hand, dismissive. "She just delivered me some components for the summoning. She's on her way out."

Ree scoffed. "The hell I am," she said. "I'm here to make sure you deliver the goods."

The Duke grinned, showing extra rows of teeth, like a shark. "A backbone. How exciting. And how do you intend to do that, little one? With those trinkets?" The Duke walked toward her, the concrete sizzling with each step his Gucci shoes made. "Do you know how many copies of Sting there are in the world? There's barely enough nostalgia in that thing to use it as a night-light in a goblin orphanage."

Ree's stomach dropped down to her ankles. *Play it cool. Let Eastwood run his con before you decide to throw down.*

Eastwood interposed himself between Ree and the Duke. "You're here to deal with me, Your Grace."

Ree heard the disdain in Eastwood's last words, which put her a bit at ease. *He's the one with the ax to grind. Let him take the heat.*

Eastwood stepped back to the table, drawing the Duke after him. Ree realized he was containing his nerves by moving slowly, deliberately, waving a hand over the five Pokéballs.

"Five souls of brokenhearted virgin suicides, to order. Now show me Branwen."

The Duke grinned again. He turned back to the cauldron, which had returned to a simmer.

Damn pleased with himself, isn't he? Ree thought.

The Duke snapped his fingers, and a plume of smoke shot up from the cauldron. Inside it floated Sionnan Reyes, dressed in her Jedi ensemble. Her clothes were ragged, burned, and dirty, and her hair had been shorn close to the scalp, with cuts and bruises visible everywhere her skin was showing. The left side of her face was a mass of welts.

Sympathetic pain hit Ree like a jackhammer, and she covered her mouth with one hand, eyes wide.

It was even worse than the cube's hologram; her mother looked haunted, strung out. But Ree's heart soared as much as it hurt. Could she reach out and touch her after all that time? Just pull her mother back into her life?

Sionnan didn't seem to be able to see them, as if the Duke had opened a window instead of conjuring Ree's mother to the room.

"Mom?" she whispered.

At that, the Duke's attention slid toward her, his bushy eyebrows raised, and he smiled. "So this is Rhiannon. How pleasant to have the family back together." He casually waved in Sionnan's direction. "She speaks of you often. Between the screams."

Ree's lips curled into a snarl, but Eastwood drew the Duke's attention by handing him a Pokéball. "Smell them yourself. They're all fresh, less than a month old."

The Duke took the Pokéball and sniffed at it like it was a rare wine. "Sixteen-year-old female. Homeschooled. And she was so very much in love. Exquisite. Give me another."

Eastwood offered the Pokéballs one by one, and the Duke sampled each of them, noting its qualities like a spiritual sommelier.

When Eastwood handed the Duke the fifth and last ball, Ree's teeth clenched. *Do-or-die time. Eastwood wouldn't have thrown down in the park if he didn't need the last soul. So whatever he did here, it either has to be crappy enough to risk a fight over or tossed together at the last second.*

The Duke sniffed the last Pokéball, eyes closed. "Sixteen-year-old male. Second-generation geek. Espresso and tomato notes. He loved his food and drink. He thought he was worthless. Quite magnificent."

Ree froze for a moment. *No. How?* She looked to Eastwood, who met her eyes, then nodded to the Duke and winked at Ree. The Duke was still lost in thought, eyes shut.

You fucker, Ree thought. She wasn't sure whether she meant it with anger or admiration. How did Eastwood do it? Did he take an imprint in the park? Maybe something in the bottle took something from Aidan, and that was what had a hold on him? *Did he only have to take Aidan to the edge? Or was it an olfactory illusion, misdirection pulled off with enough audacity and aplomb to be believable?*

"I must have this one right away. You don't mind, do you? Of course not." The Duke pushed the center button with a jagged nail, and a rush of white light leaped out of the ball and into the Duke's mouth.

The Duke took a deep breath, seeming to savor the . . . whatever Eastwood had put together. Ree watched Eastwood. He was putting on a brave face, but worry crept into his eyes, however slowly.

The Duke stretched his fingers, dropping the Pokéball as he rolled his head back and around, the cracking sounds as loud as shattering bones.

The Duke licked his lips, then raised an eyebrow. "Something's off." His eyes narrowed as he looked at Eastwood. He sniffed, then snarled at the magician, "Did you think you could fool me, whelp?"

Eastwood took a step back, hand up, placating. "The others are all real, I promise. I was so close to the fifth, but I couldn't get it. The Muse was dead, and I couldn't find another. There just weren't any more, and I couldn't kill them myself, right?"

The Chief of the Dork Lords of Hell pulled himself up to his full height, and the lights in the room flickered. With the wave of one hand, the vision of Sionnan vanished. In her place was a trio of shadowed creatures who jumped down and flanked the Duke.

All three were dressed in tattered T-shirts and ratty jeans. They looked like a perp walk of Geekdom's Worst Stereotypes. One man was tall and skeleton-thin, with a face made more of acne than skin and with hair so thin it was translucent. The other man was literally round, with hands that looked like balloons and an underbeard that failed to cover three chins.

The third was a woman with tangled and matted hair down to her ankles and a body shape more Weeble-wobble than pear.

"These three are the last of your kind to try to weasel out of a deal, Eastwood. If you give up quietly, I might even let you see Branwen once before I start your torture. And I will parade you both through your apprentice's dreams every single night."

Eastwood reached for his lightsaber and clicked it on with the signature *whoosh*.

Ree raised her shield and the sword. She left the Glaive on the ground since she didn't know how a real person could use it without hurting themself. Magic or not, Sting was still a weapon. *Right?*

She suddenly understood better why everyone in the magic underground seemed to walk around armed to the teeth.

The Duke took several steps back as Ree circled around the trio. Faced by weapons, the three hissed, their eyes turning red. The geeky servitors' hands bled. Instead of just hitting the floor, the blood solidified into dripping claws.

Eeuch. Ree stood with her right leg forward, the shield up and forward at an angle. "Time to get my Spartan on, then," she said. Eastwood nodded at her, spinning his lightsaber in slow arcs around himself as the trio spread out to encircle the older geek.

"Hey, uglies. What about me?" Ree advanced on the tall, thin man and reached out with a jab. Her opponent folded over on himself, bending backward and blocking her shot with his blood-encrusted hands. The block knocked her arm all the way over her head, and she stepped back.

Bugger's strong for being made out of skin and bones. Fucking nerd-demon magic.

The rail-thin man flipped his head backward and righted himself, facing Ree as he lashed out with bloody claws on elastic arms.

Ree took the slash on the shield, ducking under it and rising with an upward cut to his leg. He took the cut, but the gushing blood hardened almost instantly, looking like a plate greave.

"Frak me."

Turned into a bloody whirlwind, the man began raining blow after blow down on her with spindly, sharp limbs. Ree turtled underneath her shield; it was all she could do to keep from being overwhelmed. She caught a few small cuts along the ankle and shifted to keep her bad leg back, praying that the painkillers would hold out.

"How you doing, Eastwood?" she shouted, unable to see him in the melee.

"They're cheating! Blood is not supposed to be proof versus lightsabers!"

Ree threw a wide slash, trying to push the tall man back. "Uhm, I don't think their boss cares if they cheat. Any tips?" The tall man grabbed at her shield with one bloody hand, so Ree pushed into him and wrapped a cut around, slicing into his back. She felt the blood hardening around her sword as she pulled the blade back.

Now I have a chunk of solid blood on my sword. Marvelous.

Eastwood said, "*Highlander* or *Terminator,* most likely."

"Got any pipe bombs?" Ree asked.

"Fresh out, sorry."

The Duke interrupted them, saying, his voice again all around them, "You can still give up, children. Spare yourself at least *some* pain."

"Could you monologue some, maybe?" Ree held the shield forward and took the offensive, confidence building with her snark. "Call off your mooks and explain to us in painful detail the intricacies of your brilliance? Pretty please?"

Spindly grabbed her shield with both clawed hands and yanked. Ree felt her arm pop out of its socket, and the shield slipped off into his grasp. He grinned wide, his teeth bloody.

"No such luck, my little pet," said the Duke. "In a past life, perhaps. But I am not called Thrice-Retconned without reason."

Ree wanted to give another pithy response, but she was busy writhing in pain. Her left arm hung limper than an overdone noodle, and it was all she could do to keep her eyes open. She scurried away from her dance partner, who spun his elongated arms in circles. The clawed hands pulled air past her face as she kept barely ahead of the blows.

"A little help, please!" Ree called to Eastwood as she scrambled back, ripping things off the shelves to toss at the creature. She threw small boxes, bags of dice, identification cards, and caltrops, to no discernible effect.

"Still busy!" Eastwood called, dashing back and forth between the two dead geeks, lightsaber flashing. *I guess you don't spend years running with a Jedi without picking up some serious moves.*

Ree grunted, pulling an arrow out of a quiver and throwing it like a tiny javelin. The arrow stuck in the tall man's leg, the wound spilling out and adding to the blood armor. Ree grabbed another pair of arrows, but as she stood to throw, fatigue dragged on her. She steadied herself on the nearby shelf.

The rail-thin man closed on her as she found her feet, the arrow weighing twenty pounds in her hand as she fought past the fatigue. *Not now,* she thought, grinding her teeth. Grabbing the arrow with both arms, she rammed it into the man's throat. The wound spurted blood like a Sam Raimi character.

Hell yeah! Ree's eyes went wide. Her momentum back, she raised another arrow, leaped forward, and buried it in his eye. Ice-cold blood sprayed all over her shirt, which made her doubly squicked since: 1) well, blood, and 2) blood was supposed to be *warm*. She had dead man's blood on her.

At least I'm not a vamp from Supernatural.

Ree pulled out Sting and raised it high to chop the fiend's head off, kind of hoping that it was overkill but not really ready to fight someone with an arrow coming out of his eye. The sword clanged off of the cement floor with her downward stroke, and the head rolled to the side, sticking to the ground at an angle as the blood hardened.

She exhaled slowly, scanning the room for Eastwood. He'd backed up and onto his desk, using the high ground to keep the two dead geeks at bay. The Duke stood to the side, watching and buffing his fingernails.

Options unfolded in front of her like a cynical Choose Your Own Adventure.

If you charge into battle to help the man who tried to get your boss's son to commit suicide, turn to page 73.

If you take the coward's way and run the hell away, turn to page 497.

If you try to sneak up on and backstab the Thrice-Retconned Duke of Pwn, turn to page 666.

If you try to pop your shoulder back into its socket by shoulder-checking a metal shelf, turn to Chapter 21.

CHAPTER TWENTY-ONE

You Have Chosen Medical Masochism

Ree figured that the backstabbing option would get her killed pretty fast, and her sense of do-gooderism wouldn't let her abandon Eastwood. She knew intellectually how to put her arm back into its socket, but she was afraid that if she screwed it up, she might lose the arm.

Then again, if the arm is deadweight, I'm screwed if it loses me the fight. So what's it going to be?

Ree leaned against a shelf, grounded her feet, grabbed her left arm with her right, and took a breath. She lunged forward, ramming her shoulder into the shelf as she pushed with her good arm. Ree felt more than heard the *pop*, which was followed by a fresh wash of pain.

She slumped to the floor, eyes hot with tears of pain. *Holygoddamnedmonkeyballsow.*

After sobbing for a few moments, she rolled over and sat up, looking at an increasingly harried Eastwood on his desk, using the lightsaber more like a broom desperately warding off vermin than an experienced fighter wielding an elegant weapon from a more civilized age.

Not over yet. "Big Damn Hero time, Ree."

Striding down the aisle, she gathered her courage and pushed back the pain. She picked up the sword and retrieved the Captain America shield from its resting place atop the tall man's body.

"Player Two has entered the game, motherfuckers!" Ree shouted, drawing the woman's attention away from Eastwood. The same bloody claws, but her hair was also red-streaked, with arrowhead-shaped chunks of hardened blood dotting her dishwater-colored mane. Ree slashed horizontally, pushing the woman back and away from Eastwood. Carrying her cut through, she pivoted in place and cut at the round man. Her sword sliced through layers of back fat, drawing blood, more quick-harden armor forming over the cut.

As the round man rolled her way, Ree gave ground. "I got the other one with an arrow in the eye," she said, skipping back to face the dead woman, who wound up her hair like a whip, then cracked it at Ree.

Ree jumped out of the way, favoring voids over deflections to keep from giving the woman more blood armor. "Maybe they take head shots?" She caught a few cuts on her jacket and along her sword arm, but the leather took most of the bite.

I'm sorry, cows. You wanted me to think of you as more than burgers, and now I know you make awesome armor. Probably not what you were looking for. Note to self: Remember to thank Drake for his awesome coat.

Eastwood jumped to his left, dodging a meaty swipe from the round deadie. "Could be. But he parries like a master."

"Fight better, then!" Ree hid behind her shield as the dead woman swung her hair around again. The sound of the hair on the shield was like hail mixed with the floppy squeegees of a car wash. And it smelled like patchouli old enough to order a beer.

Ree cut at the hair as it squeegeed off the shield. She caught a chunk and sent it off to the side, which elicited a hiss from the dead woman. The shorn ends of the hair bled, forming a matted chunk of blood plate.

Great, now her hair has a mace in it.

Ree stepped forward, trying to cut at the woman's neck, but the dead woman spun back, taking the shot in her thick hair. Another gob of hair went flying, replaced by another mass of bloody plate.

This is going to stop working really fast.

Ree mimed a third cut, and the woman dodged back, whipping her hair around. Ree turned her wrist, pulling the cut, then swung it up again once the blood hair had whipped past. Ree took cuts along her right side and a dull blow from one of the blood plates, but she connected, tearing off the dead woman's jaw with the blade. Ree quickly cut up from the right and took the woman's head off, sending blood spraying all over Eastwood's wall of screens.

Ree shuddered. *That effect is a lot scarier in person than on-screen.*

She shook off the image and turned left to see Eastwood throw a combo, feinting to each limb before shooting straight forward and spearing his opponent through the mouth. The round man rolled back and went limp, his thick limbs hanging out from his rotund core.

Eastwood walked along his desk, holding the lightsaber out at the Duke. "Here's how this is going to go." Eastwood furrowed his brow, concentrating. "You're going to conjure up Branwen, and then you're going to get the *fuck* out of here and never show your yellow-toothed face in Pearson again."

It was the first time Ree had heard him curse in English. Not Klingon, Chinese, or made-up-SF languages, but plain ole English, and with more vitriol than she usually strung in a whole sentence of cursing.

Ree watched as the Chief of the Dork Lords of Hell reacted to Eastwood's ultimatum.

"And why would I bother acknowledging these terms, boy?

I have hundreds more where those three came from, and I know enough about you to destroy you from the demon pits just as easily as from here."

The Duke stepped forward, growing as he went. After two steps, he was more than eight feet tall, eye to eye with Eastwood, who retreated on his desk, knocking over keyboards and stacks of discs. The Duke kept growing, until he was more than ten feet tall, staring down his long nose at the now tiny-seeming geek. "The only pertinent question is how I will choose to end your miserable excuse for a life."

As the Duke spoke, Ree did her best to be unobtrusive, first sliding to the Duke's side, then inching out of his peripheral vision.

No monologuing, my ass, Ree thought. *If his mooks went down to head shots . . .* She eyed a spot on Eastwood's desk, at the far edge, where a stand of Mountain Dew cans made a tiny aluminum forest.

Well, Mom, if this gets me killed, I'll see you soon.

Slipping the shield off of her arm, Ree jumped up to the desk, knocking the soda cans aside. She pushed off with her good foot from the desk and jumped at the Duke, reaching for his shoulder and thrusting the sword at his back.

But the Duke wasn't lying about the retcons.

As she jumped at his back, the Duke reached behind, ignoring mundane things like normative physiognomy. His arm bent backward and swatted her off like a horsefly. The hit landed like a baseball bat, and Ree became an infield grounder, hitting the hard floor and rolling.

Ow. Not my best idea.

Fatigue and pain fought for attention as she tumbled. Ree slid to a stop and let the pain in for a second, paralyzing her.

She opened her eyes, seeing double. She blinked until her eyes focused, then looked around. She saw Eastwood hardpressed by the Duke, twenty yards away. The Duke had put her back in the stacks, amid an entire arsenal.

I just have to find something that will have the punch to hurt him. Eastwood would keep the most powerful weapons to himself, she figured, but he couldn't hold everything at once, not without a bag of holding, and she wasn't sure he had one of those. *I need something not powerful enough for him to already have on hand for this battle, something specialized.*

Ree heard the whooshing sounds of Eastwood's lightsaber, but instead of the crackle of blade on blade, she heard dull thuds. *What's that guy made of?*

Ree crossed lightsabers off her list of possible weapons and went back to her list. *Cross? Holy water? Cold iron?*

Now, that's a thought. If the Duke was a geek demon, he might just follow D&D vulnerabilities. The Duke struck her as more lawful than chaotic, which meant that she needed adamantine. Which didn't exist in the world, but it sure as hell existed in the geekverse, if adamanti*um* could serve as a close substitute. That depended on how much of a rules lawyer the universe was. Then again, the adamantium she was thinking about was attached to a character so beloved that he might trump the whole argument.

Mama needs a new set of Wolverine claws.

Ree hustled down the aisles, moving faster now that she was looking for one thing in particular. Again, there seemed to be no order to the props and artifacts.

"Would it kill you to alphabetize this place?" Ree shouted. If she asked Eastwood for a hint, she bet the Duke could figure it out. But her last sneak attack hadn't gone terribly well, so it couldn't hurt to speed things up.

Eastwood shouted back, his voice nearly drowned out by the whooshes and thuds. "If we survive, maybe I'll pay you to do it for me."

Ree reached the end of a row. "Gladly, but it's going to cost you a hell of a lot more than minimum wage. Where can a girl find some Wolverine claws in this mess?"

"Third aisle from the left, halfway to the door . . . second shelf, I think." His voice got softer, and Ree figured he was trading barbs with the Duke.

Ree got to the next intersection, counted the shelves as she shifted over, and continued toward the door.

Second shelf . . .

Ree passed Fleer X-Men trading cards, Versus card game booster boxes, a three-pack of the horrible Mary Jane maquette where she was washing Spider-Man's suit, a pair of giant Hulk fists (which Ree desperately wanted to try out but didn't think would have any special anti-demon effect and would likely make her go berserk), before she found a single box with a pair of yellow plastic gauntlets that advertised Tear Into Crime With Wolverine's Extendable Claws!

Bingo. Ree grabbed and ripped open the box with all the gusto of a kid on Christmas morning finally opening that last big present. She was good at this; she hadn't been a patient kid come Christmastime, even before Mom left. *Aren't you glad now, Mom? If this brings you back, I will claim the right to rip open presents with careless impunity forever.*

She sheathed Sting and slipped on one glove, then pushed the button to extend the claws.

How are you supposed to work them if you're wearing them at the same time? she wondered, then imagined that this design problem might have been why Eastwood had them on the shelf instead of in his trench coat. Holding the other gauntlet in her hand, she jogged back toward the sound of lightsaber and demon-made-of-something-that-goes-thud.

Eastwood had come down or been forced from the desk and was fighting while backpedaling down an aisle. The Duke was at least twelve feet tall, his unkempt claws now six-inch razor blades that flashed through the air. Eastwood moved with uncanny grace, weaving between some cuts and warding others off with the lightsaber. Even when he landed blows, they hit and bounced off of the Duke's expensive suit.

Ree came up on the Duke's left and led with her claws, reciting a plea to the gods of Geekdom.

Please work please work please work please work.

The Duke spun in place, swinging one hand's claws to block her own. Ree continued her plea as their claws met with a crash of sparks. She jumped to the side and tossed the other gauntlet to Eastwood, who had taken the opportunity to back off and drink some kind of blue potion. The gauntlet took him by surprise, and he dropped his lightsaber in catching it.

Mana? What is he using mana for? Ree shook her head, dismissing the question. Fight now, questions later.

Eastwood slipped the Wolverine fist on his hand and extended the claws. "How did you know I was a lefty claw fighter?"

"I didn't, but today you are whether you like it or not."

Ree lunged at the Duke again, but he was ready. He swung out a leg and knocked her aside, her claws whiffing through empty air. The blow sent Ree careening toward Eastwood, who threw his clawed hand wide and crouched to receive her.

"Huph," he said as she crashed into him. Eastwood fell back, and the two of them tumbled to the floor in a mess.

The Duke laughed. "Pathetic."

Ree found her feet, huffing. Her hands were shaking. She could run on adrenaline only so long, and when that was through, she'd be worth as much as a pile of empty wrappers. "You got any more mana potions, or whatever that was?"

Eastwood dusted himself off and raised his gauntlet forward in a guard. "In the shelves."

Ree tried to slow her breathing, find her center.

The Duke spread his arms wide, his huge form casting a shadow over both Ree and Eastwood. "A whole museum of trinkets at your disposal, and you can't even scratch me."

He's playing with us, the bastard. Ree wondered if he did this with each soul he claimed, the Greatest Game with

Gamers. A petulant gloater who toggled on God Mode and then griefed everyone who wandered into his territory.

Eastwood pursed his lips, lost in thought.

"Any new ideas?" she asked.

Eastwood waited a beat and then sighed. "Run. I'll hold him off. There's no need for you to pay for my mistakes."

"Oh, she'll pay," said the Duke. "I may have to wait a little while for her, but I still have something she wants, and she'll come crawling to me someday. Just like you did. You knew better, and yet here we are."

As the Duke grandstanded, Eastwood reached into his pocket, and Ree heard something rip.

The next thing she heard was Eastwood speaking to her. But his lips weren't moving. The words echoed in her mind like a racquetball. *I put a boomerang back to his dimension in the summoning. We just need to get him into the cauldron again and flush-goes-the-toilet. Find something to knock him over— I'll provide the distraction.*

Ree shot Eastwood a sly look, thinking, *You sneaky bastard,* but he didn't respond. Whatever trick he'd used, it seemed to be a one-shot.

With no answer from Eastwood, Ree started the charade. She lowered her gauntlet, putting on her best guilty face. "Good luck," she said, then turned and ran for the door. She heard the sound of fighting and searched her mind as Eastwood shouted taunts at the Duke.

"Fight me for real, you cowardly, Ferengi-loving, toaster-munching piece of tribble bait!"

Knockback. Something with enough oomph. Or something that pulls, if I can get it on the other side of him . . .

Ree tried to hold a list of every gadget and prop she'd seen in Eastwood's stacks in her mind, and cross them off one by one. She had a niggling feeling still. She knew she'd already seen the answer and just had to remember it.

After she heard a few more nerdly curse-streams from

Eastwood, a light went on in her mind. Ree took the stairs up to the back door three at a time and opened the door, cackling to herself all the while. Then she waited for it to close again and jumped off the stairs to land at the same time as the door slammed with its characteristic grinding thud. She hoped that Eastwood's running commentary would be enough to sell her ruse.

Ree crept over to the fifth row of shelves. She turned the corner and looked up and down the stacks, trying to find the box she'd noticed on her first visit and had misread as marking Eastwood for a big perv. *Not that he isn't a big perv, but not for this reason. I hope. The box wouldn't be open if he is, right? Plus, he has chicken legs, he'd never be able to pull them off.*

Ree saw the box and plucked it off the shelf, relieved. And then the reality of what she'd have to do in order to pull it off hit home. *Damn you, DC.* She reached down, unzipped her boots, then unbuckled her belt. Positioning herself behind the stacks for modesty—out of habit more than any actual fear of discovery—she dropped her jeans and picked up the stockings from the box marked Birds Of Prey—Black Canary's Fishnets.

For Ree, Black Canary was a perfect example of how DC Comics could be simultaneously brilliant and ludicrous. The character had been a part of some of DC's best story lines but was continually saddled with a stripper outfit, each version of which always centered around her trademark fishnet tights.

Priorities, Ree reminded herself, pulling the tights up as far as they would go, all the way to the edge of uncomfortableness and a little bit beyond.

Ree felt the power thrumming in her throat. She also felt like the camera of the universe was trying to find angles to show her from below.

Hoping that she was now prepared, Ree started the long, terrifying walk back down the room, making it at least the fifth time she'd crossed the Dorkcave in, what, ten minutes?

Oh, the milkshake I have earned.

She heard a shout of pain from the far side of the room. If it wasn't Eastwood, then the Duke sounded like a scared, tired teenage boy when he was hurt.

Stay on target. Eastwood better deliver. Hell, I better deliver.

She hoped that Aidan was all right, and that Sandra and Darren and Anya and Priya were having a good night, completely untouched by the Sharknado that her life had become.

A litany of hopes crossed her mind, and she bound them to her steps, praying as she went and adding hope to her will. She tried to hold on to all of the prayers at once, to use them to press on, to finish the fight and put this whole nightmare of a week to bed so she could rest and go back to having a normal-ish life.

Eastwood was dancing around the Duke, trying to keep his distance. The pair was fifteen feet from the cauldron, Eastwood closer to it than the Duke.

Well, shit. What now? If she rejoined the fight, it would give the Duke a chance to guess what her fishnets meant, which could ruin the whole plan. But if Eastwood couldn't get their man into place, he might get killed before she had the chance to play Dunk-a-Duke.

Ree waited, keeping her body hidden behind a cardboard stand-up of Raphael from the *Teenage Mutant Ninja Turtles* movie. She tried to catch Eastwood's eye as he dodged the Duke's attacks, occasionally counter-attacking, but largely his back was to her, the cauldron between them.

Screw this.

"Hey, Dorkass!" Ree shouted at the pair. Both of them looked. Ree grinned and flipped the Duke the bird with both hands. "Come and get it, you cut-rate *Prophecy* knockoff!"

At this, Ree had the treat of seeing Eastwood crack a bloodied, doofy grin at the same time as she saw all humor instantly drain from the Duke's face. He turned his back on Eastwood and started barreling toward her.

Definitely picked the right reference. Viggo was way hotter, after all, and there was no disputing it.

Ree had picked her angle carefully, putting herself just off-line with the cauldron so that the Duke stomped right by it in his charge. Ree fudged some math in her head, then dove sideways in her best *Hard Boiled* impression and screamed her lungs out. She screamed with all the pain of losing her mother just when she needed her most, the pain of watching her father struggle, the pain of families broken by lives ended too early—but she also screamed with hope, with her dreams, with the lives she needed to protect, even the ones she'd never asked to be involved with.

It wasn't even a word, really. The scream was nothing more and nothing less than Ree's whole heart poured out and made sound. The wave stopped the Duke's linebacker charge entirely, then picked him up off the ground and lifted him fully ten feet in the air. Ree kept screaming, but the Duke hung in the air, buffeted up by the power but not moving backward.

The Duke flailed, trying to grab the ceiling, a nearby shelf, anything, but he was stuck, locked in the air as Ree screamed and screamed, drowning out all other sounds in the room.

The moment stuck, stretching on as long as Ree's heart continued to pour out her rage, hope, fear, compassion, and everything else. What felt like an eternity later, Ree ran out of breath. Sputtering out the last of the air in her lungs, the scream ended, she fell to her knees, and her lungs threatened to implode.

The Duke dropped straight down and into the cauldron, fitting in like a circus diver dropping into a thimble. There was a crack of thunder and a flash of purple light, and then His Brilliant Marvelousness, the Thrice-Retconned Duke of Pwn, Chief of the Dork Lords of Hell, was gone.

Ree clawed at the ground and the air, trying to get her lungs to take in oxygen. *You can't die here, Ree. This is not some hateful indie tragedy.* She wobbled to her feet and looked over the lip of the cauldron, while Eastwood closed in to look as well.

She saw nothing. No Duke, no purple goo, nothing but the wrought-iron bottom of the vessel itself.

Ree continued to hyperventilate, and Eastwood's eyes went wide. He pounded Ree's back, and around the time she wondered if she was going to pass out, some physiological switch flipped and she could breathe again. She sat for a little while longer, Eastwood kneeling at her side.

When her breathing settled enough that she didn't have to force her lungs to operate, she grabbed the side of the cauldron and pulled herself up. "Holy shit. That worked."

Eastwood, who had never been a touchy-feely person in the weeks that Ree had known him, wrapped his arms around her and picked her up off the ground into a bear hug.

"Eep!" Ree said as she waved her feet, failing to connect with the ground. Eastwood set her back down, and Ree met his gaze with indignation wrapped around anger. *I'm far from done being pissed off at you, bucko,* she thought.

Eastwood's smile was as broad as the Golden Gate Bridge. "Sorry."

"Is it over?" she asked, looking around at the bodies, which started to dissolve one pixel at a time, like old 16-bit video-game characters.

"For now. Someone else can summon the Duke, and if they screw it up, he could get loose. Luckily, almost no one is arrogant enough to summon a Dork Lord of Hell."

Ree continued to smolder with pissed-off-ness, and Eastwood sighed. "I know." He turned away and looked back to the overturned table and the scattered Pokéballs. "I've . . . I've got a lot to answer for. A lot of amends to make."

"No shit," Ree said, too conflicted to know what tone to put on the words. "You tried to get my friend to kill himself. I'd shiv you myself, but I'm so tired that I'd probably fall over."

"You're right. About everything," Eastwood said, reaching

down to the floor and starting to clean up. He looked up and around the Dorkcave, taking stock or avoiding eye contact, Ree couldn't tell. "I'm sorry, Ree. I—I'm just sorry. Call me if you need anything. Anything, okay?"

Eastwood walked over to the table and picked it up, then went back to tidying, picking up bits of trash, broken props, and the bits of the maelstrom that the room had become.

Ree stood for a moment, watching. He'd spent who knew how long building this whole plan up, and all he'd gotten for it was a trashed room, a cranky apprentice, and what looked like about five hundred pounds of guilt that he wore around his neck like Marley's chains. She wanted to clock him again, but she could tell from the way he moved that he was already punishing himself. And Ree was too damn tired to add to it. At least for now.

"We're not done, you hear that? You've got four lives on your conscience, and another count of attempted coerced suicide, or whatever the hell that would be called. You're going to need to pull some serious Mother Teresa shit to even the score, Eastwood."

He didn't turn, but he nodded, fighting with a chair that had gotten wedged into the steel struts of a shelf. Ree realized that she'd never seen Eastwood look so old in all their brief time together.

Shell shock.

Ree left Eastwood to his cleaning and turned to cross the Dorkcave one more time. She ran her hands along the steel strut and tried her best to process the last few weeks, put them into some kind of context. She searched for a way to deal with everything so that she could go back to slinging coffee and playing video games and trying to perfect that strange alchemy of writing a salable script.

I've read a thousand books, seen four hundred movies, and read a bajillion comics where the hero ends the story right where I am, on the edge of the Return, trying to figure the shit out. And most of the stories don't bother telling what happens next. It's just kill the bad guy, kiss the girl, and ride off into the sunset, or get married and ride off into the sunset, or get married in the sunset and kiss as the music swells.

Ree stepped up to the landing and opened the door out to the basement entrance. *But this isn't a movie, or a comic, or a video game, even though all of them seem like they can be as real as you make them, with the right tools and enough belief.*

She stepped into the midnight air and felt cold rain on her head, heard the distant blare of sirens and the dull bass thud of a party somewhere nearby.

But where does that leave me?

Ree climbed up the steps, the dull pain in her leg where she'd taken the cut flaring back up. She sighed and walked slowly, limping along in the rain, feeling it on her face, her hair, hearing it patter against her jacket, and feeling it sploosh under her shoes.

Right here. Living. Aiming to misbehave or just trying not to fade away. Ree shook out the rain and forced a smile. I may not have gotten Mom back, but I know who has her, and I've beaten him once. So screw the pity party, it's time for a milkshake. And then I can call a cab and see what the crew is up to. And then sleep for a week, wake up, and figure it all out again.

Invigorated by the prospect of milkshakeitude, she picked up her pace and made for the Burger Bin in the U-District, planning out the specific combination of mix-ins and flavors that she would dub the Shake of Victory.

Shake It Out

When Ree woke up, daylight filled the room. She flopped in bed for what must have been another hour, stretching and yawning away the coma of recovery. Either she had managed to plug in her phone before she crashed, out of sheer habit, or Sandra had done it for her.

She never did make it out to see the gang, since shortly after she made it to her building, she passed out in the elevator. She'd been through the emotional wringer for what seemed like a straight month but really had been only about a week, between Jay, the Muse, Eastwood, the whole wild ride.

Which meant that now, Tuesday afternoon, according to her phone, she was hungry, thirsty, and probably unemployed.

Ree dragged herself into the kitchen and was able to make coffee thanks to years of muscle memory and a brutal desire for caffeine.

After the second cup of coffee, she could see color again and began to start thinking about considering making an effort to restart her life.

Ree called the café, hoping she'd catch Bryan before he left for the day. *It* is *Tuesday, right?*

"Zombie Cafe," her boss said, answering on the second ring.

"Brains," Ree said. She had meant to say "hey." She shrugged and started again. "It's Ree. How is Aidan?"

"He's fine. How are you?"

Ree blinked a couple of times and looked down to see that she was still wearing her outfit from the fight. "Alive, surprisingly. Do I still have a job?"

After a beat, Bryan sighed. "Ree, you saved Aidan. Literally saved him. You're an actual hero to my family, and for that, I will always be grateful."

I smell a but, Ree thought as Bryan paused. "But I can't keep the lights on with a hero, Ree. I love you, but I have to find someone else or promote Charlie. Things are too tight right now. I can't make exceptions, even for you.

"I know it's unfair. Wickedly, horrendously unfair. You're welcome at our house anytime, day or night. But I have to run my business. If you're done with your business, then we're fine. But we both know that no one in that world can keep normal hours."

Ree looked at her phone as if it were actually Bryan and not a miraculous device that digitized voices and hurtled them through the air to another very specific device that would decode the code and speak with her voice, leveling a hateful stare.

A moment later, she put the phone to her ear again. "Yeah. I get it. I could still bake for you sometimes, or do marketing, or babysit the twins, but right now I can't guarantee anything about what's going on with me."

"I'm sorry, Ree. You're like family."

Ree sighed. "Yeah, but like you said. Tight."

"Yeah. I can maybe ask some of the folks in the business association if anyone needs a part-timer."

Ree rolled her neck, her bones cracking every one of the 360 degrees. The pain washed away some of the fatigue, and the soreness it left in its wake was welcome by comparison. "Hold off. Give me a couple of days to get my feet and figure it out.

If nothing else, I will totally provide free Dumpster-cleaning services if you look the other way after taking out the stale bag."

Bryan laughed on the other end of the line, and Ree could see the look on his face without seeing him. "I have no idea what you're talking about," he said in a dissembling tone.

"Certainly not. I'll take Amy up on that dinner tonight, though, if it still stands."

"Hell yeah. Come over anytime after four."

"Thanks," Ree said. "And don't you fuck up the store just because I'm gone. I was keeping you in the black, old man."

"Your baking kept me in the black, but it also kept me in a 38-inch waistband."

This time it was Ree who laughed. "Damn right."

"See you tonight, Ree," Bryan said.

"Seeya." Ree hung up the phone, then looked at it again with misplaced anger.

Foul harbinger, damned herald of suck.

At least I already had November's rent paid.

That gave her two weeks to find something before all the bills in the world started to come due.

Easy. It's not like we're in a recession or anything.

Ree finished her coffee, checked her email, and wrapped herself in the trappings of mundanity for a few hours. She grilled up some chicken and assembled quickie quesadillas, wolfing a whole one down before it had even started thinking about cooling.

After breakfast/lunch/ohgodsohungry, she picked up the phone again, looking at the icon to dial her dad.

I should tell him.

No, that's a terrible idea. It'd break him. He's doing all right finally, trying to date. I can't tell him, but I should.

She owed him at least a check-in. He'd be worried.

Ree poured herself a fresh cup of coffee and dialed her father. He might be at work, depending on the timing of his last appointment.

Ring.

I can't tell him about Mom, can I?

Ring.

But I should.

Ring.

Hell no I shouldn't.

"Ree-bee?" he answered.

Ree sighed at the sound of her dad's voice, another calming force after her ludicrous week.

"Hi, Dad. How's tricks?"

"Not bad. Should I call you back, sekrit-style?"

"Yes, please. It's done for now."

She hung up and sipped coffee while she waited. Shortly, her phone rang again, showing [Blocked], and she picked up. "Hello?"

"This is Rebel Base, come in, Red 5."

Ree smiled. "Red 5 here. How are the shield generators?"

"Holding steady."

Ree launched into a wrap-up of the last couple of days, her mind divided as she went. One part narrated the story, responded to her dad's questions, and carried on like normal. The other part of her mind angsted over the decision she was talking herself toward, whether she could break her dad's hard-won emotional equilibrium by telling him what really happened with her mom.

She knew the truth that had broken their home, but she had no clue what it would do to her father. She reached the point of the story where Eastwood revealed Branwen's identity, and stopped.

All right, kid, now or never.

"And then he handed me some kind of device, like a holocron, except it had a USB port."

"That sounds handy."

A voice insider screamed, *TELL HIM!* while another said, *HELL NO!*

Ree continued the narration, delaying details about the woman in the vision. She delayed and delayed . . .

And talked right past the scene without spilling the beans.

Not now, she said to herself. Maybe someday, but not now, not here. I don't think I can handle it even if he can.

She finished the story by talking about her current lack of employment.

"I was worried that would happen," her dad said. "I've taken a collection at work from clients and some of the other hairdressers. I told them it was to send you to L.A. again, but use it however you want."

Ree sighed. "Dad, I can't do that. I'll be fine."

Her dad's voice took a stern tone. "Rhiannon Anna Maria Reyes, I raised you to be grateful when people give you things. Besides, I already deposited it to your account."

"Dad . . ." she said, halfheartedly complaining.

"Too late. You can't send it back. I'll refuse the payment. Take the money and get back on your feet."

Ree took a sip of her coffee. *You get your stubborn from him, too. Pick your battles.* "Thanks, Dad. Hopefully, I'll have more cool stories for you, but maybe the others will be more on the funny side."

"Whatever you do, I'll want to hear about it—and think about how much inspiration you have for screenplays!"

"I know, right!?" Ree said, her nervousness giving way to excitement.

They chatted for another few minutes before Ree checked the clock and realized that if she didn't go soon, she'd miss visiting hours. She excused herself and packed up for a trip to the hospital.

⚄

It had taken some judo and magic-paper flashing, but Ree had talked her way past the nurse in the recovery ward and walked down the hall to Drake's—aka "John Drake"—room.

Ree kept her head up to continue projecting confidence, but she didn't meet anyone's eyes. The less lying and sneaking she had to do, the better. The last thing she needed after losing her job was to get arrested. Not like there was ever a good time to get arrested, barring wacky schemes to break someone out of prison or the like, but still.

Her footfalls echoed down the hall, overtaken by the brisk walk of a middle-aged female nurse in bright-blue sneakers who buzzed by Ree and ducked into a room.

After the next cross-hall, she found Drake's room. She checked up and down the hall to see if they'd be getting any eavesdroppers. Satisfied that they were as alone as anyone in a hospital, Ree walked into the room, closing the door behind her.

Drake lay in the single bed, with a heart monitor by his side. The curtains had a basic checkered pattern, and a 12"TV peeked out from the corner to Ree's left.

The displaced adventurer looked much less dashing in a hospital gown, his goggles and other accoutrements gone.

"Drake?" she asked, unsure if he was awake.

Drake shifted, murmuring a wordless response.

Ree reached into the slot at the base of the bed and pulled out Drake's chart. She studied it for a few moments, wishing she'd watched *ER* or something on the way over. Since she lacked any real medical knowledge, it didn't tell her anything she didn't already know.

Please be all right, okay? Ree walked around to Drake's right, moving slowly and trying to avoid provoking a panicked response from the hero-out-of-time. She'd startled her dad once when she was fifteen, and ended up pinned on the floor.

"Drake?" she asked again, a tad louder.

Drake blinked, then opened his eyes wide, looking up at Ree. "Ms. Ree?"

Ree nodded. "Do you know where you are?"

Drake looked around the room. He spoke with some difficulty, still looking a bit groggy. "A hospital, I presume."

"Yep. How do you feel?"

He managed a weak smile. "Somewhat surprised that Eastwood was strong enough to deliver a blow that puissant."

Ree nodded, sighing inside. He should be fine. If she'd sacrificed Drake by going off after Aidan . . . She shuddered, rubbing her arms at the wave of thwarted guilt that washed over her. "He's full of surprises, it turns out. Aidan is safe, and Eastwood is about as repentant as I think he can get without shaving his head and taking orders."

"I am afraid I do not take him for the praying type, Ms. Ree."

"Not unless it's praying for an ultra-rare in a card game booster pack, no. Can I get you anything, maybe something from your apartment?"

Drake looked up at the ceiling. Then he looked at Ree and said, "I will be fine. Have the doctors said when I can depart?"

Ree walked back over to the foot of the bed and pulled out the chart, flipping through it again as much to have something to do with her hands as to read the notes. "Looks like you're free to go whenever you like. Shall we?"

Drake smiled wider, his eyes bright. "Certainly. But first, do tell me what happened."

"Anything you need. I mean, you barely knew who I was and dropped everything to dive into ridiculous amounts of danger without so much as a grumble."

"I cannot refuse a lady in need," Drake said with a grin that would be rakish, were Drake not so pure of heart.

Ree did her best to keep from blushing, but she felt the blood rush to her cheeks. "That's going to get you into trouble. Especially in this town."

"It has done so many times already and will do so many times yet to come. But each time my folly has been justified by the adventure that follows, so I see no reason to stop now."

You are too much, Ree thought, shaking her head with a bemused smile.

Ree took a seat and gave Drake the rundown of what had happened after Eastwood left the park. She dropped into script pitch mode, filling in dialogue with voices, getting up to pace around and act out some of the choreography. It felt good to take control of the story, make it her own and something she could be proud of, instead of the nightmare it had felt like while she lived it.

As far as audiences went, Drake was attentive and supportive, far more than the producers and filmmakers she'd pitched to in L.A. But he was quite a bit more invested to begin with, and it was harder to be too cool for school when you were wearing a hospital gown instead of designer denim and an untucked-unbuttoned collared shirt that cost more than a reasonable person's rent.

Ree briefly entertained the idea of taking the story that was this past week and turning it into a screenplay. However, everything she knew about hidden-society stories told her that was bad news. But no one could stop her from plucking out details here and there and sprinkling them into her fiction efforts.

When the story was done, Ree fetched Drake some more water. "Shall we?" she asked, offering a hand.

Drake sat up, then reached a hand to his head, swooning. Ree caught him as he dropped back to the bed.

"Perhaps I should stay the night," he said, a hint of shame in his voice.

She squeezed his shoulder. "Of course. I'll see you tomorrow morning, then?" she said.

Drake nodded. "Marvelous. Sleep well, Ms. Ree."

Ree faked offense. "Ree. Just Ree. We've been through more than enough to put a nail in the coffin of formality, haven't we?"

Drake smiled, looking up at her beside his bed. "My

manners are nearly all I have left of my time. Please leave me them, idiosyncratic though they may be."

Ree leaned down and kissed him on the cheek. "As you wish," she said without thinking. When she stood up, she turned away a bit quicker than she'd planned, as her ears went hot.

Don't get ahead of yourself, now. she told herself. But she didn't stop the smile on her face as she walked out of the room, a spring in her step.

⌖

After a gloriously normal dinner at the Blins', Ree took stock of the imminent clusterfuck that was Her Finances. Even with her dad's deposit, she was going to be in trouble real soon.

Ree picked up her phone and dialed Eastwood. She was too tired to make another trip out into the world, and she figured she was more likely to punch the old geek if she saw him in person, which wouldn't solve her problem.

The phone rang four times and went to voicemail. Eastwood's recorded voice said, "You've reached Eastwood's Memorabilia and Collectibles. I'm not available right now . . ."

"Hello?" a live Eastwood said, sounding half asleep.

I know the feeling. "It's Ree."

A beat. "Hey. How are you doing?"

"Do you usually pass out for thirty hours after a big case or whatever?" she asked.

"At least. I woke up from sheer hunger this morning, then went back to bed."

"So. I'm still pissed off at you, and you have a big karmic debt to pay off. Here's your first task, Hercules: You get to pay for Drake's hospital visit."

Eastwood hrmed. "That's more than fair. What else?"

"Well, I find myself in soon-to-be-desperate need of employment . . ."

Eastwood sighed, long and tired. "Yeah. Do you want to come and work for me? I could use someone to organize things around here."

"How much do you pay?"

"A little," Eastwood said.

Ree shook her head. "My bills are more than little. They're between Large- and Huge-sized—lots of hit dice."

Eastwood sighed. "I'm sorry, but chances are good that I lost more than fifty grand of stuff in the big fight. I don't think I can pay more than a little for a while."

Ree nodded to herself, unsurprised. "You could just owe me. But I was thinking of something else: What would Grognard say to getting himself his very own magically-clued-in, nostalgia-artifact-wielding, genre-emulating Geek Girl to work his bar and hawk merch?"

Eastwood laughed. "I hope you can hold your Jäger."

"I can drink a three-hundred-pound Neubauten fanboy under the table and still remember all the words to '99 Luft-ballons.' Make that shit happen."

Ree hung up, a twinge of hope flickering amid the feelings of doom. At least she hoped it was hope and not her back spasming again.

⚫

At noon the next day, Ree walked into Grognard's in a black tank, her working jeans, and a Superman belt buckle. She had her hair tied back in a ponytail and had made up her face as Death from *Sandman*. It was a different Gamer Girl look than for Zombie Cafe, going more for clued-in badass than geek girl next door.

The store was mostly empty. A thirtysomething woman with a souped-up laptop sipped whiskey in a booth, and a couple of familiar-looking faces mingled by the miniatures.

"All right, Grognard, where do you need me?"

From behind the bar, the big man smiled. He reached under the table, pulled out a bottle of Jägermeister, then lined up two shot glasses.

"First, have a drink with me. There's a lot I have to explain about this place, and it is boring to talk without drinking."

Ree strode up to the bar, and by the time she reached the shot glass, it was full. She raised the glass, and Grognard met her, saying, "Welcome to Grognard's. Hope you survive the experience."

Ree clinked glasses, then threw back her drink. It burned like *woah*, but she smiled, slamming the glass onto the bar facedown.

I've had worse. I've stared down demons, werewolves, and rorikon strega, and outtalked the nerdiest, most obstinate, opinionated geeks Pearson has to offer. Hell, I've saved lives. I've saved lives from hell.

"I just hope you can keep up, Grognard. You don't know the half of what I can do."

Grognard nodded appreciatively and poured another shot for each of them.

He lifted his glass again. "To finding out what we can do."

Acknowledgments

It takes a village to raise a child. It takes several more to help a young writer publish their first novel. Thank you one and all.

To all of my teachers, who helped me discover and interrogate the world until it yielded its awesomeness.

To the staff and denizens of The Game Preserve, for showing me how great the geek community could be. Special thanks to Bryan Roberts, Andrew Reyes, James McWilliams, and to my fellow flunkies.

To my first critique group, Scat Hardcore, for taking in a newb and showing him the ropes. Special thanks to Marie Brennan, Von Carr, Darja Malcolm-Clarke, and Alyc Helms.

To the classmates, instructors, and staff of the 2007 Clarion West Writers Workshop. You all helped me learn how to walk the path. Good Unicorn says you're the best critiquers ever. Bad Unicorn says you need to write more!

To the baristas of the Barnes & Noble café in Bloomington, IN, for teaching me the way of the all-black outfit and the perfect shot of espresso. Special thanks to Christia Osborne, my café Yoda.

To the Codex Writers Group, my geographically-distributed writing lifeline. Special thanks to Elle Van Hensbergen, Beth Cato, Rebecca Roland, Anaea Lay, Kenneth Kao, Gary Kloster, Vylar Kaftan, Steven R. Stewart, Rachel Marks, Jeff Lyman, and Randy Henderson, for the great comments on my first draft.

To Lothair Biederman, for being my last-minute military/medical research consultant.

To the awesome community of Book Country, who provided the venue that made this all possible. Colleen Lindsay, Danielle Poiesz, and Molly Barton: You've helped dreams come true.

To my agent, Sara Megibow, for being my champion and my advocate. May this be the first of many awesome projects together.

To my editor, Adam Wilson, and his team at Pocket Books. Adam, thank you for venturing into Book Country and for believing in Ree, her story, and in me. You helped me power-level the novel so it could be ready to see the world.

Saving the best for last: to Meg White, for her unending support. Thank you with all my heart.

I know I've forgotten some, and I apologize. But that's what sequels are for: things left undone, stories left untold.

Bloomington, IN
May 2012

2ND EDITION ACKNOWLEDGEMENTS

Ten years later, we're back as I release this second edition of the book. It's only minimally different, as I wanted to preserve as much of the original as possible while making just a few tweaks to remove harmful or careless language that I've learned not to use since publishing this book the first time.

Some new thank yous for this edition:

To Deranged Doctor Design for the cover art & design.

To CreativeJay for formatting and production skills.

To Kim-Mei Kirtland, for career plotting and helping make it possible to get these books back out into the world.

Thanks still to Meg, for love, support, and laser eyes.

Thanks to all of the readers that have already found these books and spread the word and thanks to the new readers for giving Ree and company a shot.

Baltimore, MD
March 2022

Newsletter

Find out more about Mike's books, appearances, get bonus stories and more by subscribing to his newsletter at michaelrunderwood.com/newsletter

Celebromancy

Fame has a magic all its own in the no-gossip-barred follow-up to *Geekomancy*. Ree Reyes gets her big screenwriting break, only to discover just how broken Hollywood actually is.

Things are looking up for urban fantasista Ree Reyes. She's using her love of pop culture to fight monsters and protect her hometown as a Geekomancer, and now a real-live production company is shooting her television pilot script.

But nothing is easy in show business. When an invisible figure attacks the leading lady of the show, former child-star-turned-current-hot-mess Jane Konrad, Ree begins a school-of-hard-knocks education in the power of Celebromancy. Attempting to help Jane Geekomancy-style with Jedi mind tricks and X-Men infiltration techniques, Ree learns more about movie magic than she ever intended. She also learns that real life has the craziest plots: not only must she lift a Hollywood-strength curse, but she needs to save her pilot, negotiate a bizarre love rhombus, and fight monsters straight out of the silver screen. All this without anyone getting killed or, worse, banished to the D-List.

For more adventures with Ree, check out this
short excerpt from *Celebromancy*.

CHAPTER ONE

Confirm & Deny

Ree was late to her first public appearance as a screenwriter, and she couldn't even blame it on a monster attack.

Ree Reyes (Strength 10, Dexterity 14, Stamina 12, Will 18, IQ 16, Charisma 15—Geek 7 / Barista 3 / Screenwriter 2 / Gamer Girl 2 / Geekomancer 2) was already on the bus talking with her father and one-man cheerleading section when she got the *Where are you?* text from Yancy Williams, director, executive producer, and her new boss as a screenwriter.

"The fuck?" Ree said unconsciously as she read the text.

"What's up, Ree-bee?" her dad asked.

"I'm late. I was supposed to be there half an hour ago." Her pulse pole-vaulted straight past nervous all the way to freaked-the-hell-out.

"How far out are you?" her dad asked, his voice level. Ree's dad was an ex-marine and had all of the calm. She tried to borrow some, consciously slowing her breath.

It's not like your writing career is hanging on this or anything.

"Five minutes," Ree said. "But no one told me there was a makeup team!"

"It'll be fine. You can't make the bus get there any faster, so just remember why you were invited. Because you earned it. You'll be great."

"Gotta go. Time for a media power-up," Ree said.

"Love you," her dad answered.

A smile wiped away her worry for a moment. "Love you, too, daddy-o."

Ree hung up, looked at the text message again, sent her *ETA 5 min* response, and then queued up one of her power-up videos.

The bus would get there on its own time, so she did her best to concentrate on "The Late Shaft" from Castle.

For most new writers, watching a single scene of a TV show would be as useful as cramming French before a Medieval German exam. But Ree wasn't just any writer.

When they arrived at her stop, Ree practically dove out of the bus, and rushed into the hotel, brushing past fancy people in furs and suits that cost as much as her entire DVD collection.

One of Yancy's assistants, a young Chinese-American woman, was waiting in the lobby. *Was her name Patricia or Vanessa?* Ree wondered. She'd met most of the cast and crew all at once, and her brain's capacity for new names was about four at a time, max.

Patricia/Vanessa spotted her and said, "Thank God." She grabbed Ree's wrist and started off like a roadrunner. "Come with me, there's no time."

Ree imagined the woman speaking in the Terminator voice. *Come with me if you want to live . . . or look good on camera.*

⋅✕ˣ✕⬡ˣ✕ˣ✕⋅

They rushed to the bathroom that One Tough Mama had commandeered for their makeup prep. As Ree stepped inside, she saw a small handful of makeup artists clustered around Jane Konrad, the owner/executive producer of One Tough Mama and the star of *Awakenings*. The bathroom had been jury-rigged into a dressing room with extra lights, a clothing rack, and three Avon ladies' worth of makeup. The room smelled of hair spray and BPAL. And in the hot seat was Jane Konrad, (in)famous actress and producer.

Jane Konrad (Strength 8, Dexterity 13, Stamina 12, Will 15, IQ 16, Charisma 17—Performer 5 / Child Star 3 / Producer 2 / Philanthropist 2 / Party Girl 1 / Geek 1) was about Ree's height, had a currently-limp mane of chestnut-red-brown hair, and had starred in many happy dreams of Ree's over the years. She wore simple sweats, which hung loose on her diminished frame.

Just two years ago, Jane had been a world-class superstar, but her career had recently gone the same way as a famous young redhead's. The Jane of now was much skinnier than when she'd last been in a movie, which the tabloids blamed on drugs but Yancy denied fervently. She'd also collected more than a few citations and DUIs, and starred on the gossip sites ONTD and WTF on a regular basis.

Ree didn't know how long Jane had been in the chair, but she still looked pretty terrible. Makeup failed to cover huge bags under her eyes, her hair was thin and lifeless, and her skin was wan. And then there were the things makeup couldn't touch.

She looked forty, not thirty-two, and was at least ten pounds underweight, far more emaciated than her normal curvy vivacity. She was operating far below her normal +3 Charisma bonus.

Skinny could be sexy, but on Jane, it just didn't work. The actress looked empty, used up, like she'd gone nine rounds with a wight.

One of the makeup artists ushered Ree to a foldout chair in front of a sink and mirror, then started working.

"Glad you could make it," Jane said. Even her voice was hollow. *Are we in trouble with this show?* If her first pilot bombed, getting another job would be all that much harder.

Ree tucked a stray lock of hair behind her ear, still a little gun-shy around the star. "Sorry, I missed the call-time message."

Jane managed a weak smile. "It'll be fine. There's no need for writers to be glamorous. They'll want it anyway, since you're a woman, but you'll be fine. Just let Brendan do his magic."

Ree's nostrils flared at the comment. She knew it was true, and the double standard of it all stuck in her craw like a jagged chunk of popcorn.

Brendan was the man with at least four hands starting her makeup, if Ree had to judge just by the speed of his work.

"Can you see without these?" Brendan asked, indicating her thick-lensed glasses. If the money from selling the script hadn't all gone to overdue bills, credit cards, and paying back her roommate, she might have been able to replace the specs she'd worn since college, or afford new contacts. But that would have to wait for a series pickup.

"Not in any useful fashion," she said.

He tutted disapprovingly and said, "Then we'll work around them. Go ahead and take them off for now."

Ree obeyed and Brendan set to work, first removing the meager makeup she'd put on herself, then starting to rebuild her look from the base up. Thanks to an Irish-American mother and a Puerto Rican–American father, Ree had the "ethnically indeterminate" look, which had gotten more en vogue, to a point. Hollywood had still convinced Jessica Alba to go blonde after praising her "exotic" look in *Dark Angel*, after all.

Brendan highlighted the Puerto Rican part of her complexion, but also drew attention to her eyes. While he did that, Jane's hairdresser did a drive-by, untying Ree's functional shoulder-length braid and giving her a quick comb and treatment with some hair spray that nearly made Ree choke in her seat.

The door to the bathroom opened, and Yancy poked his head in. "Looking good, folks. Jane, how are you feeling today?"

Jane sat up, looking at Yancy in the mirror. "I've got this.

You keep them on topic, draw attention to our new star writer, and it'll be great." Jane turned and smiled at Ree, who tried to restrain a blush. Her reflection told her she'd failed, even with the makeup.

"All right. We're on in ten," Yancy said, then disappeared behind the closing door.

Brendan flashed back and the hairstylist continued to work wonders.

Ree caught Brendan's eyes in the mirror, then waggled her phone as she asked, "Do you mind if I zone out with a show while you work? It helps me calm down."

Brendan shrugged. "Just listen for my instructions when I need you to move your head."

"Got it," she said, and restarted the scene.

Since becoming a Geekomancer, a magician drawing power from her love for science-fiction/fantasy/horror/etc. media, Ree had made the executive decision to become more organized.

Her part of the apartment was still a pigsty, but she had gotten her shit together for her new Urban Fantasy life. Over the last few months, she'd made playlists of videos to watch for short hits of genre emulation and had tagged her video collection by gleanable skills.

The short clips, she'd found, were only good for ten, maybe fifteen seconds of magic, usually just one trick. But the right trick at the right time could be a lifesaver. And with the screen only ten inches away, she wasn't quite blind.

Genre emulation was the most powerful (and rare) form of Geekomancy, and it was her best chance to not freak out and wretch during her first ever press panel.

Re-upping her connection to the feel of *Castle* could give her the cocksure charm of author Richard Castle and help her waltz through her first press conference. She got through the scene three times, trying to talk along with Richard Castle as he charmed the reporter with his spiel about *Dead Heat*, the first novel based on Lieutenant Kate Beckett.

During her fourth watch-through, Brendan said, "That should do it," handing back her glasses.

Ree put her specs back on and looked up to see herself in the mirror.

She blinked and felt her jaw drop. *Who's the hottie?*

The woman in the mirror wasn't supermodel-level gorgeous, but she was far more put-together and glamorous than Ree had felt in years. Her hair had shape that wasn't braided, and, dare she say it, volume. She had blush, eye shadow, and lashes long enough to use the D&D natural attack rules, and generally looked entirely unlike herself. It was a total violation of her residual self-image in the most flattering kind of way. She beamed, her pride boosted by the *Castle* energy buzzing in her mind.

"Wow" was all she could manage. "Wow."

Brendan's smile was as wide as the room. "Not bad, eh? You better get used to it. This is Hollywood standard."

Jane leaned over to her. The star looked better herself, her fatigue concealed behind masterfully done makeup, her hair voluminous and healthy. She still looked under the weather, but the hollow look was gone, leaving the star undeniably beautiful.

Changing into a skirt and gauzy top helped as well, focusing attention on her (diminished) curves.

Ree stood and cracked her neck, happy to not have to hold her good posture anymore. She resisted the urge to reach up and fiddle with her face. *Stay cool*, said a Nathan Fillion–esque voice in her head.

"Do we wait in here or beside the stage?" Ree asked.

"Out there." Jane stood and hugged Brendan. "Great job, hon." She turned to Ree. "Now it's our turn."

The two joined Yancy outside. Yancy Williams (Strength 13, Dexterity 10, Stamina 14, Will 16, IQ 16, Charisma 14—Scholar 2 / Director 5 / Producer 4 / Kingmaker 3 / Dad 3) was an impish kind of fiftysomething, with well-earned laugh lines, a full head of white hair, and a whiskey-barrel chest. Yancy lead the group down a short hall to the entrance of the Washington ballroom.

Yancy ducked his head into the ballroom for a second, then said, "They're almost ready for us."

Jane took Ree's hand and gave it a squeeze. "Talk slowly, and give short answers when you can. Let them ask the follow-ups.

Don't answer anything you don't want to. Except the basic stuff. If you don't answer the basic stuff, we look bad." Jane gave a lopsided smile that made her look like a normal person, not one burdened with fame or plagued by her recent past. Just one woman giving advice to another.

All right, Ree. Don't fuck this up. It's just another kind of performance, like talking to customers, pitching a script, or a first date.

Set mode to Ree Reyes, Screenwriter.

Another minute later, a young man with a headset opened the door and waved them in.

Yancy went first, then Ree. Jane would go last. Ree followed Yancy up the three steps to the stage and tried to pretend there weren't fifty reporters standing in the front rows, that there weren't another couple of hundred people behind them clapping and cheering.

Stay cool.

Ree put on her best smile and tried to look confident as she took long steps, stopping at the seat next to Yancy. There were a water bottle, microphone, and a name card, which announced her as Rhiannon Reyes, at the space.

As she turned to take her seat, the room exploded. Ree saw Jane step up onto the stage, waving to the crowd. Whatever last-second touch-ups and costuming tricks Brendan had done in the hall made a world of difference.

Jane was stunning, a L'Oreal commercial crossbred with a red carpet parade and unleashed on the room. Her hair flowed like a waterfall as she worked the stage like a runway.

She practically glowed from within; the star looked like she'd had a month's worth of yoga and good diet. Her famous curves were back, filling out her clothes and accentuating the confident sway of her hips.

Di-damn. Whatever Brendan made, he deserved a raise.

The flash of cameras was nearly blinding, and the roar of the crowd was primal, enthralled.

Jane reached her seat, gave another big smile, and took her seat. Ree remembered that she was still standing and was probably staring. She took her own seat and grasped for her water bottle with a smile, eager for a chance to clear her head as a storm of thoughts bounced around her mind like a game of *Arkanoid.*

Yo. Get a grip, she told herself. *Remember the you-have-to-talk-to-people part? The screenwriter thing?*

She answered the voice in her head. *But . . . pretty!*

Ree took a long swig of water and turned to the press, which had sat down as the roar of the crowd faded. She tapped into the Castle mojo, thinking *What Would Rick Castle Do?* and her shoulders relaxed, her smile brightened. Her connection to the power wouldn't last, thanks to the radioactive butterflies in her stomach burning away her concentration, but she'd milk it for all it was worth.

Yancy held his hands up, and the room settled. A few moments later, he leaned in and started talking.

"Good afternoon. I'm Yancy Williams, executive producer and director of *Awakenings.* I'm honored to be joined by the one, the only, Jane Konrad." He paused for applause. Facing the audience, Ree saw the enraptured look on many of the audience's faces. The press seemed less enraptured, but they were still fascinated, attentive, and sitting on the edge of their seats.

Jane smiled and nodded to the crowd for a few seconds, then raised a hand herself. The cheering died out like an orchestra, with Jane as the conductor.

Yancy started up again. "And I'm especially pleased to introduce to you the creator of Awakenings, the woman behind the next big television hit, Ree Reyes!"

The applause for Ree was a fraction of what Jane had gotten.

But it's for me. Not anyone else.

Ree beamed, waving to the crowd.

Oh, yeah. Who's the shit?

A few moments later, Yancy spoke again.

"We're very happy to speak with you about *Awakenings*. We're starting the second week of principal photography, and things are going splendidly. I'm sure there are many questions, so let's launch right in."

A young Latina with long silky hair wearing a West African shawl as a scarf stood, raising her hand. Patricia/Vanessa rushed over to hand her a microphone. She waved the woman off and projected, filling the room.

"Kelly Dominguez, *Pearson Patriot*. Ms. Konrad, what attracted you to this project and the choice of an unknown screenwriter for your return to the screen?" Kelly was a local video-blogger who had parlayed her positive but probing video reportage into a full-time gig. Ree'd been a fan for years, and it was fun to see her in the flesh.

Jane pulled her mike in, nodding to Kelly. She spoke with warmth and poise wrapped together in a perfect braid. "Hello, Kelly. That's a lovely shawl. I told Yancy that I was looking for fresh blood on the project, a new voice that I could introduce to the world, the way that he helped me break in to the industry.

"I started with a stack of manuscripts selected by our interns, which must have been three feet tall." Jane paused to laugh, drawing the audience in even more.

"There was a lot of good material, but when I came to *Awakenings*, I knew this was it. Ree has a crisp, humorous voice, and the script is one of the best pilots I've read. Television is the perfect medium for combining entertainment and social commentary, and *Awakenings* is the right show for the right time. There are a lot of shows that entertain, but precious few that go deeper, tackling real issues, and none that do it the way Ree has in *Awakenings*."

Several reporters nodded like bobblehead dolls, hanging on to Jane's every word. The star gestured to Ree, shifting the spotlight of attention. "But let's hear from the genius herself. I'm sure she'd be happy to tell you more about the show."

That's me. She felt a hundred eyes lock onto her movements, their attention as intense as a spotlight. Ree was used to performing in small crowds—stores, parties, and the Midnight Market. This was a whole different world.

Ree cleared her throat and pulled in her own mike, calling forward the *Castle* energy again.

Keep it cool.

"Thanks, Jane. I wrote *Awakenings* for a number of reasons. The biggest one is that ever since Battlestar Galactica went off the air, there hasn't been another show, for me, that tackled social issues in the way I wanted to see. So I had to write it myself.

"I grew up reading Ursula LeGuin, Frank Herbert, Octavia Butler, and New Wave SF. It's hard to do social science fiction on TV, because many viewers are expecting the eyeball kicks, explosions, and constant jokes. But I wanted to take a risk, trust that an audience would go with me on something that took the time to dig into issues between fight scenes."

Another reporter took up the mike, a thirtysomething white guy with a shaved head and big plastic glasses. He was dressed in the traditional garb of his people, the black turtleneck, as well as a finely-crafted air of self-importance.

"Alex Walters, WTF. Given the crash-and-burn failure of shows like *The Event, Rubicon, Alcatraz, Flash-Forward,* and others, what makes you think that a show that seems to boil down to a mashup of *No Ordinary Family* and *The 4400* can succeed in today's television market, especially with a washed-out flight risk as the star?"

Ree knew this guy. He was hipster royalty online, and prided himself on eviscerating everything in the world as soon as it started to smell of success, predicting failure everywhere he went. And since he had a million Twitter followers and headed one of the biggest gossip sites this side of TMZ, when he did his doomsaying, a whole lot of people listened.

Yancy looked to Ree, and she nodded, trying to indicate, *I got this.* Though she had to restrain her first instinct, which was to pull the lightsaber out of her purse and take a Dark Side point.

Ree adjusted the mike and said, "The fact that companies keep putting on shows like the ones you mentioned means that the execs and others believe that there's something to it. And concept isn't destiny. You can walk into a bookstore and find a hundred YA novels on the shelves." *Look at me being diplomatic*, she thought, when all she wanted to do was dropkick the smarmy bastard out of the zip code. "Only a handful of them have hit it big, but does that mean the others are doomed to fail, or that just because a couple of them aren't great means the others are crap? Of course not. Each show deserves to be judged on its own merits, don't you think?"

Do not engage, she told herself. *That way lies madness.*

Alex shifted his weight, eyes narrowed. "That's easy to say, but if we're supposed to judge your show on its merits, will *Awakenings* actually have any?"

Because you're the God-given arbiter of taste, right? Ree thought, restraining the growing urge to jump the table and strangle the bastard.

No one will care if I clobber him, right? The media ecosystem will survive with one less parasite.

Yancy leaned in to answer. "Ree has a wry, crisp voice, and she's given us a great world to bring to life for audiences. Our special-effects team is going to deliver amazing visuals, and Jane is putting in some of the best performances I've seen in the fifteen years I've worked with her."

Ree gave Yancy a smile, waited for him to continue or Jane to hop in. After a beat, Ree spoke again. "I can give you the basic concept, just to put everything on the table.

"In the might-as-well-be-now future, magic returns to the earth, and people around the world awaken with magic powers.

People freak out, and all of a sudden, there's a brand-new way to be stigmatized. *Awakenings* takes the one-family lens approach to tackling social issues, while always staying personal."

Ree stopped there, remembering Jane's suggestion to keep it brief, or at least brief-ish. Plus, she felt the *Castle* energy starting to run low, and wanted to keep some mojo back for other questions.

Her hands were shaking, and she took a long swig from her glass as she calmed herself down, mentally grasping onto the magical energy.

She looked to Alex, bracing for another *gotcha* or snide remark. But either he was satisfied or he was going to save the rest of the bile for his article. A half-dozen other hands stood in the air, and Ree looked to Yancy, who nodded.

The next reporter was a shorter, curvy woman with tightly curled black hair. "Vlada Janczuk, StraightDope.com. One Tough Mama has had a difficult few years. How important is it that this pilot succeed, and why shoot a pilot on spec instead of pitching to studios right away?"

Yancy's response was a guarded grin. "Every project is important, and right now money is tight for everyone."

Ree had asked this question when the production company made their offer to buy the pilot. So she knew that Yancy's answer read as *This is the last of Jane's money, and if the pilot bombs, the production company will go belly-up.*

Announcing, *Hey, we're screwed if this fails, so please watch us!* wasn't exactly a way to get people to tune in, not for a brand-new show. Some shows needed "Save Show X" campaigns before they hit the air, but no one wanted to be that show. And the show would have to be picked up to series first.

Yancy continued, "As for why to dive right into shooting a pilot, Jane has always tried to innovate with our efforts at One Tough Mama. After the success of independent productions like *Dr. Horrible's Sing-Along Blog*, *The Guild*, and *Husbands*, Jane wanted to get the pilot in the can before making presentations, which will give us more flexibility. If the networks pass for whatever reason, we still have a product, and we can go direct to the fans and use Kickstarter to raise funds for a full season."

Yancy'd said part of why they were doing the press conference this early was to help drum up interest, as well as to dispel the myths that Jane was too far gone to get through a production.

From where Ree sat, they were doing all of that and more, thanks to Jane's charm and Yancy's tact, and maybe even her own fu.

The press worked through a few more questions, getting into details about the production schedule and their hopes for the series' home (any major network, plus Syfy, TNT, AMC, HBO, etc.). Ree let Yancy take the lead, and Jane answered the softball personal questions with grace and waved off the inflammatory ones from Alex and others. Eventually, the PAs got the message and stopped giving the mike to the muckraker. After the third time he was ignored, he got up and made a big production of storming off.

Good riddance.

"That's all the time we have for today," Yancy said finally, an hour into the press conference. "Thank you for your time, and I hope you'll continue following our progress with *Awakenings!*"

They stood to another round of applause. Jane played to the crowd on the way out, and Ree heard the roar continue even through the door and down the hall as they left.

"We've got a car in back," Yancy said.

Jane shook her head, grinning wide. "No, we're going out the front. Give them a minute to gather." She looked like the cat who'd caught the canary.

A shadow passed over Yancy's face. "Careful, Jane."

Jane stretched, cracking her back. "I'll be fine. And we need every bit of press we can get."

Yancy took a halting step toward Jane, a worried, paternal look on his face. Jane raised a hand, and he stopped.

"It's going to be a hit, Yanc. And then we'll be back on top."

They waited for a minute.

Why am I getting a foreboding vibe off of this? It isn't just the worry of maybe people will throw fruit instead of cheering—it was something bigger.

"I've got a bad feeling about this," Ree said without getting the chance to censor herself.

Jane looked to Ree and smiled big.

Why worry? Ree asked herself. *It'll be fine.*

"Follow me and stay close. This is going to be a great ride."

Jane nodded to her bodyguard Danny, who had appeared from nowhere to take the lead, engaging his not-to-be-fucked-with look.

Danny Park (Strength 15, Dexterity 16, Stamina 14, Will 15, IQ 13, Charisma 10—Laborer 2 / Security 3 / Martial Artist 5 / Bodyguard 4) stood only five feet and change, but he was ripped, the muscle shirt he wore under his jacket showing enough skin to make that fact abundantly clear. He wore a short ponytail tied back, and his jeans were well worn without being patchy.

Ree followed, and as they walked through the hotel, Ree couldn't help but envision the group in their very own Badass Walk: the last or next-to-last shot of a TV credits sequence or film trailer where the main characters stride with purpose down a hallway, alley, or battlefield. Bonus points if something explodes in the background.

Her mind played a made-up theme song in the style of Nerf Herder as they walked. Danny reached the front of the hotel, and two men in suits opened the doors for them.

The crowd outside was even bigger than it had been in

the ballroom by at least 50 percent. *Where are all these people coming from?* Ree wondered.

Jane sauntered through the crowd wearing a modest smile.

The air was tight with excitement and the flow of energy as the star held court, soaking it all in like an emotional vampire. *I sure hope Dresden's White Court doesn't really exist. If they do, we're all fucked.* According to the model that Eastwood gave Ree during her brief stint as a snarky apprentice, there might be individual vampires that followed the model from Butcher's novels, feeding on emotion instead of blood, but probably not enough to be their own society. If they did, Ree had no doubt that they'd have Hollywood wrapped around their sexy alabaster fingers.

Some heroines got simple universes, with monsters and magic that followed consistent rules. As far as she could tell, magic in her world was as inconsistent and dynamic as real life, so just when she thought she understood what was going on, something would change for no discernible reason, like fashion, pop music, or Facebook.

Ree headed straight for the waiting town car, sliding in beside Yancy. Jane took several minutes to sign, schmooze, and soak up the love.

Yancy kept an eye on his star, and Ree watched out of the corner of her eye.

Jane waved goodbye to the crowd and slinked into the car with deliberate grace, proving Ree's point. She beckoned Ree in next, and Yancy took shotgun as Danny closed the door to the car, interposing himself to keep the crowds away.

Jane leaned in to speak to both of them.

"See, wasn't that fun?" Her eyes were wide, like she'd just taken a hit of something high-grade.

Yancy harrumphed. "Back to the set, please." The driver, an older Middle Eastern man in an aviator cap, nodded, and the car pulled out into the street.

"Actually, can you drop me somewhere?" Ree asked. "I've got a lunch."

Yancy nodded. Jane frowned. "I thought you were going to be on-set this afternoon?"

"I will," Ree said. "When I say 'I have a lunch,' what I really mean is 'I have work.' My boss has been good about being flexible and giving my work here priority, but I do have to help out for a few hours this afternoon." *That and take a meeting that could really go well, or really really not.*

"Just tell the driver," Yancy said, the car already in motion.

Ree gave directions to an office building across town.

Of course, that wasn't where she was actually going.

Read *Celebromancy* now:
http://michaelrunderwood.com/books/celebromancy/

About the Author

Michael R. Underwood is an author, podcaster, and publishing professional. His books include space opera *Annihilation Aria*, the Ree Reyes *Geekomancy* books, the Stabby Award finalist *Genrenauts* series, and Born to the Blade (written with Malka Older, Cassandra Khaw, and Marie Brennan).

Mike has been a bookseller, sales representative, and was the North American Sales & Marketing Manager for Angry Robot Books. He is also a co-host of the actual play show Speculate! and a guest host on the Hugo Award-finalist The Skiffy and Fanty Show.

Mike lives in Baltimore with his wife, their dog, and an ever-growing library. He also loves geeking out with games and making pizzas from scratch.